SECRETS
AND
SHADOWS

ALSO BY SHANNON DELANY

13 to Life

SECRETS AND SHADOWS

Shannon Delany

St. Martin's Griffin
New York

This is a work of fiction. All of the characters, organizations, and events portrayed in this novel are either products of the author's imagination or are used fictitiously.

www.stmartins.com

ISBN 978-0-312-60915-3

First Edition: February 2011

10   9   8   7   6   5   4   3   2   1

Dedicated to the two guys who remind me daily what love, loyalty, and friendship truly mean—my husband, Karl, and my son, Jaiden. The right words don't exist in any language to completely describe just what you both mean to me.

ACKNOWLEDGMENTS

I figured doing the acknowledgments for the second book in a series must be easier, right? But something I'm learning as I go is that things don't necessarily get easier: They're just different the second time around.

I have some different folks to thank this time. Please note: There will inevitably be people I've forgotten or whom I can't yet acknowledge because of timing. But hey, that's why it's doubly great there's yet another book in the series!

Thanks to the generosity of Karen Alderman and her husband, Kevin, who set three alarms to place the winning bid. They won the *13 to Life* ARC and swag I donated to Do the Write Thing for Nashville. Talk about understanding teamwork and charitable giving! Likewise, thanks to Myra McEntire, Victoria Schwab, and Amanda Morgan, who organized and handled the fundraiser. Through their efforts (and the generosity of authors, bidders, and others) they raised more than seventy thousand dollars in ten short days for a city in need. Jess would have been proud of their efforts—I know I am!

Thanks also to the generosity of Scott and Debbie of Texas who supported BeInANovel.com in 2009 and its charity, Operation Joy of Valley Forge, Pennsylvania. Because of their bid Jess "got back on the horse," so to speak.

To my ARC tour guides! Carla Black who immediately expressed interest in *13 to Life* and initiated a great UK ARC tour and has become one of my greatest cheerleaders after reading the book. She's already read this one, too; it has her Wolf Girl seal of approval. Thanks to Katie Bartow of Texas, who picked up a faltering United States ARC tour and spread the wolf love! To Alyson Beecher, who read and loved *13 to Life* enough to pass it along to people to read and consider carrying in their stores and libraries. It's through such efforts that books are discovered. I (and many other authors) very much appreciate such support.

To Lynsey Newton, who knew I was struggling with titles for this book and sent several awesome lists filled with great ideas.

To Jennzah Morris, who somehow got skipped over in *13 to Life*'s acknowledgments and has been a stalwart supporter of mine since Textnovel 2008! You rock, hon!

To the Class of 2k10! A wonderful group of talented debut YA and MG authors that made my debut year at once wonderful and amazingly busy. I recommend you read their books—there are some powerful voices emerging that I had the great pleasure of reading early on! You can check us all out at Classof2k10.com.

To Katy Hershberger in the St. Martin's Press publicity squad and Eileen Rothschild in marketing, who cheer me on and gladly check out things I think might be worth pursuing. These girls are awesome, and I'm so glad they're working on my series.

To Antonio Avanzato, whose local weekly radio show, *The Voice of the New Italy,* inspired a short but important moment between Jess and her dad. Thanks for allowing me to use a great phrase!

To Matt Cooper and Celina Simms, owners of Capresso—one of my very favorite places in the whole world to do copyedits. They understand when to chat and when to let me spread papers all over their beautiful tables.

To my CPs who stuck through this one the whole way: My husband, Karl, and my good friend Robin Wright. To my Book Two betas: Carla Black, Rachelle Reese, and Alyson Beecher. I appreciate the time and thought you've already given this series.

To my agent, Stan Soper, who reads my manuscripts, gives great input, and steps up when needed.

To my editor, Michael Homler, who asks the right questions and has an attitude that makes my being a new novelist not nearly as terrifying as it could be.

And, last, but far from least: to my readers and fans! I hope you love *Secrets and Shadows*!

SECRETS AND SHADOWS

PROLOGUE

A LITTLE MORE THAN A YEAR AGO

In a seemingly standard suburban sprawl outside the city of Farthington something has gone wrong. Sharp sidewalks and carefully clipped lawns hem in the town houses and flank the expected allotment of single homes. It's a quiet neighborhood, where everyone appears to know everyone else. But things are not always as they seem, and people are seldom *only* what their neighbors expect.

In one such innocuous yard a man naturally inclined to an animal grace staggers. Tall and broad shouldered like his elder son Max, and lean as his youngest, Pietr, he's dark as any Rusakova, with only a hint of silver in his hair.

Even so young a father, his life is nearly over. Not because of the poor choices he made as a younger man—choices that caused his wife to give their children her name rather than his—but because regardless of how normal the setting seems, Andrei is far from the norm.

He sways by the picket fence, the traditional American symbol for happiness, success—the elusive American dream. But to him, even pretty fences make a common cage. He glares toward the neighbor's house, a powder blue Cape Cod, and his wife lopes out of their home, crossing the yard on quick and quiet feet.

Slender and lithe as their daughter Catherine but with heavy highlights of red streaking her rich brown hair like coppery lightning, Tatiana tilts her head, nostrils flaring in question. Her eyebrows draw together, and she circles him. "Come inside," she pleads, laying a hand on his arm.

He shakes it off like a dog throwing off the rain. Face red with rage, his fiery gaze stays fixed on their neighbor's home. "The way he watches you . . ."

She blushes, fearing the shame is shared although she tempts the man unwittingly. With its very existence the animal that skitters and claws beneath her human skin calls to some men, entices and ensnares their weaker senses.

The door of the blue Cape Cod opens and the man steps out, waving boldly at her. The smile stretching his lips does nothing to mask his unwanted attentions.

The sun slips away, leaving a bloody smear across the southern mountaintops. These are the dangerous hours, when the skin feels loosest on the wolf within and the beast in the human-seeming breast grows more anxious to burst free.

"I will rrrip out his hearrrt—"

As her husband springs across the fence with a snarl, Tatiana fears that although this is not the first time a man has acted indecently toward her, this might be the only time it matters.

It's a race up the broad porch stairs to the neighbor, who doesn't even have enough sense to go inside, bolt the door, and lock himself in a closet—to wait out the dawn and pray for reason to override rage.

Instead he stands there. Spreads his legs in a fighting stance. "Off my porch, Rusakova," he growls.

The sound is nothing compared to the noise tearing out of Andrei. Coursing through his chest, the twisting growl erupts as he takes the porch's final three steps in one smooth leap.

His hands on the man who stares openly at his wife, Andrei's words are too thick with anger to be clear. A growl, a slur—language matters little when actions speak louder than words. And Andrei's actions speak wrath, revenge—*hate*. So fluently.

The man flops in his grasp, fighting stance forgotten as he screams and lands sloppy and panicked punches on Andrei's face as it twists and pulses and pops. *Changes* . . .

Someone appears at the window, shoves the curtains aside, mouth drawn into an "o" of terror. The leerer's wife—the mouse he ignores except when he publicly berates her. She thrusts her son from her side, and the curtain falls back across the window.

Behind him, the man's door clicks shut; the lock bolts into place with a slithering sound. There will be no retreat.

Tatiana pushes between the men, grunting with exertion. "Stop," she urges, eyes wide.

Lights flash, coloring the dimming neighborhood quickly falling into dusk with red, white, and blue as a siren wails its way down the normally quiet suburban street.

"Not finished with you," Andrei, half-turned, yowls. He throws the man across his shoulder and lopes around the house, into the tree-filled backyard and the shadows that threaten to solidify beyond.

With a glance toward the street, Tatiana sets her jaw and follows her husband, disappearing into the growing darkness.

A swarm of uniformed officers mount the porch stairs, as one unmarked SUV slips silently past the house, daring to scatter the darkness with its piercing headlights.

In the Rusakovas' home Catherine presses her face to the window, Pietr by her side. Unable to be much help, the twins are more than a year outside their first full change.

Pacing, Alexi refuses to change and go. His shaking fingers drag through his hair, but he rejects Catherine's pleas and ignores Pietr's threats. Begging until her voice is nothing but a reedy whine, Catherine sobs; her tears smear the glass, and the world outside seems to ripple. Pietr pulls her away, silently wrapping her in his arms.

And as vehemently as Alexi refuses to go, there is no place he'd rather be than beside the parents who adopted him and have kept his secret—that he is nothing like his siblings and is simply, horrendously, human.

The one Rusakova—the one *wolf*—able to help is missing. Spending one more night in the arms of anonymous girls, Max is living his short life as fast as he can.

In the woods not far from the backyard stands the tragic threesome. Tatiana, shaken by frustration into her ruddy wolfskin, circles the rivals for her attention, growling. Andrei releases the man, speaking to the worried wolf in a most guttural Russian. His words impeded by long and pointed teeth, he searches for an explanation, some justification. Distraught, he wavers as his metabolism—his canine bits—burns through the drug or drink that had such a hold on him.

Their neighbor looks around, contemplates escape. His jeans soiled from something fouler than the tears streaking his frightened face, he watches the werewolves warily.

All eyes suddenly focus on something—*someone*—shrouded in the shadows. The wolf Tatiana howls at the betrayal as a smile once again slides across the leerer's lips.

A sliver of moonlight shimmers across the barrel of a gun swinging into view, giving directions. Tatiana obeys, the wolf stalking to the side. But obedience is too much for Andrei and he lunges, completing his transformation in midair . . .

. . . one moment of fluid grace . . .

. . . brought down by a muzzle flash so bright it blinds.

He falls, pulled from midair with a grunt and a spatter of blood, never to rise again. The copper wolf noses the limp body of her mate, a whimper tearing at her throat. Rage empowering her, she leaps, willing to fall dead at his side, her husband. . . .

Her *heart*.

A muzzle flash tears at the inky night again and she tumbles to the earth, falling limp.

Silent.

Still.

CHAPTER ONE

NOW

"So, after the loss of your mother in the car accident, you started work to redeem her amnesiac murderer, met a new boy at school, who you hid your attraction from in order to protect a friend's feelings. Then you learned the boy was being hunted by the CIA—one of their agents who happens to be trying to date your dad . . . hunted because the boy's a werewolf."

There was a long pause. I ran over her summary, mentally ticking off the checklist of the bizarre that my life had so recently been reduced to. "You forgot about the Russian Mafia's involvement and the shoot-out we were in."

Looking at her clipboard, Dr. Jones replied, "Yes. So I did." She jotted something down. "Well. It looks like our time is up." She clicked her pen and set it down definitively on her broad ebony desk. "Your story is absolutely fascinating." She confirmed what I knew too well. "But."

I sat up, the leather couch creaking beneath me. I gave her my best *but what?* look. I'd talked forever.

As much as I hated to admit it, the school counselors were right. It felt great to get it all out and tell an objective professional. So I waited, looking at her expectantly. She could surely say more than *but* after all I'd confessed.

"But, if you really want to get past the trauma of your mother's death—which is truly the crux of your situation—you'll need to get real here." She stood, lips twisting.

Get real? I had told her everything. I had risked the Rusakovas to save my own crumbling sense of sanity.

I couldn't help it. I laughed so hard I snorted.

In the two months since I'd met Pietr Rusakova I could number on one hand the times I'd told the truth. The lies? The phrase *totally out of hand* had special meaning when trying to keep track of them.

But to finally try and straighten things out and be shut down? Not what I expected.

She blinked at me. "Seriously, Jessica. Russian Mafia? Government agents? *Werewolves?*" She laughed. "I should be like other psychiatrists, I guess, and blindly prescribe something with an exciting new name. But I want to help you get better, not medicate you. I want you to get a grip."

"You don't believe me."

"It's my professional opinion that you're screwing with me. Most kids clam up on their first visit or avoid the heart of their issues. But you"—she glanced at the clipboard—"are an editor for the school newspaper. Surely inventive. So you chose the other route, exhibiting a commendable streak of creativity. But I have a high crap tolerance."

Her voice lowered and she ruffled the corners of her freshly written notes. "You have to, working with kids," she muttered. "You're no more delusional than the average teenager."

"I killed a man." God, for all the notes she seemed to take, did she not listen?

"Yes, Jessica, so you said. But where's the body, sweetie? I'd expect some part of the aftermath of a bloodbath like you described to be seen by someone. Why wasn't there anything in the papers?"

"I told you before. The agents called in a—" I chewed my lower lip. Why wouldn't the right words come when I needed them? "A cleaning crew."

"Yes, the *agents.*" She made quotes in the air with a twitch of her fingers. "Including"—she flipped through the papers on her clipboard until she found it—"Wanda the librarian."

"No one gives librarians the credit they deserve," I snapped. "Yes. She works in the reference department and is a gun-toting government agent."

"Of course," Dr. Jones said, still smiling. "So. Creative, and probably with a large number of overdue books causing you to be creatively suspicious about librarians. Interesting."

I had no idea what else to say. I'd surely said it all.

"Anyway. It's your insurance coverage. You decide if you want to waste it on fantasies."

She turned away to look out the window—a clear dismissal. I stood, slung my purse over my shoulder, and headed out the door, as confused as when I'd first arrived.

I'd decided to adjust to my new normal. Regular counseling. A life with no mother. No more shoot-outs with the Russian Mafia. Nearly no CIA presence. And a werewolf sort-of-boyfriend who was also still seeing my not-quite-stable friend Sarah because we hoped to avoid triggering her return to absolute psychosis.

Okay, so my new normal wasn't nearly normal by other people's standards, but it was the best I could do.

I was back to horse riding and farm chores and trying to keep up with my classes and working on the school newspaper.

I still had my friends. Amy had my back, and Sophia, well, she was hanging around enough that I knew she cared—or was fascinated by the tragedy that seemed to continually wash over me. And there was Sarah—beautifully angelic and with so little of her original memory she was almost safe to be around.

I hoped.

Derek (the star of our football team) shadowed me now, too, frequently appearing and smiling at me in a way that made my heart race. I'd had a crush of *Titanic* (and I do mean like the ship that nailed the iceberg) proportions on him. For years.

Well, until Pietr showed up and everything changed.

Anyhow, my new normal should have been a good thing. Not perfect, but acceptable. Nearly sane.

In the nonthreatening beige waiting room people hid behind newspapers and magazines so old their readers were learning history—not catching up on current events.

All but one.

Catherine Rusakova waved to me and rose, following me out the door. Normally as unnoticed as a shadow slipping across shade, she was also impossible *not* to notice when she wanted.

Like now.

The office door clicked shut behind me. "Hi, Cat." I wasn't sure how to proceed. I wasn't used to being stalked by Pietr's twin sister. Werewolf number two.

Her eyes sparkled, astonishingly blue and faintly slanted, with a fringe of thick lashes. Cat's strong features and high cheekbones made her look more like a goddess of old than a werewolf.

Of course, there was probably someplace where the goddess of old *was* a werewolf. . . .

The Rusakovas were at once strong and beautiful: an elegance and brutality blended in their features. Once I'd seen what they became—what they truly *were*—it was impossible not to see some shadow of the beast slinking within their eyes, some hint of it hiding in the glint of their smiles.

"*Privyet,*" Cat greeted me. "I did not realize you were seeing a psychiatrist until your sister told me," she admitted, the faint roll of her first language softly coloring her words.

Nice. I'd have to have a little chat with Annabelle Lee later. Sometimes she was far too helpful. Just not to me.

"Does Pietr know?"

I shook my head. It was one thing I hadn't found a way to tell him. It was far easier to talk about school and books than admit to seeing a psychiatrist about serious issues.

"Considering circumstances, I agree it is wise." She smiled, and I repressed a shiver. That beautiful grin turned into a devil's nest of fangs when she wanted. "You have seen a lot of horrible things recently."

I paused by a potted plant that looked like it needed water—or proper burial. "But?"

"But what?"

"I love talking with you, Cat, but why are you here?"

Cat tilted her head and peeked at me from the corners of her eyes. "It's not often people outside our family know our truth, Jessie. It might make us nervous to hear the one who does know is talking."

"I don't want to make anyone nervous." My palms grew damp. *Nervous* was not a descriptor I wanted applied to any member in a family of werewolves.

"That is why I chose to come," Cat explained. "To get a better understanding before the boys find out. You are very important to our family, Jessie. I am convinced of that."

"Because I opened the *matryoshka* and found the pendant?"

"*Da.*"

I watched her, waiting. "And?"

She sighed. "And because of what your tea leaves said." Shaking her head, her smile ghosted away. "I must ask you what—"

"Everything, Catherine. I told her absolutely everything."

She stepped back, solemn. "The CIA?"

"Yes."

"The Russian Mafia?"

"Yes." Tears filled my eyes, threatening to spill.

"And werewolves. Jessie, you said you'd seen werewolves?"

"Yes!" I winced, closing my eyes and remembering the dreadful moment I'd seen in so many movies recently—the moment the werewolf changed and tore out a victim's throat.

I held my breath.

Nothing happened.

I opened my eyes to find Catherine gazing at me with curiosity. Predators did that, though. Studied their prey.

"I'm sorry, Catherine. I had to say something . . . had to tell someone. . . ."

Her fingers twitched by her hip.

I shut my eyes again, ready as I could be for certain disemboweling. I'd gutlessly betrayed their family, in an attempt to save my sanity. I deserved no better.

"What are you doing?" Cat's words rushed out; she stood so close now her breath was a warm breeze brushing across my face.

"Waiting."

"For what?" she asked.

"*Death?*" I squeaked, peeling one eye open to watch her—the way I watched most werewolf films.

She laughed.

My heart throbbed against my ribs.

She grabbed me so fast I nearly peed myself. Holding me in a powerful hug, she whispered, "You are a strange, strange girl, Jessie Gillmansen."

Says a werewolf.

"You should stop watching those awful horror movies."

"How did you—? Of course. Annabelle Lee."

"She is worried about you."

"Ha."

"We are not Hollywood's creations. You know that."

"Rationally, yes." Not Hollywood's creations, but rather the descendants of one of the USSR's surprisingly successful scientific experiments from the earliest years of the Cold War.

Cat nodded. "Does the doctor believe what you said?"

"Not a word."

"Excellent." She grinned her most wicked grin. "Now you can tell her the truth without repercussions." She stepped back, toying with her short, dark curls, glittering eyes fixed on me. "Might she medicate you?"

"Nope. She insists I embrace sanity without chemical assistance."

"You are such a clever girl!" She threw her hands into the air. "Strange in your methods, but clever. Oh." She pinched her ear. "Your father is coming. He should not see me here."

"Cat!" I called as she retreated down another hallway. "I need to talk to you about Pietr—"

She nodded. "I will find you. Tonight. Listen for me."

CHAPTER TWO

Sure enough, Dad was headed down the hall toward me. I shouldn't have been surprised Cat knew, but it was still odd—especially knowing *why* and *how* she knew.

When the Rusakova children each turned thirteen, strange things happened to them—far stranger than the standard hair showing up in weird places that came with normal puberty. At thirteen their ability to hear intensified. At fourteen, their sense of smell sharpened exponentially. When they turned fifteen their strength and agility increased, and sixteen was a year their bodies tried to catch up with the mutations rioting through their systems.

Then about a week ago, the twins, Pietr and Cat, turned seventeen. To say that turning seventeen had changed them would be an understatement of the oddest sort.

None of our lives had been the same since.

"Oh, Jessie!" Dad exclaimed, snapping his cell phone shut. Seeing my eyes pink with unshed tears, he wrapped me in a hug, lifting me and squeezing the air out of my lungs in one long sigh. "The first few times will probably be toughest," he said, setting me down.

He smoothed my hair back from my face. "Let's go now. You look tired." Putting his hand flat on my back, he steered me down the hall and out the building.

He opened the truck's passenger door, a mismatched green that somehow went with the rest of its blue rust-speckled body, and took his spot behind the steering wheel. The truck roared to life, and Dad twisted the knob on the old radio, turning it down.

"Why are we listening to this station?"

"There's nothin' wrong with this station," he insisted.

"It only plays the eighties."

"And I repeat—" But he didn't. He winked instead. "Livin' on a Prayer," he said, nodding toward the radio.

It seemed that's what I did most days.

Mom and Dad had both been huge fans of the big-haired bands of eighties rock. Without Mom around, Dad clung to the bits of life they'd shared even harder. Except when he reached out toward Wanda.

Blech.

I tried not to think about it as I sank into my seat and stared out the window, barely noticing any of Junction's Main Street drifting by, its little trees nearly naked as a few dried orange and yellow leaves still held tight, waving in the sharp autumn breeze. An unseasonable cold held Junction in its grasp and even back when we'd thought it was too early for Halloween displays, the dropping leaves and plummeting temperatures made it somehow fitting.

The three o'clock train shrieked out a whistle, the rattle of its cars muted by a few blocks of the town's most bustling real estate.

Dad pulled into the parking lot at McMillan's. "Just need milk and bread," he explained as he shut down the truck.

"Skipper's has better prices," I reminded.

He shot me a look that shut me right up. He would never go back to Skipper's. It shared a parking lot with the local video rental store. The rental store I was standing outside when Mom came to pick me up the night of June 17.

The same night Sarah, on a joyride, crashed into Mom's car and killed her. Dad forgave Sarah's stupidity and brusquely accepted the new subdued Sarah (amazing what severe head trauma could do to improve a personality), following my lead.

But the scene of the accident couldn't change enough for him to move on. The macadam and the surrounding buildings held too many memories. I knew. They'd frequently been the backdrop for my nightmares.

Until the night the Rusakova twins' birthday gave me vivid new imagery to replace the old.

My family had come a long way since the accident. But most days I didn't think we could ever come far enough.

I tried to ignore the decorations in the local store windows on the ride home, skeletons and glowing spiders in polyester webs reminding all of Junction that Halloween was crawling ever closer.

As was my birthday. One more celebration Mom would miss.

Maybe I looked tired to Dad (king of compliments), but my mind ran so fast I wouldn't get any peace even if I tried to nap. As soon as I got home I transferred my notes from Friday's classes. Nearly legible. I highlighted a few key concepts and tucked my notebooks away before heading to the paddock.

I thought more clearly on the back of a horse.

Rio, my chestnut mare, whickered a greeting and charged the fence—daring me to stay still.

To trust her.

She flew at me, hooves slicing up chunks of soil as she barreled forward, nostrils flared, eyes wild.

My head up, stance open, I watched her with thinly veiled amusement. She skidded to a halt, spraying dirt up from her steel shoes. Right onto my jeans.

"Rio," I admonished.

She tossed her mane, pushing her snout into my chest so I had no choice but to stroke the sleek bridge of her unmarked nose and marvel at the brightness of her eyes.

If there was one thing in life I could trust, it was Rio. Horses didn't lie. Joke? Yes.

"Let's go," I said, slipping her bridle over her head. I climbed onto a fence rail and she maneuvered into position, standing still as stone when I said, "Alley oop," and mounted.

No saddle, I felt every move Rio considered, every twitch of muscle, every thought telegraphed back to me. She didn't need to verbalize to be understood. The swivel of an ear, a snort, or a pawing hoof and I knew what was on her mind or in her heart.

When life was most confounding, Rio was the blessing best understood. My dogs, Hunter and Maggie, were seldom understood, but ever-present.

Rio and I did a few passes around the paddock—nothing fancy, nothing stressful, just the lengthening of strides, the ground-swallowing sweep of a smooth gallop and my mind drifted.

"Whoa!" I tugged on the reins. "Sorry, girl." We walked a few minutes and I tried to push everything from my mind. It wasn't happening. Even the rhythmic droning of hoofbeats couldn't push Pietr's behavior far enough from my thoughts.

Since his seventeenth birthday Pietr had become a little distant. We'd agreed he needed to continue dating Sarah, slowly weaning her away from him as he moved closer to me. More than smart not to freak Sarah out or hurt her feelings by having Pietr suddenly dump her, it was kinder, too.

But doing the kind thing made me even more of a liar. Pietr used to snatch an occasional kiss in a dark corner, grab my hand in his to marvel at my fingers, or just stare for long, breathless moments down into my eyes.

That was all before he made his first change.

Since then he'd stolen less than a dozen quiet moments with me. And it wasn't like he was moving forward with Sarah, either.

Pietr and I still talked on the phone—he seemed to enjoy integrating bits of Russian in our conversations. I knew *horashow* meant "good" and *puzhalsta* meant "please" and I could order coffee and find a bathroom if I needed to. Could I read any of it in Cyrillic? Absolutely not. To me, Cyrillic was still nothing but an elegant scrawl.

The only phrase Pietr denied me was the one I wanted most—and not because I was going to sling it around like it was nothing. But Pietr refused to tell me how to say "I love you" in Russian. Yes, I could have figured it out online, but words just sounded better coming out of Pietr's mouth. And maybe if he couldn't say it, I shouldn't want to know how to, either. It was all so confusing.

I pulled Rio to a stop and slid off her back, leading her to the barn before gently freeing her from the bridle and rubbing her down with a towel. The door to her stall was pinned open; she had options tonight as chilly as it threatened to be.

"Good girl," I assured her. "Believe me. It's not you, it's me," I said wryly, worried the words were ones I might hear from Pietr if I let the distance between us grow.

I washed the last of the dishes and set them in the rack to drip dry as the final beams of sunlight smoldered across the sky and nipped at the racing clouds. Though the wind shook the bare branches of the trees in our yard, I kept the window over the sink open a crack, listening for Catherine's signal.

A howl hurtled across our farm, and I jerked drying my fingers on the towel.

Just the wind.

Another howl and I started toward the door. This time the noise ended with leaves skittering across our small porch. I sighed and pulled my jacket off its hook.

"Where are you going?"

Jumping, I turned to face Annabelle Lee. She had been sitting so quietly reading her latest book, I'd completely forgotten she was still at the table.

"Out for a walk. It's a beautiful night."

The wind shook our home and Annabelle Lee tore her eyes from the pages of *Atlas Shrugged* long enough to give me a look that was as easy to read as Rio.

She did not believe me. Not one bit. "Is Pietr out there? Waiting for you?"

"What? Who?" Crap! Where was Dad—what were the odds he overheard us?

She set the book down. "Dad headed back to the factory. Some machine broke and spewed chocolate all over the line. Luckily no one's hurt. No blood, just foul, he said."

"Hmm. *Blood and Chocolate*. Great book. Not a flavor the factory would want, though." I shrugged into my jacket.

"Dad kissed your cheek before he left. I can't believe you missed that."

Touching the spot, I vaguely remembered the rasp of his five o'clock shadow.

Her eyebrows drew closer together. At twelve, Annabelle Lee was very bright, but she was frequently confounded by people. I often caught her (when she wasn't reading or snooping) peering at me like something on a microscope slide.

Studying me. I simply hoped her fascination meant she'd learn enough from my mistakes not to make them her own. "You really want to go for a walk?"

"Yes."

"By yourself?"

"Yes."

The door hummed under the force of the next gust.

"It's invigorating," I insisted, winding my scarf around my neck before topping off my ensemble with a sensible knit hat.

"Fine. I'm headed to bed."

Stepping onto the porch I heard Catherine's curling cry and wondered how I'd doubted I'd recognize the difference between the wind and the weaving, undulating sound of Catherine bewitching the world in her wolfskin.

I followed the sound down the slight hill behind our house and into the edge of the woods where the darkness deepened and clung like new growth to autumn's bare branches.

"Catherine?"

The forest went still.

The wind stopped.

The few remaining leaves ceased spinning on their branches and a chill climbed up my spine, ignoring my prudent layering.

"Catherine?" I whispered, surrounded by shadows. My back rigid, I realized this surely qualified as a counterintuitive behavior that—if Darwin was right—would quickly have me removed from the gene pool.

I'd need to improve my odds of survival if I was going to hang out with werewolves. I reached into my pocket, stroking the smooth and familiar surface of my pietersite worry stone. Stunned by the nerve-grating silence, my eyes strained for some clue to Cat's location. "Cat?" I tried again, eyes wide and wary.

In a darkness that made the woods unfamiliar, confused and calling a predator out for a chat—yep—I'd *definitely* be selected against.

CHAPTER THREE

"Catherine!"

Hurled to the ground, there wasn't air left in my lungs for a scream. The wolf stood over me, mouth slick, eyes narrow and blazing blood red. Heavy front paws covered in thick sepia fur pressed into my stomach as claws the length of my thumbs prickled through my jacket and shirt.

"Caaat," I wheezed.

Her mouth opened, displaying an impressive set of fangs. Death sat in those slavering jaws and terror tore at my heart as she bent down, her breath so hot it stung. I closed my eyes.

She was a werewolf. A hellhound, a skinwalker, shape-shifter—a nightmare able to gnaw my neck off.

In the movies such encounters never ended well.

She growled; the sound jackhammered through me.

Then she licked me.

A big, slobbery kiss of canine proportions stained my cheek with saliva. She sprang up, yipped like a playful pup, and stood on her hind legs to summon the change.

Sitting, my arms folded across my chest, I said, "Not funny, Cat."

"What?" she asked, all wide-eyed innocence.

"You shouldn't sneak up on someone."

She cocked her head.

"Not when you're—"

"Wolf?"

I nodded. Vigorously.

"But I am always wolf," she said. "I am *oborot*."

"Obor-what?"

"*Oborot*. One transformed." She smiled ruefully. "Can I not have fun with what I am bound to be?"

I groaned. "Can we at least agree that you won't pounce me? Or slaughter me? Or—"

Her laugh trilled through the trees. "Jessie. You must trust I will never hurt you. None of us would." She knelt, reclining in the rolling leaves, at home in the woods.

My shoulders sagged, and my hands fell loosely into my lap. I stared at them. "Pietr's hurting me—confusing me."

"Pietr is just a boy."

"Right. And you obviously aren't. Speaking of which—aren't you freezing? Where are your clothes?" I tried not to look at Cat as she rested—naked—nearby.

"Oh. *Eezveneetcheh*. I am sorry, Jessie. My temperature runs higher with the change. Alexi thinks it is because we cross from aerobic cellular respiration to anaerobic much more efficiently. Something about leaky mitochondrial membranes . . . ours versus yours. . . ." She made a show of yawning, her hand fluttering before her open mouth.

"Oh."

"Does my nudity offend you?"

How could I explain that Cat's nudity couldn't offend *anyone*. She looked so much like a classical Greek statue come to life. The only *thing* Cat's nudity offended was my self-esteem.

"In Europe, nudity is no big deal," she assured. "The things I saw over there . . ." She smiled, eyes sparking. "But we are so different here, *pravda?*"

I had to believe Russian-American werewolves were different no matter where they were. But I agreed with her. *"Da. Pravda.* True."

She giggled. "'The boys carry their clothing in their mouths, but I prefer to run as nature intended. Besides, I have yet to develop a taste for denim." Shrugging, she added, "I almost always return home before changing back."

I zipped my jacket up and pulled my knees to my chest. Seeing perfection sprawled out in front of me was making me reassess my feminine attributes. "So you guys never, like, explode out of your clothing, right?"

She laughed. "Would that not be spectacular? An expensive habit, though—at least if one had a sense of style." Her nose wrinkled and she leaned forward, cupping her hand around her mouth so the owls and rabbits didn't overhear. "I did once hear Max exploded out of his, but the circumstances were far different from what you are asking about," she quipped, adding a wink for good measure. She watched for my reaction, basking boldly under the thin moonlight.

I blinked.

"I do not mean to disturb you, Jessie," she repeated with a melodramatic sigh. "I could shift again, but it would greatly decrease the odds of my half of the conversation being understood." She grinned. "And God help us if I scent a squirrel while in my wolfskin. My attention span is . . . utter crap."

"It's okay, Cat. I'll cope."

"Eyes up here, Jessie," she teased, pointing to her face.

"Funny girl," I muttered. "So."

"Da. So. What is my little brother doing that has you confused and hurt?"

"Ugh. He doesn't kiss me as much as he did. He doesn't reach for my hand. . . . It's like we're fizzling."

"Fizzling?" The smile slid off her face when she tilted her head in wonder. "The change makes things difficult for the boys. Their brain, their communication is no longer clear. Look at Max. Nearly eighteen and stupid."

I choked and she smiled again.

"The brain of the wolf and the brain of the boy do not cooperate well. Girls mature more quickly. Our brain—our emotions—are more advanced when the change comes. Boys are beastly at seventeen whether wolves or not." Again her nose scrunched up. "He is struggling to adjust. Trying to become comfortable with you seeing him as he is. Trying to become comfortable with who he is."

"He seems comfortable enough around Sarah."

Cat laughed. "It is easy to *seem* comfortable when you do not really care."

"Seriously? It's that simple? He doesn't care about Sarah, so he can be"—taking a breath I steadied my voice—"*affectionate* with her?"

"First, things are never simple, Jessie. We are Russian-American. By definition we are complex."

I could not disagree.

She reached over and took my hand. "Second, affectionate means loving, *pravda?*"

I nodded.

"You misinterpret my brother's feelings. He is not *loving* Sarah. He is stuck with her for now. You put him in this predicament by lying about your feelings for him," she scolded. "Be patient as he works his way free."

Shamed, I considered her words. "And he's probably dealing with what happened that night," I conceded. "It's not easy. *That.*"

She nodded, releasing my hand. We'd become killers that night. Self-defense or not, we had blood on our hands. "Perhaps he feels guilty putting you in such danger."

"He didn't know any of it would happen."

"Guilt doesn't work that way. We feel guilt for things far outside our control. Entire religions work based on guilt."

I kept my mouth shut.

"Pietr takes after our father. He knows it. Father was passionate—he thought with his heart. It got him killed. And now we know it got Mother captured." She looked at the sky, watching the scudding clouds a moment. Licking her lips, she turned back to study me with grave eyes.

"Cat, I'm so sorry."

"Of course you are, Jessie," she said, eyes sparkling. "But the ones who did this are not. They have our mother, and her time is running out. Quickly." She shivered, fighting to maintain her composure. "The boys—perhaps they resist true attachment. They do not want to fall as Father did."

"So Pietr and I—"

"Will work. I know it."

"Have you seen *that* in the tea leaves, too?" I scoffed.

"*Nyet*," she said, the word wistful. "Only in my dreams. But you must believe it, Jessie. Pietr is confused. Scared."

I laughed. The memory, too fresh, of Pietr in his wolfskin, killing Russian mafiosos, didn't let me believe he could be scared. Of anything.

"Believe me, Jessie. You've seen him scared before." Her gleaming eyes anchored mine. "Stand by him. He needs you now more than ever. We must be united to free our mother."

Crap. She was right on so many counts. The night of Pietr's birthday—of his first true transformation—he was terrified. Not of the change itself but of what I'd think of him after. And if we didn't work together, how could a group of teens challenge the CIA and hope to free a rapidly aging werewolf?

I briefly wished for normal teenage problems. Zits would be fine. Oily hair—bring it on. Cramps to take me to my knees?

Okay, maybe not. But *this?*

"We must find her soon." Cat suddenly twisted away, raising a single finger in warning. Her eyes unfocused as she listened. "I must get home quickly."

"Is everything okay?" Before I could finish the question she was a wolf again, tearing away through the woods.

I headed out of the tree line and toward home.

A rustle in the bushes sent me scrambling backward. "Is someone there?"

Muffled noises—boots crunching through leaves. "Who's there?" I demanded as I quickly continued up the slope.

A radio crackled. Maybe ten yards away. "Alpha to Bravo, do you have her?"

Crap. Have who? I sped up, moving away from the noise.

"Negative. The wolf has slipped the trap." The crackling of static faded and boots tromped away.

To hunt my friend.

That was *not* part of any deal.

Finally inside and breathless from running the last distance, I grabbed the phone and called the Rusakovas.

"Allo?" Max.

"Is Cat home?"

"Da, Jessie. She just came in."

"Put her on."

"Demanding," he snorted. "I see why you like this one," he said away from the receiver.

"Allo, Jessie?"

"They're hunting you."

"Da."

"Why didn't you tell me?"

"What good would it do? They are looking for an excuse to take one of us."

"They couldn't do it if you showed up here as—*you,*" I insisted. "Max could have driven."

"I *did* show up as me," Cat's accent deepened. The phone made a noise, shifting hands.

Ugh. "Why give them the chance to take you?"

"This is who we are, Jessie," Max rumbled across the phone lines. "If the CIA chooses not to abide by our agreement let them try to take us."

The phone clicked off before I could find the words I wanted. The sudden knot in my stomach proved I missed Alexi as leader of the Rusakova household. On the outs with the full-blood Rusakovas since they learned of his involvement with the Russian Mafia, he would have been more sensible than Max. But when the wolves discovered that Alexi, long believed by Pietr, Cat, and Max to be their biological brother, was not who he claimed to be . . .

Everything changed.

That night I wrestled with sleep. When I finally closed my eyes my brain refused to stop rolling the violent images in my memory. I was thrown into the meadow at the old park the night Pietr turned seventeen.

The night Pietr became a wolf.

The unmarked SUV rocketed into the meadow, spewing leaves and bullets.

Dropped by my attackers, I scrambled to the vehicle's side, staring in dull horror at the fight raging so close. Officer Kent fell, wounded, gun rolling out of his grasp just before Wanda slid beneath the vehicle and hauled him to safety.

The Mafia dropped around us in slow motion and I barreled under the SUV, going for the gun just before Wanda reached for it realizing she was nearly out of bullets.

The leader's second, Grigori, targeted Wanda. Squeezed the trigger. Wanda rocked back, blood a blooming red flower on her shoulder. Groaning, she steadied her gun and returned fire.

Grazing him.

In the leaf litter my hand closed on Kent's gun as Grigori adjusted his aim to finish Wanda.

I fired.

Grigori's eyes rolled and he fell. Blood dribbled from his mouth, illuminated by the light of the full moon sparkling serenely above. He coughed, a wet rattling sound.

Then he was still.

The gun tumbled from my grip. I'd killed a man. Entrenched in my nightmare the sound around me muffled, my ears felt filled with cotton. The pop-pop-pop of gunfire slowed, dulled to the thump-thump-thump of an ax chopping wood.

Everything went dark and grim, the bellow of the werewolves—

slick with blood—muted by the rush of my pulse as it thrummed in my ears.

A man yelled curses at me, and I spun to see Nickolai, his gun pointed at me.

Shutting my eyes against the end, my world blinked black. I heard a roar—a cry—a gurgle . . . My eyes opened to find Nickolai staggering, his pistol dropping . . .

. . . as his head landed on the ground with the same thump as the muted gunfire. Landed two yards from his body.

In his wolfskin, Pietr stood over Nickolai, claws dripping gore, his muzzle and chest streaked with blood.

Very little of it was his own.

For the first time I saw a wildness to the glow of his eyes— something beyond the predatory sparkle of red reflection—a beast surpassing the definition spinning in my mind. *Werewolf.* Earlier, beneath the rising moon, I'd first seen him change.

But I realized then we were both changed.

Forever.

CHAPTER FOUR

Sophia caught up to me outside my literature class. In her breathy little voice she explained, "You'll need to find a new photographer for the paper. I can't do it anymore." She passed me the communal camera.

"But, Soph—"

Her lips tight, she shook her head, blond hair shimmering in the weak light of the hallway. "I'll continue to co-edit, but no pictures. And here . . ." She withdrew a stack of old photos from a pocket in her backpack.

I rummaged through them quickly. "Wait. Weren't these hanging in your locker?"

"I'm cleaning house," she said.

I didn't buy it. "Everything okay?" I thought about the recent rash of teen suicides on the train tracks that had sliced Junction up like a huge pie. We'd lost an athlete most recently. I hadn't know him personally, but he'd been part of Derek's circle.

"Fine," Sophie said, her brow crinkling. "And . . ." She inhaled deeply, like this was the worst piece of news yet. "They want us to cover a new school lunch program."

I knew instantly who *they* were. The faculty and staff. It wasn't really us against them at Junction; it was more like we worked *for* them rather than *with* them.

We technically ran the paper, but they reminded us who granted the right to have a paper at all. So we spread propaganda from time to time. Most of it was good—helpful to students. Sometimes it just felt bogus. Completely commercial.

"What's the big deal about a new school lunch plan?"

So softly I strained to catch the words, Sophia explained, "Some corporate sponsor gave the school angel funding to make lunches cheaper and more nutritionally sound."

"Woosh." I skimmed a hand just above my hair. "Right over my head. Angel funding? Like, do it or die—get angel wings?"

"No." Sophia stared at me a moment and rolled her eyes. "Like they don't want money back. At all. They donated the money for all the food. They've arranged a distributor. The school keeps whatever money we spend on lunches."

"Huh. So why aren't the lunches going to be free?"

"Thatta' girl," she agreed. "Why would the school still want a profit when they can guarantee free food for all the kids?"

"Okay, so—"

She sighed, tolerating my stumbling. Barely. "So *that's* what you're going to ask—"

Suddenly her words faded; a sound like the ocean filled my ears, ruining my focus.

Pietr and Sarah walked past. Hand in hand. As comfortable as any real couple.

Sarah smiled at me.

Sophia's hand waved before my face. "Tune in, okay?"

"Um, yeah. Who am I interviewing?"

Again with the eye roll.

"Perlson. Remember him? Our vice principal?"

"Yeah, yeah," I grouched, taking the paper she offered.

"You need to cover this fast," she urged. "The program starts soon."

"Oh. Okay."

"Jessie." Sophie snagged my sleeve, tugging me closer with a touch not nearly as soft as her voice. "Quit staring at Pietr."

"What?"

Scandalized, she hissed, "You're staring at Pietr Rusakova. *Sarah's* boyfriend?" She stepped back, her eyes larger than I'd ever seen them. That was saying something since Sophie always wore a somewhat stunned expression. "Wait. Whoa. You and Pietr?"

I scrunched my face up at her. "Don't be ridiculous, Soph. He's Sarah's boyfriend. Like you said."

A light sparked in the depths of Sophie's dark brown eyes. "Jessie. Don't get tangled up with what Sarah wants."

"Hey, Jessica!" Derek headed down the hall toward us, his smile dimpling. All-American good looks, a popular football player, and he actually paid attention to me.

Sad I didn't care much anymore.

"And don't get entangled with Derek, either," Sophie ordered, just outside the volume of her standard whispery words. She toyed with her collar and dodged away before he reached us.

Sophie still did what she could to avoid being near Derek. She'd dated him once and never again. As much as Amy and I tried to pry details out of her, she never said much about it. We'd gotten worried, but she'd assured us it certainly wasn't like he'd physically attacked her.

But that was all she'd said. And only once.

"Hey," I greeted him, focusing on the paper Sophie had pressed into my hands. Prices to be reduced to one dollar. A pretty stiff reduction. Who could reduce things that much in this economy? And who would give that much support to a public school so far from what most considered civilization?

"What you got?" Derek asked, slipping the sheet from my fingers with a brush of his hand.

"Research for an article."

"I heard about this. Sounds like a great deal."

"Yeah. Maybe too great."

Derek grinned. "Sometimes you chase stuff that doesn't need chasing, Miss Investigative Reporter."

"I just want to know the truth behind stuff. Don't you?"

"Nah. Not always," he admitted. "Sometimes the truth's harder to swallow. Why worry so much?"

"So ask the easy questions—if any questions at all?"

"Sure. Perlson's a good guy. No need to see ghosts where there's only shadows, right?"

"And that's why you're an athlete and I'm an editor," I quipped with a smile to echo his. "You can take sports at face value most times. But people?" I shrugged. "They can be harder to figure out."

"Interesting point, except people devise and play sports," he retorted, his grin tilting.

I'd swear his teeth twinkled. "Huh." I took the paper back, stuffing it into my backpack.

"Not just a pretty face here," he said with a chuckle. The warning bell rang. "Whoops. Better get to class." He jogged off.

In silent agreement I headed down the hall, doing a little mental math. Even lunch at a dollar a day might be too much to make sure there was money for Christmas. Dad's factory was still laying off workers and though we doubted he'd be cut, there was little hope for a holiday bonus.

Sarah reached up and kissed Pietr before she dodged into the bathroom for her standard between-class hair check.

Glancing up and down the hallway I decided it was safe enough to join him. We were alone. I reached out to him, but he dodged back, his gaze guarded.

I dropped my hand.

"Tomorrow night we're scouting," he said. "Neither Wanda nor Kent have contacted us about seeing Mother."

"They *want* you to scout."

He shrugged.

"Don't give me the same crap Max is pushing—that macho 'let 'em try' stuff. They have guns. Don't be reckless, Pietr."

"We have limited options. Limited time. And"—he checked the hall—"fangs and claws." A lazy grin sprawled across his lips.

My knees threatened to buckle. "So. Tomorrow night."

He gave a sharp nod and pushed back at the shock of dark hair spiking toward his right eye. "Cat wants you along. I—" Looking down at the floor between us, he seemed to measure the distance. "I don't think you're needed."

"I'm not . . . *needed?*"

He rubbed his nose and looked away.

"You're going."

"*Da,*" he said, settling his eyes on me again, puzzled.

"Then count me in," I insisted.

His jaw tightened.

"Count. Me. In."

One simple word, given so reluctantly: "*Da.*"

Sarah stepped out of the bathroom, making a beeline for us. Her blond hair was perfect. But it already had been when she went in to fix it.

I smiled and waved at her like there was nothing going on beyond two friends chatting. "Pietr," I said with a grin plastered across my face while Sarah remained out of earshot, "if you care for me—keep your hands and your lips off Sarah."

"Okay, no exploding out of clothing. Check."

Cat laughed, her voice crackling over the phone. I needed to put the receiver back in its base later. "What's next?"

"Silver bullets."

"*Nyet,* it does not take a silver bullet to kill us if the shot is perfect. That is a Hollywood invention like having to change under a full moon."

"But you and Pietr turned under a full moon," I protested.

"*Da,* because our birthdays fell at that time. The change activates after the first full moon of our seventeenth birthday. We feel increased desire to change under the moon, but Alexi believes it is because instinctively we know the light is better and easier to run and hunt by. We are the result of scientific tampering, not magic."

"Says the tea-leaf-reading werewolf. How is Alexi?"

"Alive."

I shivered at how coolly she dropped the single word.

"Next?"

"Imprinting."

I heard the smile disappear from Cat's face. "Next?"

I repeated myself.

"Are you referring to Stephenie Meyer's books?"

"Yes," I said. A little unwillingly.

Cat chuckled. "There is no shame in reading enjoyable books. But this topic is better discussed later."

"Got it."

Since we'd learned the CIA had tapped the Rusakovas' phone we were careful about chatting. Cat readily answered things she felt the CIA knew from the Soviet files. Or things that drove them insane—like sales on clothing, who needed to wax, and suitable caloric intake for girls, werewolf or not.

Some nights I thought I could almost hear agents groan.

"Would you like to speak to Pietr?"

My heart hammered at his name. "Of course."

There was a shout and the clunk of one phone clicking off as another was picked up.

"*Allo,*" he said, his voice a rumble in my ear that made my blood rush and my vision blur.

"We need to talk."

"We are talking now."

"Thank you, Captain Obvious."

He chuckled, a deep noise that welled up from somewhere unde niably close to where growls were made.

I flopped back on my bed, curling the pillow to my stomach and taking a deep breath.

"*Va chem dayla?* What's the matter?"

"I need you to stop kissing her," I admitted.

"Oh."

"I know we were going to wean her away gradually, but every kiss . . . it hurts me. I need her to get the hint sooner."

"Will she not push harder?" he asked, his voice going soft. Gentle as snowfall.

"Ugh." I sighed. "Maybe. But she'll get the hint. Soon. Once she knows you don't really want her anymore—"

"I haven't wanted her yet."

The breath caught in my throat. "She'll move on," I guaranteed.

"You're certain?"

"Once a girl knows a guy doesn't want her, she'll find someone who does."

He was quiet a moment. "That sounds—logical."

"Good. Um. *Horashow.*"

He chuckled again, the sound washing over me, warming the pit of my stomach. *"Dobray nohch,"* he said.

"Good night," I replied.

CHAPTER FIVE

The next day Pietr did not once kiss Sarah. Watching, I realized avoiding her lips was difficult. Stooping to get his backpack, her lips were in his way. Grabbing something from his locker, she nearly fell in sliding between him and his notebooks. Sarah's lips were as predictably present as acne the day of a dance.

I wondered how often people got kissed because it was easier to give in than dance away.

Pietr shot me an exasperated look after he nearly toppled into the girls' bathroom avoiding Sarah.

I stayed firm, and Pietr returned to watching the clock whenever Sarah was near.

Time meant everything to Pietr Rusakova because it was so quickly running out. The bonuses to being a werewolf: strength, agility, quick healing. The downside? A short life span and a time-bomb-style countdown ticking away in your ears and getting louder when you made your first full change.

Pietr was dying.

And he knew it.

He'd once told me time didn't matter when he was with me. The way he kissed me, I believed him. Every bit of me wanted to make time stand still for him.

In the cafeteria I opened my bagged lunch and pulled out my sandwich and carrot sticks. Fishing out the yogurt I decided how to start. "It's almost here, you know." I pulled the foil off the yogurt and dug around the bottom with my spoon to mix the berries in. The best stuff was always on the bottom. I paused. Did yogurt and society at large have that in common?

"What?" Pietr cocked his head in speculation.

"Oh. Halloween," I said.

Amy choked with laughter, setting her milk down. "You are *so* transparent!"

"What?" Pietr focused his attention more keenly on me.

Sarah giggled.

I shrugged.

Sputtering, Pietr declared, "She's right!" He reached across the table and jabbed my shoulder. "You're fishing—about your birthday, *da?*"

"Nooo," I insisted.

"Methinks the lady doth protest too much," Pietr quipped, re-loading his fork. "Wait." He set the fork down. "You said before that you always host some sort of birthday bash." His eyes narrowed.

I looked down.

"Oh," he said, realizing as he looked at my lunch.

"Crap." Amy's mood spiraled.

Dad's factory had been in the papers and on the local news again recently. Anytime a business that had been around so long started widespread layoffs, it was talked about. It only made sense we'd be cutting out unnecessary expenditures. Like my birthday party.

"I've had sixteen of them already," I pointed out, brushing it off. Though I'd brought it up.

Amy stared at my sandwich. Living in the trailer park like she did, her dad already out of work, she was as powerless in this as I was.

Pietr grinned as he chewed. "I'll have to keep Catherine out of the kitchen for the sake of the guests, but Max suggested a Halloween party. . . . More to celebrate is always better."

I didn't ask but hoped there might be a hidden meaning to his words. Perhaps *more to celebrate* had something to do with finding their mother. Or being free of Sarah. Either way, I'd welcome the news.

"If you don't mind your birthday being celebrated early, I can convince my family to hold it in conjunction—"

"What a *stupendous* idea!" Sarah said, pulling out one of her more recent vocabulary additions. Since the accident she'd developed a fascination with words, often finding ones I'd misplaced. A fascination with words, and with Pietr. "I'll help."

The joy drained out of the concept for me. "I don't want to intrude."

Pietr kicked me under the table but laughed. "Intrude? You can help with the guest list."

I looked at the chain sparkling around his neck. If he just took it off he'd have flocks of girls desperate to attend even a quilting bee with Pietr Rusakova. The Rusakovas had a strange power that could only be described as the ultimate animal magnetism. Pietr didn't need guest suggestions from me.

"Okay," I conceded. "If it's no imposition. It's really no big deal— and I don't want it to turn into one, either. "

Amy rolled her eyes at Pietr.

"Hey! Really! It's no big deal," I repeated.

This time she rolled her eyes at me. And stuck out her tongue. What a pal.

I waved my hands in the air. "Fine! Whatever."

Amy grabbed my arm. "Even *I* know that's not how you wrap up this conversation," she leered, tugging me to face Pietr. "What do you say?" she coaxed in a singsong voice, like a mother training her child.

"Thank you, Pietr." My face burned as he laughed, the low, amused sound sending a shudder down my backbone.

He refocused on the clock.

A few hours and we would be together, at least for a while.

"Have you seen it?" I asked into the phone.

"*Nyet*," he admitted. "*The Princess Bride?*"

"Yep. I thought . . . since my birthday's going to be celebrated at your Halloween party and I hope . . . well . . ." *God*. Why did I stumble and stutter around him? "I hope all this mess with Sarah will be done. That—"

"We'll be official," he finished for me. "It shouldn't take long. Many things should be better by then."

"So we can go as a couple?"

"*Da*. My present to you." He paused, and I got the impression he was taking notes. "This—Man in Black—do I look like him?"

I giggled. "Not exactly." I pointed out the most important part. "But he's the movie's hero. Only blond."

"Like Derek." The words came out sharply.

"No. *Not* like Derek. Not at all," I objected. "Do you still not get it, Pietr? I seriously like you." I'd decided not to bring up anything remotely related to *love*. "Derek's old news. There was nothing between us, and there won't ever be."

My words were greeted by thick silence.

"I can't imagine what it would take to push me away from you and toward Derek. I don't *want* to imagine."

He sighed. "So I am to dress as the Man in Black and you will be this—Buttercup?"

"Yes. *Da*," I corrected.

"Say it again."

"What?"

His voice grew husky as he repeated his request. "Say yes—*in Russian*—again."

I blushed. "*Da*," I whispered. "Will you teach me more Russian, Pietr?"

"Mmm. Only the important words," he promised.

I bit back my request for the three most important words to me. "What words would you teach me?"

"Pocelujte menyah."

"What's that mean?"

He groaned. "Repeat it tonight and perhaps I will show you. Now, though, I must rent a movie."

"You're going to do that?"

"Of course. I'm a werewolf, not a cretin. We have Blockbuster cards."

It blew my mind. Werewolves rented DVDs. At my local Blockbuster.

"I'll see you tonight," he guaranteed.

"Da," I agreed.

I raced Rio around the paddock that evening, practicing my newest Russian phrase, wondering about Pietr and Sarah, worrying about insisting on going on a scouting mission where I was the only one without freakishly good healing abilities.

I readied for bed—or the ruse of sleep—knowing the Rusakovas would protect me. That worried me, too. I didn't want anyone getting hurt *because* of me. What did Cat really think I could do to help?

I was, after all, only human.

Something cracked against my window. I jumped, rushing over to haul it open.

He stood outside, darkness draping his arms and shoulders in a long ebony coat. He wore black jeans and nothing else. Moonlight washed across his bare chest and stomach. My heart pounded.

Pietr. Dazzling in the darkness. He tilted his head, saying nothing. But I knew what the action meant.

The window slid shut with a squeak. I grabbed a sweater hanging from the edge of my dresser drawer and shrugged into it. Turning off my bedroom lights I locked my door behind me. Dad knew I did so to keep Annabelle Lee from snooping—he might not suspect anything if he came home late and found it that way.

I crept down the stairs and out the door, ignoring the need for a jacket. If Dad returned while I was gone, that'd be the first thing he'd notice. Besides, the way my heart raced so quickly and my blood pumped so hotly I couldn't imagine I needed a jacket at all.

I edged into the darkness gnawing at the soft light that spilled from Annabelle Lee's bedroom window above. She was probably still awake, reading. "Pietr," I whispered, my eyes struggling to find him among the tree trunks and the branches of bushes crackling in the breeze.

CHAPTER SIX

"Uh!" I stumbled back, startled to find him so close. He caught me, his hand hot and fierce as he yanked me up so I stood stably. He studied my face.

"*Pocelujte menyah*," I said. Loudly. And very haltingly.

Something flared in his eyes, bright as wildfire, and he grabbed me, covering my mouth with his. I gasped, and he moved his lips against mine, pinning our bodies together with his powerful arms. Every nerve ending in my body sparked like electricity rioted just beneath my skin as we breathed the same air. Shared the same tastes.

He pulled back, blinking. His eyes glowed the red lantern light of the wolf's and he blew out a breath, bracing himself.

I threw myself at him, reaching up to wrap my arms around his neck and covering his face with eager kisses.

"Easy," he said, his voice strangling in a growl as he gripped my waist and pried me off. His eyes were stunningly bright, as bold as the blinking stoplight at the edge of town. His nostrils flared, filled with my scent. His form quivered in the darkness, stuttering around the edges. He shook himself, puffed out a breath, and rubbed his head. "We need to hurry," he said, smile curling.

"Where's the car?"

"Off the road at the driveway's edge."

"Let's go." I started walking down the drive.

From behind me Pietr called, "This'll be faster."

I heard something unzip. My eyes popped realizing Pietr only wore one zipper's worth of clothing. I spun around and caught a pair of black jeans.

With my face.

I heard, "Hop on," and the wolf was beside me, casting his muzzle up in an arc to remind me to climb up.

"Uhh—" Stunned, I rolled the jeans and tucked them under my arm before climbing onto the wolf's back. Clutching the thick ruff of fur covering his broad shoulders I tried not to think about the fact I was riding Pietr.

Yeah. Not easy to forget leaning across his powerful back, my face in fur that smelled of pine-filled forests. He raced down the long gravel drive to the car, his body so hot from the change I wished I'd carried my sweater with his jeans.

The echo of his heart pounded through his ribs and spine, jolted against my chest, filling me with our shared pulses. My head spun. My stomach dropped like I was riding a roller coaster, not a were-wolf. I melted against him, and all my worries and confusion bubbled back up in my wriggling stomach.

Why couldn't things in my life be simple? Why couldn't Pietr and I just be *us*? Together. In public. *Crap*. Why must Pietr be so amazing and so complicated—so frustrating?

We stopped neatly beside the car and I jumped off him, throwing his jeans at him. "Ugh!" I cried as he changed and slipped into his pants. "You could have just carried me. As a human. But, no. You had to get naked and go all wolf—*commando*. Filling my head with . . ." I clamped my hands over my mouth.

He had the good grace to look abashed. As if he'd never consid-ered another possibility. "The wolf . . ." But he fell silent, head down as he dragged his knuckles across his forehead.

"The wolf makes him stupid," Cat finished for him, opening the door and pulling me onto the seat beside her as headlights appeared down the road.

My body buzzed. It was like the time I'd trained so hard with Rio and found out the competition was cancelled. Like there was something still to do. With a growl of my own, I clicked my seat belt together.

Cat glared at Pietr as he tumbled into the front seat.

From the driver's seat Max peered back at me, eyes glowing just beneath his tousle of dark curls. He had a charmingly sheepish look whenever he wasn't wolfishly eyeing the girls who threw themselves at him. Max was werewolf number three. A few inches taller than Pietr and broader across the shoulders and chest, Maximilian Rusakova was a daunting figure whether slinking through the shadowy halls of Junction High or driving the family's cherry-red convertible. If Max had been interested in football he could have made Junction's Jackrabbits unstoppable.

But Max had just one interest.

Girls.

And the girls returned his interest. Eagerly (at least when he didn't wear his specially devised necklace—which, regardless of how often Cat reminded me they were creatures of science, the necklace still seemed like it required a better, *more magical*, explanation).

Nuts. I was nervous. I was mentally babbling.

Nearly eighteen years old, Max was one of the most wanted seniors at Junction High, but to me, he was too much of a good thing—a little overpowering in a lot of small ways.

He rolled with laughter. "You're both so messed up," he choked out, wiping his eyes with the back of his hand. "Just do it and get it over with!"

"What?" I exclaimed, heat flooding my face. *Do it?* Okay, maybe Max was *a lot* overpowering in some ways.

"Watching you two frustrate each other cracks me up," he snorted, putting the car into gear. *"Don't* do it and I'm guaranteed lots of laughs! How crazy is it: a werewolf revving high and the human who wants him watches him date her friend!" The driver's seat trembled beneath his quaking laugh.

Pietr's face was suddenly beside Max's ear, his lips drawn back, teeth lengthening as he grated out, "Drrrive."

Crossing my arms, I scowled into the mirror at Max.

Normal, normal, normal! Why couldn't I have that? But as the car pulled away I realized as angry as I was at Max, as frustrated with Pietr, still there was no place I'd rather be than with the Rusakovas.

Dammit.

I pulled myself together on the drive. "So, tell me why I'm needed. I mean, I'll help you guys—you know that. But why do you need *me?*"

Max snickered, more hyena than wolf. "Are you asking Cat or Pietr?"

Cat smacked the back of Max's seat. "Idiot!"

My eyes narrowed, and I doubled the intensity of the glare I shot Max. "Cat."

She turned in the seat to face me. "You'll stay with the car while we scout. I do not want us to leave and come back to find it gone. There are no good places to hide it. Stay in the front passenger's seat, and if anyone asks questions, say—"

"The car stopped working and my stupid companion, who *drove*, ditched me to go find some help. We forgot our cells."

Cat smiled at me proudly. *"Horashow."*

"Spahseebuh," I thanked her in kind.

Max pulled the car over on the edge of a road running alongside one of the many suburban neighborhoods that made up Junction. I'd been here before, years ago. There was a community pool not far from a church Mom had us attend before she and Dad all but gave up on organized religion. I earned my first (and last) perfect attendance during the two years we were members.

It had been a friendly little neighborhood then. Now, in the soft light the occasional working streetlight cast, I noticed the sidewalks I'd once walked in what Mom called "my Sunday best" had become cracked and uneven.

"'There is an old church we ran past recently. A scent we recognize," Cat explained.

"Is it a brick and whitewashed church?"

Max's eyes sparked. "*Da,* Jessie. You know it?"

"I attended it. Years ago."

"Many probably say the same. It is abandoned," Cat said.

"Can you guys even—" I couldn't complete the thought.

Cat giggled. "Creatures of science, Jessie. A church is no problem. Holy water—no problem. Crucifixes? No problem."

"Crucifixes freak you out," Max corrected, staring her down.

"I simply feel it is strange to display an instrument of torture on your wall." She shrugged. "We could not get the floor plans through public records," Cat said, hesitating. "Too many questions."

"Too little time," Pietr added.

"It's easy." I chewed my lower lip, recalling details. "The main doors are probably lit. But there's the door on the right side—up a small slope—that leads into the nave, and one around back that opens into the acolyte's waiting room. There's a downstairs with a kitchen and a big room they turned into Sunday school classrooms with funky folding doors. It'll be quick to see the place."

They nodded. Cat looked at Pietr smugly. "See, it was good to bring Jessie."

I knew Pietr hadn't thought I was needed, but it suddenly sounded like he hadn't really wanted me along at all. "Wait. There's also a basement. In the classroom area there's a big wooden door in the floor. There's a small staircase, but it was bad even then. The church ladies complained when they put the season's chowchow down there before the fair."

"Chowchow? Like the dog?" Cat quirked an eyebrow.

"No, chowchow like beans, cauliflower, and vinegar . . ."

"Strange people," Max muttered.

"Seriously?" I strained against my seat belt.

He nodded.

I poked his shoulder. "Borscht-eating werewolf calling chowchow-eating humans *strange?*"

He grinned, his teeth lengthening and sharpening. "Point taken."

He tapped one growing canine tooth with a finger and chuckled as his voice lowered into the wolf's deep rasp.

Some moments I believed Max could've easily been Little Red Riding Hood's wolf. But she probably would have liked it.

"We'll return in ten minutes," Cat assured me, tossing me the keys. "We want to find her, not free her."

"Not yet," Pietr qualified, eyes glowing.

Out of the car they wolfed quickly, slinking along the shadows and hugging the hedges that marked the property boundaries of suburbia.

I hopped into the front passenger's seat and turned the car on to note the time on the dashboard clock. Ten minutes. Reclining in the seat, I promised myself I'd only worry after fifteen. I pulled out my worry stone, rubbing my thumb across its glossy variegated surface. Like Pietr's eyes it was beautiful and blue. Like what shimmered *behind* his eyes—complicated.

When fifteen minutes passed and there was no sign of the Rusakovas, I decided I would not panic.

Yet.

By seventeen minutes I'd pulled apart the car's interior looking for a weapon: a pocketknife, a pair of scissors, anything. It quickly became obvious that werewolves didn't bother with standard weapons. Teeth and claws were more than sufficient.

By twenty minutes I'd found a hefty Maglite flashlight wedged under the driver's seat. It would have to do.

Slipping the car key off the ring, I tucked it in my pocket opposite my worry stone and hid the other keys under the seat.

I was headed to the church twenty-two minutes after the Rusakovas had disappeared into the night.

And I was definitely worried.

CHAPTER SEVEN

I sneaked around the side of the church, wishing for a werewolf's hearing. Tall, stained-glass windows stretched above me, partially boarded up. A faint gleam of light warned me something was wrong. I doubted the Rusakovas needed artificial light to perform their search.

Someone else was there. Correction: had been waiting there.

People talked inside while something pounded against . . . pounded against a wall? A door? The cellar door.

Again. And again.

My heart slammed into my ribs, keeping time with the crashing inside. Pressing my back to the wall I tried to think. There were two distinct human voices. Maybe more.

I didn't have training to deal with even one.

What options *did* I have? I thought back to when I'd attended Sunday school and church here. What else had the little old ladies complained about?

One particularly wet summer water got in and destroyed the chowchow labels right before the fair. Where . . . ? I crept back down the little slope, looking for the path the water had taken.

"Ah!" I crouched beside a small—*small*—window nearly flush with the ground. Inside, the wolves growled and snapped, hurling themselves up the flimsy staircase and against the door.

With a hesitant finger I tapped the glass fixed in the crumbling brick foundation.

Things inside grew eerily still. Then the pounding against the door resumed and the window squeaked open. Cat's face was ghostly against the darkness. "Jessie! *Horashow*. It was a trrrap." She snarled out the last word, teeth in her normally inviting smile spiking to razor sharpness.

I didn't mention it was Pietr's job to state the obvious.

"They had—" Words failed her for a moment, and she shook herself, teeth dulling, eyes shifting from midnight blue to crimson as she struggled for focus—"a pelt that made us think we were on the right track."

"A *pelt?*"

"Our father's."

My stomach churned and I thought about the men inside. "How many of them are there?"

"Two."

"Distract them. Keep them near the door while I sneak in."

"Get Alexi," she suggested.

"There's no time for that. They won't keep you here. They'll want you headed to wherever before dawn."

"What will you do?"

"Try not to make matters worse. I'll come in up top."

"We will keep their attention," she promised.

A hush fell as the window shut and I circled around to the exterior acolyte's door.

I tested it, the old decorative knob squealing in my grasp. Slow and easy. I waited for the distraction, remembering the room. The door was often unlocked, until one time the acolyte discovered a deacon slumped against the wall, all the tiny cups of wine drained.

Mom had said it was no surprise, considering how many people showed up only for Communion and holidays instead of every Sunday. They weren't truly attending church, she claimed, just "paying their fire insurance." So to show our commitment we had perfect attendance. If we were going to be Saved, we would put in our time. She lived the saying "Nothing's worth having if you haven't worked for it." That applied to heavenly salvation, too.

A crash from the cellar that made the sanctuary shimmy jerked me back from my memories. I yanked the door open, the smell of mildew strong as I dashed through the small room and down the carpeted aisle lined by carved and uncomfortable pews.

In the nave I went onto the balls of my feet and stole to the head of the winding staircase. One hand on the smooth wooden banister, I peered down, looking for trouble and hoping trouble wasn't already looking for me.

Squatting, I kept below the visual barrier the banister drew in midair and I slid one leg down the stairs at a time, like a fencer practicing lunges on uneven turf. Gradually I made the distance, pushing my back against the wall as the staircase angled around to the main floor.

Curses spewed from the classroom area. The random quaking of the cellar door, so fierce it threatened to shake the church's foundations, surely rattled the nerves of the werewolves' captors.

I peeked around the corner.

"They're stronger than we were told," the tallest of two men griped.

I shuddered, recognizing his voice from when it had crackled across the radio the night they chased Cat from my farm.

"Damn straight. There. Get that table over here, too. So she says to me get this—she says—"

Darting to the double doors separating the hall from the classes, I slid behind the one that remained closed. I glanced around the door, watching the men as the cellar door and floor around it convulsed beneath the brutal werewolf attack.

"Can you believe it?" the smaller one asked. "She wouldn't tell me what she wants for her birthday, but man did she pout when she got something she *didn't* want!"

They'd moved as much furniture as they could to cover the huge door. And they continued to add to the heap. Filing cabinets, tables, chairs, a desk, an old television . . . all piled up to keep the Rusakovas down.

"They should be here soon," the smaller man decided, looking past my hiding spot and toward the church's front doors. "Unless Martinez is driving. He's as bad as a chick."

I pulled farther back, breathing heavily, my spine flat against the wall. My fingers wrapped tighter around the Maglite, its weight comforting. The best and only weapon I had.

"They should roll up anytime," the taller man agreed.

The short one started in my direction, saying over his shoulder, "Stack something else up there, too—anything you can find. I'll make sure they aren't waiting outside like morons."

The tall one returned to moving the stack of furnishings around and fighting to keep his feet whenever the old wood floor buckled beneath him.

I brought the Maglite up over my head, watching the space between the door and the jamb as the short man approached. I held my breath until my lungs burned and he appeared on my side of the door. With all the speed I could muster I cracked the flashlight down on his head.

He looked at me, surprised, before he crumpled to his knees, falling flat on his face.

Unconscious. And unnoticed thanks to the rattling floor.

"Sorry." Hooking my hands under his arms I tried to drag him out of his partner's potential line of sight. He was like a sack of stone: way too heavy to move.

Crap, crap, *crap!*

Instead, I rounded the door and headed for his partner as he examined a weary-looking upright piano. I almost lost my footing as the floor heaved again. The man turned toward me, shock lighting his face. I swung at his head, but he ducked, grazing my face with a punch. As I swung again he swept my feet from under me with a move of his own.

Landing hard on my back, the breath rushed out of me. The Maglite clattered away.

"Little bitch," he snapped, going for his gun. "You're playing a dangerous game."

Beneath the floorboards all hell broke loose. A savage howl shook the place. Every hair on my arms stood in recognition.

Pietr.

The man's gaze strayed to the hallway, where his talkative companion still lay. Made mute by Maglite.

My head against the floor I heard something grind, grate, and shift in the basement. Again and again. Glass broke, a distant, tinkling sound.

"Damn," the man said, his eyes again on me. "I didn't expect it'd take something this extreme to get him to shut up. Maybe I should thank you." He leveled his gun at me. "But I have shoot-to-kill orders." Thick eyebrows dropping down to shadow his eyes, he said, "I can shoot anyone but the bastards in the basement. So come on. Give me a reason."

I held my breath, absolutely still. Cooperating.

"Oh, hell," he said, finger moving to the trigger. "I don't really *need* a reason. And the paperwork a witness causes—"

I screamed as the window at my side exploded. Colored shards and heavy cords of leading sprayed the room, the wolf landing on the man so fast I nearly missed it.

A shot sounded, and Pietr had the man's arm in his mouth, shaking it like I'd shake out a rag. The gun clattered to the ground and I grabbed it, turning it on my would-be killer.

"Pietr!" I shouted. "Let him go!"

But the beast that was Pietr shook him harder. Joints popped, bones crunched. The man fell limp, his mangled arm still in Pietr's canine jaws.

"Pietr!" I screamed. I pulled the gun's hammer back and fired a round into the ceiling.

Plaster and dust sprinkled the wolf's face and shoulders, freckling him with white. For a heartbeat I imagined the wolf standing still and silent amidst snowfall.

The wolf froze, watching as I clambered to my feet.

"Drop him!" I commanded.

He obeyed. Hesitantly.

"We have to go."

The wolf quivered a moment and became Pietr, human and panting with effort, slick with sweat and speckled with plaster. Standing before me. *Naked.*

Glancing away I rubbed at my eyes. Seeing my somewhat-boyfriend naked so often was bound to mean I needed to find my way back to some church to confess. "We have to go," I repeated.

Before I knew what was happening, Pietr passed me out the window, dropping me onto Max's thickly furred back. Then Pietr leaped out, joining us, once again warm in his wolfskin.

I glanced at the gaping hole where the small basement window had been. The bricks torn away, each tugged free like a loose tooth ripped from a dusty mouth. "Why couldn't you have thought of that sooner?"

We slunk back to the car as an unmarked SUV pulled up outside the church; two well-dressed men carrying briefcases stepped up to the front doors to knock.

The Rusakovas, human once more, slipped into their clothes as easily as I slipped the key out of my pocket and into the car's door. I slumped into the backseat, flipping the key to Max and connecting my seat belt before curling into a ball.

Cat's hand stroked my hair like tongues of flame licking at my head. I closed my eyes, struggling not to think about the origins of the dark fur she cradled in her arms. Resting my forehead against the window as we sped away, I tried to lose my focus in the blur of streetlights and headlights.

I dozed, a moment—maybe more—my sleep interrupted by disjointed words and the sense of eyes on me—Pietr's eyes. Red and glaring one moment. Frightened the next.

"Never again. *Vwee pohnehmytyuh menya?*"

"*Da,*" Cat whispered. "I understand, Pietr."

"I've got her."

A mumble of protest raised in response.

"*Nyet,* Cat. You did enough bringing her into this." I had the strange sensation of being rocked and lifted, curled against a heater where a ticking clock raced. Wind pushed past me, snatching my hair and cooling my face.

I opened my eyes briefly, catching a glimpse of the face I always longed to see waking and in my dreams. The set of the strong jaw, the raw power of his neck and shoulders . . .

Pietr. Holding me.

Curling tighter against him, I ignored the stinging wind, focusing on the clock ticking its life away so fast. Time was short. Life was uncertain. Every moment had to count.

My window clicked shut, and I jerked upright in bed, staring. Perplexed.

I shivered in my pajamas. What an odd dream. Nudging deeper under my covers, I noticed my clothes in a neat stack by my hamper, waiting for me to decide if I could wear them for farm chores in the morning.

I lurched upright again. Because I *never* did that, even when I planned to. I blinked. Pajamas. Clothes in the wrong—well, the right—place. Grabbing my pillow to fluff it, I froze. A gun glittered there, bathed in the slender moonlight piercing my window.

Not a dream. I stroked the soft sleeve of my pj's and shrank beneath the covers, not sure what to do except try and dream all the danger away.

CHAPTER EIGHT

Unfortunately, in sleep my nightmares teamed up. They began with the story I'd learned about Pietr's father's murder. Pietr's voice, slow and sweet, with only the faintest hint of a Russian growl coloring his inflection, narrated the night his world changed forever. His words, combined with the publicly accepted account of the Phantom Wolves of Farthington, crept through my sleeping brain. And my imagination—my gift of creativity—filled in any blanks he'd left.

I watched what Pietr, Cat, and Alexi never saw that night, all under the hazy guise of a dream. Standing in shadow I saw the neighbor looking for escape, saw the way his face lit when the gun glinted. And when Andrei fell, a growl rose in *my* throat, protective and as outraged as Tatiana must have been.

The red wolf leaped up only to be shot down. And as she crashed to the ground, an SUV came into view and the wolves' bodies were pitched in its back.

"No," I moaned. It went against the newspaper reports. The SUV wheeled around and my vision trembled, shifted and changed, dropping me under the dogwood tree near Skipper's. Mom's sedan approached, and Sarah, now behind the wheel of the SUV, skidded into the lot, slamming into Mom's car, setting it ablaze. I ran forward, sobbing, unable to get her out. The nightmare stuttered again, and the car I stood by was the CIA's SUV, Mafia men firing all around me as Wanda grabbed my arm and pulled me down and I screamed out my frustration.

There was a slamming sound—cursing, *shouting*—and I sat up, gasping and chilled by my own sweat. The slamming started again.

"Jessie! Jessie!"

Where . . . ? I jumped. Recognizing my room, I struggled toward the door, falling as I fought to untangle my feet from the bedsheets. "Dad! Dad! What is it?"

The shouting stopped, and my door rattled. I unlocked it, and Dad charged in, his eyes wide. He grabbed my shoulders, staring at me. "Jessie, are you okay?"

In the hallway, Annabelle Lee stood, rubbing her eyes.

"Yeah, Dad . . ."

"You were screaming," he whispered. "You've never . . ."

"I've never screamed in my sleep before." My eyes squeezed shut as Dad reached over and turned my lamp on.

Annabelle Lee gasped. Her hand shot to her mouth and she stared at me, wide-eyed.

"What the hell?" Dad's voice rose, making my eyes pop back open. He reached out a disbelieving hand, thick fingers trembling as he pushed my hair back.

"What?" I breathed. Reaching up to touch the spot he stared at, I winced, feeling the bruise. I swallowed, remembering when the tall man had knocked me down in the church.

"How did this happen?"

My mind reeled. "I—"

"You were out with that boy, weren't you—Rusakova?" He spit the name out, daring me to defend Pietr or disagree. My mind muddled from going so quickly from the nightmare to harsh lamplight, I searched for a word, an explanation . . .

That was all it took—a moment's hesitation.

"He hit you," he declared. Shaking my head, I stammered it

wasn't true, but he'd made up his mind. Pietr was Russian. The Mafia and he had heritage in common. Therefore he was brutal. The fingers on Dad's right hand curled into a fist. "I'll—"

"No, Dad—*no!*" I clutched his wrist and pulled open his fingers so he took my hand instead. He trembled, enraged. "No," I insisted, grabbing his gaze with my own.

But his eyes kept straying to the bruise, and I knew my father had decided the same thing Pietr feared about himself: that Pietr was a monster after all. But it had nothing to do with being a werewolf. And everything to do with being Russian.

"You're grounded," he said.

"What?" I blinked at him. My cheek stung.

"No phone, no computer, no visitors. No visiting." He dropped my hand to cradle my face gently in his broad, calloused palms. "It's my job to protect you, Jessie. What would your mama say if I didn't? What sort of daddy would I be?"

I didn't realize I was crying until the tears dripped off my chin, moistening my pajama top. I looked to Annabelle Lee for support. Big surprise. She shook her head and walked away.

Dad kissed my forehead. "Now go to sleep. You're safe."

He turned off my light and shut the door, leaving me standing there in the dark.

In shock.

CHAPTER NINE

I'd never thought much of wearing makeup. Too many girls at school wore too much, attempting to show they were growing up.

Instead of looking mature, it made most look old.

But I *felt* old. And looking at the bruise on my cheek in the bathroom mirror's light that morning I decided drastic measures were needed. Some liquid concealer, powder, and blush later and I looked . . . *well* . . .

I examined myself in the mirror.

Not *entirely* whorish.

It would have to do.

It hurt to eat cereal, so I considered a radical liquid diet for the day. Coffee and orange juice to start.

"Hurts, doesn't it?" Dad asked.

I ignored him.

"Stay clear of that boy," he ordered.

"Dad. It's not what you think."

"Then tell me what it is."

At the bottom of our long, gravel driveway the bus pulled up. Early. "I will."

The bus honked, and I raced out the door, backpack and bag lunch in hand, jacket and scarf trailing as I ran.

I bounded up the steps to join Pietr.

"Makeup?" he asked, raising an eyebrow as I sat.

I shrugged, praying he wouldn't press me for a reason.

Instead, he bent toward me, sweeping a few strands of my hair away from my face. "You're hurt," Pietr murmured, his eyes darkening. Thunderstorms roiled in their depths.

"It's no big deal." I took his hand and moved his fingers lightly down the curve of my face. Content beneath his hesitant touch, I sighed, my eyes latching on to his.

His breathing hitched. "Last night," he realized, a faint line marring his brow.

"Yeah. But—" I looked down. Where were the words to explain it was nothing—a scratch, a bump, something so insignificant I could have gotten it doing chores . . . ?

His hand heated my chin as he tilted it up so my eyes had to look into his again. I tried to ignore that across the aisle gossip-queen Stella Martin and Billy (an underclassman cultivating an early mustache) burned holes into me, staring at such an intimate exchange.

"I wasn't . . . I couldn't . . ." His brow lowered, darkening his already shadowy eyes. He pushed out a breath.

"Pietr." I said his name like a protest. "Usually I'm the one stumbling for words." I smiled.

His expression was grim. "This wouldn't have happened if—"

Maybe it was the bumpy road or maybe something more, but his hand trembled and I wrapped my fingers around his wrist, bolstering him.

"If what, Pietr?" My voice faltered.

He gently peeled my fingers away, releasing my chin, his eyes the blue of the most distant piece of sky. Mouth tight, his lips grew thin as his jaw set. I caught glimpses of his reflection as he turned to the window and wrestled with something in his head.

Hand on his shoulder, I assured him, "It's no big deal. You're thinking about this waaay too much."

He whipped around so quickly Stella gasped. *"Nyet,"* he snapped, searching my face. "I never thought about it enough. That's the problem. This—" He touched the bruise so softly. . . . But I winced. His expression locked down, rage on simmer. "This could have been much worse." His hands fumbled on my shoulders and he drew me closer so I was the only one to hear. "He had a gun on you."

That was the last thing he said on the bus that morning. I wanted to remind him I'd been through worse the night of his birthday, but he would have only twisted things around to support what he just now realized: that I was simply human.

Pietr kept his distance from me the rest of that day. Whenever I felt his eyes fall on my face they seemed so sad. And so determined.

Sarah continued throwing herself at him, and, to add to my frustration, his reflexes had dulled. She landed frantic kisses on his lips twice, twisting her arms tightly around him once in a body-wrapping stranglehold of victory.

Unable to watch, I saw Derek approach.

"Hey."

"Hey," I replied.

"You look great today," Derek complimented me. "Makeup."

Why couldn't Pietr have said *that* and not wondered? "Yeah."

"You don't need it," he added. "Most girls pay—lots—to try and get the natural beauty you have."

"Ha."

He frowned, realizing he was getting nowhere. "You seem kind of down." He rested his hand on my shoulder.

Warmth tingled out from his touch, and I sighed. While Pietr's touch could be fire and flame, Derek's was a slow-building heat—sunlight and summer.

"Anything I can do?"

I forced a smile. "Nope. It'll work out."

"Sure," he agreed, giving me one of his dazzling smiles. "Sarah and I were talking about you."

"Oh." I couldn't hide my skepticism.

"It was all good," he assured. "Anyhow . . . Sarah had an idea. . . ." He motioned to her as she stood scrutinizing our body language from across the hall. She pried her arms free from Pietr.

Pietr looked past our heads, studying the wall and avoiding the questions filling my gaze.

Bopping over, Sarah paused in front of me. She clasped her hands and broke out her most winning smile. "When was the last time you went riding?"

The sting of her kissing Pietr was so fresh, I was immune to her charm. "I ride Rio almost every night."

"I mean, when was the last time you competed in an event?"

I blinked at her, stunned. "June sixteenth."

Derek's hand slid down my arm.

Pietr's eyes focused on me—until Derek took my hand.

Sarah rubbed her forehead, just beneath her soft blond bangs, where a scar still marked her involvement in Mom's accident. The smile fluttered off her lips.

Derek set his other hand on her shoulder. Her smile twitched back to life like some mad scientist's experiment in reanimation. "It's been far too long, I think. *We* think." She inclined her head toward Derek.

"It's your idea. I simply agreed," he said.

"Anyway, what if you got back on the horse—so to speak? Initiated a full competition regimen again?"

I looked past them to Pietr. He studied the floor tiles like he wasn't hearing our discussion. Or like he was considering a career in masonry.

"It would take my mind off things, I guess."

"You did *relish* competing, didn't you?" Sarah prodded.

"Yeah." Flying over fences and bushes on Rio was a rush that was hard to beat. Unless I was kissing Pietr.

"Think about it," Derek suggested, dropping his hand from Sarah to also fold it around the hand of mine he held.

"Okay, I will," I promised, slipping my hand out of his.

And I *did* think about it. All day. Almost as frequently as I thought about Pietr avoiding me.

That afternoon as I finished reviewing the assignment list for the upcoming issue of the newspaper at school, I called the Rusakovas. *Grounded* didn't stick as easily when I was at Junction High.

Cat picked up. *"Nyet,* I am sorry, Jessie. Pietr's locked himself in his room to study. He said he will not take phone calls. He seems preoccupied. *Kak dayla?* What's going on?"

"Nothing. I hope it's nothing."

Pietr nodded acknowledgment to me on the bus the next morning, but didn't move the backpack on the seat beside him. I sat, glaring at the lumpy barrier.

"Look," I said, tugging my hair back to show the barest hint of the fading yellow bruise. "Almost gone."

He nodded, a curt move of his head. His eyes remained dark. Stormy and troubled.

"I'm okay." I reached out to him.

He drew back and forced his lips into a smile. "You will be," he agreed, once more turning to stare out the window.

That day Sarah landed three kisses on Pietr, entwining her fingers into his dark hair to better capture him for one particularly long one. He didn't seem to put up much of a fight.

Probably just distracted.

Hopefully because things were going well in the hunt for his mother. But if so, he didn't mention it to me.

Back home I alternately pushed Rio to gallop and slowed her to a walk, occasionally letting her lead around the yard as Hunter and Maggie kept a silent watch. All the time I thought about Pietr. And his family. I couldn't imagine knowing your mother was alive and you couldn't get to her—couldn't see her, hug her, kiss her . . . even argue with her.

I wouldn't have done well in their shoes, waiting for someone else to decide when or if I could see her. It was no wonder they loped through the night, hunting for her while they waited for permission to visit.

I flicked the reins, encouraging Rio into a jog.

Of course, if I had the option of seeing my mom one last time, instead of knowing she was gone already and forever, I would have waited as long as it took to be with her again.

Winding back toward the barn I straightened in the saddle, seeing someone leaning on the split-rail fence. I slowed Rio to an ambling walk, wondering why *he* was here.

Derek waved at me and straightened, the breeze playing in his soft golden hair.

Rio trotted toward him and I nodded. My expression must have shown my puzzlement. "Hey." I glanced at the driveway. Mercedes. No truck. No point telling him I wasn't supposed to have visitors.

He walked around the fence and stood beside Rio. "I was thinking more about you starting competition again."

"Really? That's why you're here?"

"Not entirely. But the Golden Jumper is coming up."

The Golden Jumper. The biggest competition in our county. "Too fast. I've missed registration."

"So? Chuck and Lucy are old friends of the family."

"Charles Overton and Lucinda Walsingham?"

"The same." He grinned when my mouth popped open. "Anyhow, if you'd like to ride, I can call in a favor. . . ." He rubbed his head, short hair shimmering.

"Really?"

"Really."

"Well, um. Yeah. *Please*," I added. The deadline of the Golden Jumper competition would force me to focus on riding. "Cool. Why else did you come by?"

"I want to learn to ride," he confessed, glancing down, suddenly bashful.

As much as I was over Derek, I had to admit there was something about him.

"If there's anybody patient enough to teach me, it's bound to be you." His boyish smile dazzled me, and my cheeks warmed.

"I don't really teach," I claimed. "I mean, once at camp . . . but that was nine-year-old girls. Frankly, I'm more comfortable training horses than people."

Rio stayed still beneath me as Derek reached up to touch my leg. "Then think of me as a colt in need of a firm hand."

I blushed, images of Derek flicking through my head like clips in an old film. Derek playing touch football in the park. On the skins' team. Derek at the town pool in his navy blue trunks, water dripping from his hair. Derek smiling at me. Derek kissing me at the Homecoming game.

"What are you thinking? You're grinning ear to ear."

Embarrassed, I realized I'd mentally equated Derek to a stud instead of a colt. His hand fell away, and I cleared my throat, banishing the thought. "I'm thinking more teaching would be good on my college apps, but it takes time."

"Any good education takes time."

"And, as much as I'd love to—"

"I can pay."

"I don't—" But the idea of additional money when there was trouble at Dad's factory . . . Without a Christmas bonus, the money was quite a lure.

"Handsomely," he added with a wink.

Any other day my pride might have stepped in and made me see sense. Besides, regardless of the additional income, what would Pietr say?

I gnawed my lower lip. Pietr hadn't said much of anything these past few days. And Derek gave me his puppy dog eyes. And a tidy stack of bills like it was nothing. "Okay."

I could talk Dad into this. It was business, not pleasure.

And I could be professional. I'd be instructing him. It wasn't like we were starting a relationship. So what if he was my old crush? "Fine. Two days each week. Your choice."

"Tuesday and Thursday," he said without hesitation.

"Oh. Okay. Tuesday and Thursday."

"Will he . . ." Derek paused, looking up into my eyes as he put out a hand to help me down.

"What?"

"Will Pietr give you any problem?" he asked. "I know there's something going on between you. Even if Sarah doesn't."

"No," I took his hand, but I wasn't as certain as I sounded. I slipped my leg over the saddle to dismount. Images flooded my brain again, blurring my vision and toying with my perception. I only saw one thing clearly.

Pietr kissing Sarah.

I fell forward.

And Derek caught me.

He held me against his body, sliding me slowly down his front until the breath caught in my throat and my boots touched the ground. Nose to nose, he smiled at me. "I don't want to cause you any trouble," he confided. "Even though I think you could do much better than Pietr Rusakova."

He released me. "Tuesday," he confirmed, walking back to the waiting car.

Yeah.

It was sure to be no trouble.

CHAPTER TEN

"Sorry you're still grounded," Sarah said one morning in the hallway, *sans* Pietr.

Was there anyone who *didn't* know?

"So how did your rendezvous with Max go, you shameless girl?" she teased.

Seriously? *That* was the rumor explaining why I'd gotten grounded? My makeup application skills were surely not *that* good or the CIA would be contacting me any day about working deep cover. I'd kept my ears closed to what people were whispering, but rumors flew around Junction fast as hayseed in summer.

I refused to show shock. "It was as much a surprise to me as it was to you."

"Are you two going out?"

Pietr appeared, lugging Sarah's backpack along with his own. He watched me a moment, then searched for the nearest clock.

I focused on Sarah. She was smiling. Being supportive.

Dammit.

Her hand slipped into his, and she swung it gently. Casually. Like they were *really* together.

Dammit.

My lies and choices had led us all here, so I couldn't—well, *shouldn't*—blame her. But I did. For so much. "It wouldn't work out with Max and me." My eyes drifted to Pietr's and managed to hold them for the length of one sentence: "Although he's *amazingly* sexy."

Pietr gave no sign of hearing. He wasn't looking at me anymore. He was watching the clock.

Again.

"Sorry. Max *is* a hottie." Sarah linked her arm with mine and sighed, leaning against me. "There's someone out there for you, Jessica. Closer than you think."

I followed her gaze across the hallway.

Derek stood spotlighted in the stark autumn sunlight, blond hair glowing, bright eyes smiling to match his handsome mouth as he joked with his football buddies. He must have felt our eyes on him, because he paused and looked at me, his smile broadening into an easy grin.

"He's a looker," she confided, giving a little wave as she clung to me.

I bit the inside of my cheek before whispering, "'But I really think it's guts that matter most.'"

"What?"

"Just a song stuck in my head," I mumbled, thinking of Spill Canvas's "All Over You." And the truth.

She sighed again.

"You seem tired."

"Do I look tired?" she asked, fingers flying up to touch her face in wonder. She played with the silky blond curls that framed her face so perfectly, hiding the scar that nudged at her hairline, a reminder she'd nearly died in the accident.

The accident she'd caused.

"No. No. You look fine. You just . . ."

"I'm not sleeping well," she admitted, rubbing the spot hidden by her bangs.

"Nightmares?"

Her eyes narrowed.

"I'm the queen of nightmares," I reminded. "Have them, probably induce them in others." She still didn't smile. "If you want to talk about them—"

"No." The word was sharp with warning as she let go of my arm.

"Oh. Okay."

"*No*," she repeated, softening her reply and patting my arm. She rubbed the scar again. "It's a *conundrum* I don't want to bother you with. I'm sure I can work through this myself."

Yeah, I thought. Because working through stuff by myself was going so freakishly well for *me*.

Amy was sick of the drama and no matter what I did or said, she wouldn't let it go. "Look. He doesn't get to manhandle you in private and then parade around with psycho-Sarah in public."

I nearly corrected her, pointing out there wasn't any manhandling going on anymore and I actually missed it, but she added, "Even if he *is* hot."

My eyebrows leaped toward my scalp.

"Yeah. Whatever. Sometimes what I think just falls out of my mouth. Nice shirt, by the way."

"Laundry day."

"I *wasn't* being sarcastic. I like it."

I glanced down at the words emblazoned across my front. BEST TAKEN WITH A GRAIN OF SALT. "Yeah. Annabelle Lee's started making T-shirts."

"Cool."

"She gave me one for you."

Amy stopped dead in the hall. "Seriously?"

"Seriously." I dug in my backpack. "She thought you'd look great in green."

"She does." Amy's on-again-off-again boyfriend, Marvin Broderick, joined us. "In green, *out* of green . . ."

"Shut up," she teased, putting the shirt in front of her and smoothing it to fit the contours of her body.

Amy had me by a year and at least one cup size. She'd failed a grade along the way, but being one of the oldest in our class also meant she was one of the best built. For her, failing got her more attention than if she'd aced her classes.

Marvin was part of that extra attention. A senior, he was Amy's connection to where she should have been.

The green T-shirt was the perfect color for Amy's stunning red hair. And DEFYING GRAVITY was written right across her boobs. She grinned. "That's so wicked! May they always do so," she said with a giggle. "Thank Annabelle Lee for me. Your sister's certainly something else."

"Don't I know it."

But her grin flipped when she caught sight of Sarah, her arms wrapped around Pietr. "We need to fix this."

"Amy—don't." I grasped her arm. "If he doesn't want me . . ."

"He *does*."

"I hate to point this out, baby . . . ," Marvin joined in, addressing Amy, "but maybe Jessica's right. Sarah's got a reputation. Everybody knows she's eas—"

"-ily led astray," I finished for him. I didn't want to consider it. Yeah, I knew guys thought about a lot more than passing Trig or Calculus. *Making* passes was more their style. I would even bet Pietr thought about it faster than most guys at Junction High because of his freaky biology.

And I knew enough about Pietr's brother Max to know he wasn't one to encourage living a chaste lifestyle (especially considering the rumors going around the school). Unless he spelled it C-H-A-S-E-D. Which was what Max liked to be, by lots of girls. Still, the words slipped out of my mouth. "Would Pietr stay with her for—"

Amy sighed. "Is there a guy who wouldn't?" Seeing my expression, she quickly added, "Unless he could upgrade."

Hoping Amy's pessimism wasn't an accurate view of guys, I muttered, "I'm not interested in playing Sarah 2.0. Either he wants me or he doesn't."

I looked down the hall and watched a moment. Sarah stretched up on her tiptoes to kiss him. And Pietr saw no one but Sarah. Kiss four of the day.

My stomach balled up, sour as Amy's expression.

I'd wondered what Pietr wanted.

It seemed I had my answer.

"Vice Principal Perlson will see you now."

I smiled at the secretary and stood up, looking past the poster that discouraged students from suicide. I didn't know why so many teens in our area were killing themselves (and I certainly wasn't allowed to address it in the school paper), but I doubted posters were going to put an end to it.

I headed into Perlson's office, by this point far too familiar ground. I'd been here after I smeared my fist across Jenny's and Macie's faces. And I'd been here after the drug-sniffing dog tried to kill me because I'd made an unwise fashion choice. It hadn't been an ugly sweater, just way too big. Just because it smelled like werewolf . . .

Now, though, I was here on my terms. Interviewing the VP about the upcoming lunch plan. A plan that seemed too good to be true—except the school would make a profit off the kids.

Perlson motioned me to sit. "Good afternoon, Miss Gillmansen. It's a pleasure to have you in my office in a different capacity," he said with a flash of his broad smile. "Keeping out of trouble is the best way to go through school, don't you think?" His lilting voice went perfectly with the palm trees I associated with his native land.

Part of a special exchange program for midlevel administrators, he'd come to our district in late summer to prepare. He was entrancing, his complexion like dark brown sugar and molasses. There were few people of African descent in Junction, and although businesses claimed they were equal opportunity employers, I had my doubts about a few. So I was thrilled when the school had announced his arrival.

But my intrigue at having someone so fabulously foreign—so distinct—faded when he began to distrust me. Besides, nothing could be more foreign, or more fascinating, than Russian werewolves.

He folded his dark hands together, linking his fingers and putting them behind his head. "You have questions about the school lunch plan," he stated, relaxing in his chair.

"Yes, sir. The plan is paid for by angel funding?"

"Yes. So we never need to pay it back."

"Wonderful." I scribbled in my notebook.

"It also gives us superior food quality, considering federal standards. Better food, better processing, better distribution."

"I won't complain about that," I assured him. Federal standards were continually on the rise, but I'd read Upton Sinclair's *The Jungle* and didn't want to think too much about food between farm and table as a result. What had become unacceptable was still accepted in some places.

He smiled again, beaming at me.

"It'll remove us from the federal program, won't it?"

"Yes."

"What if the organization folds? Can we get back in?"

"We won't need to." The radiance of his smile diminished like the brightness of a bulb on a dimmer switch.

"Lots of our students get free lunch. What about them?"

"They will be allowed free lunch on the new program," he assured me. "Just a little additional paperwork."

"If the program allows free lunch transfers and is fully funded by a corporation that won't fold, why charge anything?"

His smile became close-lipped. "This may be difficult for a student to understand, Miss Gillmansen—"

"Try me."

Straightening in his chair, he licked his lips, hands sliding down to rest on his desk.

"Where will the additional money go?" I pried.

"Into a specialized fund."

"For what?"

"Discretionary purposes." His dark eyes glimmered.

"Like . . ."

"Whatever Administration decides the school needs."

"New computers?"

"Maybe."

"Water fountains that don't leak?"

"Perhaps."

"Bonuses for low-level employees and teachers?"

"No."

"I would have supported *that* one."

He blinked. Slowly. "Miss Gillmansen. Please remember that although we encourage students to try their hands at media coverage through the school newspaper and daily broadcasts, they aren't resources for inflaming the school population.

"This program is good. We want everyone on it. It will make the students in Junction better than before. The quality of the fuel they put into their bodies will be greatly improved." He rapped on his desk with his knuckles. "Make sure that's clear."

Picking up his phone he punched in a number, saying to me, "I look forward to seeing your rough draft."

"What?"

He smiled, speaking into the phone. "Yes, please tell him now's good." He glanced at me again. "Monday morning."

"Is this censorship?"

"No. Prudent behavior."

I headed for the door, not sure what to say.

In the hallway, I passed Derek.

"You okay?" he asked, touching my arm.

My anger and frustration flowed away like water running through my fingers. "Yeah," I said through what was surely a dopey smile. "Better already."

"Good," he whispered. "That's why I'm here."

CHAPTER ELEVEN

During our regular service learning assignment Pietr avoided me. Jaikin, Hascal, and Smith welcomed me back into our socially awkward clique, flirting with me as Pietr sat at the van's front, his back straight and stiff.

They marveled at what the addition of makeup did to a girl's face, whereas I couldn't wait for the day I wouldn't need it and could unclog the junk I'd jammed into my pores.

Pietr ignored us. Especially me. Determined to make him react, I flirted more boldly.

But if my playing bothered him at all, it never showed.

Twice I escorted a lizard around Golden Oaks Adult Day Care and Retirement Home with Hascal and Smith. Due to allergies Hascal carried a goldfish in a baggie on our missions to enliven Golden Oaks.

Smith carried a huge torch for me.

The situation was difficult. At best.

The highlight of those trips was visiting Mrs. Feldman on the fourth floor. She taunted Smith with the uncanny way she pulled cards from her strange and colorful deck, telling him things no one could have known.

Hascal also took a turn at having her pull cards, stupefied each time she said something that was dead on. He spent a lot of time speculating as a result of Mrs. Feldman's cards, and I loved seeing two brilliant minds blown at the same time.

I was tempted to have her pull cards for me, but I didn't want to know what my future held if it continued without Pietr. And I couldn't afford for her to blurt out the odd truth of my recent past. So I smiled and shrugged, passing up the opportunity whenever she offered.

Missing out on even trivial things like that made my days drag. At least Smith seemed interested in me—okay, maybe a little obsessed. With Pietr, every conversation (when I could weasel words out of him) was weather and homework.

I didn't know what to do.

I stopped Cat in the hall one morning to ask about things and she threw her hands into the air in frustration. "I do not know anything about it, Jessie. He is ignoring me nearly as much as he ignores you." She gave me a quick hug and loped off to class, leaving me just as confused.

Pietr made sure he avoided being anywhere alone with me—anywhere I could ask him what had gone wrong between us. I dreaded how awkward my birthday would be if this kept up.

By Saturday afternoon I'd lost my mind. Pietr filled my thoughts so often I'd poured grain for the dogs and nearly fed Rio kibble. Returning to the house I found everyone outside. The orange safety flag of our shooting range snapped in the breeze, and the sound of gunfire proved Dad and Wanda had gone for target practice.

Some people went to the movies. Or dinner. Dad and Wanda? They preferred punching paper with bullets. "Annabelle Lee?" I yelled, poking my head in each door. Nope. Probably in the barn's loft reading. Now was my chance.

Stealing the phone, I tapped in Pietr's number. Dad didn't allow it in speed dial, but I knew the digits by heart.

Cat picked up.

"Cat, it's me."

"You're grounded."

"Yeah, I need to be fast. Is Pietr there?"

There was a moment of hesitation and I heard: "Pietr." In a demand-ing voice: "It's Jessie. *Da*. On the phone now. *Da*. She's still grounded. She needs to talk to you." Then, more softly, as if she'd covered the receiver with her hand, I heard her plead: "*Puzhalsta*, Pietr. She doesn't understand. *I* do not understand."

Another pause.

Downstairs our front door opened and closed. My heart raced, but I couldn't bring myself to hang up.

Not yet.

Through the phone I heard the distinct sound of pounding on a door. "Take. The. Phone. Pietrrr," Cat growled.

Silence.

"Jessie," she whispered. "*Eezvehneetyeh*. I'm sorry. He says . . . he says he doesn't want to talk to you. I'm *so* sorry. . . ."

I hung up.

What had happened to us?

I finished my chores early Sunday morning and decided to see if Dad left any coffee on the counter. Not sleeping well and being stressed out was wearing on me. Caffeine kept me going when nothing else pushed me forward.

I paused in the kitchen doorway.

Dad was seated at the breakfast nook (what he called the "cheap seats" whenever he would tease Mom), listening to the radio. Not his normal station, but a special weekly show. I recognized it immedi-ately.

In Junction small businesses often crossed into different venues. Karate studios had Chinese buffets. Whole foods stores had book-stores. And one restaurant had a radio show.

It just happened to be hosted by the owner of the Italian restau-rant where Mom and Dad went on their first date. Every Sunday the owner broadcast Italian music sung in Italian, sprinkling Italian phrases and news throughout the broadcast and proclaiming, "You don't have to be Italian to love my music—you just have to love good music."

To Dad, it was more than a way to contact a culture other than our own. It was a way to contact the memory of Mom.

He sat, shoulders stooped, cradling something in his hand. A photograph.

Mom.

I swayed, and the linoleum floor crackled beneath me.

"Oh." He looked my way, startled, and swept his big hand across his eyes. "Hey, Jessie."

He tucked the photo into the pocket of his flannel shirt, twisting the dial on his old boom box. "No one plays the eighties on Sunday."

I crossed the floor and stretched my arm around his shoulders.

He sighed. "I miss her, Jessie."

"I know." But I hadn't known. Not really. I'd presumed he was forgetting her, pushing her memory away to make room for Wanda. Words strangled in my throat, but I managed "I miss her, too" as Dad's arms wrapped around me in turn.

We stayed that way a few minutes, sniffling and muttering and being generally pitiful. Something Mom wouldn't have stood for.

Dad was the one to point it out. "She wouldn't have allowed this," he said with a smile. "She would have told us to get up and move on."

"She would have told me to put on my big-girl panties and grow up."

"She told me the same thing once."

We stared at each other a long moment before we both burst into laughter and he clarified. "My big-*boy* pants, she said. Of course," he crowed. The tears rolling down his weathered face grew joyful.

"I'm tryin' to move forward," he admitted, "to help you girls move forward. But it's a hell—a heck—of a thing to try and move past one of the best things in your life. Your mother was the best damned—darned," he corrected, "best darned woman ever, Jessie. And you're gonna' grow up to be just like her. God. You even look more and more like her every day." He snorted. "Damn—err—darn."

I laughed. "Dad, you can't protect me from *everything*. Words like damn and hell—I've heard lots worse."

"Hmph. Well, so long as you don't use 'em yourself. Dangerous women," he continued. "That's all I'm surrounded by. Smart, beautiful, and dangerous."

Well, I'd give him two out of three. Beautiful? Parents were bound to think their offspring looked good. Otherwise what did it say about the part of themselves they'd thrown into the mix? "You wouldn't have it any other way."

"True," he admitted. "What's on your mind?"

"Does there have to be something on my mind?"

"There always is," he guaranteed. "All of you—your mom, you, Annabelle Lee . . . always thinkin'. So what is it?"

I pulled out a chair and sat. "I was thinking about riding again. In events."

"Really?"

I looked at him from under my eyelashes. Huh. Mascara did make them seem longer. "Yeah."

"I wasn't sure you'd want to, not after she died. It was—"

"Yee-aaah," I dragged the word out. "It was our thing."

"Do it."

My head popped up. "What?"

"Do it. Sometimes going back to those things—things that'll never be the same—it's good, anyhow. Helps you move on. She'd like it, Jessie. I know she would."

"Golden Jumper's coming up," I said casually.

"You missed registration," he said. "Not that I looked."

I snorted.

"But there should be another jump event coming soon."

"I've got an in for Golden Jumper."

His eyebrows rose.

"The boy I'm teaching to ride. He can get me in."

One eyebrow crawled back down. "What's he expect in return?"

"Nothing, Dad."

The skeptical look was hard to miss. "Jessie."

"I swear, not all guys . . ."

He blinked at me.

"Okay. Even if he *did* expect something—which he doesn't—it doesn't mean I'd provide it. Geez, Dad. I'm not stupid."

"Lots of girls who aren't stupid provide boys with all sorts of things."

"I'm *not* lots of girls."

"Okay." He raised his hands. "But if he even *thinks*—" He shook his head, grumbling.

"I shall inform him that you will beat the tar out of him, sir. And then I will ask him if he knows the proper definition of *tar*," I drawled.

He laughed, but his eyes lingered on my cheek. On the faded bruise. "Good enough."

Sarah called to give me the weekly Pietr Report. It seemed an even greater punishment the one person Dad let me get calls from while grounded was Sarah. Dad said since I was hell-bent (he realized he couldn't substitute "heck" there easily) on reforming her, maybe I'd be reformed in the process, too. But I knew what he really hoped would change my attitude was hearing Sarah go on and on about Pietr.

Her boyfriend.

I'd managed to avoid a few of her calls, but not enough.

"He keeps watching the clock," she complained. "Every five minutes. It doesn't matter what we're doing. It's like he's got some clandestine existence he's dying to get back to. It's frustrating," she whined. "He simply can't focus on me."

"Sarah," I began, searching for the right words. "Maybe he's got something else on his mind—I mean, other than making out."

"You haven't dated for a while, have you, Jessica?" she said with a giggle. "It's *all* they want to do."

Niiice.

"Have you considered that maybe Pietr's a deeper thinker than that?" Oh. God. I was actually going to give her advice to help her. To keep Pietr. Hand on my forehead, I fought to keep my brain from exploding out the front of my skull.

This was bad.

But helping Sarah might help Pietr, too.

Wasn't that what I wanted—what was best for Pietr?

I winced. "Maybe you should try more talking. . . ." My stomach rebelled at the thought of them building a real bond. Physical attraction changed, but real emotion was harder to undo.

I knew, because I couldn't undo the real emotion I felt over Pietr; instead, it threatened to undo me.

I fell backward on my bed with a groan.

"Are you okay?"

"Yeah. Look. Sarah? If you really, *really* want Pietr—and I mean *really*—talk to him. About everything. He's brilliant." As much as I wanted to be the one talking to Pietr, it wasn't working out that way.

"Jessica, some of us don't worry so much about how brilliant a guy is," she grouched.

"Sarah, talk to him. That's what he really needs."

Silence on the other end.

"I was thinking about other things he might need," she admitted coyly.

I struggled for breath, my eyes screwed shut against the image of Sarah working her wiles on Pietr. "Sarah," I ground out. "You're smarter than that."

She sighed. "Maybe."

I couldn't take it anymore. "I-I gotta go." I hung up the phone and lay on my bed, shivering, curled around my pillow as my tears darkened its case.

I rode Rio out of the paddock and down the hill that night. Together we tore around the farm, looking for anything to jump. For anything to challenge us.

We didn't return until we were sprinkled with sweat and flecked with foam.

I made up my mind on that ride. I would prepare for the Golden Jumper. I would remain Cat's friend, helping the Rusakovas as I could. I would consider dating Derek and move past Pietr.

My broken heart would heal.

Things would return to normal.

I would embrace my new, new normal life. Horseback riding, farm chores, school, the newspaper and a handsome non-werewolf boyfriend with a potential football scholarship.

Normalcy. Life would be good again.

Because it had to get better than this.

CHAPTER TWELVE

"What the—"

"Whoa," Amy echoed as Pietr took a seat at our lunch table.

"I know—it's awful looking, isn't it?" Sarah whispered dreamily, reaching up with a brazen fingertip to touch the bandage stretching from Pietr's eyebrow to his cheekbone.

Everyone at the table paused, gawking.

Everyone except for Pietr and our most recent addition, Cat, who had switched classes to eat lunch with us. Pietr loaded his fork and began to eat.

Cat shook her head, lips pursed as she played with her straw until it squeaked.

Most of us had been there when Pietr nearly knocked his head off during a risky ATV ride. We'd spent ten fear-filled minutes as he lay in the mud, bleeding . . .

. . . dying.

Cat and Max revived him and he recovered remarkably quickly. I'd been ready to believe in magic then. But that wasn't it at all. It was cold, hard science that kept Pietr alive. He'd worn a small Band-Aid a few days thanks to his extraordinary healing abilities.

This bandage was much—*much*—bigger. Which meant he'd been much, much dumber.

"What did you do to get that?" I demanded.

Pietr didn't answer. He glowered at me and shot a look over my head. To the clock.

Cat answered. "He fell out of a tree. Onto some rocks. Head first." She looked at him, her jaw tight.

Amy winced for me.

"Why were you in a tree?" I pressed.

Cat again: "Curiosity."

Amy grinned. "But curiosity killed the—"

"Cat? *Da*," Catherine responded, never missing a beat. "Ironic, is it not? Except that curiosity only gets Pietr started. Stupidity will surely finish the job."

Pietr rolled his eyes to her. Then back to the clock.

"Who patched him up, Cat?" I asked, realizing that talking to Pietr was a lost cause.

"Max." She shrugged. "They're spending a lot more *guy time* together recently."

Not reassuring. If I'd looked up *hedonist* in the dictionary I was fairly certain I'd see a picture of Max grinning wickedly back at me. His theory was simple: Do what feels good, live in the moment. Just have fun.

And why not? As the eldest true Rusakova, Max was closer to death than the others. His internal clock would start running down almost as fast as it had been wound up.

When Pietr rose to empty his tray, I followed.

"Listen, jackass," I began. "I don't care if you don't want to see me anymore. I'm over it, okay? Have all the fun with Sarah you want. With my blessings."

"But for God's sake, Pietr," I continued, tone wavering. "Remember, I'm still your friend." I grabbed at his arm, and he pulled back, glaring. "Stop trying to kill yourself. As mad as I am, I don't want you hurt." The last words came out softly, a sad whisper of fact. "I'm still your friend. I care what happens to you."

Derek was suddenly beside me, looping an arm around my shoulders he glared at Pietr on my behalf. "Is he giving you trouble?"

"More than you can imagine," I admitted, breaking free of Derek's hold and storming off.

That afternoon as I scrambled to swap books for my next classes, I saw something out of place at the bottom of my locker. More than something out of place (which described most of my locker's contents), something new. A note. From Pietr.

> *Jess.*
> *I can't be your friend.*
> *Sorry.*

So I wrote him one back. A simple note that summed things up for me at that moment.

> *Jackass. You idiotic jackass.*

I slipped it in through the grate at the top of his locker's door, hearing it flutter and flop onto whatever was inside. I took a breath.

And remembered my mother's words: "Never write anything you might be ashamed of later."

I fumbled with the locker's handle, rattling the door. It held. We had computers in constant blue-screen and water fountains that leaked more often than they worked. Pietr's locker, however, was the one thing at Junction High that seemed absolutely fine. *Of course.*

"You okay?"

Derek.

I spun around. He leaned against the lockers on the other side of the hall, arms crossed, head inclined, watching me. Amusement grew in his blue eyes as I struggled.

"Yeah," I grumped, giving the door a last try. And a kick.

He crossed the hall and picked up my backpack, brushing against my shoulder.

My body tingled in response. "I can carry that."

"I know. Just let a guy do something nice for you for a change, okay?" He winked at me. "We're not all jackasses."

I blinked and let Derek walk me to class.

I rode the bus each day, like normal. Most days Pietr arrived late; some days he left early. I tried not to notice.

Sarah grew more tired by the day, the results of exhaustion accumulating and showing themselves when she'd snap in anger before pulling herself back together. She was quick to apologize for anything she said (except to Amy).

I wasn't sure which part of her was quicker to react—the good girl seeking a better way, or the vicious girl she had been. She wouldn't open up about her problem, but I bet something was chasing sleep from her.

Derek walked me to classes regularly. Tempted to ask about his ex-girlfriend, Jenny, I caught her watching us once. He simply stepped over to her, spoke a few soft words, and touched her shoulder. She smiled dully, but even that was a big improvement considering how sad she used to act.

Derek sat beside me when the opportunity arose. He didn't join us for lunch—it seemed that was still Pietr's turf. But he made his presence known. As well as his dislike of Pietr.

He reached out for me every chance he got, taking my hand, stroking my arm, touching my cheek. He tried to kiss me once, but I dodged so fast he nearly nailed a locker with his lips. It wasn't that kissing Derek wasn't appealing—it just seemed like a betrayal of Pietr.

Though Pietr was far from kissing me.

Things blurred in my life as I focused on survival. I was a robot, every move mechanical, none inspired. I did my chores, did my schoolwork, rode Rio, and avoided Wanda.

Everyone moved forward except me. I was mired in the past and what could have been. Maybe that was normal, too.

It didn't seem a good sign that my favorite werewolves (and Pietr—currently my *not* so favorite) wouldn't eat the school lunch the first day of the new program. I'd never seen Pietr poke at the "food" congealing on his tray. Of course, he'd never given it time to congeal, either. He always wolfed it down, giving me a clear understanding of the origin of the phrase.

But instead of eating the mystery meat, he glanced at Cat and then back at his tray, seemingly determined to allow it to solidify into some frightening Jell-O mold. Warily I looked at Cat as I opened my bag lunch. Her delicate nostrils flared, and her lips pursed. When it seemed no one was looking, she shook her head at Pietr.

I bit into my apple.

They exchanged a look, eyes pausing on the school lunches in front of Amy, Sarah, Sophia, and Marvin.

The rest of them ate without complaint.

Cat sighed, a soft sound I wondered if anyone but Pietr was meant to hear. Then with a growl she proclaimed, "You disgust me, Pietr Andreiovich Rusakova!" She slammed her tray into his, sending food flying.

"*Da?*" Pietr snapped, pounding his fist on the table so the trays shook and spattered. "Well, you are an absolute *bitch!*"

Cat's eyes flared, but I saw humor in their depths.

"Hey!" Amy griped, their food dappling her tray.

"Pietr," Sarah said in a tone of definite warning. "Apologize to your sister."

"I don't want an apology from that flea-bitten *dog*," Cat proclaimed, slamming her milk down with such force it gushed out the container's top like a frothy Vesuvius.

Sarah was drenched.

Cat barely hid her glee.

Across the cafeteria I saw Max itching to join in. He just needed a reason to disentangle himself from his female flock.

Why not?

"You're all horrible!" I declared. "Especially that brother of yours—Max! Nothing but a common *cur!*" *Huh.* When else would *that* sentence work so fittingly against someone? I grabbed something off of Cat's tray (I wasn't going to waste *my* food) and hurled it at Pietr.

Whatever it was slapped wetly onto his T-shirt. Brown. Well, brown-*ish. Ew.*

But, God. It was satisfying, seeing the look on his face.

Sophia backed away from the table, watching the food fight grow (and narrowly missing becoming collateral damage).

"Cur?!" Max growled, suddenly in the aisle. He plucked something off of Pietr's tray and hurled it, his eyes bright, mouth curled so wickedly at one corner the end of his lips nearly touched his eye.

I felt the impact as a glob of mystery meat smeared across my face.

Cat twitched, grabbed a napkin in one hand and the back of my neck in the other. "Wipe that look right off your face," she snarled, swiping the offensive goo away from my mouth and nose with a heavy hand as she shot a warning look at Max.

A food fight *and* exfoliation. Not what I'd imagined as a suitable combination any day.

I snagged a fistful of Cat's hair and wrestled her to below table level. She totally let me do it.

"What the—?" I asked, seeing peas fly overhead.

"There is something in the food. A strange scent."

"Coriander?" I asked. "That sets me off."

She grinned. "*Nyet.* Something—I don't know—but it seems strange, as if a foreign compound was introduced."

"Like a drug?"

"I can't be sure. But I would not eat the cafeteria food."

"Amen."

There was an earsplitting whistle.

Coach Mac was on the scene. A few more globs of food flew, and the whistle blasted again.

"Cease and desist!" Perlson's voice reverberated through his megaphone. "We will not have such behavior at Junction High!"

There was a smattering of laughter.

He redoubled his efforts. "Our Junction Jackrabbits do not behave this way. We will determine who started this and they will receive the appropriate punishment."

Cat sat up, rolling her eyes.

Max settled beside me, draping his arm across my shoulders, grinning at Pietr possessively. Sly as the Devil himself. "Hey, Red," he acknowledged Amy. "You're rockin' that T-shirt."

"The name's Amy, *cur*," she said, something more than defiance lighting her eyes.

Marvin grinned at the verbal slap and Max snorted.

As Sarah worked on cleaning him up, Pietr resumed watching the clock.

Derek breezed over, perfectly clean. Where the heck had he been to miss the barrage?

"Jessica," he said, clearly ignoring Max as he sprawled across me. "May I speak to you, please?"

"Umm . . ."

Max yawned and released me, making it clear that Derek was no threat. Cat watched my face and although Pietr kept his eyes on the clock, his fingers began to tap the table.

"Sure." I slid into the aisle.

Derek slipped his arm around my waist. "Walk with me."

I did.

"Look, Jessica. I really like you. You know that. But I'm starting to think the Rusakovas are a bad influence on you. They start a lot of stuff. You're a good girl, and I don't want to see you falling in with the wrong crowd."

I snorted. "Derek, you don't know me as well as you think." *I wrote a scathing anti-jock article for the school paper. I'm moonstruck over a teenage werewolf who's probably going to do the horizontal mambo with my psycho best friend. I've broken into a church and killed a mobster in self-defense. And my grade point average has fallen into C territory.* "I'm not as good as you think I am. Life around me—it's not normal. *Seriously.*"

He grinned, dimples so deep they must've jabbed into his jawbone. "You're nothing I can't handle." Challenge glinted in his eyes.

"You're not as bad as you think," he whispered, backing me against a wall, arms boldly bracketing my body. "And if you want to be bad, you can certainly be bad with me."

I shuddered, watching his pupils enlarge, eyes darkening just before he closed them and pressed his mouth against mine, silencing my protest.

Someone cleared their throat and Derek pulled back from me, fingers tight on my upper arm as he swung around to see who dared interrupt. My eyes opened and I saw Amy and Pietr standing across the hallway, students rushing between us, released from the cafeteria.

Amy glared at Derek with all the venom she had, hands balled into fists by her hips. She hadn't had a problem with me liking Derek until Pietr showed up. It seemed he'd changed everything.

Pietr was staring. . . . I blinked. At my pendant.

"What are you looking at?" Derek flared, his gaze jumping from Pietr's daring eyes to my neckline. "Wait," he commanded as I moved to tuck the amber heart back beneath my collar. My fingers twitched and paused. I looked at Pietr.

Pietr's eyes slid to Derek's—cool and uncaring.

"Is this yours?" Derek snarled, slipping his hand between the pendant and my collarbone, throwing the words at Pietr.

Pietr watched him, still as stone.

Derek shook my arm, and I faced him. "This is his leash—his choke chain. You're smarter than wearing some necklace he gave you while he's *dating* Sarah."

I looked down.

"Aren't you? *Dammit!*" There was a snap and I gasped, feeling the slender chain give way under Derek's grip. He hurled the pendant at Pietr.

In one fluid move Pietr had the pendant—my heart—in his hand, his eyes never leaving Derek's incensed face.

"Get this through your thick skull, Rusakova. She's not yours. Not anymore."

My stomach knotted, my chest so tight it was hard to breathe.

With a growl, Derek towed me away.

Pietr finally really watched me.

Leaving.

Derek deposited me at my next class. I fought the whole period to concentrate on anything but the fact that Derek had achieved what Pietr had wanted.

Derek had made my split with Pietr undeniably clear.

CHAPTER THIRTEEN

In social studies class the next day Pietr sat in the back of the room instead of the spot beside me in the front row. Derek took the empty seat, saying he thought his grades would improve if he sat closer to the teacher and someone as smart as me.

I wondered what that implied about the intelligence of our football team members since I was only pulling B's and C's at best and he originally sat with *them*.

Derek took ample notes throughout class, even circling a phrase Mr. Miles repeated twice that I somehow overlooked. I was usually more together in Mr. Miles's class, but sitting beside Derek was like sitting beside the sun. I couldn't help noticing how he shined.

When the bell signaled the end of class Pietr brushed between Derek's desk and mine, heading straight for Mr. Miles. I tried not to eavesdrop, but the temptation was too great. Slowly I put away my pen. My pencil. My notebook. My textbook. My ears perked for any bit of their conversation.

My resolve to establish a new normal excluding Pietr had wavered almost as soon as I'd caught sight of him again. *Stupid heart. Stupid girl.*

"I do not change service learning assignments without need, Mr. Rusakova." Mr. Miles looked grave.

Change his service learning assignment? My throat constricted. Sure, Pietr and I didn't actually talk during service learning anymore, but it was still better to have him nearby than not. Most of the time. When it didn't hurt me.

Oh, hell.

Pietr glanced over his shoulder at me, peeved I was still not out the door. Derek's buddies passed by, slapping him on the back, jostling and joking with him. Each tried in his own way to coax Derek away with them—away from *me*.

I was no cheerleader. I was much farther down the social food chain. Nobody wanted a football jock dating an editor of the school paper.

Derek finished loading his backpack and propped himself against the neighboring desk, waiting for me.

I invented reasons to stay. I rearranged my pens and pencils. I adjusted my stack of textbooks, ordering them neatly by period. I straightened my notebooks. Everything I'd put away, I took out and redid, buying time.

Derek waited, beaming. Handsome, strong, charming. Impossible to ignore.

Pietr leaned toward Mr. Miles, hands ruffling against stacks of papers as he spoke softly.

Mr. Miles frowned and shook his head. "I certainly don't change service learning assignments because of a lover's spat. Imagine how often I would be rearranging things if I did."

Pietr hung his head.

Derek's mouth slid into a smirk. "Come on, Jessica." He straightened, shouldering his backpack. "We don't want to be late."

As cool as it was that Derek used "we" to refer to me and him—*together*—I couldn't leave. Not yet. Two months ago I wouldn't have given Pietr Rusakova a second glance if Derek had shown any interest in me. But he hadn't. "I'm sorry, Derek. I have to talk to him."

"Don't waste your time. Sarah will give him whatever he wants—*if* you know what I mean."

I did. *Everyone* did.

"But you"—he set a hand on my desk, so close I could smell the cinnamon scent of his breath—"you have *higher* standards."

I wanted to disagree, stand up for Sarah and say she and I were cut from the same cloth. But it was such a lie. The truth was I couldn't even afford a yard of what Sarah'd been cut from.

Instead of disagreeing with Derek, I said, "Go on. I'll catch up to you later."

He shrugged, not worried. Derek was top dog at Junction High School.

Before the werewolves moved in.

"I don't think there's anything you can say that would make me change your service learning assignment."

Pietr groaned.

I stood and slung the backpack over my shoulder, heading for the door. I'd just taken a position outside in the hallway, my back cooled by a locker, when Pietr stepped out. My stomach tightened, quivering in anticipation.

He knew I was there before I said anything.

"Why are you doing this?"

Mr. Miles closed the classroom door. Students completed the race to class, leaving us alone in the hallway.

Pietr stood silent, looking down at me.

"I don't know what to do," I confessed. "I thought—when I had time to think—we'd come through everything stronger. I didn't expect *this*. You choosing Sarah, Derek choosing me. . . ."

"You said a girl will know when she's not wanted. She'll move on," he said, shoving my logic back at me. The logic I hoped would work on Sarah. It hit me in the chest, a strike to my heart that left me gasping.

"I'm not—you don't—oh. *God*." My hands covered my ears, but it didn't matter. His words spun in my head, mixing with my racing pulse. Like Rio's hoofbeats thudding at full gallop.

"*Eezvehneetyeh*. I'm sorry, Jess. It's for the best."

"God! How can you just"—I fought for breath, for words, for hope—"how can you *hurt* me like this?"

Red seeped from his pupils to stain the edges of his irises purple. He grated the next words out, saying, "Things. Change."

"I know that, Pietr. Things change, life goes on, it's not you it's me, all's fair in love and war . . . boys become men—or more . . . or is it *less*, Pietr?"

I stepped forward, closing the distance between us for a heartbeat before he closed his glowing eyes, clenched his jaw, and stepped back.

"Pietr. I *know* you've changed. But what I saw *then* wasn't half as horrible as what I'm seeing now."

Opening his eyes once more, he avoided looking into mine.

"You want to know what makes a man a monster? *This*." I waved a hand at the thin space between us.

Stoic, he took it. Where had his fire, his *fight*, gone? I'd seen it the night of his seventeenth birthday. I'd been both mesmerized and terrified by it. Now all I wanted was some glimmer of that strength, some hint of that passion pointed in my direction.

I dropped my backpack. "Don't you feel *anything* for me, Pietr?" I lunged and hooked my hands over his shoulders, stretching to cover his mouth with mine, willing my lips to do what words would not.

He pushed me away. Voice strangling, he replied, "*Eezvehneetyeh*. I'm sorry, Jess. Take care of yourself." He stormed away, red eyes flashing.

I didn't have the heart to watch him go—couldn't bear that he wouldn't look back.

I wound up late to biology, struggling to cool my heart. I was fine until I noticed the dissection trays and pins.

Amy was at our station, carving up the detached head of a pig. My world wobbled and I was back at that night, in the old park as Nickolai's head was torn free of his body.

I tugged back my hair, barely knotting it at the nape of my neck before my throat tightened and I latched my hands onto the cool toilet seat. And threw up.

Again.

I fumbled with the toilet paper dispenser and tore free a wad of the rough stuff to wipe my mouth, tossing it into the bowl before I closed my eyes and flushed.

The door to the bathroom squeaked open and I tried to regain control of my swirling stomach. No good. I lurched forward and heaved more of my guts into the waiting water.

"Jessie?" Amy's voice froze me, though my insides quivered mutinously. I flushed and rustled through the contents of my purse for mints.

"Jessie!" She pounded on the stall door. "What's wrong?"

That was Amy: straight to the heart of a matter—no *How are you doing?* when she could guess by the sound and the smell that I was far from okay. Hoping the mints worked, I stepped out, purse dragging behind.

"Ohhh." She wrinkled her nose and looked me over. "You smell almost as bad as you look."

I reached into my pocket, digging for my worry stone. Its touch did little to combat my twisting stomach. "I'm fine."

"Liar."

I shrugged and headed to the sink.

"Are you pregnant?"

My head snapped up and I glimpsed myself in the mirror. Not good. "Not unless I've been chosen for immaculate conception."

It took her a moment, but she got it. "So." She grabbed a paper towel, wet it, and rubbed at the ends of my makeshift ponytail. "Why are you puking your guts out during bio?"

"I just . . ." How could I explain without giving everything away? Or making her think I'd lost it? "Something must not be sitting right with me."

"Bull. Is it the dissection? You got a soft spot for pigs? You can opt out and use that computer program."

I tried to imagine the process on a screen instead and headed for the toilet again. Dry heaves rattled me until my head ached. Even on a computer screen dissection—the slow examination of anatomy— would remind me of death. Of violent nightmares spiraling out again and again in slow motion.

Amy knelt beside me, stroking my back. "I had to do this for my mom a couple times," she confided. "But she was dumb about drink. You're not suffering from the same thing, are you, Jessie?"

I shook my head—slowly—not sure what to do with my mouth. There were plenty of words to explain the situation. But none of them were believable.

"This has to do with Pietr."

I could give her that much, so I nodded. *Ow.*

"Bastard. Why are they always such bastards?"

"Marvin seems okay," I suggested.

She let go of me and adjusted her sweater. "Yeah, he does seem pretty okay, doesn't he?" Her eyebrows drew together as the wheels in her head turned. "Sure, Pietr's dating Sarah, but that's not new. So what's really got you tied up in knots—what happened with Pietr you didn't tell me about?" I felt freshly sick. "What happened the night you sneaked out?"

"You know."

"No. Not the first night you sneaked out. The night of Pietr's birthday. What happened between you two?"

"Was that when I went to see Max?"

"Ha!" Amy snorted.

"That's what Sarah probably believes."

"And you can thank me later for talking to her long enough to create an interesting reason you'd get grounded."

"*I'd* never stay out all night with Max."

"Lots of girls would . . . Hey! Don't change the subject. What really happened?"

My eyes slammed shut in self-defense, like I could wall out her words and worries. But the darkness behind my eyelids drew me back to that evening, and—my stomach made a noise and Amy dodged out of the way. "False alarm," I apologized. Rising with a grunt I returned to the sink. Surely there was nothing left in my stomach.

Amy reached into her purse and withdrew a small bottle of mouthwash.

"You're not supposed to have that in school."

"Well, hell-o, Dick Tracy." She pressed it into my hand. "Do us all a favor and break this rule. Mints aren't working."

I opened the little bottle and took a swig, swishing it into all the unholy flavored nooks and crannies of my mouth.

"I'm going to ask one more time," she chided. "Okay, no, that's a lie. I'm going to keep asking until I get the truth. What happened the night of Pietr's birthday?"

I swirled the mouthwash around until it felt like every taste bud on my tongue had peeled off. Where would someone in my position start? With the CIA, the Russian Mafia, or werewolves? I spat and cupped a hand for water.

"We learned a lot about each other. He surprised me." *Not with a bouquet of flowers, either. With fangs. And far more body hair than the average guy ever developed.*

A crease appeared between her eyebrows. The next words she said fell out of her mouth one by one, cut from the other. "Did. He. Hurt. You?"

"No! No. Geez, Amy. *No.* It's just—we're really, fundamentally, so different." *He changes into a frightening wolflike thing and tears through the woods eradicating the rabbit population. I like to watch an occasional reality television show.*

"People can be different, even be dating, and nobody in the pair winds up kneeling before the porcelain throne when they take a scalpel to a pig's head."

I shrugged. "You've told me before you don't follow my particular brand of logic."

"You're still not giving me the whole story."

I made a show of trying to fix my hair. The results only reinforced what I already knew: Sometimes trying to fix a thing only made it worse.

"Dear God," Amy said. Pulling out a brush, she freed my hair from its impromptu ponytail. "Ask for help, for once. For a change."

I glared into the mirror and let her do her best.

"So what happened the night of Pietr's birthday that makes you freak when you see the head of a dead animal?"

I seized the sink to brace myself as the image of Nickolai's beheading overrode my vision, as fresh as the night I'd witnessed it.

"What the—?" Amy held me by the shoulders, supporting me as my legs wobbled and threatened to give out.

"Sorry." I fought for control, locking my traitorous knees in place.

Someone brushed Amy aside, taking all my weight even before I realized who else had joined us.

"Catherine," I whispered.

Then I fainted.

CHAPTER FOURTEEN

I woke in the nurse's office. Catherine and Amy whispered to each other, voices as animated as Catherine's hands.

"Of course my brothers are idiots," Catherine agreed. "It comes with testosterone. I believe its letters T-E-S-T are not a reference to male anatomy, but a warning to the opposite sex. They *test* us. Repeatedly." She sighed. "You have a brother?"

I tried to sit, but my head felt lead-loaded.

"Yes," Amy said.

"Has he never been an idiot, a disappointment?"

I could only imagine what raced through Amy's mind. She loved her brother, but he'd walked out on the family, enlisting as soon as he was legal. When she'd needed an ally most.

"Yes, he's been an idiot," she admitted.

I rolled over on the cot to watch through slitted eyelids.

Catherine sat back, arms folded. "But you love him."

"Of course."

"*Da. Kohneeshnoh.* Of course." Cat stared directly at me. "And Jessie says things can't work between she and Pietr?"

"Come on. He's totally blowing her off. And hanging on to Sarah even tighter than before. I mean, *gross*. I just don't get it. What happened to push Jessie and Pietr apart and throw Jessie and Derek together?"

"Hello, Miss Gillmansen." The school nurse stepped in front of me, blocking my view and pinching my wrist for a pulse.

"I feel much better."

"Congratulations. Your pulse is normal. How long have you been purging?"

"What?" I sat up. And hated myself for doing so. My head pounded. "Purging?"

"Yes. Bingeing and purging."

I blinked, realizing. "You think I'm bulimic?"

"Aren't you?"

"No."

"You collapsed after vomiting repeatedly, according to your friends."

I bent around the nurse and glared at Amy and Cat.

Amy shot me a look that clearly meant, *If you'd told the truth to begin with . . .*

"If I could keep stuff in my stomach, I'd be happier."

She put a hand on my forehead. "You don't feel warm, but let's take your temperature. We've had a few students in here with headaches and stomach trouble. Did you eat anything questionable yesterday or today?"

An odd question. Maybe there was something wrong with the school food. Luckily I'd had none of it. "I don't think that's the problem."

Catherine leaned forward in her chair, waiting.

I looked pointedly at them. "Aren't they going to get in trouble for sticking around? Missing class?"

The nurse agreed and hurried Amy and Cat out. Cat raised an eyebrow at me. Amy stuck her tongue out.

"So, Miss Gillmansen, if it's not food-related and you have no temperature"—she placed a thermometer in my mouth—"what do you blame for your vomiting?"

Why did nurses ask questions when you had to keep a thermometer under your tongue? Like dental hygienists getting chatty while they cleaned. "Nightmareth."

"What?"

The thermometer beeped and she yanked it out, examining it, and me, critically.

"I've just been really shaken up. I'm having some nightmares and not sleeping well. That and the smell of preserved pig flesh . . ."

"When was your last period?"

"Seriously. It's nightmares."

She nodded. "Then you have to see someone about them. If your nightmares can trigger this reaction . . ." Her lips pressed together. "Have you spoken to Counselor Maloy?"

I sighed. Previous discussions with Maloy made me wonder why *he* wasn't starring in one of my nightmares himself.

"If not him, find someone else. A professional."

I considered Counselor Harnek from middle school. She'd come to my rescue once and wanted an update, anyhow.

The nurse tugged open a drawer in her desk, taking my silence for noncompliance. "Call her. She's new but well recommended."

I glanced at the card she set in my palm. Dr. Sarissa Jones. A string of letters rivaling the alphabet followed her name, proclaiming her academically proven abilities. Of course *hers* was the card I'd be given. *Been there, done that.* "Thanks."

"As a precaution, don't eat anything spicy. Try saltines, ginger ale. Keep things simple," she suggested.

"Yeah. Simple." She had no idea how attractive *simple* sounded to me.

"And, Miss Gillmansen?" the nurse called as I hit the door. "I'll be checking up on you."

It seemed everyone was checking up on me. Outside the nurse's office they'd lined up, oblivious to the scolding by the lone substitute teacher stuck on hall duty: Sophia, Amy with Marvin, Catherine with Max—even Stella Martin paused to give me a once-over (and Max a long look) as she hurried to class.

And of course there was Sarah, Pietr's arms wrapped around her like a blanket.

His eyes were the first on me, and first to pull away.

Amy tugged free of Marvin and joined Sophia and Catherine, forming a wall in front of me. "Well?" she asked.

"Stomach flu."

Amy shook her head. "It's *not* going around."

"Heat stroke," I tried.

"It's autumn in Junction." Her fists landed on her hips. "Tell me the truth or don't bother telling me anything."

For a moment I looked over her shoulder and caught Pietr's eyes. They were the coolest blue I'd ever seen, and still my knees threatened to buckle.

"Fine!" Amy snapped, stalking off, grabbing Sophia and Cat by the arms so they had no choice but to follow.

Sarah stepped out of Pietr's shadow and touched my arm. "I'm okay. It's not worth worrying about."

Pietr's eyes bored into my forehead accusingly, like he was shouting the word *liar*. But only until he knew I'd seen him.

Suddenly another face was in front of mine, blocking Pietr from my sight. Derek. The guy who'd starred in my dreams before they'd been overridden by nightmares. Handsome—actually, consistently stunning—and I, well, the only thing stunning about me was my breath. And not in a good way.

"I heard you fainted." He looked me up and down, maneuvering between Sarah and myself to slip an arm around me. My backpack hung over his shoulder, beside his own. "Sarah, I'll take over." He grinned at Pietr, his look full of challenge.

I didn't care. At least that's what I repeated over and over, fuzzy headed, as I let Derek lead me away.

Behind us a very satisfied Sarah said to Pietr, "She's always adored Derek."

The classroom door opened, and the nurse glanced at my teacher and pointed to me. I ducked my head and stepped out. "I was thinking more about your situation and decided to call your father to pick you up."

"I'm fine," I protested.

She ignored the statement. "He was at work, but said a family friend, Wanda, would pick you up in twenty minutes."

I groaned.

"Get your things. You can wait on the bench by the office and watch for the car."

My feet dragging all the way I obeyed.

Catherine passed me in the hall, bathroom pass in hand. She arched an eyebrow at me. I shook my head.

I'd barely gotten myself situated on the bench when she showed up again.

"What'd you do, lap the place?"

She shrugged, sitting down beside me. "I didn't really need to go. I like to roam." She glanced at my backpack. "Heading home for the day?" She clicked her shoes together when I nodded. "No place like home."

"Yeah."

"I'm sorry my brother's being such a jerk." She paused. "But you probably aren't helping things by kissing Derek."

"I don't want to talk about either of them."

"Hmm. Jessie, I need to ask you to do something—"

The door opened, and Wanda stood before us amidst the swirling leaves, her severe blond ponytail flapping in the wind.

"Crrrap," Cat snarled.

"Nice to see you, too."

Cat's head whipped around so she looked only at me. "Please inform Wanda that I do not wish to speak to her directly."

I glanced at Wanda. "What she said."

Wanda peered down the hall. "Please tell *her* that it is imperative we meet and discuss plans. I understand we left on—uncertain—terms, but we are running short on time. In several ways. And certain recent behaviors on the part of her family—"

I swallowed, remembering the night at the abandoned church.

"May lead us to take more extreme measures."

"Baiting a trap isn't extreme enough?" Cat retorted.

"I had no idea that was being done. I can only guarantee you that with full cooperation, such things won't occur again."

"Full cooperation?" Cat weighed the words. She turned and glared at Wanda. "How is our mother?"

"Aging. Rapidly. But she has been since her first change, hasn't she?"

A growl built in Cat's throat, and I slapped my hand down on her thigh.

"So you need to talk about the Rusakovas seeing their mother and what you want in return." I looked at Cat. "Soon."

"You must be there, Jessie," Cat concluded.

"Why?"

"We may not be able to stop from shredding her if you aren't there to remind us of our humanity," Cat stated very matter-of-factly.

"She's grounded," Wanda pointed out. "I'll bring additional agents. For safety's sake."

"You'll never get in alive. No extra agents. You and one sidearm. Jessie as negotiator."

"I'm grounded," I echoed. The last thing I wanted to do was be between a pack of angry werewolves and the well-armed government agent keeping their dying mother imprisoned.

Wanda squinted at Cat, measuring her intent.

"Make an excuse," Cat instructed. "A girl's day out."

Despite my skyrocketing pulse rate, I laughed. Loudly. "Sure. We'll go shoe shopping, Cat. What color's fashionable for jackboots?" I doubled over, patting the tops of my sneakers and fighting for breath. "Ugh. Fine." I stood. "Cat's terms."

"Fine," Wanda agreed. "Let's get you home."

Nearly out the door, I looked over my shoulder to say good-bye to Cat and I noticed Derek. Cat followed my gaze, glaring at him.

He said, "Bitch."

Cat responded, "Manipulative bastard." Derek shrugged as if to say *touché*. Wanda tugged me out to the car before I had too much time to wonder about their brief exchange.

CHAPTER FIFTEEN

The next day Sarah caught me between classes, no Pietr in sight. She towed me into the girls' bathroom. I'd spent so much time in Junction High's bathrooms since Pietr's arrival I expected to start paying rent.

Even Sarah's perfectly done makeup—yes, I realized, startled, she was back to wearing makeup—couldn't hide the faint bags beneath her eyes. "Is there anything you didn't tell me about that night?"

Crap, crap, *crap!* What night? I'd racked up quite a few lies about particular nights recently. Now it seemed the trick was knowing which night she meant. I was too tired to guess. Just one more thing people never told you: Not only was lying morally wrong, it was exhausting. "What night?"

Something small shifted in her eyes, like someone in the background waking.

Amy sauntered in, whistling. "Hey. Heard you were here," she addressed me. She paused, seeing Sarah. Amy tossed her long mane of red hair and cracked her knuckles.

Sarah ignored her. "June seventeenth. The night your mother died."

Amy resumed whistling, spun on her heel, and retreated to the hallway. Or maybe class. Some of us still tried to get to class from time to time.

"Umm." There was a lot I hadn't told Sarah about that night. Like the fact she'd caused the accident. Or the fact I hauled her, unconscious, out of her car and to safety because my mother told me to. Or that by saving Sarah I'd doomed my mother to a fiery death. Or that forgiving her was essentially my mother's dying wish.

Man. I hoped Mom wasn't hung up on *that* one.

Where to begin? The truth seemed foreign stacked against such heaps of lies. And what good would the truth do when Sarah tottered on the brink of returning to her old, nasty self? Would knowing help or hurt her?

And how dare I try to make her a better person? She'd seemed quite content being evil. At what point did my desire to make Sarah "better" become some weird God-complex? Shouldn't she know the truth, make her own choices?

I rubbed my forehead, a headache threatening. "Okay. There's actually—"

The fire alarm blared.

"Shit!" Sarah exclaimed.

My heart sped up. The new Sarah was big on word choice: Why use profanity when you could be creatively clean? But the original Sarah . . . I shivered. "Let's go." We stepped into the hall and were quickly separated by the evacuating classes.

Standing outside in the blustering breeze, I wondered if the fire alarm hadn't been some strange cosmic intervention. Maybe I wasn't supposed to tell Sarah after all. Or maybe not yet. *Ugh*. If the fire alarm had been a sign, couldn't it be clearer?

I hopped up and down to stay warm. Rumors spread through the crowd. ". . . an electronic malfunction . . ."; ". . . the library's on fire . . ."; ". . . somebody in Beany Belden's class lit a match . . ."

My IQ slipped as I listened.

Max appeared, followed by his gaggle of giggling girls. He slipped behind me and draped his arms across me.

I stiffened in his grasp. "What are you doing?"

"You look cold."

"So do half the girls around here. And you'll get way further with them than with me," I assured.

"Geez, Jessie, give a guy some credit," he purred, his mouth so close his breath singed my ear.

"Ohhh, I give you credit, Max," I returned. "But it doesn't mean I understand why you're hanging on me."

He lowered his voice, his whisper as tangible as the rasp of a cat's tongue on skin. I ignored the goose bumps rising on my arms in response. "Look. At two o'clock."

I glanced ahead and to my right.

Pietr was wrapped around Sarah's slight form, his head turned in our direction. His eyes glowed a faint red.

"We could make him jealous," Max offered. "It's a bit of a dirty trick to play on my little brother, but—" He yawned, and I knew his eyes were taking on the sleepy appearance of someone *very* comfortable. What some older folks called "bedroom eyes."

I'd seen Max play a similar game before. Even without looking I knew what Pietr saw.

"Whaddya' say?" Max rumbled. "Maybe a kiss . . . ?"

"Don't you dare. Besides, I don't want him to be jealous. I want him to be smart."

Max's laughter shook through me, his body tight to my back. "Good luck with that," he intimated. "Pietr's seventeen. He has a girlfriend who throws herself at him. Smart won't be easy." His tone changed faintly. "Why couldn't you have shaken him off on your other friend? Amy? The hot redhead. We could have taken them apart and I would have been her shoulder to cry on."

"Amy's with Marvin."

"Yeah," he droned. "I noticed that." He snuggled closer, and I resisted the urge to elbow him in the groin. "She's smokin'."

"Leave Amy alone, Max. She's happy with Marvin."

"And if she wasn't?"

I growled.

"That's actually sexy." He purred like a lawn mower was lodged in his chest.

Ahead of the crowd teachers waved us back toward the school building. Sighing, I slid out of Max's embrace and ignored the jealous glares of his groupies.

"So, no to making Pietr jealous?" he tried once more.

"What would you do in my place, Max?"

He looked away from me for the span of one heartbeat, but I caught the path of his gaze.

"I don't know, Jessie."

Leading his pack of admirers, he skulked away.

I waved to the couple he'd spotted just before stalking off. Amy tugged free of Marvin's hold and waved back.

Lurking outside Counselor Maloy's office, it didn't take long for him to ask to see me, wondering what was wrong. I made it clear. I wanted to talk to somebody about my issues. Not him. Counselor Harnek.

He wrote the pass, relieved. At least I wouldn't be his problem anymore. He could return to focusing on filing state-mandated tests and know someone was looking over my shoulder from time to time. He'd save on colored paper clips, too.

The wind whipped through Junction Friday morning, giving us a taste of winter's coming power. I hurried from the bus to the school's glass double doors, dodging around people seemingly unaffected by the cold.

But the chill of the snapping breeze wasn't nearly as startling as seeing Sarah in Pietr's welcoming embrace inside. It shouldn't have surprised me, but somehow it still did.

The doors flew open at my touch. Crisp autumn air pushed past me, snarling my hair out ahead of me, tangling in fall's frosty fingers. The same wind that rattled me rustled the spiking dark mop of hair hanging over Pietr's eyes.

He raised his head to the breeze, nostrils flaring as his eyes closed, shutting out the world. Something tightened in his face and he leaned over Sarah, murmuring so she laughed. He nuzzled his nose, his lips, into the soft blond hair that whispered along Sarah's face and down her slender neck.

Where was Coach Mac and his PDA-seeking whistle? I stumbled out of the path of other students but couldn't pull my eyes away from Pietr. He looked at me, holding my gaze boldly, eyes tinting the red of hellfire, her scent—her *taste*—tearing down his throat. Lingering in his lungs.

That was the first morning I looked for Derek. It took only moments to find him. He glanced up from where he sat chatting with Marvin. And as soon as he saw me it was like nothing else mattered.

I let him lead me to a quiet and poorly lit corner of the math wing. I didn't stop him when he tried to kiss me. Instead I linked my arms around his neck and hung on, letting his lips smother mine, all the while wishing he was Pietr. When the bell rang I hurried away to show my guidance pass to my next teacher before heading down the lengthy hallway connecting Junction High to the middle school.

I paused outside the middle school's main office: I'd been burned before. I took a deep breath, readying myself. Reminding myself Harnek hadn't betrayed me. She actually rode to my rescue after I took down a tag team of cheerleaders. My hesitation gone, I figured if there was anyone I could trust to help sort out my heart and my mind, it was my old counselor.

In I went. The receptionist looked at my pass. "Oh. Jessie Gillmansen." Her tone changed, eyes softening in realization. "I'm so sorry about your mom, Jessie. . . ."

I looked away and closed my eyes; pushing the breath that had caught in my throat out, I regained control. How could people do that? Wreck me so fast with just a mention of Mom? "Thank you." The answer was stiff. I couldn't put the right emotion behind some stuff anymore.

People would learn to cope. Or leave me alone. Sometimes I wondered which I'd prefer.

The tag marking Harnek's door glinted and I shoved toward it, oblivious to the receptionist's warning, "She's busy—"

"Ms. Terrence, Ms. Terrence!" A couple kids bumbled in, their high, demanding voices seeking attention. And the receptionist was overrun with requests from everything from toilet paper for the restrooms to paperwork for a teacher requesting supplies. And there were photocopies to be made.

Her protest was drowned out and I pushed on the door, easing it partway open, not wanting to disturb Harnek but not wanting to be stuck in the milling madness of a filling office.

"I don't want to see!" someone hissed from inside the room. Open a crack, the door allowed me a slender line of vision and the advantage of watching without being seen.

Harnek stooped over, holding the attention of whoever sat in the huge chair opposite her desk. "You *have* to. It doesn't matter that you don't want to—you *have* to. Otherwise . . ." She shook her head. "You know."

There was no reply beyond a deep sigh. Finally a muffled voice—male—agreed. "If it's absolutely necessary."

"It is."

I knocked on the door, opening it further with each light rap of my fist.

"Jessie!" Harnek straightened, smiling, hands clasped together. "Come in. Maloy mentioned you'd be seeing me. He didn't say *now.*"

"Is it a bad time?"

"No. Nooo. We were finishing up, weren't we?"

There was a creak of leather. Derek stood up from the glossy seat, his expression a far cry from the frustrated one I'd expected.

"Yeah. Hey, Jessica." He did that thing that came so naturally to him. More than a smile—a *gleam* that lit his whole face. I couldn't help but smile back. He glanced at Harnek. "Thanks for your time."

"Anything for you, Derek," she replied. "Jessie. Sit."

Derek squeezed past me, pausing to peer into my eyes. He rested a hand on my arm and smiled, leaning in.

My breath caught; I was mesmerized.

"Nice to bump into you, Jessica," he whispered, his sparkling blue eyes skimming my face.

"Derek, we'll see you *later,*" Harnek hinted.

His dimples disappeared and he nodded.

Struggling not to stare as he left the room, I blushed and sank into the seat.

"You're having nightmares?"

I nodded.

"Tell me about them. And don't worry. I'm entirely nonjudgmental. So no matter how weird or scary it sounds, hit me with it."

She propped her heels on her desk's corner and settled in for a long story. Boy, did I give her an earful.

That afternoon Derek caught me before I made it to the bus. There was no dim corner. He shoved the backpack off my shoulder and tangled his arms around me, kissing me with a passion that made my eyes widen before I remembered who was kissing me and slammed them shut to forget.

It wasn't that he was a bad kisser . . . far from it. And yet . . . my mouth stopped moving in time to his.

I *didn't* want Derek.

As fast as the thought was formed it whisked away, my mind flooding with images of Pietr. Holding Sarah. Kissing Sarah, his eyes filled by *just* Sarah.

And I kissed Derek back. Not Pietr. *Derek*. With his blond hair and boy-next-door looks and his scent like sun warming a field of wheat. He pulled away a moment, blue eyes gone dark as his pupils widened, nearly eclipsing their color.

My knees shook when he landed one final, long kiss on my lips, scooped up my backpack, and settled it on my shoulder.

"Better get on the bus," he said with a grin.

I nodded and stumbled away, pouring myself into my regular seat without a care for staying on one side or the other. Pietr wasn't on the bus home, anyhow.

CHAPTER SIXTEEN

"Shoe shopping?" My father's surprise echoed my disbelief.

"It's a way for Jessica and me to spend some time doing girl stuff," Wanda assured him. "We won't buy anything outrageous."

"Only sensible shoes, Dad."

"What about Annabelle Lee?"

Nuts. That's what I'd forgotten.

Wanda and I exchanged a look. I got the feeling I was about to be thrown under a bus.

"The thing is"—Wanda's volume dropped as she confided—"Jessica says she wants to talk. I think she needs to talk to a woman. In private."

"Oh."

I did not dare imagine what Dad thought we'd discuss. A preemptive blush scorched my face.

"Well, hell, Wanda. You know I trust you." He patted her hand, and my stomach squeezed in rebellion.

I wished I could tell him all the reasons he shouldn't trust her. Or even one. One might be enough.

He dug out his wallet and pulled a few twenties free. "Take your time and treat yourselves."

We got in the car before Dad could second-guess. Driving in silence we were two people absolutely at odds with each other. I tucked the money away; it might be useful later.

Cat greeted us at the Rusakovas' door. She gave me a quick hug. Wanda looked like she considered hugging me, too, but decided a hug wouldn't help her case.

Thank God.

"Come in, Jessie. And *you*." Cat glared at Wanda.

As soon as the door closed behind us, Cat was all business. "Since we agreed to one sidearm, I'd like you to carefully produce it. Then Max will pat you down."

"Not him," Wanda said, slowly drawing her gun from her ankle holster. "He's handsy."

Max barked out a laugh. "My reputation precedes me."

"Pietr," Cat instructed.

From behind Max he came. Not even sparing me a glance, he took Wanda's gun. "Ten shots. Three for him, three for me, two for Cat. Two left. Alexi and Jess," he presumed. "Good thinking. You might get out alive." He ran his hands over her arms and legs, skimming down her front and back. "She's clean." He handed the gun back to Wanda.

He didn't miss her look of surprise.

"You can't take away our teeth or claws—we shouldn't take away your weapon, either."

"Now do Jessie," Cat commanded.

His upper lip curling, Pietr glowered at his sister.

"You're the one who suggested limiting her involvement. Your attitude toward her has changed. So search her."

Pietr looked to Max for support.

"I'd search her for you, little brother, but I'd enjoy the job." He grinned, regarding Pietr smugly. "And I'll bet I could make Jessie enjoy it, too," he rumbled, the challenge clear.

Pietr stayed perfectly still a moment, eyes closed, waiting like someone praying for a stay of execution.

"Do it," I snapped.

Pietr's face a study in control, he bent to the task. His nostrils flared and I knew he caught the scent of Derek's most recent kiss on my face, Derek's body on my hands and covering my clothes. Well, good for him. I hoped it stung his sensitive nose.

He ran his hands along my arms and slowly down my ribs, his touch so light it tickled. He brushed over my hips and my breath caught treacherously as his fingertips stroked down my legs and traced along my ankles. Then he stood, his gleaming eyes hooded, expression masked. "She's clean."

Peering past him to me as if to say, *See?* Cat darted a glance at Pietr's hands, noting how they trembled.

I looked away, unsure how she could mistake loathing for something like interest. "Let's get this over with," I urged.

We took up positions in the sitting room, facing each other in well-stuffed seats like some bizarre war council.

"I'll start since I'm mediating. I expect your people"—I addressed Wanda—"to let them see their mother as soon as possible."

I turned my attention to Cat. "I expect your family's cooperation giving Wanda the samples she needs. Blood, hair, and tissue, right?"

"For now," Wanda said with a nod.

"And what later?" Cat snarled. "Marrow? Sperm? Eggs? Gray matter?" She clicked her teeth together. "I want all the terms clearly defined. Here and now."

I just wanted to go. To no longer be the one spot in the room Pietr's eyes never went to. But they'd asked for my help. And I knew too well that sometimes the greatest help was the thing that hurt the most.

"Wanda. Tell the Rusakovas exactly what you expect and what they get by agreeing."

She began to open her mouth.

"Without threats."

Her mouth shut and she rethought her words. "Blood, skin, hair, fur, marrow. A baby tooth, if available. You get to see your mother—

alive and in good health—in a contained and safe facility under un-obtrusive observation. You will be allowed into her environment—"

"Her *environment?*" Cat's nose wrinkled. "How is she being held?" Wanda looked at me.

Squeezing my eyes shut, I took a breath. "We're only talking terms, now, Catherine."

"These are the *terms* of our mother's imprisonment, Jessie," she protested. "If your mother was alive—"

I winced.

"Wouldn't you want to know her condition?"

"Wanda," I said, "are you in charge of their mother's captivity?"

"No," she whispered, leaning forward, her eyes slightly wider than normal. She read the contempt in Cat's glowing eyes, and I knew that in a moment Wanda might go for her gun.

"Then, Catherine, you cannot—can *not*—hold the terms of your mother's captivity against Wanda. Do you understand?" I paused, praying it sank in. "No matter how she's being held . . . Wanda's *not* responsible. Tell me you understand, Cat."

"I understand." She bit off the words. It was something.

"Wanda."

"She is in a twenty-by-twenty-by-ten cubicle in a secure facility. Nearby. She is provided with all the essentials and some of the com-forts high-ranking political prisoners are granted." She looked at me again. "That's all I'm at liberty to say."

Cat sighed. "Does she ever get to go outside? Can she see the moon or stars?"

"'That s all I'm at liberty to say," Wanda repeated, Cat's frustration shared.

"Can she be released?" *Pietr.* Asking the hard question.

"I do not have sufficient rank to warrant her release at this time."

"Then why the hell are we all here?" Max snarled, baring his teeth. "She's committed no crime, and she's probably never seen a courtroom except on TV. She should be *here*. With her family."

"I wish it was that easy." Wanda stared at her fingers. "Techni-cally your family defected from the USSR decades ago. You are U.S.

citizens because you were born here, but she's an illegal. If I push too hard, they could deport."

"They'll be waiting for her in Russia," Catherine said. Her head tilted, and she faced the room's open door. "*Da*, Alexi?"

He stepped into the room, his dark hair disheveled, shirt buttoned wrong. I wondered how long he'd stood outside, uninvited but certainly not uninvolved. There were hollows beneath his eyes where shadows nestled. Being labeled a traitor by his family wasn't working well for him. "*Da*. They'll be waiting to take any of us." He tapped off his cigarette, letting the ash and embers fall into his open hand. He didn't seem to notice the singeing of his flesh. "Better a jail in America than a hole in Siberia."

"Okay." I threw my hands into the air. "Then let's leave it like this—visitation on Wanda's terms. Samples given the day of visitation, except for marrow and fur. That can be after a successful first visit. Release can be discussed later."

Alexi nodded. "Wonderful. Except we can't stay."

"What?" Wanda and I asked in unison.

"We will shortly be out of money. The Mafia no longer supports us, and my skills are—negligible—anywhere but in a black-market economy." He grinned like a ghost smiling up from a grave. "If we stay, we'll be on the street in under a month. What can your people do to keep us?"

Wanda flopped back onto the love seat and yanked on her ponytail. "Take five." Cell phone in hand, she stepped out of the sitting room. The door to the porch opened and shut.

"Jessie," Alexi muttered, sitting in the spot Wanda vacated. "You're doing a good job, but why did Cat bring you into this?"

"We needed a mediator," Cat said.

The strain in Alexi's voice spilled across his face. "You could have asked me," he said.

"You would have sold us out all over again!" Max roared.

Alexi leaped up. "When did I *first* sell you out, brother? Tell me!" he demanded. "I stood beside you on the field of battle. I bled as you bled and when you face down the Devil you don't even invite me to help?"

"I'm facing down the Devil right *now*," Max snapped, eyes glowing, nose to nose with Alexi.

"Stop it!" Catherine shouted. "Both of you. Sit!"

Something in her tone brought them both down.

She rested her head in her hands, elbows on her knees. "This is precisely what I hoped to avoid by not inviting you, Alexi. By having Jessie take your place."

I rose, crossing the room to stand beside Cat. Reaching over I gave her shoulder a squeeze.

"Our family is broken. Why must you boys rip it further apart?" Her head against my hip, she looked up at them, eyes damp and imploring.

Max grumbled and shoved his hands into his pockets. But Alexi stared at Cat as if seeing her for the first time.

"*Eezvehneetyeh*, Ekaterina," he lowered his gaze. "I am so sorry . . . sorry for any part I played that hurt this family."

And then he was gone.

Wanda reappeared in the doorway. "Why do I get the feeling I missed something big?"

"It was nothing," Max growled. "*Absolutely* nothing."

"Uh-huh." She pocketed her cell phone. "Well. The good news is we can see our way clear to grant you a stipend and, uhmm, *specialized* health care as government employees. The bad news is there's no way it'll do everything the Mafia money did."

"We'll take it," Catherine said. "Jessie, thank you. *Spahseebuh*. I think you two had better go." She grabbed my hand, yanking me down so we were eye to eye. "Things will get better between you two," she promised.

CHAPTER SEVENTEEN

When Wanda showed up announcing a spectacular sale on purses at the mall, I knew something was up. Dad smiled, gave me cash like money didn't matter, and wished us luck purse hunting. Annabelle Lee stayed curled on the couch, reading *All the Pretty Horses* as if she hadn't been overlooked again.

I felt a twinge of sympathy for her. No one wanted to be forgotten, but I had a job to do.

"What's going on?" I asked, climbing into the car.

"We have a delivery."

"Ohhh-kay."

We hadn't gotten far when Wanda pulled the car over. "I need to know something, Jessie."

"What?"

"Whose side are you on in all this?"

I raised an eyebrow at her. "Theirs."

Wanda nodded. "That's what I figured. I'm not going to waste your time trying to explain how we'd like to save the werewolves—"

"They have names."

She just plowed ahead. "To find a cure for their abbreviated life spans," she said with a wave of her hand.

"No. Wait. You want to do *what?*"

"We want to fix the werewolves, and not in the trip-to-the-vet way."

"Huh."

"It's come to our attention that having a more normalized population is more beneficial to the ongoing success of both military and government operations."

"Okay. I don't believe you."

"I knew that would be a risk of my being honest with you."

"How would you benefit from undoing their time line?"

"Imagine. You're forty—or younger, in their case, as they're doubly full-bloods—and you collapse in public. A good Samaritan gets you to a hospital. Doctors find you've got the liver and heart of a ninety-year-old. And some parts of you, internally, are just sort of melting. Is it a new disease? Quick, get the CDC on the phone! But faster still you've got NBC and ABC on the phone. And . . . disaster. And that's if your werewolf hasn't triggered and destroyed the E.R. So. Fix the life span and there's less chance of them making the evening news as some bizarre focus spot. Less chance of an inquiry into the experiments we did during the Cold War, and before—"

"*We* did? Our scientists did stuff like this, too?"

Wanda paused. "No. Not like *this*. We were the good guys."

I squinted at her summary. "Seriously? It was that black and white? We were the good forces of democracy and they were the diabolical Communist Reds?"

"Ugh. Look. It doesn't matter who did what. The fact is, we made some bad choices—did some unethical experiments. But that's history. We just don't want it being rehashed. So."

"So?"

"We want to help them, but it takes time," Wanda said.

"Yeah. Their most precious commodity."

"Exactly. So while we're scrambling for a cure—based on the samples you got them to agree to give—we need to keep a better watch on them so they don't do something stupid."

"Have you *met* Max?"

"Precisely."

"Why not tell them the truth? Give them some hope?"

Her eyes slid toward me. "You know the truth isn't always accepted. Or believed."

"Yeah. They don't trust you."

Wanda nodded. "So I need a huge favor. I need you to plant a bug."

"What?! I. Will. Not."

"Jessie. This can alert us if trouble starts or if somebody gets hurt. We can get someone there to prevent it from making the papers." She touched my shoulder with her free hand.

I shook it off.

"If the public found out, they'd be hauled away, you know? There'd be no more—"

"No more Rusakova family." She was right. If Pietr wondered what sort of monster crawled beneath his skin, what would the public demand the government do to find out?

"What if the Mafia returns? They'll need backup."

Another good point. "You do it."

"They'll be watching me, Jessie. I won't have a chance." She fished around in her purse and pulled the bug out.

Such a small thing, really.

"They trust you."

"That's because I won't betray them."

"Right. You won't. You'll *protect* them. If there's trouble, we'll know about it. We can get there and help." Opening my hand she placed the bug in my palm. "Help us help them, Jessie."

"Where?"

"Under a table in the sitting room."

"Okay. But if they catch me we're both in big trouble. I *will* throw you to the wolves. Like a juicy bone."

"Nice." She pulled back onto the road. "Glad to know you haven't become jaded by helping your government and friends."

"Yeah. What were the odds of that?"

———————

The wad of cash Wanda presented to the Rusakovas went a good distance toward cementing their agreement. Alexi quickly divided the
money into mortgage, utilities, food, and incidentals. The last two
piles were thinnest.

"They'll need to hunt," he pointed out. "Otherwise we can't maintain their calorie count."

Wanda glanced at each of the Rusakovas in turn.

"You don't want them roaming hungry, do you?" Alexi asked.

"No. *Crap.*"

"Not so easy being a werewolf keeper, is it?"

"You are not our keeper," Max snarled.

Alexi braced himself. "I *am* my brother's keeper," he said. "And,
like it or not, I am still your brother."

Max paced. Growling. I heard joints snap, changing. Without
looking, I knew his eyes glowed red with emotion.

"Max . . ." I stepped back.

He swung his head toward Alexi, jaws long and lined with sharp
teeth, eyes glowing like banked coals—holding his transformation
mid-change. It seemed even more a threat—seeing the wolf's head
on the broad human shoulders.

Max puffed out a breath. "Brrrrotherrr." He swung his heavy
head toward Pietr. "Brrrrotherrr," he repeated, looking to Catherine.
Swinging his head back to center, he lunged, snapping at Alexi; his
teeth closing a hairsbreadth from Alexi's face.

I jumped.

Alexi simply sighed. "You want the job?" he asked Wanda as Max's
feral features sank back into his human face.

"Hunting." She hit something on her cell phone. "Signal's not so
good in here." She stepped out of the sitting room, followed by the
Rusakovas.

It was my chance.

They trailed her past the staircase. The back door made its regular whine of protest and I dropped to my knees, reaching under the
marble-topped table to plant the bug. It stuck easily. I was preparing
to stand when I heard him.

Which meant he *wanted* me to hear him.

"Lose something?" Pietr asked.

"Just—"

"Don't lie to me, Jess." In two quick strides he closed the distance between us. "What have you done?" So close his breath warmed me all the way down, he dropped to all fours, the grace of the wild animal within ever-present.

He stood again, a lithe move that set my heart pounding far more than my fear at being found out. Encircling my wrist with his fingers, he towed me onto the front porch.

"Why . . ." He released me to rake a hand through his hair. "Why would you bug us?" He arched toward me, his height accentuated as he threw me in shadow. His searching eyes clouded with anguish, and I felt a pang in my stomach. "Why betray us?"

"No, Pietr—no betrayal—" I rested a hand on the wall, throat burning as my heart and lungs battled in my chest. "A safety precaution," I gasped. "Please. *Puzhalsta*. Believe me." I reached up to touch his face.

He flinched, closing his eyes.

"I would *never* betray you." My hands walked down his arms. His skin was chilled by my touch; goose bumps rose wherever my fingers traveled. "Believe me, Pietr. Take the bug, crush it."

"How did Wanda convince you to do this?"

"Things are so volatile right now, and if you get into a bad situation, the CIA may be useful."

He opened his eyes to marvel at my hands. Clinging to his arms.

"Pietr. What if the Mafia comes back? Don't you want some firepower on your side?" I stepped deeper into the shadow he cast, resting my head on his chest.

He stiffened, frozen like a rabbit who'd just spotted a hound. "You smell like *him*," he murmured, the words tinged with disgust. But his heart sped at my nearness, racing even faster than normal. "Stop," he begged, nudging me back.

"I can't stand the idea of you being hurt. I'll do anything to protect you," I swore.

He sighed, a ragged, beaten sound. "We'll discuss important things in another room."

"What?"

Sunlight sneaked across me as he stepped back. "It stays. I don't trust Wanda, but in this, she could be useful. Are there any other bugs?"

"Not that I know of. I mean, the phone's still tapped. . . ."

"*Da*. We make few calls that interest the CIA."

"Yeah. Thursday's weekly pizza order probably doesn't top their list of concerns."

He chuckled.

"I miss that," I said, examining the wood floor of the expansive porch.

"What?" he asked, voice going gruff.

"Your laugh." I raised my eyes to his, hoping he read the emotion in them.

He looked away, intrigued by the dining room window.

"I miss a lot of things," I said, advancing. My hand reached up and rested on his chest, the heat of him scalding my palm. "I miss holding you. And you holding me. I don't want Derek."

He winced at his name.

"I want *you*." I took another half step forward, pinning my hand between us as I stared up into his glittering blue eyes. "*Pocelujte me-nyah*," I begged, lips reaching up to soften the hard line of his mouth.

He roared, knocking me back with the sound. Hunched, nostrils wide, lips curled to expose his teeth, he glared at me with wildly glowing eyes. "You do *not* underrrstand," he seethed.

"What the—?" Wanda came crashing out the front door.

Pietr dodged around her, his feet pounding all the way up the stairs. A door slammed.

Wanda looked at me. "You okay?"

I nodded.

"Great." Her eyes scoured my face and body, like she searched for physical wounds. "Time to go. The hunting issue's resolved. They won't starve now."

"Good."

She put a hand on my back and slowly guided me down the stairs and to the car. She opened my door, and I fell onto the seat. Wanda reached over, dragging my seat belt across my body. Watching me the whole time, she clicked it together before fixing her own.

She started the car and pulled it away from the curb. "Um. I—" Staring straight ahead at the road, she suggested, "Maybe you should step back from this. It's a lot to handle. We'll deal with the werewolves."

"They have names," I insisted.

"So? They're werewolves."

"But it's . . . it's like you're . . ." I blew out a breath. "Like you're dehumanizing them."

Wanda glared at the road.

"Maybe it makes it all easier. Hunting them and throwing them in for testing. If you don't use their names, don't think of them as human . . . it's gotta' make it easier."

"You're too close to this," Wanda accused me. She pounded the steering wheel and mumbled something that sounded suspiciously like, "Maybe I am, too." Her fingers curled around the wheel. "Take a break, Jessie. Let me handle this. I'll make sure they get a fair shake."

"They don't trust you, Wanda."

"Yeah. But I think you need to be better protected."

I turned. Looked at her.

"They're monsters."

"That's what Edward thought."

"Oh, yeah? He a friend of yours?" Wanda asked.

"No, Miss Librarian. Just a main character in a wildly popular vampire series."

"Huh. And what did that series teach you?"

"A bunch. Partly that sometimes good people don't get the chance they deserve to prove they're good *people*."

She sighed, reminding me suddenly of Dad. She was too rough to compare to Mom. "Your dad wants to protect you. That psychiatrist you were seeing wants to protect you. I think maybe I should consider protecting you, too."

"Don't do me any favors. There's nothing to protect me from. Other than rampaging CIA agents. And the Russian Mafia."

"Protecting your body's one thing. Protecting your heart—you're overlooking that. It's easy to do first time out."

I looked at her. *Really* looked at her. It was the first time I'd wondered about Wanda. What was her story, anyhow? No one just popped into existence as a CIA agent wading through old files the USSR dumped in an attempt to extend a hand of friendship to a Cold War enemy.

"I think I love him, Wanda."

"That's a very grown-up sentiment."

"My mother's dead. I've learned the world's a hell—"

She shot me a look.

"The world's a *heck* of a lot weirder than I ever dreamed. I've been shot at and I've killed a man in self-defense. Pardon me if I'm starting to feel I have the right to grown-up expressions of emotion."

"Love's big."

"Yeah."

"That's why you were sent home sick."

I didn't bother answering.

"He's dating your best friend."

"*One* of my best friends," I corrected.

"A little advice from someone who's been there?"

"Why the *heck* not?" I shrugged.

"Go out with the football star. He's really something. Just—look out for yourself first."

"Is that what you're doing with my dad?"

"Aw, crap, Jessie." She shook her head.

"Because he needs protecting, too." I focused my eyes straight out the windshield at the leaves bouncing across the blacktop. "Seems that's my job. Jessie Gillmansen—protector of *werewolves* and grown men. Don't screw with the people I love, Wanda."

CHAPTER EIGHTEEN

Dr. Jones peered up from her seat at the desk when I entered. "Miss Gillmansen. I didn't expect you to come back."

My shoulders rose in a shrug. "I figured you might have filled my appointment slot, but it was worth a try."

"Really?" Her gaze threatened to level me.

"Yes. Those things I said last time . . ."

She crossed her arms and leaned back. "Yes. About the Russian Mafia, the CIA . . ."

"And werewolves."

A smirk tugged at her lips. "Who could forget *werewolves?*"

"Those things I told you were—" The corner of my lips twitched.

"Lies," she concluded.

At least *I* hadn't needed to say it.

"Would you like to start again?" She glanced at the clock.

"Yes."

"Shall we focus on your expression of grief at the loss of your mother?"

My throat tight, the words burned a trail toward my tongue and stopped. Dried up like dust and clogged my mouth. My eyes stung. But I nodded, pulled my hands from my pockets, and sat.

Dad was outside, the truck running. I'd made him agree to wait in the parking lot instead of suffering more of his rib-crushing bear hugs outside the doctor's office. He was whistling.

"Ah, crap, Dad. Is Wanda coming over again?"

"Nope. She should already *be* over at this point."

"Funny guy," I said.

"Hey, who's to say your imprisonment can't at least be fun for one of us?"

"It would be fun if my friends could visit," I sniffed.

"Tomorrow," he promised. His fingers drummed on the dash. He backed the truck up. "Don't even say *his* name," he dared.

So I did. "Pietr's my friend." Dad didn't know it wasn't true anymore.

He white-knuckled the steering wheel at the mention of his name. "Leave that boy to Sarah. I know he seemed to be warmin' to you, but you get round him and you do stupid things. And I know you say he didn't hit you—what—you *fell*, right?"

I nodded. I had fallen. While being walloped by an attacker of the CIA variety.

"So you do stupid stuff *and* get clumsy? I don't know. There's somethin' not quite right about that boy. He's dangerous."

"But Wanda, with her collection of firearms, is—"

"Well prepared and charmin'," he quipped.

"Wow." I'd thought about forcing her out of the picture, but I needed her to get me back and forth to the Rusakovas'. I just never thought . . . "Eeeww, Dad. *Charming?*"

He grinned. From ear to ear.

"Have you *met* Wanda?"

"I've done more than that," he said, puffing his chest out.

I blushed for us both. "Daaad . . ."

"Kissin'—kissin'! Geez, Jessie. See what I mean? Even talkin' about that boy gets you thinkin' stupid stuff."

In a blink we'd blown through Junction and I'd missed my favorite part of therapy: Main Street.

Dad parked the truck and looked at me. "Pietr's trouble, Jessie. He's the reason you lie—"

"No." Pietr had been the most honest part of my life. Until I corrupted him.

Wanda stood on our front steps, pistol case in hand. I rolled down my window, looking her way. Our signal.

Dad shook his head. "He's the reason you sneak around. And this last time . . ." Dad jumped, Wanda at his door, knocking.

Though I'd never thought I'd thank *anyone* for Wanda, I silently thanked God. Yes, she was too rough, too quick to jump, and knew way too much, but that was all probably part of CIA job requirements. And she was my ride. I couldn't risk losing *that*.

"Hey, handsome," she said.

Dad unrolled his window to greet her.

I looked away as they kissed. It hadn't even been six months since Mom died. I wanted Dad happy. I did. But happy was different from dating. And kissing. And dating and kissing—when I could wrap my mind around my Dad doing that—*shouldn't* include Wanda.

"I was just tellin' Jessie why she and that Rusakova boy shouldn't be seein' each other right now."

Wanda's expression went grave. "Still grounded?"

"Until tomorrow," my father reported.

I wondered if Wanda playing chauffeur didn't wear on her, too. The excuses she came up with to get me out of the house were very un-Wanda-like things to do. But Dad never batted an eye when Wanda suggested doing girl stuff with me.

He surely hoped it eased the pain of losing Mom. But shopping couldn't do that. Maybe time would.

Eventually.

Wanda pushed the pistol case into my arms as soon as I climbed out of the truck. "Be a dear and carry that."

I grunted, following them down the hill. I set up the safety flag to show the outdoor range was live. Stapling up two targets, I wondered if we shouldn't stand under cover in case the heavens suddenly dumped; the sky stretched above our farm was heavy with clouds painted gunmetal blue.

The breeze kicked up, blinding me with my hair.

Wanda jerked a rubber band out of her pocket. "Tie it back," she said, laughing at me.

"Safety glasses," Dad reminded me, and I tucked their arms behind my ears, coloring my world glare-free amber. I plonked a pair of earmuffs on to drown out the eventual gunfire.

Opening the gun case I paused. The gloss of oil-slicked steel contrasted with the wood and bone of the two revolvers' grips. Wanda leaned down and offered Dad the one in bone. "Model nineteen, four-inch barrel Smith & Wesson; .357 Magnum."

He held it more like it was a baby bird fallen from the nest than a deadly mechanism born of fire and metal.

"I'll take this." Wanda picked up its mate.

Orders were abbreviated on the family range. I looked around before announcing, "Ready on the right? Ready on the left? All's clear. Commence firing."

They emptied their six-shooters quickly, Wanda finishing first. She stuck her hand out expectantly, and I shook six more rounds into her palm. She spun the cylinder, dropping bullets in with a speed that spoke of hard practice.

She snapped it shut. And handed it to me.

Dad watched, unwilling to hide his curiosity. He took the brick of ammo out of my other hand. "Wanda and I were talkin' about you and your potential. We agree you should take up shootin' again."

I examined the pretty tool of death in my hand. "I don't—"

"You never know when the skill could come in handy," Wanda added. "Could save your life."

"I don't want to fall back into competition shooting. That was"—I glanced at Dad—"your dream, not mine."

Dad's face remained expressionless, but I knew wheels in his head were turning. He hated that I'd waste a gift—that I had an ability I didn't take advantage of. Silent, he waited for me to break.

"Ugh. Maybe I'll compete—a little. But only rapid-fire." Rapid-fire would let me defend myself. My eyes locked on Wanda's, forcing her to read them. She nodded, a silent agreement that medals meant little if you didn't live to display them.

She winked over my head at Dad.

"Okay, Jessie," he conceded. For now.

I faced the targets and chose the one that looked cleanest. Dad's. Raising the revolver, I relaxed my shoulders and hands, and eased out my breath. . . . Found the sight picture and fired. The muzzle rocked up and when it drifted back down, I fired again.

The sky darkened, the target dissolved, replaced by Grigori as he advanced on us that night. I squeezed off another round. Again. Again. And again. The gun loose in my grip, I stared straight ahead, struggling with the fact there was no threat.

Just me, punching paper.

Wanda eased the revolver out of my hands. "You really cleaned out the center of that one."

Dad grinned. "All clear?"

I nodded and he jogged forward to check what was left of the target. He let out a whoop of joy, and I forced a smile.

"Great shootin', Jessie," he congratulated from downrange. "It's like you barely took time off."

Wanda watched me. She grinned for Dad's sake, but her soft words were full of warning. "You know you won't get to take that much time in the field. It'll be pop-pop-pop. No time to release that breath and settle, no time to let gravity pull the muzzle back down. You may have to muscle it." She made a show of patting my back. "Great shot, this kid!" she yelled.

"I didn't want any of this," I hissed.

She looked at me, the dopey grin sliding away quick as lightning. "No one wants this, Jessie. But we handle what we're dealt or we die."

"Geez, you all looked real serious for a moment," Dad said, jogging back to us.

"Wanda was reminding me that practice makes perfect and I still have a lot to learn."

Her gaze hardened a moment. "Yes, we *all* still have a lot to learn," she agreed. "Hey, I could arrange a match in a couple weeks. I'll loan you the perfect piece."

"Great," Dad agreed, giving her a peck on the cheek. "What do you say, Jessie?"

I thrust the word through clamped teeth. "Great," I conceded. "I have stuff to do in the barns."

"Lunch at noon," Dad called, meaning: *What're you cooking?*

"Burgers," I announced, heading back to the barns to fuss with the feed and tack I'd already rearranged twice in my boredom. I considered my new, new, new normal: regular therapy; no Mom; non-werewolf boyfriend; horse riding; farm chores; school; newspaper; and shooting competition.

Swell.

CHAPTER NINETEEN

I was flipping burgers out of the sizzling pan and onto buns when Wanda's phone blasted "Hungry Like the Wolf." She set down a fry and snapped her cell open. "Wanda," she said amiably.

Something about her had changed faintly—a narrowing of her eyes, the way her jaw slowed as she continued chewing. "Well, of course. I'll pop right over and lend a hand. Mind if I bring Jessica?" There was the briefest of pauses. "Great! Yep. We're on our way!"

I raced to the door with my jacket and purse, trying not to be obvious as I shifted from foot to foot. Wanda didn't move this fast unless there was trouble. And the only trouble she welcomed me to was trouble at the Rusakova house.

"Gotta race off to the library—major research mishap. If we don't reconcile it fast, the seniors at Junction will have a heck of a time with their projects."

"Go, woman," Dad chuckled.

Wanda dashed out the door I held. She sprinted to the car and I hopped in, barely buckling up before we launched forward.

"What's going on?"

"Our bug picked up a huge fight at their place. Call your boy-friend. I need to know what's up."

Instead of protesting that Pietr wasn't my boyfriend, I hit the number. The phone rang and rang. "No answer." Something cold crawled along the base of my spine, climbing toward my stomach.

"Damn it." She shot through stop signs.

"What do you think . . . ?"

"You've studied wolves. What happens when the leader of the pack gets displaced?" She nailed the accelerator, and we sped through town. "Thought they were smarter. . . ."

I squeezed my eyes shut and pinched the bridge of my nose. A fight for dominance between wolves was brutal, but between Pietr, Catherine, Max, and one too-human Alexi . . . ? It couldn't end well. I tried to steel myself to the fact it could be Pietr and Max fighting. Max was older by nearly a year, broader in the shoulders and heavier with muscle. Quicker to react, he was faster to let the wolf inside his skin leap out.

Pietr was more agile. Brighter. Fear set my nerves jangling. Imagining the full-blood brothers fighting, I shuddered.

We were in their driveway before I could consider all the possibilities. Wanda bolted out of the car with me beside her. Even outside the house the brutal noise of glass shattering and cursing shook us.

Onto the Queen Anne's shadowed porch we flew. Wanda kicked the door open. Any other day I'd suggest she try the knob first.

The foyer was strewn with signs of battle—pictures torn from the wall, glass splintered across the ornate Oriental rugs that ran the hallway's length. There was a crash in the sitting room. Pushing past Wanda I froze, mouth gaping.

Stunned.

Max had Alexi pinned to the floor, his hands on his elder brother's neck. "Pretenderrr . . ." The word stretched from three to seven syllables under Max's primal rage.

"Jee-ZUS!" Wanda sprang between them, throwing her weight at the choke hold Max had on Alexi, desperate to break his grip. "Dammit! Let him go!"

Eyes bulging, Alexi's face reddened as Max choked the life out of him.

Alexi fought. His fingers, slow and clumsy, battled for their own grip on Max.

Helpless, I looked on. Where were Pietr and Catherine?

Wanda knelt beside the warring brothers. "Alexi, stop fighting."

Alexi's eyes rolled to Wanda.

"Stop fighting. Submit," she said, so calm the words and tone seemed as opposed as the brothers she aimed them at. "I know. It's counterintuitive. But *I* can't stop him. *You* can't stop him. The others aren't here to save your sorry ass. And I don't know if they would if they were."

I stumbled forward, crouched beside her, hands struggling to peel away even one of Max's fingers. My knuckles screamed with effort. Desperate to break his stranglehold, my attempts never rated a single glance from Max.

Alexi's eyes rolled back in his head.

"MAX!" I shrieked.

Wanda's voice stayed cool and even. Tempered and rational. "You know you have to trigger that part of the beast in him, Alexi. You did a great job triggering his attack instinct," she commended with a sneer. "Now submit. Or die."

Alexi gagged, veins rising across his forehead. His eyelids fluttered. Closed. His hands dropped away from Max, arms limp. His whole body seemed to collapse in.

"Ohhh, God . . . ," I wailed, my hands on Max's as his fingers loosened and he dropped Alexi's body to the floor.

Panting, Max rocked back on his heels, his eyes losing their wildness. "Shit," he whispered.

I smacked him—a crack of my hand across his cheek—a second before Wanda knocked me to the floor.

Pietr straddled us in a sprinter's pose, lips peeled back from teeth already lengthening.

Max's eyes flared, his face stretching. The noise of joints slipping wetly from their sockets warned his body was beginning the shift.

I grabbed Pietr's arm, a mad attempt at begging him to stop. But backing down wasn't in his nature.

Wanda shoved me away from them, pushing me against the love seat. "He nearly shut down that dominant wolf response. What were you thinking? Trigger it again—aim it at you?"

"No . . ." My eyes blurred. So did Pietr's and Max's forms, their spines rippling as the wolves inside wriggled free of human clothes and human skins.

"No!" I screamed.

Jaws snapped, teeth clicking cruelly together as they dove for each other. Pietr, fully furred, the tall, dark hair along his back rising in a thick crest, circled Max until his shoulder struck a side table.

Max pulled up to his full height on all fours, a reminder to Pietr of the difference in their size. The love seat's carved legs bit into my back, and I yelled, "Pietr! Drop! Submit!"

I covered my face as Max lunged at him. Pietr twisted out of the way, letting Max vault past. And slam into the wall.

A photo of St. Basil's Cathedral crashed onto Max's back and he shook it off, spraying the room with tiny shards of glass like a biting rain. Max growled, the noise rising from the darkest part of him. He spun, claws gripping the floor, shifting the carpet and gouging the hardwood as he launched himself at Pietr again.

With a *woof* he connected, rolling Pietr into a table that collapsed on them both.

Pietr tore free of Max's toothy grip and the tang of blood stained the air. Pietr rose, red trickling from a slice in his shoulder. Shaking out his pelt, he spattered the room with crimson.

I blinked, reaching up to touch something warm and wet on my cheek. Blood on my fingertip, a tremor rocked me.

Pietr charged, heading right and turning left at the last moment—a bold feint—cutting under and up, his back on the floor. Belly up, his teeth locked on Max's throat.

Wanda stood, going for the gun under her shirt.

"No!" I leaped up, wrenching her hand away.

"This can't end well," she snapped.

"Keep your hand off the gun," I said, looking down at Pietr lying in his wolfskin, jaws clamped on his brother's throat, prepared to crush his windpipe or open a jugular.

Max whined. Pietr readjusted his grip.

"He'll kill him," Wanda stated.

"No." Before I'd thought my actions through, I was beside Max, arched across his back and neck, staring into Pietr's eyes. "Let go, Pietr."

His jaws moved. *Chewing.*

Max whimpered.

"His eyes are glazing," Wanda said.

"Do you see me?" I leaned over further, unbalanced by more than my precarious posture. I reached out to place my hands on either side of Pietr's head.

"Don't touch him," Wanda warned. "He'll bite your hand off as happily as he'll lap up his own brother's blood."

Pietr snarled as if in agreement. Startled, I yanked my hands away.

"Unbutton your shirt."

I whipped around to see Catherine leaning against the door frame. "What?"

She shrugged. "We're animals, after all, Jessie. Survival and dominance drive us. Pietr's deep in his desire to dominate, and Max isn't smart enough to submit."

"She's right," Alexi coughed, rolling over to watch with detached curiosity. "Give him something else to focus on."

"I doubt unbuttoning *my* shirt will get Pietr's attention."

"You might be surprised," Alexi muttered.

My gaze flicked to Wanda.

"Do what you have to before I do what *I* have to." She tapped the holster snuggled just beneath her shirt.

Max started sliding forward, eyelids drooping. I fumbled at my top button.

"Pietr," I whispered, stooping back over to catch his eyes. The first button opened.

Pietr's eyes narrowed.

I opened the second button. "Pietr, don't do this," I pleaded, focusing my eyes on his. He watched my fingers work, watched them tremble and flounder. His eyes widened when he got a glimpse of more bare skin.

"You're no monster." I drew down a deep breath. This was not what I'd ever imagined as a moment with my werewolf ex-boyfriend. Not me unbuttoning my shirt. And not in front of an audience.

I tried to think of it as an actress playing a part with a strange actor. Necessary. But nothing to do with anyone's relationship. I fought back the fact I'd earned a D in Drama. My life now should rate extra credit.

The third button opened, and the tension left Pietr's jaws. He let go. There was a clunk as the back of his head hit the floor. He rolled to right himself, lying on his furry stomach, canine attention absolutely fixed, tongue lolling. To the credit of his animal instincts his eyes stayed hopeful, entranced by what remained beyond button four.

Max flopped to the floor with a whine. One eye still open, it also lingered on my fourth button expectantly.

Catherine howled and I blushed, buttoning up in record time.

"What have I said, Jessie? Men can be total *dogs*," Wanda said, blousing her shirt around her holster.

I kept my eyes on her to avoid the distraction of two naked guys slipping back into the clothes their wolflike counterparts always slinked out of.

Max spoke first, back in his pants and running his hand through his tangled hair. "Thanks, Jessie," he said coyly. "For everything." He grinned and rubbed the wicked bruise already fading on his throat.

Pietr's head snapped up, the first rumblings of a growl beginning. Blood streaked his shoulder, but the long cut mended as I watched.

I stomped a foot. "See that, Pietr Rusakova?"

He rolled his eyes from my foot to my face, only pausing briefly on my shirt's buttons on the way up. "*Da*," he said thickly.

"That is me putting my foot down. No fighting with family."

He arched an eyebrow at me.

"And don't expect me to"—my tongue tangled in my mouth and heat rose to color my cheeks—"to do *that* for you again, either." I crossed my arms.

His lips twitched. "I wouldn't dream of it," he whispered.

Max snorted. "It's all you'll be dreaming of now, little brother!"

I kicked him in the leg. Not hard. But it was better than getting his attention by unbuttoning part of my shirt again. Far more satisfying, too. "You almost got your head chewed off."

"Because you threatened Jess," Pietr said levelly.

Max rubbed his jaw, remembering my slap.

My hand ached. Max was thick-skulled in more than one way. I'd probably remember the slap longer than he would.

"I'd never hurt Jessie."

"Damn rrright you won't," Pietr said.

Heart in my throat, I reminded myself this wasn't about me. This was stupid alpha and beta wolf stuff, nothing more. I was territory to piss on. And man, did it piss me off.

Max looked at me and lowered his gaze. Submitting for now. "Sorry, Jessie. Are you all right?"

"Yes. I'm fine," I insisted. "Why is everyone so worried about *me?* Ask Alexi how *he's* doing."

Alexi bowed his head, looking away.

"We'd have to care before we'd ask," Max said, his simple logic chilling.

"He's been your brother for years," I reminded them.

Catherine frowned. "He's *played* our brother for years. He is no relation. We share no blood or DNA. No kinship."

"But you share a bond."

Three pairs of eyes met mine. Assessed me as if they were once again more wolf, more ferociously feral, than not.

"The bond of your secret."

"And that means he's a liability," Max stated.

"Am *I* a liability, Max?" I stepped forward.

Wanda hissed. "Do you have a death wish?"

"I know the same thing Alexi does. Will you try to kill me?"

"Don't you have any common sense?" Wanda wondered aloud. "Nonconfrontational!"

"Well, Max? When will you try to choke the life out of *me?*"

Max dragged a finger along the carpet's edge. "I won't." One shoulder rose. "You're strange—"

"Says a werewolf," I muttered. Wanda swore. And not for the first time since we'd entered the room.

Max smirked. "I trust you, Jessie. I *used* to trust him. But now, he just needs to go."

"Unfortunately that won't work. He's the only one of legal age to play guardian," Wanda pointed out.

"A few months from now . . . ," Max growled as he rose, reminding us all of his upcoming eighteenth birthday. He crossed his arms and widened his stance, readying for a confrontation.

With a sigh, Wanda continued. "If he goes, you all wind up wards of the state."

"Foster care," I realized.

"Yes. Probably split apart because groups are harder to place."

The three full-blood Rusakovas grumbled.

Alexi sat up straighter, rubbing his neck with slow and ginger hands.

"How do we trust him again?" Pietr voiced a subtle protest.

"Maybe you don't. Remember: 'Keep your friends close and your enemies closer,'" Wanda quoted.

"Good advice," Max agreed. "Exactly why we keep you around."

"We should go," Wanda suggested, snaring my arm. Obeying, I felt Pietr's gaze follow us out the door and all the way to Wanda's car.

CHAPTER TWENTY

Dad opened the door and I slid along the metal wall, whispering soothing words to Rio as I backed her out of the trailer. All around us horses and riders warmed up for the Golden Jumper. I'd have to thank Derek for getting me in—and thank him again for not attending. I told him I needed to focus. It was true.

I was returning to normalcy.

This would be my first jumper competition since Mom's death. As much as I'd practiced, and as good as Rio was, I knew the stands would be quieter without Mom intermittently screaming and gasping for us.

I reached for my worry stone but wanted the amber heart pendant. Some sort of anchor. That morning I had put Mom's netsuke rabbit necklace on. Warm against my skin, it was solid. A connection to my past. "Let's walk," I said to Rio. "Stretch those legs."

Dad glanced my way, his face filled with what mine hid. He was forever beside Mom at these things, Annabelle Lee following. This was hard on all of us. The truck pulled away.

I eyed the course. Eight jumps; one very wet-looking liverpool.

Totally doable. Rio pranced, eager for eventing. This was more than a competition—a way to return to a part of my life I'd nearly lost when I lost Mom—it was a reward for Rio.

When Pietr turned a cold shoulder and Annabelle Lee was wedged deep in a book and I had no one but Dad looking at me with disappointment deep in his eyes, it was Rio I went to. She deserved to have some fun on a jump full of rails and water.

I did, too. There was no lying between horse and rider. Every move she made, every muscle she twitched told a subtle truth I recognized and read. And the only way to win a jumper competition was with good communication.

Open and honest.

When Pietr and I fell apart, Rio and I grew together.

It was only right Rio got to play over fences and race through the flats and mixed terrain of an exciting course. I wanted her happy. And if I won?

Bonus.

A number of riders in my class had already gone when Georgia Main was announced. I moved Rio back so I could watch. The time started, and she raced through the course, her horse—one I'd admired a while—nimbly approaching fences and flying, beautifully, over each one. A nearly flawless run—a great time, but I knew enough about Georgia to know she'd be humble about her performance. Being a rising star didn't go to her head.

They announced us and I mounted, guiding us onto the field. I snugged my helmet's chinstrap and waited for the signal. Scanning the crowd I found Dad and Annabelle Lee in the stands. Annabelle Lee set aside her book to watch.

But something else caught my eye. Not one to fit in easily with the jumper crowd myself—they were polished, elegant and generally moneyed—I easily noticed others who didn't fit the given mold. And there were several of them. Men. Broad-shouldered, tall, with a rigidity to their stance and a hard expression that spoke of surviving tough times.

They seemed more uncomfortable here than a novice rider on her first course. Not the regular crowd. Although they stood apart from one another, they seemed to communicate. A glance from one to another, the raising of one cell phone moments before the next.

One of them looked toward the stands. Then two. Three. And four. All at once they were staring at Dad and Annabelle Lee. The crowd was peppered with werewolves, not the type that made my blood hot, but those that chilled me—marked men—Mafia.

Rio leaped forward when the signal sounded, snatching me from my fear. It was a public place. Crowded. Dad and Annabelle Lee would be fine. I focused on the task at hand—helping Rio show how amazing she was when she leaped and soared.

A beautiful beast, Rio's legs folded high and evenly, her neck stretched, graceful as a swan's over each jump. Ears pricked forward, she ignored the stress I telegraphed.

I wasn't worried about the course; I was worried about what would come after. If we flew through the jumps cleanly we'd have to ride out and get Dad and Annabelle Lee's attention, hoping we could get to the truck before the Mafia made their move.

But if we *didn't* jump cleanly . . .

Rio never faltered, though my heart thudded in opposition to her hoofbeats. She took the verticals easily until we headed over a broad oxer, two rails across. Her hind hoof clipped the rail, and I took my chance.

I slipped from the saddle, falling as the crowd groaned. Tuck. Roll. It sounded so simple, but it was bone-jarring—my back popped, my legs tangled, and my teeth rattled with the impact.

I came to a stop, face first, in the turf.

Ow.

Rio stepped back around, nudging me with her nose and snuffling, confused.

Medics rushed me, fingers probing my neck and easing me into a collar before they rolled me onto a board and lifted me.

"I'm okay," I assured them. But not too much.

Rio was walked out with me, her head bobbing alongside, ears twitching as she snorted.

"I'm okay," I repeated.

Off the course Annabelle Lee and Dad caught up to us.

"Seriously," I said, watching the Mafia men group and disperse. "I'm okay. I want to go home."

Dad looked at the medics. "Does she check out?"

"We'll look her over in the ambulance," they said. "You can pull alongside."

Dad took Rio and scrambled to get the truck and Annabelle Lee situated. Watching them go I considered holding my breath until they reappeared.

"Jessie," a voice called, and I turned to see Georgia. *Ow.* "I never thought I'd see *you* fall," she admitted. "You okay?"

"Yeah." The medics helped me stand. "I'm fine." They shone a light in my eyes, and I resisted swatting them. "Hey. Congratulations on a nearly flawless course."

Georgia ducked her head and smiled.

"Gracie's a great horse." Someone grabbed me for a pulse. It would escalate if the Mafia reappeared. "Don't you have to go and accept a prize or something? You don't want to be late."

"Yeah. I thought you two would blow past us. I kinda wish you had. It would have been a great comeback story."

"Things change," I said, struggling to keep the smile alive on my lips when I realized I'd quoted Pietr. "You totally deserved the win."

She smiled and headed toward the waiting judges.

The medics announced what I'd been betting on. "She'll be stiff, a little bruised, but other than that, she's fine."

They eased me into the truck, and Dad got us home quickly. The whole way I watched the side-view mirror, wondering why we hadn't been followed—hoping I was wrong about the men lurking in the Golden Jumper's crowd.

At home I pulled up Google. If I was going to deal with Russian Mafia members, I wanted to know something about them. This time I'd gotten lucky.

Not surprisingly, Russian Mafia members looked like many men. It was like Nickolai had said, many of them started as good men— military men—who returned home from war to find the promises their government made weren't kept. Disillusioned and without support, they turned to the streets for survival.

The mob took them in. Trained them and gave them new orders. They were to have no family outside the mob. No affiliations. No connections. What they had, they took. In the mob there was only honor in what I'd been taught was dishonest dealing. Men who once protected Russia now carved her apart because they didn't see another choice.

And now they were *here*.

I wanted to see pictures—were there some I'd recognize? But my search produced a whole other world of images. A world filled with nearly as much ink as blood. Tattoos branded mafiosos as participants in Russia's underworld.

Even the saber marking the full-blood Rusakovas was a military insignia and an increasingly common tattoo for Mafia men in America. They called themselves "werewolves"—human and slyly unnoticed by day; they reveled in people presuming them monsters by night.

Seated before my computer I was astonished by the life stories that could be read in a mobster's tattoos. Each spire on a church represented a murder committed. A spiderweb illustrated being tangled up in addiction. A pair of stars on their chest or knees meant they were captains in the Mafia's own military.

My stomach queasy, I shut down my computer. To go from being protectors of a people to their biggest internal threat . . . And to realize they'd been forced in that direction . . . I wasn't sure what was more disturbing. But I was beginning to realize choices weren't merely black and white. We all muddled through various shades of gray.

And too often the most difficult decisions were based on survival.

Unfortunately the end of the weekend didn't guarantee the next week would be an improvement at all.

The Rusakovas scouted and Cat told me how they continually came up empty. Pietr told me nothing. I pored over map after map of Junction, but nowhere seemed suitable for hiding a werewolf.

Monday we sat on the bleachers in the gymnasium for class pictures. Tuesday the school mourned the loss of another student to suicide and Derek was down another friend. Noticing he wasn't in school, I decided to make it the first time I called him.

"Hey," he said. Cheerfully.

I paused. "Hey. You weren't in school today."

"Did you miss me?" His smile was audible.

"I thought—I'm sorry. I'm sorry about Mike."

The other end of the line went silent. "Oh. Yeah," he said finally. "He was a good football player."

"It must be hard . . . losing a friend."

Again I was faced with silence. I waited.

"Umm, yeah. I guess it all got to be too much," Derek said, somber.

Got to be too much? What? The Mike I knew was always joking, laughing. House near the Hill, two parents and a younger sibling. Decent grades, too, if I recalled correctly. Of course, Mike wasn't in my circle of friends. So I didn't *know* him much at all, really. I paused, straining for some answer I wasn't getting on the phone.

"Yeah. It sucks," Derek concluded, his voice grave. "So how was your day?" he asked, his tone brightening.

Uneasy, I made small talk until I could find an excuse to get off the phone.

Wednesday we got our class photos. Sophia held hers, puzzling over something, her face fierce.

"You look beautiful in it," I assured. "Picture perfect."

Startled, she hissed, "Mine's so blurry." She squinted.

"Really? Lemme see." I took the photo and peered at her again. My lips tugged together and I licked them. "Blurry?"

"Maybe it's allergies," she said, taking the picture back. She rubbed her eyes.

"It still looks blurry?"

"In lots of places." Her mouth pressed into a pale, thin line. "It's not blurry at all, is it, Jessie?"

"No."

"*Crap.*" She jammed the photo back into its manila envelope.

"Soph—what's going on? You won't do the newspaper photos, you clear out your locker, and—" I balked, remembering the brainstormed list with its barely hidden message.

The crowd of kids passing from class to class had thinned, but Sophia looked frantic about being asked so openly.

Too soon the tardy bell would ring. Why did I always have to ask hard questions between classes?

"Into the girls' bathroom with you." I guided her down the hallway, shouldering the door open. "You're freaking me out. The photo's fine. So what's wrong? Are your eyes giving you trouble? Do you need to see a doctor?"

She laughed, and bumps rose on my arms. "A doctor won't help— maybe a witch doctor." She giggled. "If it was my vision . . . My eyes are definitely giving me trouble." She stepped away from me long enough to check each stall until she was satisfied we were alone.

Feeling she didn't mean exactly what she said, I asked the next strange question. "Remember when we brainstormed that article and Derek and Jack came into the teachers' lounge?"

"I remember *I* did most of the brainstorming."

"True," I admitted. "Did you know there was a message in what you wrote?"

"A what?"

I set my backpack on the sink and pulled out my school newspaper notebook. "Here." I passed the paper to her, running my finger down the first letters in each of her hastily written sentences.

BEWARE.

Stunned, her volume rose. "Now you're trying to freak *me* out."

"No," I insisted. "I didn't know what it meant at first. But then— well, something weird happened later that night. And BEWARE seemed like a fitting sentiment."

"I can't believe this."

"What's going on, Soph? Does this happen to you often?"

"*This?*" She waved my notepaper and shoved it back against my chest. "No. *This* doesn't happen to me often."

I swallowed. Just like a normal person living a more than normal life. "Do you see strange things?"

"We're in high school. We all see strange things." Soft-spoken Sophia was gone, replaced by the same anxious and angry Sophie I'd witnessed confront Derek that day.

"There's more to that photo than you're saying. What sort of strange things do you see?"

"Maybe I don't want to say. Maybe I'm perfectly comfortable letting you and Sarah be the crazy girls at Junction High."

"Niiice. Maybe if you tell me, I can help you."

"You can't undo what was done to me," she scoffed. "This thing I have, it's permanent. I'd rather not get into it. Let's leave it with the fact that I've tried to get rid of it."

"What is *it*?"

"God, Jessie. You're so frustrating sometimes." She blew out a breath. "Fine. I'll let you into my crazy little world." She pulled the photo back out of the envelope and pressed it flat across the bathroom mirror. "What do you see there?"

"Our graduating class. Well, plus a few people who probably won't graduate with our class."

She rolled her eyes. "Awesome. Pen, please."

Puzzled, I looked at her.

She snapped her fingers. "Come on. Chop-chop."

I obeyed, watching as she scribbled all over the huge photo, the mirror reflecting back her look of extreme concentration. She pulled back, frowning, but seemingly satisfied. "All that?"—she ran her fingers along the scribbled-out areas—"blurs."

"Really?" I pulled my picture out and compared it. There were a handful of places she hadn't scribbled out. "What about those?" I asked, touching them one by one. VP Perlson, Derek Jamieson, Pietr, Cat, Sarah, Sophia.

Me.

"All those members of the junior class look clear?"

"Crystal."

"Why?"

"I've thought about it a bunch. I think it's about intentions.

Motivation. I feel like . . . like these people have clear goals. Beyond making a living, getting good grades or scoring. In football or with girls." She smirked. "It's almost like they—*we*—have a calling. And we're already on the path." She handed back the pen. "Crazy, huh?"

Whatever inside me had reconciled with the existence of werewolves only briefly freaked at the idea. "Can you, like—*read* their motivation? See what their calling is? What drives them?"

She shrugged. "Maybe someday. I just know we're different."

"Can you do that with any photo?"

"Not so much. It needs to be new. Maybe it's an energy thing. I'm trying to research it, but what do you put in a Google search for *this*? It's all so frikkin' weird."

"Welcome to my world." There was a spot just away from the bleachers that Sophia had carefully left un-scribbled, too. A vaguely human-looking shape. I tapped it with a finger. "And this?"

Sophia grinned. "Ready for the *real* ride into crazy town?"

"Most days I'm driving the bus."

"Fine. Sometimes I see a woman. She's hazy. Like she's not quite here and not quite"—she waved a hand—"there. Wherever *there* is."

"Like a ghost?"

Her lips smooshed together and shoved from one side of her face to the other. It was the first time I'd seen Sophie look ugly. "Yeah."

"Who is she?"

"Your mother."

My world froze for a minute, and I staggered. The photo fell from my fingers, and Sophia snatched it back as it drifted.

"It gets better. She has a message for you."

I swallowed, the noise crackling in my ears. The lump in my throat refused to budge.

"I've only gotten part of it so far," she admitted. "Actually"—she tugged my notepaper out again—"it seems *you* got the same part I did."

BEWARE.

CHAPTER TWENTY-ONE

It was my strangest trip to service learning yet. All day Pietr kept his distance, but every time Derek came close, Pietr's gaze found me. He never said more than a cool word, never even brushed against me when we passed in the hall.

On the ride to Golden Oaks, Pietr sat up front. Hascal, Smith, and Jaikin were quick to resume our standard flirting game, but my heart wasn't in it.

"Jessie," Hascal wheezed, "you're not really here, are you?" He waved a hand so pale it was nearly translucent.

"Sorry, boys. I—"

"Is it Derek? It's got to be Derek. He's been giving her a lot—*a lot*—of attention recently," Jaikin rattled.

"Or Maximilian Rusakova. He's been hanging on her."

My three favorite nerds looked at one another, nodded sagely, and turned back to me.

"Nope." I popped the "p" on the end for emphasis. "I'm just exhausted. Stressed. My head's pounding."

Smith petted my arm, his clammy touch raising gooseflesh.

"Have you tried a nice herbal tea?"

"Mmm. Chamomile ith my favorite."

I glanced at Hascal. He was starting to lose his s's again—an unfortunate side effect of his severe allergic reaction to anything in the canid family. Allergic to dogs, wolves, jackals and evidently werewolves.

"I highly recommend it," he concluded with a sniff.

I nodded and cracked a window. Pietr's was open. "Thanks, guys, but I don't think tea is going to help. Hey, while I've got the three brightest guys from Junction High at my disposal"—they blushed—"what do you guys think about this recent teen suicide trend?"

"Tragic," Smith concluded.

The others nodded.

"Okay, I'm rephrasing. Why do you think we're seeing a sudden rise in teen suicides?"

Smith cracked his knuckles, the sound reminding me of the noise Pietr's joints made sliding from their sockets during his change. "I tend to believe we aren't seeing a rise in teen suicides but rather with the growth of media coverage we are more able to bring such stories to the public."

"You think there've always been the same number of suicides in the area?"

"There are, of course, differences in the numbers related to the growth of population. The easiest way to confirm my belief would be to do a quick comparison chart between the populations over the past few decades and the numbers of teenage suicides, breaking it into a ratio or percentage—your choice."

"A chart? Yee-aahh. Anyone else have an opinion?"

"It's not so much an opinion as a bit of information I read online." Jaikin signaled me to lean in. "I'm not allowed to name my sources." He grinned.

"Oh. *Them,*" Smith muttered with a roll of his eyes.

"What? Who's *them?*" I asked.

"Jaikin indulges in fantasies of a conspiratorial nature," Smith said, picking at his fingernails and clearly disapproving.

"Are you a conspiracy theorist?" I teased Jaikin.

He blushed. "I give room to all possibilities."

"He flat out denies Occam's razor," Smith remonstrated.

I wondered what Smith would think if he discovered he was sitting two rows behind a werewolf. "Have you considered that sometimes life is so complicated, slicing things down to the simplest answer like Occam suggested isn't good enough?"

Smith got quiet. He was crushing on me—he wouldn't argue.

"You're fascinating," I assured Jaikin. "Tell me about this theory related to the suicides."

"It seems the most recent suicide victims left behind interesting notes, journals—"

"Actually a blog," Hascal interjected, wheezing.

"Right. The blogger journaled every night, leaving detailed notes of what he did and what he saw."

"Did they have something in common?"

Hascal pointed to me and touched his nose. "Yeth!"

Jaikin continued, "They all either wrote something, drew something, or claimed to see something related to werewolves."

I stiffened in my seat. "Werewolves?" Without looking, I knew Pietr's body language mimicked my own.

"Now she sees my point," Smith declared. "Not so much fascinating as gullible, aren't they?"

Jaikin said smugly, "You're just jealous. You want to be fascinating to Jessie, too."

Smith glared back.

"Werewolves," I whispered.

"It's one of myriad possibilities." Jaikin shrugged.

I rubbed at my arms, chasing a chill away at the thought the Rusakovas were linked to the suicides. "Tell me what else you've heard."

"Since you asked . . . these werewolves—some call them loup-garous or hamrammr—"

"Or *oborot*," I added.

"What language is that?"

"Russian."

All three sets of eyes turned to Pietr. Smith twitched, and Hascal's eyes widened behind his thick glasses, giving him a distinctly owl-like appearance.

"What? I can't know something from time to time?"

Hascal patted my arm. "You're fathinating, too, Jethie."

Jaikin concluded, "So, one group believes the werewolves have set up people to be killed on the train tracks."

The memory of standing blindfolded on the tracks moments before Pietr shoved me out of the way was so fresh in my mind a shiver rattled me. "Why?"

"Do they need a reason? Would a werewolf—a creature at least as much beast as man, a *monster*—hold to the same principles we do? Maybe it's just fun."

I couldn't fathom what raced through Pietr's mind.

"Murder as a pastime? Sounds like pure human evil to me," I proposed. "Any other opinions?"

"Some have suggested it's not the werewolves doing it, but people who want to keep the werewolves secret," Jaikin added.

"What? The werewolves are spotted and some clandestine organization takes out the witnesses?" My heart sped at the possibility, but I shook my head. "Any other options?"

Smith cleared his throat. "The only other option *is* the option. Teens have a reputation for being dissatisfied. Our hormones are horribly out of balance, choking off our brain's higher functions whenever we notice someone has a nice rack."

"That must be why you can't do calculus whenever you're in the same room with Jessie," Jaikin chuckled.

Pietr's shoulders shook with laughter.

Smith looked like he'd sucked on a lemon.

"So," I said. "Smith, you were saying . . ."

"Most of the time we're simply unhappy with what life hands us. We struggle to find our place. In the world and in our families. Life is tumultuous. As the stressors become greater, it's only natural the will to survive becomes less in certain members of our species."

"So to you, suicide is an example of survival of the fittest?" I hoped my dismay could be read on my face, but uncertain, I added, "That's cold, Smith. I may agree with you on lots of other things, but . . ."

The van pulled up to Golden Oaks and I hopped out first. I shot a look at Pietr and he sighed, resigning himself to meet the greater good. We quickly clarified who was partners with who and taking which of the local animal shelter's animals on our rounds.

Smith was miffed that Pietr and I had reunited. "Is this because you're angry with my answer?"

I gave him a peck on the cheek. "I'd think with a brain as large as yours there'd be room for more compassion."

Climbing the stairs with Pietr due to his aversion to elevators, a mix of emotions stirred my stomach. "We need to talk."

"We had nothing to do with the suicides," Pietr assured me. In the crook of his arm the calico kitten, Victoria (now a regular with Tag, the pug), mewed. "Did you have to ask?" He rubbed his nose and blinked at me, his eyes going red for an instant as we paused on the steps.

"Sometimes hearing stuff helps. Are you angry?"

He blinked until the red was gone. "*Nyet*," he muttered, motioning up the stairs with a jerk of his chin.

I changed the way I held Tag and, on the move again, I asked my next question. "So why do they all appear to be related to werewolves? Like they've seen something?" I paused, my teeth grinding together. "Is Max being careful?"

"Max? *Careful?* Those words should never be put in the same sentence. You should know that," he said, a note of warning in his voice.

"Okay. Let's say someone spotted him. Who would want them dead because of what they saw?"

We looked at each other and said in unison, "The CIA?"

"I mean, Wanda and Kent have been trouble," I admitted, "and in the church it seemed like that guy really might . . ."

"Kill you?" He gave me a leveling look. "*Da.*"

"Okay. Yeah. It really seemed he was going to shoot me."

"Exactly." He rubbed his nose again.

"Allergies?"

Shaking his head, he blinked red at me.

"But I'm starting to wonder if it's normal for a government agency to act so . . ." I shrugged.

Looking back, I caught him with his nose buried in Victoria's fur. I raised an eyebrow. "Does she smell good enough to eat?"

He chuckled. Uncomfortably. All traces of red bled from his eyes. Watching me, they went clear and blue as Arctic ice. His mouth pulled into a taut line. "What if there's a new player?"

"Who else? Holy crap, Pietr—we're already dealing with the Russian Mafia and the CIA. Who else might want a piece of you?"

"Who doesn't? It's a dog's life, right?" He opened the door for me. "Or perhaps people aren't who they say they are. Things are seldom what they seem."

Says a werewolf.

Hazel Feldman watched Pietr with far greater interest than she'd shown the first time she'd met him—when she'd agreed that *Romeo and Juliet* wasn't much of a romance. "I'm glad you're doing your duty again," she said.

He quirked an eyebrow at her. "I didn't stop. I've been doing my service learning assignment steadily."

"There's a difference between doing an assignment and doing your duty, boy."

He shrugged one shoulder and passed Victoria her way.

"She's a beauty, isn't she?" Feldman marveled. "But such sharp little fangs. That's the way the world is, isn't it? The prettiest things often have the worst bite."

"You speak in riddles, Mrs. Feldman," I said with a smile. "I always leave here with lots to think about."

"Good, good," she said, petting Victoria with such a heavy hand the kitten's head bobbed down and her eyes widened with each long stroke from her head to her tail. "Are you ready to give in, Jessie?"

Out of the corner of my eye I noticed Pietr tilt his head, observing our exchange. "I don't know," I confessed. "I'm not sure I want to know my future."

She glanced at me, wizened eyes narrowing further so her wrinkles deepened into crevices. " '*Que sera, sera,*' " she muttered. " 'Whatever will be, will be.' "

"*Da,*" Pietr agreed. "But doesn't that song continue with the idea we don't get to know our future?"

"I hate that song," she sniped. "Perhaps if I start with *your* cards, Pietr." She pushed Victoria back into his grasp and dug into the folds of her voluminous skirt, withdrawing her beautiful deck of cards. "Shuffle."

Reluctantly Pietr crossed to her door, shut it, and set Victoria down. After checking the window was closed, of course. He had learned that much from his first trip to service learning. He took the cards and paused.

"Don't be scared. Shuffle. The future is an amazing gift."

"Some of us don't get time to unwrap it," he muttered.

"What?" She cupped a hand to her ear.

"He said he's sorry he's being so taciturn."

He looked my way, but only briefly. He shuffled the cards like a pro, his hands quick and sure. "I draw."

She grinned. "You've done this before."

"*Da*, I have a sister with a fascination for such extraneous activities."

"If you think what she does is extraneous, she's not very good at it yet." She took the cards and fanned them in her hand, holding them facedown. "Perhaps I'll make you a believer. Pull one for your recent past."

He did.

"The Tower. You have recently faced great change."

"I'm a teenager. Things are always changing."

"Shall I be more specific?"

Undaunted, he replied, "You may try."

Holding the card, she closed her eyes a moment. "Your most recent birthday was filled with surprises."

My teeth pinned my lower lip.

Pietr didn't show any sign she'd struck a nerve. "Go on."

She ran a thumb across the card, contemplating. "You expected to be hurt that day, not betrayed. But someone close to you surprised you. No. Two surprised you. One with near betrayal, one with acceptance," she corrected.

Pietr's eyebrows lowered.

"Another card? For the near future."

"*Da*." He yanked another free of the fan.

She turned it over. "Oh." Her lips slid across her face as she considered the meaning, or perhaps the words, to explain it. "There is death ahead."

His eyes closed for one sharp second, and he swallowed.

"It is a repeating cycle, a loop meant to close. You can fight it, but it is coming. Quickly."

I reached for him, but he stepped smoothly away. "Pietr . . ."

"This is nothing I don't already know. If you want to make me a believer in magic, you'll need to do far better."

"Fine," she said, lips twisting in a devilish grin. "One more card. For a secret you're keeping."

He reached forward, and she jerked the cards back.

"No. Think about it. Hold it in your mind. What do you want to keep hidden most? What secret do you dare not share?"

He licked his lips. His jaw set like stone. Slowly he slid a card out and showed it to her.

Her eyes flicked from it, to him, to me. "Leave the room, Jessie," she ordered.

CHAPTER TWENTY-TWO

"But . . ."

The faint line of a vein appeared by Pietr's hairline.

"Okay, I'm leaving," I mumbled, slipping out of the room with Tag still in my grasp. Only when the door clicked shut behind me did I hear the faint noise of people talking resume. Sighing, I took a tour of the hallway. Could Mrs. Feldman have learned Pietr's greatest secret? Was she—right now—revealing to him she knew he was a werewolf?

Pietr swung the door open and I jogged back, searching his stony face for some sign. I wanted so badly to touch him, to assure him, but my hand didn't dare twitch from where it held Tag, Pietr looked so fierce.

So utterly unforgiving.

Mrs. Feldman looked at me. A smile crackled her face into a thousand wrinkles. "Come now, Jessie. Shuffle the deck and learn your future."

"I don't believe in magic," I confessed, my eyes never leaving Pietr's face.

He sat, no—*perched*—on a chair in her room, seeking the corner's solitary shadow.

"What is it with you children now? Either you believe in magic, spelling it with a terminal k, as if accepting anything else might indeed be terminal, or you cling to science, dismissing all other possibilities. Has no one taught you they blend? They interweave. Can we explain the magic of birth as science—yes. Sperm meets egg," she confirmed, clapping her hands on the deck. "Until"—she bent forward on her bed as if sharing some secret—"until that first moment a mother or father looks into their child's eyes and realizes there is indeed magic dwelling within."

She shuffled the cards, hands amazingly quick considering they were knotted and gnarled and freckled with spots. The gaudy rings on her fingers sparkled. "Creation. Amino acids encountering the right atmospheric pressure, temperature, and conditions to start life. Science!" she proclaimed. "And yet, where has it happened in our universe? Only here." She pointed with a vehement finger. "On Earth. *That* is a kind of magic."

My eyes followed her hands and she raised them, baiting me as she shuffled and danced the cards back and forth. "They work together, magic and science. And any scientist worth his salt will confess to feeling something magical anytime he or she learns or discovers something new. Have you never thought it is most suitable that science and magic should blur together here in a town called Junction?"

"I never thought about it at all," I confessed.

She fanned the cards and snapped them shut. "Shuffle."

I did, my hands fumbling with the hefty deck.

She took them back, carefully spreading them. "Now pull."

I drew, holding the card out to her, aware how intently Pietr watched my hand.

"Hmm. You worry too much."

Pietr snorted and looked at me, his jaw loosening enough for him to speak. "And you say *I* always state the obvious."

I thought the ghost of a smile twitched there on his lips, but it was gone too fast to be certain.

"You are surrounded by people who want to protect you."

I shrugged, wanting to stand as firm as Pietr.

"Draw again."

I did.

"These people who want to protect you are keeping information—keeping secrets—from you."

"Why?"

Her gray-and-white curls bobbed as she shook her head. "Only to protect you. If they thought it would help . . ." She glanced at Pietr, but he silenced her with a look. "It is important to remember they have the very best intentions."

"The road to hell is paved with good intentions." I gazed out at Pietr from beneath my eyelashes.

He was unmoved.

"One more," she urged.

I sucked in a breath and rolled my lips together, pulling one last card.

"Ahhh. But the secret far bigger than any they're keeping from you is a secret flowing within you. There is hope in you."

"That's no secret," I murmured. "But it's wearing thin."

"No. It is too great a part of you to ever wear," she assured me. "The dog." She motioned.

I held out Tag, and she gave him a cursory pat. "Excellent. Now go."

"Thank you," I said, letting her words dance in my head.

"Pietr."

He paused behind me, and I waited for him by the door.

"Hold on to hope," she said. "It is the only way to live."

He shook his head and closed her door behind us.

"Wait!" Feldman shouted, and I heard a faint tap on the door as I sprang toward it and threw it open.

Mrs. Feldman was pale, staring at the door as it swung wide. "Careful," she breathed, pointing at my feet. A card lay between the toes of my sneakers.

"In all my years . . . Bring it to me, child."

"Why's it . . ." I stooped to retrieve it.

"It flew out of the deck." She looked it over. "This is troubling."

We'd had death and dramatic change and *now* we had the truly troubling card?

"What does it mean?"

"Beware."

I stumbled backward. Into Pietr.

"Ohhh." In her wrinkled hand the deck vibrated, the stack shimmying.

A single card slithered forward from between the others. Mrs. Feldman's eyes found mine and she freed it the rest of the way. "The boy. Beware the boy."

"Thank you," Pietr scowled. "Now if she'll just listen."

We rode back to the school in silence.

The newspaper sat on our kitchen counter, headline blaring "Gas Drilling to Begin." Fabulous. I moved it to the far side of the counter and started pulling stuff out to make dinner. Nobody wanted the gas drilling—it was dangerous to the environment probably well beyond the span of the studies they'd done. But nobody could blame the farmers around Junction for leasing their land, either. The economy was in the crapper, and people were desperate for assurances and cash. Generally not in that order.

I was digging around in the fridge's vegetable drawer when I heard the newspaper flop open.

"Dad?" I asked, glancing around.

No one was there. A chill ran across my arms, and I rubbed it away. Maybe I'd left the door open. Ignoring the newspaper, I stepped to the mudroom. No. The door remained shut. Locked, even.

The newspaper rustled again, and slow as a victim in a horror flick, I turned to watch as the sections and pages rearranged themselves as if a person pawed through them.

Or a ghost.

The sections slapped apart, one falling at my feet. The local. "Teen Train Track Suicides Stump Cops."

"Mom?" I squeaked.

Nothing.

"I'm totally losing it. Thank you, Sophie." I picked up the paper gingerly, setting it by the sink. I read snatches of it as I made dinner. It mentioned the werewolf connection Hascal and Jaikin had suggested, but only in passing. Instead, they focused on the idea the victims had seemed depressed and might have used drugs causing hallucinations (although they admitted finding no trace of illegal substances in their systems).

Weird. Werewolves showed up in Junction, then the CIA, and the Russian Mafia, and now there were even more suicides. Maybe normal wasn't achievable anymore.

I made it through dinner by pushing my food around the plate more than eating it. Dad called to say he'd be working late at the factory, so he wasn't there to examine my every move. But Annabelle Lee was. Over the cover of her newest book she watched me.

When I finally rose to scrape my plate, she spoke up. "I saw them kissing."

My back straightened.

"Pietr and Sarah."

I sighed. It was one thing to put on a show around me, but to be kissing elsewhere . . . My stomach clenched, and I was glad I hadn't eaten much.

"I'm sorry he's so stupid."

I set my plate in the sink with a clank. "That's the problem, Annabelle Lee. He's not stupid. If he was, I wouldn't be so, so messed up over him."

"I'm sorry he's—" She paused, and I looked at her, waiting. "I'm sorry he's with *her*," she concluded.

"Me too."

That night as I finished changing for bed I heard a long and wavering cry outside, a howl that twisted the air the same way it twisted my insides into bows.

"Oh my God, what's *that?*" Annabelle Lee raced into my room, dropping her book on my bed as she zipped past me to yank open the window. "A coyote?"

The call reverberated off the walls, filling my bedroom with its rich song—distinct, distressed, and powerful. My blood rushed in recognition.

Pietr.

"No," I whispered. "Definitely a wolf."

She looked at me as I joined her at the open window. "You don't seem worried about the horses."

"They're safe."

"What do you think it eats?"

"Everything," I said with a grin. "But not horses."

"Why's it out there? Is it hunting?"

"I don't know."

"Well, what does it want?"

"I honestly don't know." I grabbed the window frame. "Come on. It's cold." I realized, closing the window, I didn't necessarily mean the weather outside.

"Why is he watching you like that?" Derek asked, grinding each word out as we stood in the hall between classes.

I looked around his shoulder. Sure enough, Pietr's eyes were fixed on me. Sarah was nowhere in sight. "I have no idea. Maybe he needs to tell me something. . . ."

"Go." Derek didn't bother to mask his disgust but dismissed me in a very kingly fashion. Which irked me. A lot.

Although no hallway in Junction was particularly expansive, something about crossing from one side to the other—to Pietr's—made me feel like I was embarking on my longest journey ever.

"What's going on?" I asked, keeping my tone light. "Other than you watching me makes Derek grouchy."

"I didn't mean to stare."

So much for my little ego trip. *Stupid heart. Stupid girl.*

"We have a lead," he said, eyes glowing. "A place we think they're keeping her. Cat and I are going to snoop around more today to pinpoint things. Then we'll free her."

"That's great!" But the thrill drained away, replaced with a sudden and daunting dread as I realized what it meant. "You'll break the agreement. The CIA will—what'll they do if you . . . ?"

"Try to free our mother?" His eyes narrowed.

"You can't."

He drew back, as far from me as the hallway allowed, his back to the wall, eyes hooded.

My mind scrambled. "Don't you want to get a look inside first? See the lay of the land?"

He stared at me.

"Pietr. Think." I glanced up and down the hall. Derek's eyes burned into my back, and I changed my posture. Stiffened—going for an indifferent-seeming stance. Just another lie as my heart threatened to spill out of my mouth. "I know you want her out. And she'll get out. *We'll* get her out. But why risk angering the CIA? What about our progress?"

"Their *progress* has slowed to nothing."

Struggling with a reply, I pressed. "What if we wait a little longer? Play this out? Do it their way so we can see how the place is set up inside?"

"Cooperate so they take us into its heart?" He rubbed a hand across his chin and I shivered, remembering the feel of his jaw, the touch of his fingers.

"Yes. Cooperate first. Maybe they'll still give us what we want," I insisted.

He closed the small distance between us before I could catch my breath. He reached out, but dropped his hand, casting a look over my shoulder. At Derek.

"Please," I begged. *"Puhzhalsta."*

His eyes snapped closed and he shook his head, fighting some silent inner battle. When they reopened they were the brilliant blue of a clear summer sky. "Fine," he breathed. "They can take us into the heart of their operation. But understand," he said, eyes locking with mine, his voice clipped and cold, "if they do not give us what we want, we will tear that heart out."

My head jerked down in agreement. And fear.

I wondered if it was possible the CIA's poor handling of the situation could turn normally sensible Pietr into the monster he feared was so much part of his nature. What did it take, after all, to make a man a monster?

CHAPTER TWENTY-THREE

For once, the CIA's timing worked in our favor and Wanda drove me to the Rusakovas' that afternoon, pausing briefly to pick up Officer Kent. I called ahead to let them know our numbers had changed and the agents brought good news.

I hoped I wasn't lying by proxy.

The car was stifling, warm and thick with an overpoweringly spicy scent. "Your car deodorizer is a bit much."

Kent chuckled from the back seat.

"Can you even *taste* your coffee?" I asked, peering into the flip-down passenger mirror.

He just raised his ever-present mug in my direction in a silent toast.

When Catherine opened the door to the house, ushering us within, Wanda smiled, pausing just inside the door. "It's a nice day," she commented. "Let's take a walk."

"Take a walk? You promised good news," I reminded her. "Do we get to see their mother today?" I asked, aware of the way the Rusakovas bristled and shifted, surely wondering.

Kent grinned and adjusted something inside his coat. Pietr and Max moved in to stand on either side of me. Cat sidled up behind, and Alexi crossed the floor to stand beside her.

"We do," Wanda assured.

Kent opened the door again, letting the autumn breeze waft through the foyer.

The Rusakovas straightened, drawing up to their full heights, and I saw their noses wrinkle, faces pulling into masks of absolute distaste.

"Perhaps Officer Kent needs a shower," Max snarled, his eyes narrowing.

"Or a drowning," Cat suggested, covering her nose.

Wanda winked and tugged a pouch from her shirt pocket, dangling it before me.

I sniffed. "What the . . . ?" The same stink as the car's hung from her hand.

"I guess we won't need these," she said, looking at Kent. "Once they know where we are, diluting our scent won't matter. They'll find us whenever they want." She shrugged.

I repressed a shiver, wondering what Wanda's group had that made them so confident about handling any unscheduled meetings with the Rusakovas.

She tossed the pouch into the wastepaper basket by the door. Kent dug into his jacket pocket and withdrew a matching pouch, shook it for sheer devilment, and tossed it away too.

The full-blood Rusakovas sneezed.

"What's in that?" I asked.

"An old remedy to deal with pesky tracking dogs—and werewolves," Kent added, flashing a smile.

"Shall we go now? Times a-tickin'," Wanda reminded.

Max stifled a growl, and the group of us, an awkward alliance, stepped onto the porch. Alexi pulled the door shut and I was thrust into the middle of an argument.

"Why are *you* coming?" Max asked his adopted brother. More than a question, it was a challenge to Alexi's previous role in the family.

"She's my mother, too," Alexi said.

Catherine wedged herself between Max and Alexi, placing her small hands on Max's wide chest and peering up into his face.

"He's right. And Mother would want to see all her children, no matter if they've strayed from the pack."

Looking over her head at Alexi, Max agreed. "I just wouldn't want to be *you* when Mother learns how you betrayed us."

Alexi sighed, shoulders slumping.

We walked only a few blocks, out of the Victorian and Queen Anne sections of Junction, and into the smaller remnants of a Colonial farmhouse area.

Wanda paused by a mailbox before passing through a hedgerow dotted with rosemary and other aromatic plants. The place stank of herbs. The dirt around their bases had only recently been disturbed, the plants fresh this season and not meant to last a Junction winter.

I wondered if any of us were.

We walked down a pathway of large, flat rocks and stepped up onto an old stacked stone porch. Here the suburbs and modern living caught up to the past and tried to swallow it whole. What had once been a large farm plot with one home on several hundred acres had been reduced to a single house, an old garage and gas station at its back. Strange, a fieldstone Colonial, just a few hundred yards and a postage stamp worth of a backyard away from the broken-down Grabbit Mart at its back.

Wanda stepped to the doorway, knocking out a strange rhythm with her fist, and I was surprised when the door swung open revealing two very neatly dressed men. Two men most comfortable when armed—the two from the abandoned church. I gawked, realizing what their presence implied. "Seriously?"

Where were the thick metal doors that slid open when the right person put their palm on a special sensor? My eyes scanned from the ground to the roofline. One small camera pointed toward the road, the type anyone could get from RadioShack.

If this was the facility where they contained a secret like were-wolves, where was our tax money going?

"Step inside," Wanda directed us with a curt nod.

Warily we obeyed. Like most Colonials the house was small,

close. The impression of intimacy it gave only made me feel less at ease.

Clustered together in what served as the main hall, we looked expectantly at Wanda and Kent for instructions. That the Rusakovas stood in a house so near their own and yet so well hidden only made them more anxious. Max shifted from foot to foot, eyes glittering.

"Where is she?" Catherine asked.

The two men looked at Wanda and Kent.

The shorter one spoke. "First things first," he said. "I believe part of the deal was that we would get blood, skin, and hair samples before any of you see her."

The heat rolling off Pietr and Max at mention of the delay threatened to smother me. I kept my tone controlled. "Almost there," I promised. "We'll see her soon. And what an amazing building." Casting a glance from one end of the hall to the other, I patted Max's arm and smiled at Cat. "Just a little longer."

Pietr watched me, cooling as my logic—and my unspoken suggestion to observe our surroundings carefully—sank in.

"So, are we ready for testing?" The shorter man didn't look at the Rusakovas but kept his eyes on me.

I wondered if he remembered my Maglite-wielding capabilities. Nodding, I smiled at him, my voice steady as I said, "Yes, that's what we agreed to."

"Lead on," Max commanded. "Let's get scraped and leaked."

The agents headed down the hallway, looking over their shoulders frequently to make sure we were coming. I noticed the tall one's arm was in a heavy cast. He wouldn't be so fast to level a gun against me again. The Rusakovas healed swiftly, but the same couldn't be said for those of us who were simply human. Wanda and Kent fell in behind us, bolting the door before dogging us from one small room to the other.

We quickly came to an area where a staircase had been added. The taller of the two men opened the door that led under the stair and stuck out an encouraging hand, signaling us to head inside.

Max grabbed Alexi, scooting him in front. "You first, brother," he said, the bitterness clear in his voice.

Alexi grimaced, but started down a dimly lit set of stairs as the Rusakovas' point man, head moving quickly from side to side, eyes alert. Catherine snugged up behind him, one hand gripping the banister tightly, the other reassuringly on Alexi's shoulder. Max followed her, sandwiching me between Pietr and himself.

I counted steps. The stairs went deeper than I expected and I turned, looking past Pietr and up to Wanda. "I didn't know there were any places like this in Junction."

"At one time, this was one of the most northern stops along the Underground Railroad," Wanda mentioned, the research librarian in her showing through. I liked her better as a librarian than a gun-toting CIA agent. But then, I didn't like her much as a librarian, either.

"Before the staircase, there was a simple trapdoor leading into a small pit that the previous owners had walled with random boards and stones. Not much comfort to be had if you were an escaped slave on the run."

"There's never much comfort if you're trying to escape an unjust government," Alexi said. Loudly.

I swore I heard Wanda grind her teeth from nearly ten steps above.

Between us Pietr stayed stiff and aloof. I doubted he had any interest in the building's past. He only wanted to know how it connected to his present and his mother's future.

I noticed no cobwebs in the basement, no mold or speckling of mildew. The musty smell I expected was nonexistent. Instead, the smell matched my memory of the garden in springtime. The scent of damp and freshly turned dirt.

I reached my left hand out, noticing how the texture of the wall changed. Cement, fresh and pale, ran smoothly where my hand traced along the stairway. Thirteen steps. Fourteen. Fifteen . . .

Pietr said, "You haven't been here very long." His statement thinly veiled his surprise.

I didn't need to see Kent's grin of satisfaction to hear it in his words. "Pietr, you turned seventeen, what—a little over a month ago?"

"Considering you have our house bugged and our phones tapped," Alexi said, pausing to turn and face the rest of us from the front of the line, "I'm sure you know our birthdays, Officer Kent."

Cat's hand tightened on his shoulder.

"Perhaps rather than suggest the government raise taxes next term, the CIA could make ends meet by becoming administrative assistants to the occupants of the houses they bug. Since you know everyone's business, you can at least make sure none of us criminal types miss a meeting."

Alexi may have lost the title of alpha in the Rusakova household, but to me it sounded like he'd just pissed on Kent's shoes.

"No one accused any of you of being criminal," Wanda spat.

"Then release our mother," Catherine said so casually there could be no doubt of threat.

Following the verbal ping-pong match, I stood between them on step seventeen, my back to the cool wall.

The smile faded from Kent's voice when he next spoke. He motioned us forward. Eighteen, nineteen . . . "We started construction almost a month ago. We move very fast when there's a reason." He paused. "The entire basement was expanded. . . ."

As if on cue, we came up short at the bottom of the stairs. Twenty. I glanced down the final stairs, concluding my count. Twenty-four. The men leading us stood by a door. This at least seemed more impressive. Larger than normal and of heavy steel construction the door was a pale gray, contrasting with the faintly warm color of the cement. It reminded me of doors I'd seen on cold storage rooms at a butcher facility we toured in elementary school. I trembled at the comparison.

A small number pad was integrated into a spot just above the door's hefty-looking handle. The shorter of our two escorts tapped out a rapid succession of numbers; the number pad blinked green twice, and the door opened with only a hint of sound.

Now that *was* impressive.

We'd come to a tunnel of sorts. Again cement lined the walls, smooth and angular, and I imagined they paid a pretty penny to hire a construction crew and mason to quickly set up shop. Maybe *that* was where tax dollars went.

Fluorescent lights coated us in an unhealthy-looking glare as we walked along the lengthy underground hall. Certainly a suitable location for fluorescents, the hellspawn of lighting.

We came to another large door. "Okay," I said, "I know we're no longer under the house we entered. We've crossed beneath the backyard. On the other side of this door we should be under the Grabbit Mart."

"Absolutely correct," our shorter escort agreed.

"We nearly had to quit construction when the locals put up a fuss about the way we were tearing up the old Grabbit Mart parking lot and gas tanks." He chuckled. "We said due to newer OSHA and EPA regulations the old tanks couldn't stay. And unfortunately, the old Grabbit Mart had an extensive, and leaky, system of pipes running beneath it. The whole neighborhood could go up in a puff."

"Or so you said," Alexi surmised.

"It calmed them down," his partner agreed. "As you can see," he said, opening the next door, "everyone has profited by our progress." The area widened into numerous office spaces, and beyond that an additional set of heavy doors lined another wall.

"How far does this place go?" I asked, awed.

"Just a little farther now . . ."

CHAPTER TWENTY-FOUR

Through the next set of doors was a bustling science lab. Our last stop before the Rusakovas could reunite with their mother. Cat and I released a breath together. A little of the tension in Pietr's shoulders eased.

It was probably in a place like this where the genetics that enabled the Rusakovas to shift had been tweaked out: a high-tech science lab with machines that looked like they came out of the latest big budget sci-fi movie.

As the doors sighed shut behind us, all activity inside ceased. Men and women in white coats turned to stare, wide-eyed. Pietr, Cat, and Alexi moved in tighter around me and Max puffed up, well aware they were the center of attention.

A balding man—smaller even than the shortest agent (was the CIA trying for werewolves and *gnomes?*)—trotted over to us. "It is my distinct pleasure to meet you." He grabbed Max's hand and shook it vigorously. "Maximilian Rusakova," he announced.

The women sighed.

Max was in his element.

"The alpha male," the scientist added confidently.

I nearly reached up to tug my eyebrows back down. It was a bold thing to announce in the midst of a pack. Either these people had no idea how dangerous these wolves were, or they didn't care because they knew something we didn't. Hoping it was the former, I forced the nagging fear out of my throat, past my rattling heart, and back into the pit of my stomach.

The little man (Henry, by his name tag) reached for Pietr.

Pietr did not respond as eagerly.

"Pietr Rusakova, the beta male," he said, his expression going wary. Until he spotted Catherine. "Ohhh," he said, grabbing her hand and pulling her out front. "Ekaterina Rusakova. The female."

"Smart man, not calling me *the bitch*," Cat answered.

Henry quickly snapped orders at his fellow scientists, who seemed to mill around, watching more than doing. The full-blood Rusakovas were seated for samples to be taken. The female scientists jockeyed for position to get samples from Max.

And Max enjoyed the show.

Moving over to stand beside Pietr, I said, "Thank God you wore your necklace."

He wrinkled his nose and pushed the red out of his eyes with effort. "I'm here to see my mother, not pick up girls."

"You don't have to get angry," I muttered.

Cat chuckled like she'd been let in on a joke without me.

Max was done giving samples and was peeling off his shirt to the *oohs* and *aahs* of the crowd.

"Max!"

"What?" He looked as sheepish as a werewolf could. "They wanted to see the saber."

I thought I should at least be thankful he hadn't taken the request as innuendo and been taking off his pants.

Alexi edged up beside me. "It's a zoo. *Always* a zoo. You want the job of zookeeper?"

I snorted, watching the women examining the saber-shaped birthmark on Max's left shoulder. All full-bloods were born with one. "No. Definitely not the job for me. Besides, I don't even rank the beta male's attention anymore."

"Funny what we presume," he intimated. "Since Max is bigger, more brutal, he must be the alpha, *da?*" He crossed his arms. "We give too little credit to intellect, to plotting and planning."

"Hmm."

Henry was speaking again, Max tugging his shirt back into place. With help. Where was his necklace?

"The makeup of the werewolf—no offense"—Henry ducked his balding head in the direction of the Rusakovas—"is fundamentally different due to the changes occurring during adolescence. If we take Maximilian's blood, for example"—he grabbed the slide and placed it beneath the large microscope's lens—"you'll notice the shape of the individual red and white blood cells is different—" He motioned for us to take a look.

"—From—" He reached out to me, signaling for my hand.

I gave it, watching him take a fresh needle and prick my finger. A single drop of blood welled up, and he touched it to the edge of the microscope slide so it crawled onto the glass.

"—Simple human blood." He sandwiched a thinner piece of glass over the top and bumped Max's slide over, pushing mine in. A quick adjustment of a few knobs, and he motioned me over. "Here."

He was right. The edges of the doughnut-like cells seemed somehow softer, rounder than the stickier looking werewolf sample. "Look," I said, pulling Cat over to take a peek.

"Straight human blood has a different quality to it." Henry glanced at me. "So to speak. Of course there are many things that we've noticed are different between our interrelated peoples—werewolves have a significantly larger spleen, which acts as a reservoir for red blood cells. When the change is triggered, the spleen dumps those additional cells into their bloodstream for an extra burst of power. After they've returned to their human form their platelet count jumps. We presume it's to help with clotting. It seems the scientists who tweaked your DNA figured you'd change, get wounded, and need to stop bleeding fast."

"It's like they knew you," I mumbled to Pietr as he, Max, and Alexi took turns at the microscope while the other scientists moved hesitantly back to their work.

"You're really, very fascinating," Henry admitted, rubbing his hands together. "Have you all seen the slides?" he asked.

Nods all around. The Rusakovas were starting to get itchy again.

"Can I, one more time?" I asked.

"Certainly," Henry said, cheeks pinking. "Which first?"

"Umm . . ."

He bumped them together, and blood seeped across the two slides, mixing.

"Ew," I said. "Hey, Max. You and me all gross together."

"If that's the way you like it," Max rumbled.

A woman nearby pulled the pencil out of her hair, letting it fall free and grinning at Max like he was lunch.

"Oh dear," the man said.

My thoughts exactly.

I peeked into the microscope. "Huh." I bumped the other slide across. "Ohh-kay. Yeah, those samples are totally trashed."

Henry took a look and swabbed away perspiration suddenly beading on his forehead. "Oh. How odd . . ."

Alexi pushed between us for a view just before Henry snatched the slides away. "I think it's time for your visit. Isn't it, Frederick?" Henry asked the guard by the door.

The man nodded. "Sure, Doc. Let's go."

Beyond the lab one last set of doors whispered open at the guard's touch.

I bumped into Max, not realizing he had stopped. Ahead of me the Rusakovas had formed a more-than-human wall.

"What . . . ?"

No one answered. The Rusakovas were transfixed by something just beyond my range of vision. I ducked down, I slid to the side, I stood on tiptoes. I couldn't even catch a glimpse of whatever it was that held them frozen, stunned to silence, their breathing shallow and rapid.

I finally wedged myself between Pietr and Max, stubbornly pushing forward until I could see. And I joined their ranks, quiet with heartbreak. Slipping my hand into Pietr's, I squeezed it for reassurance. He pulled away. But slowly.

Before us was a large glass cube. Twenty feet long and the same wide, it was a clear box designed to allow the inhabitant no privacy. Had the creature inside been on display at some zoo I might have thought little of it, but what lived inside this cage was Pietr's mother. In one corner of the glass house was a small cot; in another, a few books were scattered. And in the third corner, back and to the left, was a stainless-steel toilet and sink. There was no privacy for the woman dressed in a tank top and khaki pants, her long hair an unkempt tangle of browns and reds. Sitting by the final corner, her back was to us.

"She often pretends to ignore us," the taller of our two escorts pointed out. "Maybe a self-defense mechanism?" He rubbed his chin, looking at the remaining Rusakovas in speculation. His eyes settled on me. "Do they ignore unpleasant things?"

"They're ignoring you now," I pointed out.

The escort blinked at me. He cleared his throat so he could project his voice more powerfully. "You have visitors."

There was no reaction from Mother except to raise a single, specific finger in our direction.

Our escort laughed, and I dug in my heels and clasped Pietr's arm against me to keep him from leaping at the man. His back unnaturally straight, he was so stiff his muscles twitched beneath my fingers. He didn't look at me; he was far too comfortable with the anger pumping through him faster than even his blood.

"Stay calm. They'd love an excuse to lock you up, too."

Our escort's eyes flickered in my direction, confirming my fear. I watched the lump in Pietr's throat slide as he swallowed. He shut his eyes for a moment. "Mother?"

She spun so quickly I didn't see the movement, only the result. Nose pressed to the glass, head cocked to one side, and fingers splayed across the thick invisible barrier as if she would claw her way to us, she asked, "Pietr?" Her voice was scratchy, raw from disuse. Her eyes focused on Pietr just before she screamed his name like a battle cry.

He closed the distance to her in two ground-swallowing strides. His hands mirrored her own, pressed flat against the glass like the force of his will alone could get him inside. Her lips moved, but I couldn't hear her words. Pietr rested his forehead on the glass, his shoulders slumped, all the rage draining from his body.

Max and Catherine flanked him, Alexi close behind.

I hesitated, suddenly aware of how different I was, how much more like the scientists and guards holding her captive than her wild and graceful children. It may have been my battle, but it was not my family.

My mother was gone; theirs was alive. And a prisoner.

I bowed my head and folded my hands, determined to wait while they tried to catch up with the parent they had long thought dead.

"Jess."

Pietr looked in my direction, signaling me over with a move of his head. My heart stopped, seeing the look on his face. I tried to keep calm. Not to run to him. To breathe.

Eyes down, I crossed the distance between us, nerves jangling, unsure of how to act around a mother who was also a werewolf. As soon as the thought formed, I realized the flaw in my logic. Pietr was a werewolf. Max was a werewolf. Catherine was, too. And most times I was quick to forget the fact. Often our shared humanity overrode our distinct differences.

Cat reached out and threw an arm around me, tugging me before the glass wall. "This is Jessie," she said.

CHAPTER TWENTY-FIVE

Their mother studied me, her lips thin, eyebrows lowered. Crow's feet branched around her glinting turquoise eyes—what were once laugh lines ran into furrows of worry and anger. God, she was so young and yet so old. . . .

"It's nice to meet you, Mrs. Rusakova. . . ."

Behind me, Max said to the guards, "We were told we'd be allowed inside."

One guard pushed a button on the wall. An intercom buzzed, blaring a reply. "Yes. Allow them all inside the cubicle."

I spun out of Cat's grasp. "No. Two in, three out," I said, heart pounding. How hard would it be to just not unlock the door once you had all the werewolves you could want in one cell?

Cat echoed my suggestion. "Max and I will go in first. Then Pietr, Jessie, and Alexi."

Their mother gave me a smile, and my heart jumped. "Cleverrr girrrl," she said, her words equally strong with a Russian purr and a werewolf growl.

A set of four more armed guards entered the room as a precaution. Alexi and I looked at each other. We were doing the same thing: taking careful mental notes. Numbers, weapons, speed of response.

A code was tapped into a number pad by her door, and a guard pressed his palm onto the surface of the pad. Lights flashed and a siren purred "Red-red-red" as a seal broke and a door slid open, nearly seamless in the transparent cubicle.

Cat and Max stepped inside, the door sealing behind them. I shifted from foot to foot beside Alexi.

Pietr had already left me to stand by the door.

There were hugs and tears, and Tatiana—Mother—pulled the single chair over and sat. Max, the family bad-ass, sniffled and fell at his mother's feet, resting his mop of hair against her knee. Tatiana sighed and played with his dark curls, doting on him as if they had all the time in the world. Cat sat by her other knee, posture rigid, absolutely alert.

She was seeing what I had noticed: stress, strain, and age marring the natural beauty of a woman without her family. A woman whose love was lost.

"Who is she?" Their mother pointed at me again.

"Mother," Cat's voice rose. "I said her name is Jessie."

I looked at Alexi.

"Senile dementia begins early in the species," he whispered.

"I am not senile, Alexi," their mother barked. "And I hear quite well. I want to know who Jessie rrreally is. Who is she to my family?"

I got the impression it was not my place to define my connection to them. And what would I say, anyhow? *I almost dated your youngest son, but my sometimes-psycho friend got to him first, so we just sort of messed around behind her back until he changed and now I'm dating the one guy at Junction High he seems to really hate?*

Not a way to endear myself to Pietr's mom.

Cat said simply, "She opened the *matryoshka.*"

Their mother's head nearly ripped off, it moved so fast. "She opened it?"

Alexi nodded.

"Then . . . ?"

"Nothing," Alexi reported. "I have no answers yet. I am at a loss."

I got the feeling they were talking over my head. About me. Cat, Max, and Pietr looked like they were out of the loop, too. All eyes were on Alexi.

"Therrre arrre no acceptable losses," Mother said, her eyes glittering red.

"Heart-rate-is-elevated," the siren announced.

"Of course it is," she snarled.

"Mother," Alexi said. "I am doing the best I can with limited resources."

Now I was certain the CIA was taking careful mental notes, too, trying to decipher their conversation.

She shook her head, long hair tumbling. "I do not doubt you, Alexi. No matter what steps you had to take to get to this moment."

Max looked up at her, his expression clearly reading stunned. "You knew? You *know?*"

"Alexi knew there would be a time he must make hard decisions—his life has been full of harsh truths." Her face filled with pain, and Alexi dropped his gaze. "My poor boy," she whispered. "He has done his best to protect you, has he not?" she asked Max pointedly.

Max blinked. "But the Mafia . . ."

"Did he call them to take you?" she prodded. "Or did he stand beside you? Help you?"

"You know about that?"

"They talk," she muttered, motioning toward our escorts and guards. "Gossiping like ill-bred girls to get a rise out of me." Her eyes flashed, then calmed. "You should not doubt Alexi, either," she admonished her eldest full-blood son. "Just because we do not share a direct heritage does not mean we do not share a legacy. Life is a puzzle, is it not, Alexi?"

"*Da.*"

"And you are missing one piece?"

"*Da.* A very important one."

"Then there is still hope."

"*Da,*" he said, reluctant to commit.

"There is always hope," I confirmed, though I didn't know exactly what we were hoping for.

Alexi rested his hand on my shoulder. His fingers shook. He hadn't had a cigarette since sometime before we'd left the house, and his nerves were starting to show. "You need to quit smoking."

"You arrre smoking?" Mother growled.

Nuts. Werewolf ears.

Alexi stepped back, hanging his head in shame.

"You are my son, Alexi. Not by blood, but by choice. We adopted you. I will not tolerate one of my children endangering themselves with something as deadly as . . ."

I couldn't handle more railing against Alexi. He'd been a wreck recently. Before I could stop myself I blurted out the rumor running through school: "Max is having sex with multiple partners!"

Oh. *Crap.*

Mother looked at Max, her eyes glowing.

"Heart-rate-is-elevated," blared again.

Max went a shade paler. No. Three shades. "Mother, I—" He flopped onto the floor belly up, covering his eyes with his arm. He groaned.

"Maximilian?"

"Mother, I—am—*not.*" He sighed. He shot me a look. "Not since Paris," he qualified softly.

"What?" Pietr, Cat, Alexi, and I asked in unison.

Max focused on me. "The things you presume," he chuckled. "I have a reputation," he confirmed. "A healthy one."

His mother rumbled.

"But I only flirt!" he protested.

"Continually," I groaned.

"And you kiss," Cat reminded.

He shrugged.

"And grope," Pietr added.

Max sat up, glaring at him. "So what? You're continually trying to bash your brains out because you can't—"

Cat silenced him with a look, eyes sliding to me.

"What are *you* doing, Pietr?" Mother asked, eyes narrow.

"I am struggling," he muttered. "This"—for a moment his eyes were on me before they darted away—"is not easy. It is not easy knowing I am dying already and that trying to live endangers others."

Cat rose, tugging Max to his feet. She caught the guard's attention. "Switch," she said. "Jessie, you, too." She hugged her mother, as did Max, and then, in a few tense moments as the guards looked on, rifles at the ready, the siren blared, the lights flashed, and we exchanged places, Cat and Max glaring at the guards, Pietr, Alexi, and myself staring at Mother.

Pietr's mother grabbed him and hugged him, only pulling back to search his face. "You are not sleeping," she surmised. A glance at Alexi and me and she repeated herself. "Why is no one here sleeping?"

"We've been searching for you," Pietr whispered.

"All of you?" She glanced at me.

"Not anymore," Alexi answered on my behalf. "We simple humans are out of action."

She nodded. "They like you enough to keep you around. I searched for you as well," she recalled. "There was a brief time I was free. I followed your scents as far as I could, stumbling through horse farms and parks. . . . But the river made things difficult." She sighed. "I found your school just before they recaptured me."

"It was you in the high school that night," I realized.

I dropped to the floor and sat Indian-style. I thought back. "But in the rain that other night? That wasn't you."

"Why must you bring *that* up?" Max asked. "I was scouting. And I ran back from that little encounter with a limp."

My lips curled in over my teeth, realizing.

"When is the logical response to a wolf attack ever to nail the animal in the groin with a big stick?" he asked me.

Pietr, Cat, and Alexi fought back smiles.

"Sorry?" I tried.

He snorted.

Mother was the one to refocus us. "If you opened the *matryoshka*, where is the pendant?" she whispered, looking at my neckline. "Is that . . . ?"

"No," I admitted. "It's my mother's netsuke."

"Did you not give her the pendant?" Mother asked Alexi.

"*Da*, Pietr did." He looked at him, confused.

Pietr had not told him he'd been given it back.

"Pietr?"

"I have it."

"Give it to me." Mother thrust her hand out.

Pietr retrieved it from his pocket and handed it over.

"This is yours," she confirmed, dropping to her knees before me. "You opened the *matryoshka*. You are important to us."

"How?" I whispered. "I don't know how I'm important to your family. I'll help however I can—you have to believe me—but . . ." I shook my head.

Her hands were warm on my face. "Shhhh, Jessie," she soothed. "Sometimes we do not know what role we play until it is thrust upon us and we can only then do our best to carry it off." She reached around, fastening the chain behind my neck.

I glanced at Pietr. The chain was new. Heavier. Stronger.

Mother looked at us both. "You had all better go—time—"

The siren blared, "Thirty-minutes-thirty-minutes."

"Time is up."

A few quick hugs, another tear or two, and we were out of the cubicle and headed (with our armed escort) to find Wanda and Kent.

We pushed into the lab, where Wanda was having a very animated discussion with Henry. "And what am I supposed to do about this? Hope there are no bodily fluids exchanged? Play keep-away with—"

Henry's pointed look stopped her midsentence.

"Dammit," Wanda muttered. "I'll take care of it," she assured him. "Sooo," she said, facing us, her smile thin. "Was Mommy happy to see you?"

Max's face soured at her use of the endearment.

"We were all glad for a chance to meet," I said, stroking Max's arm. He calmed beneath my touch, though I was certain I'd get an earful later about ratting him out to his mother.

"Wonderful," Wanda chirped. "Let's close this little get-together up, then, shall we? We'll want a marrow and fur sample before your next invite. I'll let you decide when. After that? We may need to do a little renegotiating."

Cat's chin rose. "Renegotiating?"

"Cat," I warned. "She said *may.*"

Wanda nodded. We trailed behind Wanda to the door like lost puppies. Out and up the stairs, I recounted each one. If we had to do something drastic, it might be dark. Counting stairs might save us from tripping down them.

Finally outside, Wanda slapped her hands together against the cold. "I trust you can find your way home," she muttered, "since it's really just around the corner."

Wow. They'd gotten arrogant.

Wanda's gaze slid from Pietr to me as if weighing some danger. "Jessica, I'll be back to take you home soon."

"Don't bother," Max retorted. "I'll drive her back."

Again she measured Pietr with a glance. "Huh. Okay." Wanda shrugged and slipped back inside.

A half-dozen bolts clicked into place behind us.

"I cannot do this," Cat murmured as Max pulled out of their driveway. Her voice cracked. "I cannot become like her so soon. . . ."

"Cat," I insisted, "You still have years. You all do."

"Not as many as you will," she said. "Why can I not be normal—not *this?*" she asked. "As normal as Jessie?"

I resisted the urge to explain that *normal* was a relative term, and right now it was so relative it didn't seem to relate to me at all.

From the front passenger's seat Alexi looked over his shoulder at her. "You are blessed in many ways, Ekaterina," he said. "You have much that many would kill for—and many have."

"I would give it all away," she confessed, "to live out a normal life and reach a normal old age."

I couldn't keep my mouth shut any longer. "Some normal people don't live very long, either. What if you give up your gifts—your healing, your agility, your wonderful wildness—and die in an airplane crash? Or crossing a street. It happens, Cat. There is no normal life span. Only average."

"Perhaps this is simply what we're destined to be," Pietr added. "Wild and powerful, and then . . . nothing. Should we not embrace what is carved into our genetics, be all that we may be for as long as we can be? Live life fiercely?"

Max turned the car up my driveway. "Live fast, die young," he mumbled.

The car stopped, and I couldn't get out fast enough. "And what do you leave behind?" I snapped, leaning back in to the open door and scowling at Max because my stinging eyes proved I didn't dare look at Pietr. "Who do you leave with only memories of you? How many hearts do you break when you risk too much and die too young?"

I slammed the door shut and stalked into the house.

CHAPTER TWENTY-SIX

"That boy of yours is on the phone," Dad said, holding the receiver out to me.

"Who?"

"Derek-the-man-Jamieson," Annabelle Lee called.

I took the phone. "Hey."

"Hey. I was thinking about you."

"Oh." I tramped up the stairs. "That's nice." I took off my sneakers with a clunk and peeled off my socks, holding the phone between my shoulder and cheek.

"Your party's tomorrow night," he reminded.

"It's really more the Rusakovas' Halloween party."

"Trying to be difficult?"

"No. I'm tired. Things have been pretty weird around here lately." I took off the rabbit netsuke and left the amber heart. "I was thinking of skipping the party."

"You can't do that. It wouldn't be a party without you. It sounds like it'll be quite the bash. Nothing like we throw on the Hill, but it's sure to be talked about." There was a long silence. I wiggled out of my jeans and slipped on my pajama bottoms. His voice deepened, became more focused. "I would have thrown you a party."

"My father wouldn't have allowed it."

"He thinks I'm trying to get something for my good deeds?"

I paused, pulling my tee up. When had I mentioned that to him? "He thinks you're trying to get something from me, yeah."

"I only want what you want to give," he assured me.

"Mmm." I nearly dropped the phone as I pulled off my shirt and undid my bra. "Hold on." I set the receiver down, looking for my flannel top. Tugging it over my head, I retrieved the phone.

"You're getting ready for bed," he said, voice rasping.

I spun to my window, half-expecting to see him clinging to it. "Uh, yeah. Lucky guess."

"I better let you go, then," he said with a sigh. "I'll pick you up tomorrow for the party. Sixish?"

"I was actually going with Amy and Marvin. . . ."

"Fine. I'll see you there." He paused. "Dream of me."

"Good night."

The next morning a shiny Mercedes pulled up outside my house as I was drying the last of the breakfast dishes. It had to belong to Derek's family. Mercedes were not frequently found in Junction.

Hunter and Maggie went nuts when Derek sprang out of the car with a bouquet of flowers. Hunter even rediscovered his inner alpha and growled.

I pushed them back from the door. "You're early. By hours."

"A dozen roses," he said, opening the screen door and stepping inside as I booted the dogs out. Hunter promptly found the Mercedes and anointed its wheels. He must've wanted to keep it. "I thought about things a lot last night," Derek said, heading to the kitchen. "Vase?"

"Um, yeah." From under the sink I brought out the only glass one we owned. It was dusty with disuse. I reached over to rinse it out, but he took it from me, moving my hand away from the faucet with a firm touch of his own.

Taking up the kitchen shears, I began trimming stems. "They're beautiful, by the way."

He smiled. "I figured, how often do girls get to really celebrate their seventeenth birthday, right? Shouldn't it be a little bit of a big deal? Yeah, I know that's like an oxymoron or something." He shrugged. "So I called your dad this morning. Yes. At the factory. No. He's not in trouble because I called."

I closed my mouth.

"I know people, remember?"

It was hard to forget.

"I asked if I could keep you out. All day."

"Wow."

"He said yes."

Double wow.

"Since it's nearly noon and you've done your chores . . ." He glanced at me for confirmation.

"Yep. Everyone's fed, water's checked; supposed to be beautiful out these next few days, so they're mainly hanging out in the pasture. No mucking to speak of."

"No mucking," he snickered. "Let's start with lunch. And we'll do a couple things on my list."

"You have a list?" Derek never struck me as a planner.

"I'm absolutely scheduled out for today, baby," he said, leaning in to kiss me.

"Don't call me that," I said, pulling back as his lips brushed mine. "I'm not anyone's baby."

He shrugged. "Ready?"

"Yeah, let me just go and get my costume. And change . . ."

"Sure." He put his hands behind his back, swaying and whistling jokingly as I dashed up the steps.

I grabbed my dress for later. Frikkin' Buttercup. My Man in Black had probably made new plans since we weren't together. I wondered what he'd be going as and I tried to *not* wonder even harder as I peeled out of my work shirt and freshened my deodorant. I was rummaging through my closet for a change of clothes when my door squeaked open.

Derek stepped inside. "Sorry. I thought I'd grab your costume. Not ready yet?"

"Um." Too aware I stood there in only my bra and jeans, I tugged a random shirt free and nearly blackened my eye as the clothes hanger swung toward my face.

Derek's hand stopped it in midair, his breath warm on my cheek. "Careful." He'd crossed the distance remarkably fast. Unnaturally fast. My heart raced.

His eyes rested on the amber pendant I'd slept in, but he said nothing.

"Costume's on the bed." I pointed.

He let go of the hanger and turned to get the dress.

I tugged the shirt over my head, watching him. "Step outside. I need to finish changing."

"Again—sorry," he whispered. "I'll wait by the car."

"Good idea."

As soon as I was certain he was gone, I squashed down my questions and shimmied out of my dusty jeans and pulled on a clean pair. I pounded back down the stairs and scrawled a note to Annabelle Lee.

> *AL,*
>
> *Unexpected Dad-approved date with Derek. Off to celebrate becoming seventeen. Back late tonight after party at Rusako-vas'.*

I called the dogs in and closed up.

Derek stood waiting by the car as promised. He gallantly opened the door for me and, sliding in beside me, he nodded to the driver. "Princess Buttercup," he said nonchalantly.

"Uh, pretty much," I said, puzzled.

"Great minds think alike." Reaching across to the front passenger seat as I buckled my seat belt, he pulled out a pair of black leather pants and a black satin shirt.

The Man in Black would make an appearance tonight, after all. Seeing my expression, he took my hand.

Fuzzy-headed, I blinked. I was in a broad room painted in gold, blue, and white, surrounded by walls decorated with Junction High pennants, football trophies, and jerseys. I swallowed hard, realizing I sat in its center. On a bed.

I shoved the heels of my hands into my eyes, trying to clear the remaining blur from my vision. A football jersey bearing the number twelve shimmered on the wall. The single word across its top read *Jamieson*.

My hands gripped the comforter and I realized where *here* had to be. Derek's bedroom. My stomach lurched as I tried to make sense of things.

I shook my head to clear it but gasped as pain shot through my temples, blinding me. There was a door off the side of the room, light glowing around its edges, water splashing. A bathroom. Inside, Derek whistled the same cheery tune as earlier.

On the nightstand a phone in the shape of a football rested in its cradle. I grabbed it, punching in the numbers.

"*Allo?*"

"Max," I whispered. "I need a ride."

"Jessie? What number are you calling from? Where are you?"

"Umm . . . a bedroom. On the Hill."

Across the miles I heard a door slam. "With *him?*"

He had to hear me choke on my shame.

"Shit. Address?"

"I don't . . ." I'd crushed on Derek for years. But I'd never looked up his address or phone number. I'd never had the guts to try a ride-by.

I heard Max's car door slam and the convertible snarled to life. "It's a piss-poor day for tracking," he grumbled. "Jessie."

My stomach curled in my gut. "Yeah?"

"Stay clear of him. Don't let him get his hands on you."

"Okay."

"Jessie, you hear me? Don't let him touch you."

A smile dimpling his face, Derek took the phone and set it on the nightstand. *Not* in the cradle.

"Who are you talking to, Jessica?" he asked, loud enough for Max to hear. "Someone coming to pick you up?" He reached for me, and I scooted away. "Shhhh. It's okay."

I trembled. "How did I get here, Derek?"

"My driver brought us. Don't you remember?" He snagged my wrist, and my head filled with images of us curled in the backseat of the Merecedes, kissing. But it was strange—the view skewed somehow.

"I don't remember—" I began, but the visions pushed back into my head, stealing my words as he covered my mouth with his.

He dragged his lips across my mouth, assuring me, "You will," as his hand shifted its grip and he pulled my arm over my head and pushed me down.

For a moment I thought I heard the Rusakovas' convertible roar to its fastest speed, squealing through the phone's receiver. And there was cursing. In Russian. Though I didn't understand the words, the intent was clear, even across the distance.

Then everything faded away and there was only the warmth of Derek's hands. As if miles away, I heard him coax, "This is all so much easier this way. . . ." and I felt something flutter through my mind, my brain like the Rolodex that Counselor Maloy kept on his desk. Spinning. "Interesting," Derek whispered, his lips tracing across mine, their warmth blurring my worry, blunting my fear, washing away my cares. . . .

I sighed, sinking back, head filling with pleasant images; pictures of Pietr floated to the surface. Kisses scorched along my face and neck. "Pietr . . ."

There was a growl, and I felt fingers at the waistband of my jeans. The button opened and a hand traced along the top of my underpants.

"No," I said.

The kissing resumed, harder. "Jessica." The word rumbled in someone's throat. Not Pietr's. To him, I was *Jess*.

"No," I insisted, trying to pry my eyes open. Something was wrong . . . Not Pietr . . . I pushed at the chest above me, my eyelids stinging as I willed them apart.

"Relax . . ." a voice said, lips dragging along the corner of my jaw, filling my head with honey, sticky and sweet. . . .

There was a crash, and my world snapped into screamingly sharp focus. My head quaked like it'd been jackhammered open. My eyes wide, I saw Max reach for me. "Button your jeans," he growled.

What? *Oh, God.* I fumbled, buttoning up.

Neanderthal-style, Max slung me over his shoulder. Derek clambered to his feet.

"Don't you ever touch her again," Max demanded.

Derek just grinned.

Sensation swirled in my head—kissing, touching, a single word— "No . . ." I was going to throw up. I was certain.

What had Derek done?

Max headed to a door hanging by a single hinge, and fast as a striking snake, Derek lunged, clutching my wrist. Images ripped through my head, twisting, quivering, fogging and evaporating—stealing my thoughts and wrenching away my memories. Something jolted through me like lightning. . . .

Muscles cramping, I convulsed.

Max roared, spinning back to Derek.

My world went black.

Silent.

The ocean crashed in my ears, surf tearing at sand, grinding away the ground beneath my feet.

"Jessie. Jessie. Jess-ie," someone crooned my name.

I covered my ears. "Shut. Up." My brain—or what was left of it— was on fire. It danced and jumped in my skull, threatening to burst free.

"Good girl. Wake up." Fingers snapped. "Snap out of it. Jessie . . ."

"Max?" I blinked, sunlight stabbing into my eyes. I squeezed them shut with a whimper. "Where the—?"

"Jessie." He shook my shoulder with his huge, hot hand.

"God, you're so loud . . ." My eyes popped open, and I grabbed the steering wheel as a horn shrieked at us. "Stay on *our* side of the road!"

His attention snapped back to the road. "How do you feel?"

"Like—" My head was folding in on itself like my brain had landed on the lip of a black hole. "Like you better pull over if you want this all-leather interior to stay smelling *anything* like leather."

It was the fastest I'd seen a Rusakova pull a car over. I opened my door, Max's hand undoing my seat belt. I tumbled out.

As did the contents of my stomach.

"Oh. Boy."

Leather creaked as Max leaned across and the glove compartment squealed open. Napkins were thrust into my shaking hand.

I swabbed off my mouth and slid carefully into the car. I rubbed the back of my hand over my forehead. "How did we get here? *Why* am I here?"

"What do you remember?"

"Waking up in the car. Vomiting in the grass."

"*Nyet.* Before that."

"Uhhh. Derek was taking me for lunch. He showed me his costume for the party. *Ohhh.* The party, *tonight . . .*"

"Do you remember anything after that?"

I shook my head, instantly regretting it.

He muttered something.

"What?"

But Max was still muttering, ". . . never thought . . ."

"Max, what are you talking about?" My head screamed, so I rested it in my hands, trying to keep it from flying to pieces.

He ignored me and flipped open his cell phone. A string of Russian words rolled out of his mouth. All of them too loud. I heard an answering set of words flinging back in kind. Cat's voice.

"*Da*, wiped. Can he . . . ? Shit."

"Cat'll get on you about your language if you don't stop," I warned. *Ow.*

"*Nyet.* She smells okay."

I most certainly did *not* smell okay. Not after my vomit-fest.

"*Nyet*, Cat. He didn't . . . *nyet*. I'd rip his ba—"

Cat plowed through more Russian.

"*Nyet.* I'm bringing her over," Max barked.

"What?" I asked.

"We need to talk, Cat." He hung up. "Buckle up," he commanded, checking his side-view mirror.

"Damn it, Max. I may not remember how I got here, but I'm not stupid. What's going on?"

He reached across me and tugged the door shut.

My hands fought with the seat belt until it clicked. Images rushed me. Derek and me curled up and kissing in the backseat of the Mercedes. No. Impossible. I struggled to examine the memory more closely. Something was off. The perspective? I was seeing more of me than Derek. Like *I* was Derek. Like the memory was . . . I held my head more tightly, hoping I could keep it from tearing down the center.

My stomach rioted as I realized. I *never* went anywhere without my seat belt buckled.

"Stop," I said as he readied to pull back into traffic. My head was going to split open like an overripe melon. I slung open the door just in time to throw up again.

"Max," I whispered, "I need to know what's going on."

"Here, drink some of this." He passed me a Gatorade.

I rinsed and spit with the stuff before taking a tentative drink. I gulped down a few sips and screwed the cap back on.

His voice cool and measured—*cautious*—he said, "You were out with Derek. You had some food and started feeling really sick and the jackass didn't know what to do, so he called me to get you since he knows I drive and we hang out." His gaze darted to me again.

"Eyes on the road," I reminded.

He obeyed. "Jessie, food poisoning will wipe you out." His jaw worked silently. "Derek's selfish. Unreliable." He opened his mouth, then snapped it shut again before saying through a grimace, "Jessie, you need to stay clear of Derek. For me."

"Max . . ." The clock in the dash glowed cruelly. "My appointment! How did I forget? I *have* to get to counseling. If I don't . . ."

He nodded sharply, did an absolutely illegal U-turn, and didn't say another word as he drove me to Dr. Jones's office.

CHAPTER TWENTY-SEVEN

"Are you sleeping well?" Dr. Jones asked, her voice skipping around in my hollowed out skull. *Loudly.*

"No," I groaned. "I keep having nightmares."

"Mmhmm." She scribbled something down on her blasted clipboard. Also loudly.

"Your father is concerned."

"I know."

"He's more concerned since he found the gun."

My head jerked up and I winced. "What are you talking about?" Unease crawled through my stomach, tying bows in my guts.

"The gun he found under your pillow."

The one time Dad beat me to the laundry and it hadn't occurred to me that there was no longer a gun under my pillow. I was way too new at all this subterfuge stuff.

"Are you scared of someone?"

This time I moved my head slowly, but I still felt utterly disoriented looking straight at her. "No."

"Why would you sleep with a gun under your pillow?"

I thought. *Hard.* "I'm a competition shooter. I was loaned a new piece. An old training technique includes keeping a gun at hand almost all the time to familiarize a shooter with it. Like the way cops wear holsters even when they're not on duty." I paused. "Did Dad tell you where the gun came from?"

"He confirmed that a family friend, Wanda, loaned a gun to you. For competition." She tapped the pen on the clipboard, frowning. "The mind is amazing, explaining away things that deeply bother people in oddly logical ways. Your father may accept your excuse. And I admit I'm not well versed in the subculture of competition shooting. But I'm also not one hundred percent convinced there isn't more to a gun being under your pillow." She frowned. "Do you want to hurt yourself?"

"No. I'm trying to get a grip. Have a more normal life."

Scribble, scribble.

"The number of suicides in the area has recently escalated," she commented.

"The train track suicides. Yes, I know. And yet, here I am. Thrilled to be in counseling. Weren't we supposed to be focusing on a healthy expression of my grief?"

Scribble. "You seem disoriented. Have you been drinking?"

"I have too few brain cells naturally to waste any on a temporary buzz."

Scribble. "Drugs?"

"Just write *See Above*—the same philosophy applies. Look, I had a really lousy lunch. Food poisoning of epic proportions. It's messed me up."

"I'd like to get a urine sample."

"Give me your coffee cup."

Scribble, scribble, scribble.

She stood, her heels clip-clopping a rhythm on the floor. Thrusting a plastic cup into my hand she said, "Down the hall and to your right."

I shuffled away, found the rest room, and peed into the cup. I stayed in the bathroom a moment longer, resting my hands on the cool sink and peering into the mirror at my image—thrown back to me under harsh fluorescent light.

Not a good thing.

There were places where fluorescents should be hung over mirrors—like in hell (or public school bathrooms—hey, they had things in common), and in underground CIA corridors, but not somewhere you hoped to improve a person's attitude about themselves. Standing there, my brain felt like mush.

It hurt like this when Amy found me in the bathroom vomiting over nightmares and flashbacks. Food poisoning probably just heaped the effects together. *Man.* I barely remembered anything from when Derek picked me up all the way to losing my lunch by Max's car. It was . . . hazy. Even arguing with Max—had he been on the phone with Cat while he drove? *Totally unsafe.* Even that memory was like looking at a painting someone had smudged before it dried. Like I'd slammed my brain against my skull with so much puking that there wasn't much brain left.

Maybe I'd just go home and sleep.

But the party . . . everybody would be there. It'd suck to miss my own birthday bash.

I deserved to have a little fun. I still had a few hours to recoup. What had the nurse suggested last time? Saltines and ginger ale? I could manage. Rehydrate, relax, prepare to party. A phrase lodged itself somewhere between my brain and my lips. "I'll sleep when I'm dead," I stated. The way my head ached, that might just be tomorrow. Remembering Pietr's words, I looked into the mirror at myself. "Live life fiercely," I urged my reflection.

By my session's end my head felt clear, my attitude improved, and my stomach had calmed. Everything was better.

Walking out to the parking lot, I paused and tried to remember exactly what I'd discussed with Dr. Jones. Vague bits and pieces of conversation stuttered around in my head. *Tired.* That had to be it. Being so suddenly sick made me tired.

"Hey, Max." I smeared on my best smile.

In the afternoon sun, the Rusakovas' stunning red convertible was even more brilliant. Max paused where he stood, polishing a fender, and scowled at me.

"You cleaned the whole car while I was getting grilled?"

"I kept busy. Keeps me from overthinking."

I hadn't really thought Max was ever at risk of *that*. "See, I would have thought you're being so freakishly industrious because you're hyped up for something."

He tilted his head, studying me. "You okay?"

"Much better. Good session. Hyped up for the party tonight?" I wondered aloud, noticing my costume in the back.

"Why do I have to be *hyped up* about anything because I'm being industrious?"

"I've just never seen you so *involved* in anything. Other than chasing girls." I rubbed my eyes and shrugged.

Max watched me, chamois in hand. "You're okay," he muttered. Like it was a surprise.

"Therapy's freeing. Maybe this is like some girls say."

"What?" His eyes grew small—intense.

I'd used his favorite word again.

Girls.

He opened the door for me, asking, "What do girls say?"

"That guys who are—*frustrated*," I teased, cheeks catching fire at my boldness, "get antsy."

He slammed the door and went around to the driver's side. I thought I heard him mutter, "She's okay," as he climbed in. He looked at me again, a smile twisting his lips. "So if I'm careful about the car's appearance I'm *antsy—frustrated?*"

"Are you? Itching for something?"

"Why, Jessie?" he purred, and the Big Bad Wolf was back and grinning. "You have a girlfriend who'd like to scratch my itch?"

I sank into the seat, every bit of skin on fire. "Down, boy," I muttered.

He chuckled. "Maybe the hot redhead. Amy?"

"Dating Marvin," I reminded him.

"Yeah." He frowned. "I was thinking about changing that."

"Don't mess with Amy," I warned. "She seems happy."

He nodded solemnly. "Sometimes, Jessie, things aren't exactly what they seem."

Says a werewolf.

Max threw the car into gear.

His arm around my shoulders, Max guided me into the Rusakovas' dining room and pulled out a chair. "Sit."

I did.

"Ekaterina!" he roared.

"You have to," Cat argued upstairs. "I do not care how uncomfortable it makes you. You will do your part in this. This is the path *you've* set us on."

"Ekaterina!"

"*Da!*" There was movement at the top of the stairs. "I mean it. Get yourself togetherrr," she warned. "I'm coming!" she thundered back, racing down the stairs. She stopped in the doorway and straightened, pushed one rogue curl back into place and regained her composure. She smiled at me. "Jessie!" she greeted me, giving me a big hug and—a cursory *sniff?*

She conceded to Max, "*Da*, you are right."

"What did you say?" He looked toward the stairs.

"Nothing except he must step up. Now."

"Hi," I said. "I'm right here and yet—somehow not involved in the conversation at all."

Alexi stepped into the room, hearing my complaint, arms loaded with books. "Welcome to the club," he griped, setting the stack down.

"Wow. What are those, Alexi?"

"Grandfather's journals."

"Seriously? So these have information about . . ."

"About their creation?" He nodded. "Close. I'm missing a volume."

"Lemme guess. *The* volume."

Cat bent over me, murmuring, "How are you, Jessie?"

"Fine. Other than a bout with food poisoning, I'm fine."

Alexi was still rambling, ruffling the pages of one journal. "*Da*. Extrapolating the information to find a cure . . ."

That last word scored my full attention. "You think you can?"

"*Da*, but it may take more time than we have," he admitted.

"See," Cat whispered behind me. "She's fine. *Tabula rasa* can be a blessing," she assured.

"Ignorance is bliss?" Max returned.

"Why rock the boat?"

Max echoed her tone, "Because the boat may be sunk with the wrong captain at its helm."

"Nothing we cannot handle now we know. Stay between them," Cat insisted.

"*Between* them?" Max sighed. "Do you understand what you are asking me to do?"

"Precisely. I have asked even more of Pietr."

"*He* is why she is here."

I flipped. "Look. I want to know why you're both talking over my head—and behind my back." I spun to face them, gripping the back of the chair. "Let's get a couple things straight. I am not here because of Pietr. Not anymore. It may have started that way, but that's obviously not what he wants. And what I want . . ." My throat tightened. "I'm here to help your family if I can. Say what you have to say."

Cat kissed my forehead. "You know everything you need to. There is nothing *to* say."

I blinked.

Max looked toward the stairs.

"Come," Cat said, gently taking my hand, "let me get you some crackers. You rest while we decorate. Food poisoning can be ruinous."

Although I protested, Cat filled a plate for me with crackers, poured some ginger ale, and sat me on her bed. I flailed a moment, sinking into a giant marshmallow of pink and lace. "Eat, drink, and get some rest. Everything looks better after a nap."

"Really, Cat, I'm fine."

She smiled at me. "I know, Jessie. I just want you to have a terrific time at your party, and since Derek won't be attending . . ."

"Wait. What?" One of the reasons Dad had been okay with me attending a party at the Rusakovas' house was because Derek would be my escort. Not Pietr.

She studied my expression, squinting to peer into my eyes as if I reflected back the sun. "A boy who would dump you on the first friend of yours with a car—when he knows you are sick . . ." She shook her head. "Such moments tell you much about the man he will become. Derek is not growing into a man you should be with." She pulled the door shut after her.

I stared at the door for a long while before gnawing through the saltines and sipping some soda. Finally I relented; burrowing into Cat's ridiculously soft bedding, I closed my eyes.

When I woke and fought my way free of the frothy pink bed and stumbled out of Cat's room, things had been transformed. Fake webbing hung from all corners, orange, purple, and red lights sparkled downstairs, giving the place a creepy glow as fog crawled around the base of the staircase. From somewhere far from sight came the feedback and static of a sound system being checked.

Wow.

"You're awake!" Cat exclaimed. "How do you feel?"

"Great. This is—*amazing*, Cat."

"*Horashow.* The guests will be here soon," Cat said, "We'd better get dressed. You"—she looked at me—"need a shower." She marched me into the bathroom.

Turning the faucet on over the big claw-foot tub (was I the only one without claws around here?) I heard her outside the door again. "*Da.* I know she smells like him."

Pietr. Grumbling.

Then Cat: "You will need to make a decision, brother. Before it is too late. You have already pushed her too near the edge. Tell her the truth."

The idea Pietr was lying was laughable. Pietr simply didn't want me. Still, hope clutched at my faltering heart at the idea Pietr lied. How twisted that I hoped for *that*?

With Pietr choosing Sarah, and Max and Cat determined to keep me away from my selfish, evidently bad-lunch-buying boyfriend, the party in my name seemed one I'd attend alone.

Happy frikkin' birthday to me.

I stepped into the tub, pulled the curtain around and, not wanting to hear more, let the shower rain down over me.

CHAPTER TWENTY-EIGHT

"Beautiful!" Cat exclaimed, seeing me in my costume. "Buttercup the day of her wedding."

I winced at her assessment and mumbled, "Buttercup the day of her *rescue*."

Cat nodded, stroked the sleeve of the soft blue fabric, and adjusted the neckline of the dress's shift slightly. "Just in time to greet the guests with Max." She reached up to my hair and moved the fake pearl crown the tiniest bit. "Perfect," she announced. "One more thing. Your present."

"What?"

"This is your birthday party. You have gifts."

"The *party* is my gift, Cat," I protested.

"It is the gift from all of us, *da*. But . . ." She looked down the hall. "Pietr!"

He stepped out of his room, slowly, and the breath stuck in my throat. In black jeans, engineer boots, a dramatic black poet's shirt, and with a black bandanna around his head, Pietr was enough to make a pirate blush. My Man in Black. No, I reminded myself sharply. Not mine at all.

He carried a large rectangular something, wrapped with a precision that demonstrated an eye for detail.

His eyes raised and he hesitated, seeing me. For a heartbeat I thought his chest stopped moving as his eyes went so fast from blue to red they appeared purple. "Your birthday present," he whispered, blinking.

"Thank you." I took it, my hand brushing his, sparks flying at such a simple touch. My stomach flopped, the electricity I still felt at his nearness made my nerves scream and my chest ache where my heart had been. *Stupid heart. Stupid girl.* I slid my fingers beneath the tape, sliding a poster frame out. I turned it over. "Wow."

In the simple black frame was an illustration of a girl in traditional Russian garb creeping through a darkened forest. Illuminating her way was the eeriest of torches: topping a long stick, a skull's empty eye sockets glowed. "It is Bilibin's work," he said. "*Vassilissa in the Forest.* He was a renowned illustrator of Russian fables and folktales, and Vassilissa—" He fell silent, staring at me.

"Is the heroine of our favorite," Cat concluded.

My eyes glued to Pietr, I whispered my singular thought: "Amazing."

"I will put it somewhere safe," Cat announced, wrenching it from my hands and leaving Pietr and myself standing at the top of the staircase alone. Together.

"Pietr . . ."

"I can't do this," he ground out, his eyes glimmering red once more. "This party . . . you . . ."

"Guests!" Max bellowed from the porch.

"You need to go. This is your party. I am"—he blew out a breath, digging the heels of his hands into his eyes and snarling like he had one hell of a headache suddenly—"*not* ready to celebrate." He backed toward his door.

I leaped, pressing my lips to his so fast his eyes jumped wide open, red as warning as his nostrils flared and he stumbled back. His fingers slid around my neck, tangling in my hair, and he dragged me with him, kissing like he'd devour me. "Ow!" I pulled back, my tongue stinging, blood in my mouth.

His teeth pointed, he groaned and dodged into his room, slamming the door shut in my face. The lock slid across, grating like my nerves. I pressed my ear to his door. He was a solid inch of oak away from me. And panting.

What a way to start a party.

I clumped down the steps to stand beside Max, putting what I hoped passed for a happy expression on my face. He put his arm around me and together we greeted the guests pouring into the party. Music blared inside, shaking me as I stood on the porch.

At a break in the crowd streaming in, Max asked, "Pietr in his room?"

I nodded bleakly.

"Good for you," he said.

"What aren't you telling me?" I demanded, but Max's eyes fixed on someone on the stairs.

Before I could push for an answer, Sarah had called my name. She climbed the stairs and smiled at me sweetly.

"Well," Max rumbled. "Isn't this embarrassing? You're both the same character." Pietr's movie rental had evidently educated the whole family. And Max was right. To my astonishment, a much daintier Buttercup faced me in the cool pink dress of the dream sequence, richly appointed with gold filigree. Balanced atop her blond hair was a tall golden crown.

"Wow, you look beautiful," I said. And I meant it. Compared to Sarah I was reduced to something far closer to Buttercup on the farm than Buttercup in the castle. Nuts. Sarah definitely reigned. "Pietr's in his room being miserable," I explained, pointing. "Maybe you can cheer him up."

She brushed past me, lifting the hem of her dress slightly to get up the stairs without tripping.

Max moved his arm off my shoulders and looked down at me. "Maybe I'm stupid," he began.

"Cat might agree some days."

He blinked. "Don't you want Pietr? You're miserable and yet you push her toward him like they should be a couple."

"She's my friend. If she makes him happy," I continued, "who am I to get in their way?" Max was shaking his head long before I finished. "I want Pietr happy. Maybe I'll find happiness somewhere else."

As if on cue, the Mercedes pulled up and Derek slid out of the back, light bouncing off his tight leather pants and black satin shirt. He was radiant as a dark angel. Something fluttered in my stomach at his approach and my palms grew damp.

Max's arm slipped around my waist, pulling me close, and the growl building in his belly made mine tremble.

Derek hesitated, one foot on the top step, one on the porch. He flashed a smile at me, reaching in my direction.

Max shoved me behind him, one hot hand holding me like he feared I might bolt for the Mercedes. "Back down," he told Derek. "Jessie doesn't want you here."

"I don't believe that," Derek countered, stretching his hand forward again as he moved up one step.

"You need proof she doesn't need you?" Max challenged. Smooth as silk, Max spun me a step away from Derek, sighed as if resigning himself to some duty, and bent me back in his arms. His lips met mine, eyes commanding as he opened my mouth with his. My eyes flickered shut and he pressed me against his muscular body, curving me to match him. Dazed, I let him kiss me. *Expertly.* For one looong minute. He released me and I stared at him, breathless.

There was clapping from inside. "So *that's* what the birthday girl's getting," someone laughed.

Derek's hand returned to his side and he glared at me. He didn't dare glare at Max.

There was a noise from the doorway and Sarah jounced onto the porch, her eyes wide from Max's display. "Present's on the table," she said with a little wave.

"Your presence is my present," I assured her.

"Trust me, you'll prefer what's in the box," she grumped. "Pietr won't come out, and you've got your hands full," she mentioned, her eyes racing across Max. "Without Pietr, it's not much of a party," she added, disappointment flooding her face.

Derek held his hand out again, this time to Sarah. "Let's you and I go somewhere and hang out. For old times' sake."

She took his hand and waved to me over her shoulder as she and Derek headed to the waiting Mercedes.

"What just happened, Max?"

"Worst-case scenario? I just pissed off a very dangerous guy by kissing you."

I snorted. "Doubtful. Football player"—I nodded toward the retreating car—"werewolf," I whispered, jabbing his ribs.

"Yeah. Seems that simple," he agreed. "Best-case scenario? I just helped you break up with a total prick and got a decent kiss out of the deal."

"Hmm." I considered a moment. The idea of breaking up with Derek didn't bother me nearly as much as losing time with Pietr did. "Max," I said, looking up at him, "I love the Russian heritage you guys are so willing to share, but I'm not so thrilled with the French."

"What?" His brows lowered. "We're not French."

"Great. So the next time you feel the need to kiss me, keep your tongue out of my mouth."

He roared with laughter and pulled me inside. "So where are your other friends?"

"Huh. I saw Sophia slip past, but—hey!"

Amy attacked me from behind, giving me a huge hug. "Happy, happy birthday!"

I grinned, hugging back and letting any last niggling doubts about inadvertently dumping Derek drain away.

"Great party, Max!" Amy congratulated.

Marvin hung back, watching their exchange.

"Anything for Jessie," Max muttered, but his eyes were completely on Amy.

Amy dressed as . . .

"Little Red Riding Hood?" I gulped. *Uh-oh.*

"The same." She laughed, doing a little spin so her hood fell back, her short cape ruffled and her brilliant red hair whipped loose. A low-cut blouse did double duty, exposing the thinnest hint of both cleavage and midriff.

Max gaped. "You even have"—he stuttered—"a—an amazingly well-packed basket of goodies."

Ohhh . . . I looked. Thank God. Amy was actually carrying a basket. "I doubt your grandmother would let you out like that, Red," I choked, grabbing her by the wrist and guiding her into another room.

Marvin followed, moping.

"And you, Marvin? You are?" I asked, glancing at the fake fur on his shoulders and the mask he held under one arm.

"The Big Bad Wolf," he blustered.

I caught Max's eyes and knew we both thought, *Hardly.*

Into the basement we headed, Max picking up girls as we went. The music blasted, throbbing against me as the heat of the dancing crowd rose to greet us. Amy shoved me onto the dance floor, Marvin lagging behind. I quickly got separated from them in the crowd and only briefly glimpsed Cat and Sophia.

Max was always visible, though, and that was how he liked it. He danced, he pawed, he gyrated, and flirted, and the girls fawned all over him. Indecent and entertaining at the same time.

As the music slowed and I moved to the edge of the crowd, I caught a glimpse of Amy across the room. Marvin was nowhere in sight; that was probably better because the way Amy watched Max run his hands up and down Stella Martin, it wouldn't have mattered if Marvin had been right in front of her. He'd have been invisible.

Starting across the floor to tell Amy to put her eyes back in her head, I saw him. Marvin. Watching Amy. Watching Max.

Faster than I could find words to warn her, he caught her. The look of surprise—and fear—on Amy's face made me scramble toward them. He was hauling her up the stairs. Away from the crowd. Alarm bells rang in my head.

Where was Pietr? Or Cat? With a growl, I pushed toward Max. "I need you!"

"Finally you admit it!" he called back, grinning.

"No, idiot! I need help. Now!" I raced him to the stairs.

His brow lowered, nostrils flaring; his concentration shifted. Could he smell her fear? He passed me on the climb, plowing ahead.

Upstairs kids were scattered around the hall, lounging on furniture and the next set of steps, swaying to the music drifting up from below. I glanced up the next staircase, but Max hooked my arm and pointed to the sitting room.

"There."

The only closed door. Not nearly enough to make Max pause.

"What the hell—" Max cracked the door back on its hinges as he bounded in. I followed, close enough to feel waves of heat pour off him.

Marvin spun to face us, hand so tight on Amy's arm his fingers were white as winter, his expression equally cold.

Amy found a spot on the floor to focus on.

"Are you okay, Amy?"

"I'm fine."

Marvin shook her. "Don't you look at him."

"Get your hand off her," Max warned, the volume belaying the ferocity behind the words.

"Time to leave, baby," Marvin ordered, shaking her again.

"No, Marvin," I said, stepping forward, a hand on Max. My fingertips stung, nerves on fire from the contact. "If you need to leave my birthday party, go ahead. I'll make sure she gets a ride home with me." My tone sounded remarkably steady in my own ears considering the way my pulse raced.

"Let go of her," Max said, coloring his tone so to the uninformed it sounded like a suggestion—not an order.

Marvin released Amy's arm and she adjusted her sleeve to better hide the color it was becoming.

My heart sank, realizing it was a practiced move. I wasn't the only one lying about things.

Between clenched teeth, Marvin said, "Let's go, love."

She fluttered a glance past Max and pasted her gaze to the floor once more. She stepped forward. Obediently.

Max turned his head away, the heat draining from him.

Marvin grinned. Victorious.

"I need you to stay, Amy," I sputtered.

She glanced at Marvin, his jaw was so tight veins rose by his hairline. "Don't make me choose," she begged.

I reached out to hug her, but she flinched at the motion. Flinched from *me*. I ground my teeth and sidestepped to block her view of Marvin. "I need you to stay."

Her eyes glistened, lower lip trembling.

"Come on, *sweetheart*," Marvin snarled. "Don't upset me."

Amy shivered.

Max's spine straightened, chin up. "Don't threaten."

"It makes Max angry," I explained, holding Amy's gaze reassuringly.

"And you wouldn't like me when I'm angry," Max stated. He crossed his arms and looked at Marvin. *Down* at Marvin.

"I'm not threatening," Marvin backpedaled.

"I should go," Amy said.

Max raised an eyebrow at her, his mouth a firm thin line. Without verbalizing, he plainly told her *no*.

"Unless you need help cleaning up," she offered.

"Please!" I said.

Marvin shifted behind me.

Max shifted to shadow him.

"Fine!" Marvin puffed. "Call me tomorrow." Exiting, he bumped purposefully into Max. Marvin rubbed his arm from the impact. Max hadn't even noticed the attempted aggression. He was enthralled by Amy's unusually quiet demeanor.

"Umm . . ." Stella Martin appeared in the doorway, lifting a feathered mask to peek into the room at us. "Max . . . don't you wanna dance? Instead of standing there looking all . . . statuesque? We plan on shaking it"—she did an impressive pop-and-lock move to demonstrate—"like a Polaroid picture, if you're lucky." She winked, then grinned at him, her gaze traveling the length of his body.

Max smiled, some of his tension draining. "Quite an invitation."

Another girl peered in. "Max . . . ," she cooed, batting her eyelashes. "Come dance."

Max groaned.

I planted my hands on my hips and shot him a measured look. Things would be easier without him. "Looks like you lost your necklace," I commented.

He snorted. "I prefer livelier accessories." Stella and the other girl slunk in and draped their arms around him. "See what I mean?" He shrugged, wistful and seemingly helpless to battle the power of his own animal magnetism. Another anonymous girl danced in and grabbed his hand, leading him away with such a sway to her hips I wondered how she didn't throw her back out. Max looked over his shoulder at us. Well, at Amy.

The front door slammed and Max glanced toward the sound, his mouth curling in satisfaction.

Marvin was gone.

"Come on!" Stella yelled.

He glanced back at us, eyes lingering again on Amy.

"Go, you dirty dog," I chuckled.

He closed the door between us, muffling the party's noise.

Amy went limp, flopping onto the love seat. "What a player," she said in disgust. But there was something else in her tone too. A wistfulness to match Max's.

"Yeah," I agreed. "So."

"Marvin's not always like this, you know," Amy justified.

"Not *always?*"

"I knew you wouldn't get it."

"What's to get? He *hurt* you, Amy. He was nasty. I'm glad he's not always like that, but—" I blinked. "This isn't the first time?"

The music outside the door cranked and a howl of appreciation rattled the house.

"Bets on who's shaking their bon-bon now?" Amy asked, flicking a dust mote with her finger.

"Take off your shirt."

"What?" She looked at me, startled.

"You heard me. Take it off."

Her cheeks flamed.

"I know you, Amy. A few months ago you would have torn it off on a dare and done power poses. What happened since then?"

"Nothing important."

"If it involves you, it's important. Take off your shirt. Prove what I'm thinking is wrong," I challenged.

Silent, she stood. Heartbreak shone in her suddenly streaming eyes.

"Amy—"

She undid the clasp of her red hood and cape combo, letting it fall to the floor. She turned her back to me, bent over, and tugged the shirt up over her head, her long auburn hair slapping down across her shoulders as she straightened.

"Oh, shit."

All across her soft skin, tucked beneath the back and occasionally obscured by the narrow straps of her lacy bra, were over a dozen different bruises. Each the size of Marvin's palm or fist, all in differing shades of brown, purple, green, and yellow—a rainbow of rage marring her beautiful back in a chronology of cruelty.

I was so stunned I didn't hear the door open.

"Son of a—"

"Max!" I shouted as Amy reached for her shirt.

But he was gone.

"I have to—" Stop him. Crap, crap, *crap*!

"Go. Go—" Amy wriggled into her shirt.

"You stay here—" I demanded, dashing out the door. The name always on my mind leaped to my lips first. "Pietr! Pietr!" I shrieked over the music, hands on the staircase's banister as I bellowed.

He leaped from the second floor, caught the banister, and landed in a crouch at my feet, eyes glowing in the party's dim light. His nostrils flared, checking the air. "Are you okay?"

Nodding, I caught my breath and raced through the words. "Your brother's gonna kill Marvin if—"

He blinked. Nodded. "I'll stop him," he promised, out the door so fast its lacy curtains flapped in his wake.

"God, I hope so," I whispered before turning back to the sitting room for Amy.

It was empty.

Dammit.

CHAPTER TWENTY-NINE

Scouring the party, there was no trace of Amy. Finally I figured out where my cell phone had gotten to and selected her name. "Pick-up-pick-up-pick-up," I chanted, sitting on the Rusakovas' back porch and wondering if Marvin had gotten himself killed, if Max was going to be locked up, and why Pietr couldn't stand to be near me. Yep. Normal concerns.

"What?"

"Amy! Where are you?"

"A cab."

"I need to talk to you."

"I need some time to think."

"Have the cab bring you back. You can think here. Or over at my place. Dad won't mind."

"No, Jessie. I ruined your party. I think I've done enough damage for one night."

"Are you going home?"

"I don't know."

"I'll wait here for you until midnight. Then I'll head home. You can get me—catch up to me—either place."

Silence.

"Amy, I'm worried about you."

Her voice crackled, and I checked my signal strength. Fine. "I—I'll be okay," she assured me. And she hung up.

The party wound down and broke up without Max and the girls playing around on the dance floor. When he and Pietr finally got back I didn't ask either one of them why they avoided me and went to wash up first. I quickly updated them and returned to the back porch to sit, dangling my legs off the edge.

Max joined me, his hair damp, stubble shading his jaw under the yellow light of the single bulb. "*Eezvehneetyeh*, Jessie."

I frowned up at him. "Sorry for what? Wanting to beat the pulp out of somebody abusing my best friend? I'm fighting the same instinct. Here." I patted my lap, and he rested his head on my leg. "You're a real dog sometimes, but you're also amazingly loyal." I toyed with the dark curls shadowing his face. "You've got great protective instincts. The makings of a hero."

Closing his eyes, he protested. "I'm far from a hero."

"Well, you, Cat, Alexi, and Pietr are some of the very best people I know."

"*People.*" He snickered, the noise bitter. "You'd probably be one of the only ones to qualify us as that after knowing what you do."

"It's nearly midnight," Pietr said from the door. "She's not coming here tonight."

Max raised his head, stretched up into Hunter's play pose and, eyes glinting, slid forward so his breath heated my entire face. Then he *licked* my cheek.

"Oh, geez!" I hissed, wiping my face clean as he rolled over and jumped up, grinning.

"Come on." He put a hand out to me. "I'll take you home."

Pietr just stood in the shadows, watching.

The next morning I threw hay to the horses and called Max before even considering breakfast. "I need a ride."

He didn't ask questions. I didn't volunteer answers.

We wound up at Park Place, a rough little trailer park on the edge of Junction.

"Stay," I commanded.

He nodded, turned on the radio, and played with his necklace while I got out. But I felt his eyes follow me as I walked to the yellow and tan trailer and knocked on the dented metal door.

Amy's father came to the door, eyes bloodshot, breath stinking of stale alcohol. His factory had closed its doors and shipped operations off to some third-world country that supposedly needed the work more than we did. Glancing at the empty beer cans and teetering stacks of old pizza boxes behind him as he stood wobbly-legged in the doorway I couldn't imagine a third-world country being any worse than that trailer.

"Amy!" he bellowed. He looked surprised when she didn't reply. "Did she stay out with that guy she's seeing?"

My stomach dropped, and I clutched the bent metal banister. "I don't know. Do you know where he lives?"

"Up toward the Hill. Pretty good family—some money. Makes a big difference, money," he grumbled.

"Really? I thought money didn't matter. Not like love."

Max was behind me, latching his arm around my waist and tugging gently. His words brushed by my ear, "I know where they are."

Amy's father swayed, squinting at Max. "Who's he?"

"Just some guy," Max muttered.

"No. Probably the hero du jour." I stalked back to the convertible, Max trailing me.

"*Hero's* a big word."

"You're a big guy. You can grow into it."

He started the car. "So that's her dad."

"Yeah. They've got issues, right?"

"I'm not judging," he said with a grimace. "Remember? *Werewolf.*"

"Good point. So how do you know where he lives?"

"I was almost there last night, before Pietr caught me."

"The nose knows," I said.

"Yeah." Max punched the accelerator and peeled out, the convertible's tires squealing and slinging gravel. "How can anyone think it's okay to . . ."

". . . hit a girl?"

"Hit *anyone*."

I avoided mentioning his willingness to rearrange Marvin's face. "I don't know, Max. I really don't know."

Even in brooding silence, time evaporated with Max driving.

"You really like her, don't you? Isn't your interest in her a little . . . sudden?"

His brow lowered.

"Max . . ." I paused.

"Jessie." He blew out a breath so hot the car's windshield fogged a moment. He pawed it clear with the back of his hand and just shook his head. "You don't know everthing, okay? You can't. You're not . . . *omniscient*." He blinked, and I closed my gaping mouth. She's hot," he justified, but the words weren't as flippant as usual. "Here."

Topiary figures flanked a herringbone brick driveway just off a cul-de-sac. Max pulled in and rolled his window down to take a whiff. "This is it." Ahead was a huge white house with a broad porch and fat white pillars. It looked like some misbegotten southern mansion had been reassembled in Junction to lord over the commoners.

"Nice looking, huh?" I asked.

"Looks like heaven. Wouldn't know there's a devil inside."

I nodded. "You stay here, quiet and out of sight. I don't want him thinking you two are messing around."

"Yeah. And, Jessie, if you need me—"

"I'll yell."

I didn't expect Marvin to live in such a huge house. And not on the Hill. Not direct neighbors, he still shared a neighborhood—a realm—with Sarah. And Macie, Jenny, and Derek. The Hill was *the* neighborhood in Junction, with houses that peered down on the rest of the town, raised above the rabble.

For a girl like Amy . . . No. The thought rephrased in my head. *For a girl coming out of a situation like Amy's*, being on the Hill was huge. I had to remember that. "If you walk a mile in another's shoes—" Mom said. Man, to have that sort of perspective without the pain that came with it . . .

With a swing of my hand the door's big brass knocker announced my presence boldly with a harsh thump. I took a deep breath but was unprepared when the door swung open.

A woman smiled out at me. "Well hello."

She was pretty. Fine-featured, with hair that nearly matched Amy's natural shade, she wore fashionably conservative clothes—a neat blouse, a knee-length skirt, and heels. Around her neck was a hefty strand of pearls.

They nearly hid the bruises.

It was official. I was in over my head.

But so was Amy. And I'd been so self-involved recently—she deserved a friend who'd swim into shark-infested waters to pull her out when she was drowning.

I refocused on the woman's face, smiling back. My stomach clenched at the thought I was seeing Amy's future. "Hi. Mrs. Broderick?"

"Yes." The smile wavered. "I'm sorry. You are—?"

"Jessica Gillmansen. I go to school with Marvin. You can call me Jessie."

"Oh. Wonderful. What can I do for you, Jessie?"

"I was wondering if Marvin's home."

"He's eating breakfast. I could set you a place."

"Oh. Um. Thanks but—" My stomach growled, betraying me.

"It is the most important meal of the day."

"Yes, ma'am," I agreed. I thought of Max waiting in the car. Obedient as a hound. At least I prayed he was.

"Marvin," she called. "One of your friends is here." She opened a door into a dining space that put both my breakfast nook and the Rusakova's dining room to shame. Even combined.

Light flooded in from a bank of tall windows, setting the elegant glassware and silver ablaze.

"Jessica." Marvin said my name like he'd just gotten a bitter taste of something. I hoped he had.

Amy, at his elbow, raised her head, undeniably nervous.

I remembered wearing that look once when my family stayed at a really amazing hotel. I kept waiting for a member of the staff to realize we didn't belong and kick us to the curb.

"I'm setting Jessie a place for breakfast," Mrs. Broderick explained as she took utensils from a fanned display on the buffet. She paused. "Jessie. Wasn't your party last night?"

"Yes."

"Did Marvin thank you for inviting him?"

My brain stuttered to a halt, letting my tongue rattle loosely in my head. "Errr . . ." No. I had a werewolf kick his sorry ass out. Not much to thank me for, probably. Unless he had the cake. The cake was good. *Not* made by Catherine.

"Marvin," she scolded.

"The party was lovely, Jessica. Thank you for inviting me."

I nearly believed him. *Bastard.* "My pleasure." *Kicking you out, that is.* I smiled and took a seat.

"Then today's your birthday, isn't it?"

"Yes."

"Well. Happy birthday, Jessie. I hope it's a great one."

"Me too. Thank you."

Mrs. Broderick ladled out steaming diced potatoes, heaped scrambled eggs dotted with mushrooms (wild, I bet) onto my plate, and added a slice of ham the size of my head before topping things off with a buttermilk biscuit (doubtless not from a can) and freshly stewed strawberries. "Oh. I'm so sorry, Jessie. I didn't ask if you'd prefer French toast and bacon instead." She lifted the lid on another dish.

Max was gonna kill me. I hoped he had beef jerky in the car. The good kind.

"This is fabulous, Mrs. Broderick." It was the best breakfast spread I'd seen in years. I carefully chewed everything, tasted everything, considered the nuances of flavors, savoring every moment. I almost forgot I wanted nothing more than to slowly choke Marvin into unconsciousness for beating Amy. Until she spoke.

"You're making yummy noises," Amy whispered, smiling.

Guilty, I blushed and took a swig of freshly squeezed orange juice. It was all so perfect. Until someone got mad. "You do all this yourself?"

"Of course." Mrs. Broderick blinked at me. "My men love breakfast. And I love to keep my men happy."

The last bite of ham was hard to swallow as I considered the implications of having an unhappy man in Marvin's household. I swept a bit of biscuit around my plate and popped it into my mouth. "Can Amy and I help you clean up?"

"Well, the maid usually . . ." Mrs. Broderick blinked at me again. "Actually, yes. That would be—" She looked at Marvin for—*permission*?

He nodded.

"That would be delightful."

"Great," I said, gathering plates. "Lead the way. Come on, Amy!" I called over my shoulder.

If looks could kill, the maid would have been cleaning up my corpse, courtesy of Marvin's hatefilled glare.

"That's fascinating, Mrs. Broderick. So your husband's often away on business?" I shook my head. "I think I'd want more attention than just seeing my guy weekends and holidays."

"Some men are better at business than at home, Jessie. They get unhappy if they're caged."

"Huh. I guess they might."

She dried her hands on the delicate apron hanging around her narrow waist. "In real, lasting relationships you make sacrifices. A little of your happiness for some of his."

Amy stared at the floor.

"But there's a limit, right?" I pressed. "Some things people shouldn't ever give up for a label like *lasting relationship*." I framed the last two words with air quotes.

"Like what?"

"Dignity."

Amy's eyes slid to me.

Mrs. Broderick blustered, tugging at her pearl necklace. "Of course," she agreed. "It's not love if there's no dignity."

I nodded. "I appreciate your hospitality. But Amy and I really need to be going. I have a car waiting."

"Oh. Maybe your driver knows our driver."

"Maybe. Max often surprises me."

Amy's head came up at his name. "We'd better go."

We hurried to the door, but didn't make it out before Marvin caught us.

"*Baby*," Marvin snapped out the endearment like the cracking of a whip. "You'll be back for dinner."

"Sorry, Marvin," I said with a shrug. "I think tonight we need to work on fixing Amy's heart."

His eyes were cold. Daring.

"The biology project. You know, Marvin, the model heart that's due soon," Amy whispered.

"Yep. It seems it's gotten a bit confused and it's a huge project fixing a heart if you've gotten it so wrong."

His eyes narrow, there was no doubt he knew what I meant.

"You know biology's not my best subject," Amy reminded him.

"Fine. Your choice," he snarled.

"Marvin!" his mother called. "Getting good grades is the right choice. You should support it. How is *your* project going?"

He stared at her.

"I'll help you," his mother promised, her voice dropping.

I grabbed Amy and dragged her through the grand doors and out of the beautiful hell she was courting.

"Back to the real world." I shoved her into the front seat.

"What'd you do in there," Max asked, "stop to eat?"

"Umm . . ."

"I snagged you a biscuit," Amy said, reaching into her purse and opening a paper towel.

The look Max gave her was definitely related to hunger, but I doubted it was about the biscuit.

"Thank you." Their hands touched as he took the biscuit from her. *Sparks*. And complications.

"Drive, Max," I instructed. "Buckle up, Amy."

Things were quiet, each of us thinking. Maybe not Max. But Amy and I were lost in thought until she broke the silence.

"He's old money, you know."

As if that justified it. "So were the Hapsburgs," I griped.

"What?"

"The Hapsburgs. Old European powerbrokers. They made marriages all over based on cementing their hold in society."

"And?"

"They had issues. Trying to hold all that money and power made them crazy. Sometimes literally: big jaws, small minds. Old money, new money. Too much makes people nuts."

"Too much or too little," Amy corrected.

CHAPTER THIRTY

Back at the Rusakovas' house, we quickly forgot about biology projects and got into an argument.

"I just think—"

Amy shook her head. "You don't just leave a guy like Marvin."

I sighed. "Why not?"

"He gets crazy without me. He needs me," she stated. "Leaving him makes things worse. Look. This isn't some black-and-white thing," Amy said.

"No. Black and blue," I snapped.

"Marvin loves me. He just gets out of hand sometimes."

"Have you seen your back recently?"

"Seriously? How often do people ever look at their backs? That's why our worst bits are back there—so we don't see."

"It's not—" I glared at Pietr and Max, who lay on the rug between us, smirking at Amy's logic. "It's not funny. He hurts you. There's nothing funny about that."

Max nodded soberly. Pietr looked away.

Max puffed out a breath, admitting, "I was ready to—"

"Give him the scare of his life," Pietr concluded quickly, shooting a reprimanding look at Max.

"*Da.*" Max snorted and rolled onto his back. "*Pravda.*" He rolled again; rising to his hands and knees he stalked to Amy's seat, muscles sliding, bunching and coiling beneath his cotton T-shirt. Even fully human I saw so much wolf in him I wondered how Amy could miss it. "Drop him," he purred, placing a hand on either side of her on the love seat's cushion and coming to a kneeling position so he was nose to nose with her.

"I—" She swallowed, pinned by his eyes.

"You need a reason?" he whispered, voice hoarse. I wiggled in my seat and looked away, aware I was seeing the beginning of something tremendously personal. But my eyes kept returning to them: my best friend and Pietr's older, definitely hot brother.

Amy sat stock-still, captivated as Max leaned in and kissed her. Like he knew her. Like he was working out some impassioned promise with his lips.

Harder than watching was *not* watching.

Pietr cleared his throat, catching me peeking.

Max pulled back, slow and easy, head tilted, eyes never leaving Amy's face as it went from warm pink to deep red.

"I need more than that," she whispered.

Max leaned in again—

"No!" she laughed, pushing him onto his heels. "I didn't say more *of* that. You dog!" she taunted.

"You have no idea," Pietr said with a yawn.

Max leaned back again. "What do you need to be rid of him?"

Pietr suggested a backhoe.

Amy looked at me for help, but I crossed my arms. "Name your price. Evidently Max'll give you as much of"—I waved my hand in the air—"*that* as you need. But what do you really need to stand up to Marvin? To break it off?"

Amy played with her fingers and worried her lower lip between her teeth. Her eyes shut a moment. When they opened, they were pained and pointedly honest.

Max set his hand on top of Amy's, stifling her twitching. "What do you need?"

Never had I seen sadder eyes. Although she said, "Protection. A place to sleep," I heard hidden beneath it: *a hero.* Her face screwed up in an anguish she must've masked for weeks. She pushed Max's hand away, collapsing forward, head on her knees. She shook with a single sob, covering her head with her hands.

Max looked at me, stunned. Helpless.

I glared at him. A beautiful player, Max knew how to line the girls up. The last thing Amy needed was to get into line like the rest. I thought about Stella Martin. How would she feel if Max just threw her away? Like Sarah would if Pietr chose me. Devastated and betrayed. *Dammit.*

Amy needed a hero and as much hope as I had I doubted Max was ready for the job. Not yet.

"Move," I ordered, shoving him aside. I looped an arm around her and stroked her hair. "You'll have it," I promised. "We'll figure it out somehow. It'll be okay."

She hiccupped in my grasp, a kitten instead of the tigress I'd grown up with, the girl I always thought I understood.

In the corner Max slunk into the shadows, his spine rigid, chin up. I wondered what he was thinking.

And then I saw the chain glittering around his neck and realized as much as he wanted Amy, he didn't want her to come to him like the others had. Maybe he was closer to playing hero than either of us imagined.

I had never been one of the girls truly able to understand guys. Max and Pietr didn't make me feel any more capable when Monday morning came. And the fact Wanda left me a text message warning me to stay clear of the Rusakovas . . . Considering how strange everything was, I stayed even closer to the werewolves.

Weirdness reigned.

Max might as well have been dating me, the way he kept me just out of Derek's reach. He could not have possibly made it to class. It was the weirdest game of keep-away I'd ever been involved in. While Max hung on me and kept Derek at bay, being his big, gruff self, Pietr watched everything with wary eyes—like there was something even he hadn't been told.

"So, what's going on?" Amy asked me in the girls' bathroom between classes. I was starting to believe we spent so much time here we should redecorate for comfort. Or at least better lighting. "I feel like we're being guarded by the sexiest thug brothers around."

I raised an eyebrow at her in the mirror. "You broke it off with Marvin, right?"

"Yeah. Over the phone."

"That's safest, considering."

"Max got my stuff from Dad's trailer and officially moved me. It wasn't pretty, but I'm living at the Rusakovas' now, I guess."

My eyebrows would not come down. "Where exactly?"

"Basement."

My heart resumed its regular rhythm. "Good. Then just accept your status as guarded, like I guess I'm supposed to do. Docilely."

"Not that I'm complaining . . ."

"But."

"But why is Max all over you and Pietr's obviously coping with watching me? Shouldn't they switch assignments?"

"I don't know what's going on between Pietr and me. But I intend to find out."

Amy held the door open. "Well, you may just get your chance. It seems ours isn't the only social shakeup. Derek's keeping Sarah pretty close, too. Maybe she's done with Pietr?"

"Doubtful." I considered things. "I want some answers."

"Not me," Amy said. "I've seen enough crap in my life already to know sometimes it really *is* better not to know too much—you'll only be disappointed by what you find."

I reached out and gave her a hug. "It'll get better," I assured. "So. Wanna help *me* get the answers *I'm* looking for?"

"Anything for you," Amy said, and we stepped back into the restroom to plot some subterfuge of our own.

Amy absolutely knew how to yank Max's chain. Maybe it was a were-wolf thing, but ever since Halloween and the Red Riding Hood outfit, Max couldn't keep his eyes off her. Correction: didn't bother keeping his eyes off her. Stella Martin had been the first to notice. I still didn't know how Max had handled that, but Stella was moving on, Billy from the bus worshiping her the way only the most gallant of mustache-bearing freshmen could.

So when Amy shamelessly suggested Max walk her to classes and Pietr deal with troublesome me, Max's eyes nearly fell out of his head.

Pietr was less impressed.

I tried getting Pietr to tell me why I was the ball in some game of monkey-in-the-middle, but he didn't have great answers, either. So I shot Amy *the look* and she twisted her ankle. Sometimes the classics worked. Cute redhead writhing on the floor and the werewolves raced over like monsters in the movies.

I'd decided my best shot at answers was with Derek. He could tell me why I had no memories from our date or . . . well, I didn't know. But I was on the lam. I should've guessed I wouldn't get far with Pietr on my trail.

He caught my elbow, shoving me against the cinder block wall, his powerful arms braced on either side of my shoulders as he peered down at me, a wild gleam lighting his eyes. "Don't make me hunt you," he snarled, his breath a desert breeze across my cheeks.

The late bell rang and he rolled his eyes. "How can I pass math if I'm *never* there?" His forehead resting against the wall beside me, he took a deep breath and jumped back like he'd been stung, eyes blar-ing red. Rubbing his nose frantically he squeezed his eyes shut. I heard a *pop*.

"Crap!" I yelped, eyes wide in realization.

And then I heard something else. Just around the corner. Coun-selor Harnek.

"I know what's going on, Derek. And I expect better from you."

Another pop as Pietr battled the wolf within. Crap! Why now? I thrust him back against the wall—not an easy task this time—and warned, "Get ahold of yourself."

In the next hallway Derek sputtered. "You expect *better* from me?"

"You've been reckless and selfish. The stunt you pulled at Homecoming, getting the crowd riled up when you pretended to be hurt, getting buzzed from that was one thing. But the way you're handling Jessie . . . you need to back off."

"I doubt you fully understand my part in all this."

"I understand you've screwed things up royally," Harnek stated. "The Rusakovas are on alert. Remember what happened with Sophia when you got sloppy?"

"I didn't know any better," he snapped. "I didn't mean to trigger her. Things have changed. I doubt the company's let you in far enough to really understand my assigned role."

"You think I'm out of the loop with the company?"

I leaned back against the cinder-block wall, sliding closer to the corner to catch their words as Harnek's voice dropped. Pietr's fingers touched mine in warning.

"I was the company's first contact in Junction. With my degree and my location, they came here offering help for our students through *me* first. Your job is simple, Derek: be an extra set of eyes so we can better protect the students."

"I've done that."

"Yes, and you've done a fair job. You're amazingly gifted. But I think you're using your knowledge and influence in dangerous ways."

"Why shouldn't I get a little something back, considering everything I do?"

"That's just it," Harnek soothed. "We protect people. Unselfishly. I don't expect to gain anything doing my part."

"That's exactly why you aren't on the company's fast track anymore." The sneer marring his face was obvious in his tone. "I don't think you really grasp their objective."

"*A stronger, better youth to light the future's path*? I don't grasp that?"

"You really don't know, do you?" There was wonder in his voice.

"Daaamn. I don't think you're allowed to talk to me like you're my superior anymore. This conversation? This thing of preaching to me about what I should and shouldn't do? Over."

Footsteps faded farther down the other hall. One of them walked away.

I let out a deep breath and looked at Pietr, his eyes once again clear and blue, breathing steadied. What the heck was really going on in Junction?

CHAPTER THIRTY-ONE

"You need to take the hint," Pietr insisted, pushing through the stairwell doors at Golden Oaks, kitten in hand. "Don't push me, Jess. Even she's told you, *beware the boy*," he said, opening Feldman's door. "I *am* the boy."

"Bull and shit," Feldman snapped. "Close that door."

Cowed, I obeyed.

"Are you so egotistical you believe everything is about you, Pietr?" she asked. "Just because cards are pulled or produced in your presence does not mean . . ." She puffed out an exasperated breath. "If you are so fascinated by yourself, perhaps I should stroke your ego and tell you more, hmm?" The cards zipped and buzzed like angry bees as she shuffled them furiously. "Touch nothing," she commanded when he reached to draw. "I will pull your heart out and display it here. Now."

She tossed the cards in a seemingly random spread and bent over her lap to examine them. "Oh," she whispered, looking up.

I grabbed Pietr's arm and his eyes flashed red at me, bright as fireworks.

Feldman gasped. "Oh, no. I did not . . ." She scooted back as far as the wall allowed. "I didn't realize what you are . . . I didn't guess you would find me here—I have *tried*," she swore.

"What the . . . ," Pietr muttered, blinking his eyes clear.

"Mrs. Feldman, what are you talking about?" I set Tag on the floor at her bedside. The amber heart slipped free of my neckline, swaying between us. Mesmerized, Mrs. Feldman's mouth opened and closed like that of a fish out of water.

"Oh, no wonder you are with him . . . You've opened the *matryoshka*."

My knees felt filled with rubber.

Pietr crouched beside her.

She gasped. "I swear I've t-t-tried," she stuttered, "but I haven't found the way to cure you . . . not yet. Please, *please* don't hurt me."

"Mrs. Feldman, no one will hurt you." I patted her hand and tried to make my legs support me. "What do you know about the *matryoshka*?"

"That"—she jabbed a bony finger at my pendant—"was inside. I prescribed its design at my father's bidding." She held her head and rocked back and forth, muttering incoherently.

"Hazel Feldman," I scolded. "No one here is going to hurt you. Stop this nonsense and talk to us."

The rocking stopped. Her eyes slid warily to Pietr and back to me. "He is *oborot*," she confided. "A werewolf."

"Yes. And they have very good ears," I added. My mind raced. If she hadn't known Pietr was a werewolf earlier—what secret did she see in his first reading? "Who are you? CIA?"

"No." Her eyes grew round. "The CIA's involved?"

"Never mind," Pietr said, his voice as rich as cream. "You've been working on a cure? What do you know about all this?"

"What don't I know should be the question," she insisted. "My father was your creator. . . . The lead scientist on Project Oboroht. He was deemed a failure when the first generation wasn't markedly different, but then, only seventeen years after the project was closed, he heard tales of strange children, horrible murders . . . suicides and monsters." She shivered. "He realized his project was not completely a failure, but ran along a canine chronology. He tried to gather your—*people*—back up, find them, and redeem himself, but . . . you die so young. . . ."

Pietr looked away.

"He became a changed man. He could not return to the USSR knowing his research had led to such a tragic circumstance. To create such things and set a genetic timebomb . . . He came here to better track the offspring of Oborot, to study and find a cure. But I wanted none of it. I"—she pointed to the cards—"chose a different path. Then I believed science and magic were mutually exclusive. If one existed, the other could not."

She looked at Pietr again, studying his face. "You are different than I expected. He is handsome, isn't he?"

I blushed. "Yes," I agreed. "Amazingly handsome."

"And you know and yet . . ." Emboldened once more, she asked, "You will not hurt me?"

"*Nyet*, I will not," he agreed, solemn.

"Let us test that theory. She has seen you—ahhh—" Her eyes sparkled. "On your birthday, yes?"

"*Da.*"

"She knows the truth of who you are."

"He only shared the truth with me because of this," I tapped the pendant.

"That is not true." He rose to his feet.

"You thought it was a sign because of the rabbit netsuke."

"The rabbit netsuke," Hazel mumbled, smacking her forehead like it was all so obvious now. "Your *mother*? I gave her the rabbit in Brighton Beach."

"What? I need to sit down." I landed in a nearby chair gracelessly. "Alexi's mother was the Coney Island con woman—How do they connect?"

"Alexi's mother—oh." She paused. Took a deep breath. "They are—*I am*—one and the same," she said. "Perhaps you should brush up on your geography, child. Brighton Beach and Coney Island are not so very far apart."

"Why did you give Jess's mother the rabbit?" Pietr pressed.

"It was foretold." She shrugged.

"No. Things are foretold? Our destiny's already written in the stars? No. That's too Shakespearean. Too tragic," I gulped, thinking about *Romeo and Juliet*. "You mean to tell me I have no choice in life—there's some almighty plan I don't have a chance to change?"

"Shhh," Feldman soothed. "Just because something's written in the stars does not mean our destinies are fixed. The stars may not *seem* to move, but they are moving as our universe starts the return from its Big Bang. Fixed is not what we once thought it was. We have choice. But some things come *highly* recommended." She smiled. "I expect it is highly recommended I call the nurse to fetch my lock-box."

Pietr's eyebrows rose.

"Proof that though I was the prodigal daughter, I did not abandon my father's search for a cure." She pressed the button by her bed and a nurse appeared. "Bring me box HF169, please." The nurse disappeared. "While we wait, perhaps you can answer my questions. The boy your parents adopted—"

"Alexi," Pietr said.

"Ah. Is he well?"

"*Da.*"

"Good, good. What is he—what is my son like?"

"He is smart, and strong and handsome," I answered, adding that last one even though I didn't see Alexi that way.

"Good, good. And . . . the night of your birthday . . . Jessie accepted what you are?"

Pietr nodded, slowly, as if he was still unsure.

"Did you imprint?"

I straightened at the question.

"*Nyet,*" he conceded.

"Interesting." She glanced at the cards still spread on her bed. "Not an easy task to accept one who isn't sure if he is man or monster," she credited me.

"It's not difficult if you care for him," I stated.

She nodded. "So why? Why are you trying to stay away from her now? Have you imprinted with someone else?"

"*Nyet.*" He flexed his fingers, cracking his knuckles. "I am trying to protect her."

"By not being with her? Interesting. And is she safer now you maintain your distance?"

"*Da.*"

"*Nyet!*" I countered. "There were mafiosos at the Golden Jumper. I threw the competition just to get us out of there."

"What? Why didn't you tell me—?"

"When, Pietr? When you were making out with Sarah? When you refused my phone calls? When you locked yourself away at my birthday party?" I stormed through the list, my face heating with rage. "You've forgotten that there was no time you gave me . . . I was hurt worse falling off my horse than taking that punch from the guy in the church."

Pietr was before me, gripping my arms, his eyes red as rubies. "*You've* forgotten I am the boy you're being warned against."

"Mrs. Feldman?" The nurse pushed open the door. "Is everything all right in here?"

"Yes, yes," she waved her hand. "Merely a demonstration of teen drama."

"Oh," the nurse set a numbered box on her bed with a key. "*Romeo and Juliet?*"

"I certainly hope not," Feldman scoffed as the nurse bobbed her head and exited. "Close the door," she reminded her.

She opened the box and withdrew a journal that looked amazingly like the ones Alexi had been poring over searching for a cure. "Take this when you leave. You should now have all thirteen journals. My notes are in the margins."

I nodded.

Pietr dropped his hands from me and held my eyes with his. "Do you see *this*, Jess," he whispered, widening his eyes so I could not mistake the red color glowing in them.

"Yes."

"This is why I can't . . . why I don't . . ."

The deck of cards smacked into Pietr's face and dropped to the ground.

"You are *not* the boy, Pietr Rusakova," Feldman snapped.

He rounded on her. "How do you know?"

"This message came from a specific source. Does one of you have a spirit hanging around?"

I sighed and Pietr stared at me as I slowly raised my hand. "A friend of mine thinks my mother's coming through."

Pietr's eyes widened.

"Big surprise, right?" I mumbled. "Werewolves, ghosts. Happy Halloween."

"Big surprise," he echoed. Like he meant it.

"I'm sorry, Jessie. I did not realize," Feldman lamented. "Sometimes spirits get stuck. In a time, or a place . . . Some can work themselves free, but others?" She shrugged. "When your mother was alive . . . Who was the boy you talked about with her? Was there a boy there when she died? It could be either."

I collapsed back into the chair. "Oh. It's both. Like you," I said to Mrs. Feldman. "One and the same." Seeing the concern on Pietr's face, I assured him, "It's not you. It's Derek."

CHAPTER THIRTY-TWO

Annabelle Lee turned to a fresh page in the book she was reading over the dinner I'd prepared, acting like she hadn't heard Dad's words. But I knew better.

"Dad, it's perfectly safe. I need to get Rio to try different stuff. The old park's perfect."

"You considerin' the competition schedule again?"

I nodded. "You know what they say: *'Get back on the horse.'* I botched the Golden Jumper. I want to do better."

"Hmm." He speared a piece of broccoli. "Make sure you're out of there by dark," he warned. "Never know what sort of trouble may drift in."

I shuddered, remembering the shootout. "Yeah." I pushed in my chair and headed for the door, grabbing my jacket and a flashlight in case the path home was ridden in darkness.

I needed time to think—to get things straight in my head. And whereas before I might have gone to Skipper's and stood beneath the dogwood to search for some modicum of peace after Mom's death, my life had been rattled by more than her loss. I needed to face the spot I had lost what was left of my innocence. The place I killed a man and watched Pietr do the same.

Rio warmed up quickly and we jogged into the old park through what used to be its main entrance. The wooden sign had long ago been defaced, most of the marigolds stolen, and the few remaining rose bushes were seasonally trimmed back by visitors with bud vases to fill.

I'd played here as a child, on swingsets that were now rusty skeletons of headless horses, the chains that once squeaked along their bellies long gone, the moments my feet nearly kicked the clouds to earth—all but memory.

I nudged Rio into a trot, passing the wobbling water fountain and broken benches where parents used to watch their children play as they gossiped about their neighbors (until their neighbors joined them and they gossiped about others).

Down a narrow path we went, only pausing when it opened into meadow. I steadied myself and felt Rio tighten beneath me in response. "S'okay, girl," I soothed.

In the slanting light of late afternoon the image before me was pastoral, far from the night of Pietr's birthday. I slid out of the saddle, pausing by Rio's shoulder, looping the reins around my hand and running my fingers along her soft snout.

"Come on, girl, let's walk."

She matched my pace, ambling beside me as I kicked leaves and scanned the area. I'd hoped to find some answers here, some peace. This was the place everything changed for Pietr and myself—for him very literally. Was there any way to get back to being us? To have a normal relationship, considering the facts stacked against us? I had to believe we could. But I needed him to believe it—to want it—as much as I did.

I kept my feet moving, shuffling through the crackling debris of autumn while I tried to forget the blood the ground had drunk down and the leaves had covered up.

The sky turned colors, the blue deepening to purple, and the world around me took on an eerie and unfortunately familiar cast. My stomach tightened and my mind argued against it.

I shivered and led Rio to where most of the action occurred, reminding myself silently I had nothing to fear. The threat—the danger—had passed. Casting aside the blaring memories of blood and gunfire, my mind drifted.

And I realized there were no definitive answers here. I could only get the answers I wanted from Pietr. Suddenly the knot of emotion nestled inside me began to loosen. "Let's go for a ride." I slapped Rio's shoulder and slipped my foot into the stirrup to mount.

We moved from a trot to a lope to a ground-swallowing gallop. We terrorized the park's vacant trails, spinning back the way we came at the lightest touch of my knee to her ribs, making hairpin turns, testing our abilities.

And then, down one trail long abandoned we found my favorite obstacle: a fallen log. "Rio," I whispered, leaning forward to prick her ear with my breath. "Let's give it a go." We trotted back a few paces. "Ready?" I asked, and I felt her muscles coil in anticipation.

"H'yup!" We raced down the narrow trail, leaves flying in our wake and as we neared the downed tree I rose up in the saddle, leaned forward and straightened my back. Rio flew across the log, her legs long, extension perfect. A little jolt at touchdown, but the thump might as well have been my heart falling back into place after a great jump.

"Awesome!" I cried, thumping my palm on her neck as she continued forward at a rapid clip.

One of her ears pivoted to the right and I felt her tense beneath me. "Easy, girl," I soothed just before I heard it.

The hair at the nape of my neck tickled as it struggled against the rushing breeze to rise in warning. A half stride behind and holding steady something raced through the brush and brambles on a parallel course.

Something big.

I gave Rio her head and felt her stride lengthen, a spray of foam flying out of her mouth and off her neck. The pounding of her hooves on the old packed path rattled me. I gathered the reins and tried to hear beyond her heavy breathing and thundering hoof beats.

I caught a glimpse of something zipping along the undergrowth, dodging the worst of the briars on astonishingly nimble feet. My heart raced to outrun whatever challenged us, beating so fast it quivered in my chest instead of pumped.

The light bled from the sky, violent shades of red and purple twisting in agonizing beauty above us. I wouldn't be out of the park by dark, regardless of my intentions.

Ahead the path widened, the brush separating us from our challenger disappearing as the trails merged in a small clearing. "We'll know soon," I muttered, lying across Rio's stretched neck, my jacket sleeves sopping up her sweat.

The brambles between us were suddenly gone and a shadow leaped out—huge, canine, and wild. But not a simple wolf.

Rio panicked, rearing up, dancing on her hind legs and kicking out with her front.

She screamed and the beast was no longer a wolf, but Pietr, grabbing her reins in a move so fluid Rio turned with him and I plunged from my saddle.

Into Pietr's powerful arms.

"Down!" he commanded Rio, his voice so low I barely caught the single word.

Rio heard it clearly. With a squeal of indignation she obeyed, rolling her eyes and stomping her hooves.

"*Eezvehneetyeh,*" he whispered toward Rio. "I didn't think I would frighten you since we've known each other . . ." He blinked and focused on me, still in his grip. "*Strahsvoytcha,*" he said, his choice of greeting allowing him to roll it under a thick purr. He set me down, my hands slipping along his naked chest.

Naked.

I blushed so fiercely my face could have set dusk back an hour or two. I turned my head away from him, concentrating on Rio. And breathing. My knees shook. I didn't dare look at him.

He seemed confused. His brain still hadn't puzzled back together with the wolf's.

"Hello," I echoed lamely. "Pants," I said.

"*Da.* Pants." A wolf again, he dashed down the trail. I heard him stop, curse, and wrestle with some sort of plant. Then he returned, pants on, T-shirt in hand. "Sorry," he said. "I drop things sometimes."

"Mmhmm. Like clothes and girlfriends," I alleged.

"What?"

There was no fooling me. Pietr's hearing was remarkably keen. "You heard me."

"I'm sorry."

"You need a new line," I retorted. "That one's old."

"What do you want me to say?"

"Say that the past was all a nightmare."

"You know better. *This* is what I am," he hissed.

"That's not the past I want erased. That's not what needs to change."

"Then what?"

"Say that you're breaking up with Sarah—cleanly—and choosing me. Say you never wanted her but you didn't want to hurt her. For me. Tell me you know you're not the boy I've been warned against."

"I—" He looked away.

"Damn it, Pietr," I said, unable to hide my disgust, "Why bother to run with us, to talk to me now, if you're going to keep hurting me? It's one thing to play guard dog at school, but I need more than that from a friend."

"I can't be your friend."

"Liar."

"You know I don't lie . . . not like that." He pawed at his eyes and groaned. "I mean it, Jess. I can't be your friend."

"Jackass."

"I don't want to hurt you, Jess. I want you safe."

I blinked at him.

"Why are you here tonight?"

"I lost something," I muttered. "The night of your birthday. I wanted to find it again."

"What was it?" he stepped closer.

His scent flooded my senses—all woodland and wild—and my world wobbled. "Shirt," I whispered, too near his bare chest for clarity of thought.

"You lost your shirt?" His expression twisted. "I don't remember that."

"No. *You*. Put on your shirt."

He nodded, raising his arms to pull the thin tee over his head. The move only accentuated his well-muscled stomach. "What did you lose?"

Oh, God. It was time for the truth. I'd lied so much recently, I wondered if I remembered how to tell it.

"What did you lose?" he repeated.

"My heart, Pietr. I lost my heart."

He sighed. His forehead touched mine, searing the spot just above my nose, eyes blurring a shade of violet, hanging between sky blue and stop sign red.

"Have you seen it, Pietr?" I asked. "I gave it to someone to guard, but I'm not sure he wants to anymore."

He sighed again, his body shuddering, his eyes screwed shut against my words. "Perhaps you're right," he whispered hoarsely. "He may not want to hurt you, but I don't think he can help it."

My jaw hung open, eyes wide.

"There are things—things beyond his control . . ."

Oh, God . . . What could I say? "Control is learned. It just takes time."

He pulled back far enough to shake his head. "Some of us are short on time." His hair brushed my forehead. "It's beyond my control."

My heart clenched and as much as I wanted to babble until I somehow stumbled across the right words to say, nothing came.

"You were right about him," he confided. "He *is* a monster."

"No."

"Do you know why?" He didn't wait, but plowed ahead: "Because he lost something that night, too."

My lips quivered as I formed the single word. "What?"

"His soul."

I slapped him. "Don't you ever say that again, Pietr Andreiovich Rusakova! You may have thrown away my heart, but you have not— *not*—lost your soul." I pounded on his chest with my fists. "That night . . . you did what you did to save my life."

And then it hit me.

"Oh. God." My vision wavered. "I thought you were trying to hurt me, or avoid me, but . . . You *are* trying to protect me . . . everything you've done . . ." I swallowed.

Stepping back, he sank into shadow like it was second nature.

"No. You stay right here. You talk to me. Who are you protecting me from, Pietr?" I thrust out my hand to tick off my current threats. "Sarah, who could snap at any second and go back to being a social nazi?"

He tensed, but that wasn't it.

"The CIA? They still believe they need me to keep tabs on you. The closer we are, the safer I am."

He shook his head, doubtful.

"Is it the Russian Mafia? Did you think by being separated they wouldn't look for me? They found me at the Golden Jumper. If they want to they can find me again."

Thick in shadow he stood even taller, lips open to show the tips of his teeth.

"Oh. Pietr." I reached out to him.

He stepped back again, going even deeper into the darkness.

"It's all that and you. You're afraid you can't protect me from you." I grabbed his arms and held on.

He tried to twist away, but it was a half-hearted effort. "You don't understand the danger, Jess," he insisted, words grinding out like gravel lined his throat. "I—I'm not myself."

"You *are*, Pietr. You are absolutely who you're supposed to be. And you're perfect," I swore, stepping so near that when he inhaled his chest brushed against me. "Don't fight who you are."

"Ugh." *Pop.* He stepped back again.

"What?"

Voice deeper, he rasped a confession. "You're *killing* me."

"What? How?"

"Every time we touch . . . whenever I catch your scent . . . or see or hear you flirting . . . I just want . . ."

"What?"

He looked away.

"What do you want, Pietr?"

"I want *you*."

"Wha—? *Ohhh*." I stepped backward. Stumbling, I tried to reason it out. "It's because of your bizarre metabolism, isn't it? Like—your biological clock is ticking or something. You guys mature at a different rate, right, so it's your normal . . ."

He barked out a laugh. A very nervous laugh. *"Da*. My normal." He rubbed his eyes, clearing the red. "Alexi says I'm running hot—my system's not synched up yet with the changes."

"This—was this . . . ?"

"My secret. I want you," he grated out. "And I can't . . . I need to be focused to find a way to get Mother out. I can't be thinking about *you* every seven minutes. . . ."

"Every seven minutes?" Wasn't that how often my Health Ed book postulated guys thought about sex? Why did I remember *that* and still struggle with the order of planets in our galaxy?

Pietr's burgundy blush confirmed my hypothesis.

I fumbled for my worry stone, trying to get a handle on a lot more than just it.

"Wait. Sarah can hug and kiss you and . . . ?"

His mouth turned up in a cruel smile. "Nothing."

"But . . ." I stepped forward, resting my hands on his chest.

Tenderly he took my wrists and stepped away. Again. "Let's not test my self-control." He shivered, letting me see his human-form quake and his eyes glow, the wolf dancing just beneath his skin, begging to run free.

"What would happen if you *did* lose control? Oh." I drew back. "It's not like in those vampire books, is it?"

This time, he laughed in earnest. "No. We may not be Romeo and Juliet or Lorenzo and his Jessica, but we certainly aren't *them*, either. I have no desire to drink your blood."

"But what you *do* want to do—"

"Neither of us is ready for. It doesn't matter. The wolf's winning most of the time—confusing my impulses and reactions. When I've tamed him, we'll have . . . other issues," he said like a promise, no threat at all.

"Huh." Issues I had plenty of.

"Being away from you hasn't helped," he admitted. "I've used Sarah's scent as a shield too often. I've built a tolerance."

I tugged at my hair. "Pietr, Sarah's . . ." I couldn't say it. Didn't want to think it.

"*Da*. I know. Every guy's already congratulated me for *nothing*. She must have really been—"

"*Popular*," I concluded. "Ugh!" I hopped from foot to foot in frustration. "This sucks. So I'm not allowed to hug or kiss you . . . until when?"

"Until my self-control comes back."

"Do you have an ETA on that self-control?"

He snorted. "I've been working on it," he groaned. "Believe me, Jess. I'm struggling. You—you're my Vassilissa—"

From the illustration he'd given me for my birthday—the illustration that now hung above my bed.

"My light in this darkness."

I sighed. "Just to review—you lose control and—"

"Change."

"And—what? Hump my leg?"

"*Nyet*." He chuckled. "But it'd be bad if a wolf ran loose between classes."

"Point taken. Wait. How come after you tried to change your service learning assignment and I kissed you, you didn't—?"

"I fought like hell," he groaned, scrubbing at his hair with his hands. "And then I did a few laps around the track. My personal best, by the way. I beat you to class by moments."

"Oh." It was an ego trip of huge proportions. I could make a guy crazy and not in the set-a-fire-in-the-shape-of-my-name crazy sort of way. And I was making the right guy crazy. Okay, probably poor Smith, too. But he was collateral damage. Pietr was my target.

And I was right on.

"You can't be my friend?"

"*Nyet*. I want so much more than just friendship from you."

"Huh." *That* I could deal with. "We're not between classes now," I murmured.

I grabbed him so fast he didn't have a chance to dodge. Lips crushing his, I moved my mouth with a fervor I'd never felt before, and he reciprocated with unmatched heat and hunger: my kiss full of all the confusion, pain, and hope I'd been feeling since he first changed—his kiss strong as our mutual need for reunion. And in a moment my human Pietr fell back, blurred, and the wolf burst free of his clothing and raced away.

I pushed the shredded outfit with the toe of my boot. He wouldn't wear *that* again. I'd have to correct Cat about wolves exploding out of their clothing.

I laughed my first real laugh in weeks.

My cell phone rang. "Yeah, Dad. We're on our way. Rio did great. Yeah—I didn't do half bad, either."

CHAPTER THIRTY-THREE

The autumn breeze snatched at my hair and nipped at my neck as I stepped off the bus. Glad the school doors were only a few quick steps away, I was surprised to find Sarah waiting for me. More than surprised. Frightened, actually.

She let out a long sigh and raced over. Before I could think to defend myself she grabbed me in a fierce embrace. I struggled to mask my shock, peering over her head full of soft, angelic blond curls and searching for a clue about her behavior up until the moment she released me.

"What's going on?" I asked, trying to keep the apprehension from edging into my voice.

She pouted, her lips perfect for the expression. "It's Pietr," she said.

"Oh. What happened?" I hoped the question sounded better to her ears than it did to mine.

"He broke up with me."

"Oh." What could I say? Not I'm sorry you broke up, because I wasn't. I couldn't lie about that. "I'm sorry you're hurt, Sarah," I managed.

As the morning continued, I started believing Pietr wasn't coming to school at all. Although Sarah was hanging around, Derek, her current cohort, was seldom seen. Of course, Max was constantly throwing Amy and myself in shadow, totally on guard.

Even playing the gruff guardian there was a new light in Max's eyes everytime he looked at Amy.

I became comfortable with Sarah not knowing Pietr'd broken up with her for me. But when Sarah announced, "He broke up with me over the phone," I thought almost exactly what Amy said.

"That gutless wonder!" Hands on her hips, Amy became the enraged female representing all females. "How could he do that? How dare they expect us to invest our time and emotional energy and then, when we really feel something for them, we get *the call*." She shook her head, auburn hair tossing. "Just because the guy's good looking doesn't mean he shouldn't step up and say it's over to your face."

"You broke up with Marvin by calling," Sarah pointed out.

"Totally different circumstances," I assured; wincing.

"Besides, I don't think it's over," Sarah confided. "I think he just has roaming eyes. In Russia, some married men keep a mistress or two—a *paramour*. Did you know that?"

I glanced at Max for confirmation.

He shrugged. "It happens everywhere."

Sarah ignored him. "He just needs to know things are different here," she continued. "When he realizes what he's missing out on, he'll—"

"What?" Amy asked. "Come trotting back?"

"*Galloping* back," Sarah corrected. "Fast as *quicksilver*."

I swallowed, patting her shoulder. "Sometimes things don't work out like we want. Maybe it's better this way. I mean, I'm sure there's someone just waiting for you. What about—" I gulped, thinking of Sarah and Derek getting back together. Officially. What if he'd been part of the reason she'd been so horrible before? Sophie wasn't the only girl who shared a past with Derek. "What about Derek?"

She shrugged. "Derek's okay as a friend, but we're just not that way anymore. You know?"

Amy tried to help by adding, "Well, you're young, attractive, bright . . . . I'm sure the right guy's out there."

"The right guy," Sarah said, "is Pietr."

As if he'd heard his name, Pietr appeared, taking my hand and smiling as if we were the only two people in school.

Crap.

"Pietr." Sarah looked at him, then at me, and her wistful gaze settled on our hands. Together. "Oh."

She shot a look at Amy. "How bizarre," she hissed, eyes narrowing. "You were *actually* trying to make me feel better."

Amy shrugged. "I like to try everything once."

Max rumbled, hopeful. *Bad boy.*

"So, is there anyone here that didn't know about this little development—other than me?" Sarah raised her hand in mock encouragement.

No other hands went up. Not even Sophia's, although I'd never told her any part of it.

"Great," Sarah said. "Everyone knew except me. So how long have you been . . ." She paused, the word she wanted suddenly gone. "How long have you been—*plotting*—this?"

"I never planned—"

"No," she snapped, and I saw the old fire, the old danger, rising in her eyes. "You *had* to plan. Not one of my boyfriends ever left me without some"—she paused, grappling with words—"some *conniving* girl laying plans or getting *laid.*"

Pietr bristled at the implication.

"Look, Sarah, I'm sorry." I remembered how pitiful the words sounded coming from Pietr, but hoped they seemed more authentic from me. They were still just words. Ugly little syllables that meant so little.

"Oh. Well, then it's okay. As long as you're *sorry.*"

I watched her like I'd watch a copperhead.

"Pietr." She slid up to him, boldly pressing herself against him and sliding her hand between ours to shake his free. She raised her face to him so he could easily read the heat and promise in her eyes. "I know what you know. We're not over. I understand temptation," she confided. "And maybe if I haven't found someone else by the time you get tired of Jessica—I mean, how long can that really take?—maybe I'll take you back. *If* you're lucky."

Max and Pietr both stiffened as Derek slid up behind Sarah and settled his hands on her shoulders.

"Come," he whispered, looking at me as he took her hand.

I trembled at his tone.

Together they stalked off, Sarah adding a little wiggle to her walk for Pietr's benefit.

Pietr's arms wrapped around me like a shield and he held me so tight I knew he tested his resistance. I slipped out of his grasp. He was being bold. Trying so hard to give me what I wanted and what he struggled with.

"Yee-aaah. Psycho," Amy said, giving a long, low whistle.

"Super Freak psycho," Max confirmed, humming the old song.

"Okay." I gave Pietr's hand a quick squeeze. "That could have definitely gone better. I mean, wasn't this what we were trying to avoid?"

"*Eezvehneetyeh.* Sorry, Jess. We broke up last night."

"Yeah, over the phone," I reprimanded.

Amy socked him in the arm. "That's for women everywhere," she added. "Psycho and sane."

Sophia's mouth tilted into a little smile. "I don't know how you get into so much trouble, Jessie," she said in her soft voice. "But you're always entertaining."

"Niiice." I let go of Pietr long enough to brush my fingers through my hair. "I think we'd better cool things for a while."

"What do you mean?"

"No huggy-kissy. Hold hands occasionally, but nothing Sarah could misinterpret as rubbing it in that we're together. Not in public. I don't want this to be harder on her than it already is."

Max grumbled on Pietr's behalf. "Eventually, Jessie, you'll need to throw the dog a bone."

My cell phone buzzed, vibrating across my bedside table, and I snatched it up to stare bleary eyed at the name. *Wanda.* Why couldn't she leave it be? Ever since our first visit to see Pietr's mother, Wanda had been vehement about me not seeing Pietr. She always dressed her messages up in the guise of being worried about me—my health, my heart . . . But I knew there was some other motivation—some hidden agenda—she was keeping.

And her interference was botching her relationship with Dad because he was finally trying things my way. Dad had insisted Pietr show him his grades and luckily they earned Pietr a reputation as worthy of tutoring me. So Pietr helped me with school and I helped him with life. And acceptance.

We enjoyed several days of peace and quiet, Pietr and I curled up on the love seat at the Rusakovas' studying. I briefly believed my grades might be salvageable. Those days Alexi and Cat were scarce, and Max and Amy were everywhere, laughing and flirting outrageously. But beneath it all the stress of not having Tatiana, their mother, free was wearing on us all.

The Rusakovas had all gone back to visit a few times, but the CIA (an organization I increasingly doubted was what they claimed to be) kept making excuses about freeing Tatiana. They kept asking for more samples. And more time.

I didn't even look at Wanda's text before I erased it, glanced at the clock, and called Max. He picked me up as soon as Dad and Annabelle Lee were fed and my chores were done.

Back at the Rusakova house, we gathered around the thirteen journals as soon as Amy headed out for a run. Max went along with her, still worried Marvin might do something stupid. Amy promised to go slow and easy on him, but Max suggested he could go as fast as she wanted, boldly pointing out he had *amazing* endurance. All said with an undeniably wolfish grin.

Lying on the floor, Pietr sprawled beside me (testing his own endurance). I flipped through the old books. "So this really is the one we need," I said, tapping Hazel's offering.

"*Da*," Alexi said. "Now it's a matter of putting it all together. It appears your Mrs. Feldman got further in this than she suspected." I did not question his reluctance to call her something more familial. "Her notes are quite promising. This, my research, and Grandfather's . . .

We may have something. We just can't define these last two ingredients my grandfather suggested. They don't make sense when you read them in Russian."

"Well, what do they say?" Before he'd opened his mouth I specified, "In translation. Seriously. Russian is lovely, but you might as well speak Greek to me for all the good it'd do."

Alexi sighed. "I thought Pietr was teaching you Russian."

I blushed and Cat giggled. "None that deals with chemical reactions." I thought for a second. "Or maybe it does," I said with a snort.

Pietr groaned.

"I don't want to know," Alexi insisted. "What's annoying is it seems he tried to disguise his list. Like he didn't want his ideas to fall into the wrong hands."

"Luckily nobody knew enough about his research to go after any of it until very recently."

"Here," Alexi tapped the page. "I'm warning you—Grandfather fancied himself a poet. This ingredient is described as: Ancient tears from sappy eyes whose pining tops brush 'cross the skies."

"Amber," I said.

They all looked at me.

"What? You guys must totally suck at crossword puzzles. I'll bet I could trounce you in Boggle, too. Ancient tears, sap, pine. Amber. The pendant . . . next?" I challenged.

"This one is wolfsbane," he mentioned, moving down the short list.

"Seriously?"

He nodded. "Most legends are based on real things."

"You'd like my history teacher. So. You have any, Alexi?"

"Wolfsbane? Of course."

Pietr snarled. "Nasty stuff."

"Easiest way to ground an unruly werewolf," Alexi chuckled. I looked at him briefly. Ever since the first visit to Mother, Alexi was looking better. Healthier. Letting his pseudo-siblings know he was doing what was needed all along—having Mother's stamp of approval—made a huge difference. "And this is something like: The life, which liquid, runs in part from trembling hand to heavy heart."

I shrugged. "Blood."

"Whose blood?" Cat asked.

"Wait. Um . . ." Alexi slid out another journal. "Grandfather postulated that opposites attract for a reason, that everything had some strange balance or equilibrium it sought out. Like, once two very different things came together, you could find their commonality."

I looked at Pietr. "We're very different, and yet we're together. What if it's my blood?"

Pietr cringed at the thought.

"At the lab the day they did the initial tests . . ." Alexi closed the journals. "Your sample looked like it was fighting Max's."

I gulped. "It's my heart," I tugged out the amber pendant, dangling it before them. "My blood. Holy crap. I'm the cure?" I flopped onto my back. "That's why Wanda . . ."

"What?"

"She's been absolutely refusing to drive me here. She and Dad got into an argument. She wanted me grounded for going off with Max to Marvin's place and not saying anything."

"The CIA knows what we've known all along," Cat said. "You're a real part of this."

"Ugh. But, Wanda said she wants you all to be cured—to be normal," I insisted.

Pietr sat up, looking into my face. "A: Max will never be normal. B: How is it the one werewolf movie you haven't seen is *Dog Soldiers*?"

"It's a soldier movie with werewolves, not a werewolf movie with soldiers," I returned.

"I agree with Pietr," Alexi said. "The CIA doesn't want them cured. They need to make more of them and unfortunately they only have directly related purebloods at this point, so they can't risk breeding them."

"We're right here, you know," Cat said in disgust.

"*Eezvehneetyeh*." Alexi continued. "So to have any chance at replicating their genetics they need all the DNA they can test before it breaks down too far with age."

My heart squeezed. "Most human DNA starts breaking down

at an *early* age." I rubbed my forehead and looked at Alexi. He knew. "Oh, God. Your mother's DNA," I said. "It can't do the job. Her . . ."

Pietr nodded, realization dawning. "Her usefulness has reached its end. Except as a lure to us." His eyes closed, and I pulled myself up to wrap my arms around him.

"We need to get her out." I said what everyone knew even more acutely now.

"And we need to have the cure ready," Cat stated.

"I'll do whatever I can to help," I promised.

Cat took control. "*Horashow*. We'll need a sterile kitchen knife, a bowl, and your arm."

I peeled myself away from Pietr to gather supplies from the kitchen. In the dining room I set down a bowl, a knife, and a mortar and pestle I'd cleaned the dust out of.

Cat brought bandages, and Alexi contributed a pretty awesome chemistry set. Cat pushed up my sweater sleeve as I sat at the table and she swabbed my arm.

Alexi muttered, "If these notes are correct . . ." He reached for the pendant I gladly gave over. My heart was the least I'd give to help the Rusakovas. "We shouldn't need much of the amber—or much blood—to make this work."

He set the pendant in the mortar and handed both it and the pestle to Pietr. "Go ahead. You broke her heart before. This time do it for a decent reason."

Pietr growled, forcing the pestle into the mortar, and I heard the pendant crunch apart. He ground it slowly, deliberately, so he didn't stir the fine dust and lose any of the precious stuff.

The front door opened and for a moment we all froze, expecting Amy to bound in and up the stairs for a shower. Max surprised us instead, scoping out the situation. "Back in a minute!" he called out over his shoulder.

I felt a slice as the knife zipped across my arm and a warm trickle as my blood ran.

Max was rooting around, looking for something in Amy's backpack. "That girl's going to wear me out," he admitted, withdrawing a sketchpad and pencils. He grinned. "But I'm loving every minute. Everything okay in here?"

Alexi nodded.

I looked at the red puddle gathering in the bowl by my elbow. "And human blood doesn't . . ."

Max snorted and Pietr chuckled.

"Jessie," Cat admonished. "We aren't sharks. Or vampires," she added wistfully. "Human blood doesn't do it for us."

"Far too tainted with chemicals and preservatives," Pietr whispered. "The only time it's attractive is if it's laced with a substance a oborot has a major attraction—"

"—or addiction to," Cat added. "Heroin, meth, cocaine . . ."

"Pizza," Max whispered, eyeing me devilishly. "What did you have for lunch today, Jessie?" he growled, licking his lips.

"You're such a pain," I muttered.

"Stating the obvious," Pietr pointed out.

"Hey," I called to Max. "Has Amy started drawing again?"

"*Da*. But she'll kill me if I show you. Mostly they're nudes," he puffed out his chest. "Of *me*."

"Liar," I called his bluff. "What's she really working on?"

"*Me*," he declared with a wiggle of his eyebrows. "Almost as much as I'm working on her." He winked roguishly.

"The blood's coming faster," Pietr marveled, leaning over my arm to watch.

"Because your brother's pissing me off," I snarled.

"I can show you one I drew of her. . . ." Max pulled a loose sheet of paper from between the sketchpad's pages, holding it up proudly.

A stick figure with a red scribble of hair and boobs stared back at me, smiling.

"Max!" I snapped.

He tucked it away and shrugged. "Yeah. She said: *No more paper for you!*"

"That's plenty of blood," Pietr announced, and Cat bandaged me up.

"Glad to speed the process," Max teased, placing a sloppy kiss on my forehead before heading back to Amy.

Alexi carefully measured the ingredients, mixing some of the powder and dried wolfsbane into the blood before pouring it into a beaker and slowly applying heat.

Max reappeared in the foyer to rummage for something else. His nose wrinkled. "Gross."

I agreed. "Definitely pungent. That—"

"Smells like Cat's cooking," Max concluded.

"Very nice, Maximilian," Cat pouted. "I do not recall you complaining when you licked the meatloaf dish."

"I did that purely in self-defense. If I hadn't eaten it, it would have come for me," he protested.

Cat threw a notebook at him.

Max dodged, laughing. "We'll be on the back porch. For . . . An hour?"

Alexi nodded. "*Horashow.*" He checked the temperature of the mixture and turned off the heat. "Well. It should be that simple. Amazing what might be undone if someone's willing to make a small sacrifice and take a risk."

"So what now?"

"We'll need to test it. See what it does to a sample of their blood on a microscope slide."

"Do you have a microscope?"

Pietr hissed something at Cat.

Alexi nodded, ignoring them. "Upstairs. I'll go get it. We'll test our cure against their blood and see what happens. If we get a result we can decide if it's to be ingested or injected."

Pietr hissed again.

"It will take a little more time, but science generally does," Alexi explained.

I couldn't help it. I turned away from Alexi to see what Pietr was complaining about.

"Cat!" Alexi cried out, staring in horror.

"Time is precisely what we don't have, Alexi," Catherine said apologetically. She smiled, her teeth stained a sobering dark red and brown with my blood. "Weren't you the one just talking about sacrifice and risk?"

"*Da*," he whispered. "But, it's like medicine . . . the dosage . . ."

"Will be fine," she assured him. "Ugh."

"What? What is it?" he demanded, giving her a little shake.

She wrinkled her nose. "Little—aftertaste. I think I should sit down. Or—" She looked at me.

"Head to the bathroom?" I was closing the bathroom door behind us when she finally nodded agreement.

"Are you okay?" I asked.

She swayed, and I helped her sit on the cold tile floor by the tub. "I will be far better than okay if this works, Jessie," she confided. "To be a normal human—have a normal life span—that is better than anything I have ever dreamed of."

She clutched her stomach and groaned. "Ohhh."

"I'll get Alexi—" But she grabbed my arm and said plainly, "*Nyet*. I don't want him to see me—like this—*ohhh*. Pietr. Get Pietr." She sagged against the side of the tub, eyes narrow and unblinking.

I barely had time to turn the knob before he slid past me to kneel beside his twin.

"I heard," he whispered. "It hurts, *da*?"

"*Daaa*." She bit her lower lip to keep from crying out.

"Like the change?"

"Ugh. More—*noise*," she panted, pressing her hands to her ears. "Oh. I think—"

I screamed when the wolf flashed into being, wiping out Cat. Eyes burning, tongue darting between snapping teeth, it lunged at me.

Pietr was between us in a heartbeat, crushing the breath out of me as he pinned me against the bathroom door. Alexi shouted for us to let him in from the other side. Pietr's heart beat so hard it threatened to leap out his back and into me. This was new to him, too.

Not reassuring.

"Catherine. Ekaterina!" He growled something at her in Russian, and his body burned as fur sprouted all along his head, neck, shoulders, arms, and torso. There was a crunch as if all the bones and joints in him struggled to shift at once. With a wail that rocked me he melted from human to wolf, T-shirt pulling apart. Slick jaws snapping, he stooped toward her, the hair on his body rising and making him look even bigger—even more terrifying than I'd ever seen him in his wolfskin.

Still wolf, Cat whined, throat trembling out a final threat as she dropped to the floor and exposed her soft belly. Submitting.

Pietr's jaws clamped shut on the ruff of her neck and he pulled her up, shaking her soundly before dropping her back down. He snorted out a breath so hot it fogged the bathroom mirror.

Cat shivered on the floor while Pietr slowly regained his human form and his senses.

"What's happening?" Alexi demanded, pounding on the door so hard it rattled me.

"She changed. I don't know." I tried to explain through the bathroom door, my hand on Pietr's bare back. "It's like she poofed into her wolfskin and now . . ."

"*Not* my week to clean the bathroom." *Max.*

"Get back to the porch and keep your girlfriend busy," Alexi demanded.

"Hard to keep her focused with so much noise," Max grumbled, marching back down the stairs. Beneath his grumpy facade I heard real frustration as he worried about Cat.

"Now what, Jessie? Can you let me in?"

"No. Sorry. Cat said you weren't allowed."

"Dammit." His fists thundered against the door again.

"She'll be fine, Alexi," Pietr reassured, his voice steady. I was the only one to see the way his hands shook. To see the fear reflected in his eyes.

Suddenly the wolf convulsed, giving one long shudder that shook her from snout to tail and she tore straight down her center, ripping in half as simply as I'd separate a paper towel from the roll. Catherine flopped forward, out of the wolfskin, spattered in gore. Simple, human, and exhausted, she smiled in vindication.

CHAPTER THIRTY-FOUR

Strangely, things between Sarah and me improved. It was almost like we were back to our pre-Pietr time, Sarah swallowing books whole— Shakespeare's *Macbeth* and Orwell's *Animal Farm*—and me not doing any PDA. Max and Amy made up for my lack of public displays of affection, though, and I worried, catching Marvin glaring at them one morning before Derek led him away, hand on his shoulder. Sophie followed our antics from a distance, watching thin air with quiet curiosity almost as frequently as she watched us.

"Is she here?" I asked after everyone had scattered to classes.

Sophie's forehead creased, her focus somewhere else, like she was trying to hear something a great distance away. She nodded. "She gets clearer," she breathed, "when she really tries. I think she wishes you could see her, too."

I looked at the same spot that held Sophie's rapt attention. No luck. "It's enough I know she's around occasionally," I assured.

"She's always around," Sophie corrected.

"Oh." Thinking about my mother as witness to the quick make-out session Pietr and I had had the previous night, I muttered, "I am *so* grounded when I die. . . ."

Sophie chuckled.

"What's she doing?"

"Hear no evil, see no evil . . . I think she means she knows when to cover her eyes and ears."

"Mom always had a strong sense of humor."

"She's glad you're staying away from Derek, too."

"Yeah. I wish I knew why that was so important. I mean . . . I know he's mixed up in some weird stuff here, but . . ."

"Stay clear of him, Jessie," Sophie intoned. "No matter what. You've been really lucky so far. But even luck runs out."

Mr. Belden stepped out of his classroom, glaring. "Tardy bell in three—"

I rushed the door . . .

"Two—"

. . . slid across the floor . . .

"One—"

. . . and into the seat by Pietr.

The bell rang. Belden slapped a pink slip of paper on my desk. "Detention," he declared.

"What? I made it . . ."

"Running in the hall." ·

"That is absolutely unfair," Pietr muttered.

"What was that Mr. Rusakova?" Belden asked.

Pietr paused, coming to a decision. "That's unfair. It absolutely *sucks.*"

Another pink slip was produced. "One for you as well." Belden seemed quite satisfied.

But Pietr was more so.

We were mired in quadratic equations when the desk behind me lurched and I felt something hot and wet spatter across the back of my shirt. "Oh. God." I'd know the smell anywhere.

Vomit.

Out of our seats, we all stared as Kylie Johansen convulsed on the floor, fountaining like a lawn sprinkler set on random. Belden was on the intercom, nurse on the way as Pietr and I pulled desks away from Kylie's writhing body.

The nurse shouted for us to clear the room. EMTs arrived so fast I wondered if Junction High kept them on stand-by. The classroom door shut. Stunned, my mouth wouldn't. I looked at my classmates. Stephen Marx held his head like he had a migraine to beat anything, and Lynn Marretti clutched her stomach, pale and quivering. In fact, all of my classmates except Pietr looked like absolute crap. And *I* was the one coated in spew.

Mr. Belden looked at me as the EMTs rushed Kylie's body down the hall on a stretcher. "No detention," he muttered, wrinkling his nose as if I was the worst thing ever smelled in his classroom. "You've been punished enough."

Pietr served detention, and Max insisted on taking Amy and me out for coffee after school since I'd ditched the nasty sweatshirt and just looked like one more raving fan of the Junction Jackrabbits, wearing my school gym shirt in public. It was remarkably civilized of him— no drive-thru or Grabbit Mart coffee for us—he parked in front of the newest and most European of the cafés crowding Junction's Main Street. As our small talk waned to nearly nothing, he caught my eye.

"Pietr, Alexi and I are going out tonight."

"Oh." My heart sank. "Tonight?" It was suddenly too soon, too frightening. I knew time was running out. I knew the CIA wasn't cooperating. They'd keep Mother as long as she lived *if* it guaranteed them access—and a sense of control—over the Rusakovas. But when Wanda started trying to keep me from the Rusakova family, the wolves decided it was time to make a move against them. To get Mother out and consider a new strategy. Maybe a new location.

Dammit. With Cat cured, it left only two werewolves and one human against a nest of agents. I had strictly been told by my occasionally canine guardians I was not allowed to go.

I ran my straw along the bottom of my cup, sucking up the last bits of mocha and caramel. They didn't taste nearly as sweet now I knew.

"How bad could it be, Jessie?" Amy punched my shoulder. "They're going out for *one* night. In Junction. Pietr's not looking to hook up with anyone but you." She slid her finger around the inside of her cup to scrape off the last bits of whipped cream.

Max stared. I totally understood the title of the song "Hungry like the Wolf."

Oblivious, Amy licked off her finger. "I mean—how much trouble can they possibly get into, in Junction?"

"Yeah," Max said, his voice suddenly an octave lower. "How much trouble could I—we—how much trouble could *we* get into in a town this small?"

"With you at the wheel, too much." I kicked him under the table for emphasis.

A brief stop at one of the half-dozen local pharmacies—seriously, how many did a town the size of Junction really need?—and the Rusakovas were again stocked with bandages, salves, and an assortment of painkillers and first-aid-related items.

Amy looked at Max as he filled the cart, and he shrugged, smiling. "You know Pietr has a predisposition for injury."

Amy nodded, surely remembering the ATV ride when we were both so scared Pietr was dying. That had been well before I knew Pietr had basically been dying since he turned thirteen and normal things—like concussions and near-death experiences—meant little to his overall health.

I gawked. "I may know *that*, but I sure didn't know you knew the word *predisposition*."

"Not just a pretty face," he snorted.

Amy grinned.

"So, if you guys are going out tonight, what are the girls going to do?" Amy asked.

"I'm staying over," I mentioned.

Amy was ecstatic. "Sleepover!"

"We have strict rules about pillow fights," Pietr stated.

"*Da,*" Max drawled. "No pillow fights unless the boys are present to watch." A sly grin twisted his lips.

Amy shoved him, and Max stumbled back like her little push mattered. "We can watch a movie . . . play some games," she suggested, shrugging a single shoulder. "It'll be great."

"Yeah, but it's still a school night," I pointed out. "I need to get this stupid heart project done for Bio, and we should all be asleep at a reasonable hour." Hopefully I could get Amy squirreled away downstairs before the boys came back with Mother. Amy was a heavy sleeper. . . . It might just work.

I suddenly realized I didn't know what was supposed to happen if the boys succeeded. Why hadn't I been told?

Cat spoke up. "I may have to leave early in the morning—catch a flight, I hope." She continued before either Amy or I could ask *a flight to where?* "So I might need one of you to handle breakfast."

"Please," Max agreed.

Cat rolled her eyes at him.

"Anyway, we'll be out all night," Pietr said.

"Imagine us at Denny's," Alexi suggested to us. "Wolfing down gigantic helpings of pancakes."

"I will." At least I'd try. It was far more pleasant than what they'd really be doing.

We ordered pizza. There was an air of celebration about things. And when the moment came for the boys to leave, I got twitchy. Terrified. I knew I couldn't go. Knew I'd be a liability. I wasn't stealthy, I wasn't strong. I surely couldn't handle getting shot. But the idea of sitting in the old Queen Anne house while they risked their lives to free their mother . . .

Standing on the front porch, Pietr brushed a strand of hair back from my cheek and tucked it behind my ear. His fingers trailed gently down the side of my face until he cradled my chin, peering into my eyes. His breath hot against my lips, my heart pumped so fast under his intense gaze I could no longer pick out individual heartbeats; it seemed to hum along. Pietr pressed his lips against mine, his hands tracing the curve of my neck and slipping over my arms and onto my back. He wrapped them around me, pulling me closer.

I slid my arms up and around his neck, closing my eyes and turning off my senses except those absorbing him.

I heard only Pietr's breathing. I tasted only Pietr's lips. I smelled only Pietr's wild woodsy scent. And I felt—I felt . . . Pietr's chest rising and falling against me. Pietr's arms like hot steel bands squeezing me close. Pietr's lips racing along my jawline and pausing by my ear. He filled my head with his words: "There is so little time. We need to make every moment count."

My fingers twined into the dark hair curling slightly at the nape of his neck and his breathing grew ragged. For the moment there was only us. "Easy," he whispered. "Jess, easy." I saw the fire crawl up in the depths of his eyes.

"I'm scared."

"Don't be," he commanded. "I can't worry about you tonight—I need to focus."

"Of course. Don't worry about me. But—"

"What?" he whispered, eyebrows drawing together as he looked down at me.

"Come back to me, Pietr. In one piece."

"As you wish." He crushed me to him, reminding me of the power he kept hidden beneath a surprisingly human-seeming skin. He covered my mouth with his and kissed me with his eyes open so I could see the slow burn I'd started.

I held on to him, fingers knotting in his shirt, sneakers climbing on to the top of his. "I'll do my best, Jess," he promised. "For you, I always do my best."

Alexi grabbed him, shoving him toward the car, already running in the driveway. "Come on, Max!"

Max hesitated for a moment on the porch. He looked at Amy. She met his gaze, undaunted, and answered his unspoken question. "I don't kiss somebody who's looking to kiss anyone but me."

He didn't even blink but grabbed her, dipped her, and kissed her until he'd guaranteed her knees would quake.

"Seriously?" she asked when she'd caught her breath. "You're going out, but—*you're* going out . . . ?"

"What sort of reputation do I have around here?" he muttered, watching Amy's expression from half-closed eyes.

"A well-earned one," I answered.

"Yee-aaah."

"Go. They're waiting for you."

He did, bounding down the steps and leaping into the car.

They sped away, and we turned back to the house. A house that felt oddly vacant without their wild energy.

I dropped my hand of cards when I heard the car in the drive. *Too soon*, I thought. I saw the same words—the fear—etch across Cat's forehead.

"What is it?"

Cat and I looked at each other, then at Amy. We'd imagined a different time line. We thought she'd be asleep when the boys rolled back in, successfully freeing Mother.

But, now . . . she was awake and aware.

We lunged for the door, Cat's fingers closing on the knob an instant before mine. Back in the dining room our chairs clattered to the floor. Cat looked at me, eyes wide, and sucked down a ragged breath. She flung the door open, gasped, and tore down the walkway.

I stood frozen in the doorway.

"What's going on, Jessie?" Amy asked from behind me. "You've lied a lot since your mom died. And I get it. The truth sucks most days. But—"

I felt the change in the air as Amy turned to look the way Cat had run.

Between us, the words died, strangled in our throats.

In the thin starlight I barely made out the silhouettes limping toward us. Two figures half-dragged, half-carried one between them, and Cat, the smallest, dashed around the edge of the damaged trio, speaking Russian in low and urgent tones.

"You should head to your dad's tonight."

"Hell, no. Tell me what's . . ."

I rounded on her, my eyes starting to sting as tears threatened. "If you won't go, at least get out of my way." I edged her farther inside as they climbed the steps and were bathed in the soft glow thrown by the porch's single bulb.

Alexi's weary face was smeared with blood, his shirt torn and spattered with red. Pietr was worse. A gash across his face marked a graze by a bullet. His shirt was ragged, the holes that tattered it edged in crimson. There was blood. Lots of blood. I reached for him even as I realized he wasn't the worst. He, at least, was walking.

Max, though—Max was a different story.

"Holy shit . . ."

"Inside," I ordered Amy.

She scrambled to obey.

"Phone down." It was all the reminder she needed that the Rusakovas did not dial 911.

She pocketed her cell as we pushed past. "What . . . ?"

"Sometimes it's better not to know, right?"

She nodded, swallowing the logic she'd spouted earlier.

Cat closed the door behind us, and together we eased Max onto the love seat in the sitting room. "I get tired of replacing furniture." Cat's voice wavered.

I reached beneath the marble-top table, brushing the wood with my fingers, remembering the bug I'd left. But I found nothing. Pietr smiled at me, a grim turn of his lips as blood trickled into one eye from another cut. Knowing the way Max ran his mouth, he'd removed the bug before the risk outweighed the benefit.

"You're last on the list," Cat informed Alexi. "Do we need to set a perimeter?"

"*Nyet*. They'll be picking up pieces for a while."

I didn't realize Amy had left us until she dashed back into the room, carrying an assortment of bandages and ointments.

"Good girl," Alexi congratulated her. "Now go home."

Cat snatched the packages out of Amy's hands and tore into them. "Pietr. You sit there and try not to bleed all over the upholstery. Max."

She stooped over him. "Max!" She slapped him, her hand cracking across his face.

His eyes pulled open as he fought for focus. "Sisterrr," he croaked.

"Wake up, idiot! I need to know where every bullet landed. Your body's trying to seal. And I'd bet they've spiked the ammo."

"*Da*," he agreed groggily. "They're not stupid. As long as they can get one of us, they'll have what they want."

"What the hell is he talking about?" Amy asked.

"Nothing," Cat insisted. "He's been hit on the head. Makes him even more stupid."

"But . . ."

"Get me the Leatherman by the door," Cat commanded. "Have you kept it sharp?" she asked Alexi.

"As a razor."

"*Horashow*. We need markers, too. Otherwise we might lose one . . . Sharpies are in the drawer."

Taking Pietr's hand, I made him press the gauze tight to his own head wound while I found markers.

"You boys run the risk of not being so pretty," Cat muttered as she swabbed the Leatherman's blade with alcohol. "Or so alive." She looked at me. "Get Pietr's shirt off and circle each entry wound. Then look for exits."

Nodding, I hesitated. How could I get his shirt off without hurting him more?

Cat's gaze flicked to me and she ordered, "Tear it off," as she focused once more on Max.

I grabbed the neckline of Pietr's shirt and pulled, the sound so like Cat's final transformation I froze. I fought to keep my eyes open, to view the wounds that marred Pietr's beautiful body, so pocked with holes. Hand trembling, I circled each one.

Pietr snared my wrist, steadied me. "It's not so bad, Jess," he said, catching my eyes with his own.

My vision blurred, eyes filling with tears. "I'm the liar in our relationship. Don't you start."

He leaned back, watching through narrowed eyes as my hands stumbled across his body, circling the wounds already trying to close.

"I need to see your back."

He grunted and rolled awkwardly over.

"Is it good or bad there's one exit wound?" I asked.

He insisted, "It's fine," but the last word came out with a wheeze.
"Liar," I protested.

"*You* do it!" Cat shrieked at Alexi. "Damn human hands—not
steady at all." Shaken, she stood by Max, the blade bloody in her
hand.

Alexi reached up and took the knife, making soothing noises.
"Circle the other wounds," he whispered. "I'll cut. I have more practice with my damn human hands."

"Here." Amy was beside me, kitchen knives in her hands, blades
bright and stinking of alcohol. "Take them all out?"

"Yes, every single bullet."

She nudged me. "Scoot over. Should we clean our hands?"

"I—" Regular infections didn't seem to matter to werewolves, but
what to tell Amy? At what point were lies more harmful than the
truth? Probably always. "Just get the bullets out."

"'Lucy, you got some 'splainin' to do,'" she said in her best Ricky
Ricardo impression. She set a hand on Pietr's stomach, nestling
the tracing of the bullet hole between her spread index finger and
thumb.

Pietr gasped when the knife dug in and I grabbed his hand.

"They heal so fast. . . ."

"Yeah." No point denying it.

She reached her fingers into the hole, digging around for the bullet's metal head.

Pietr writhed, face contorting, and I pulled my hand free of his so
I could rest all my weight on him. My face inches from his, I stared
down into his glinting eyes, ignoring the pinch of pain in his features
and the way Amy apologized each time she withdrew another bullet's head from Pietr's rapidly healing flesh.

Instead, I kept my best smile pasted across my lips and told him
about the things we'd do when winter arrived. I promised snowball
battles, sled races, and icicle sword fights ending with hours wrapped
up together by a roaring fire, sipping tea and hot chocolate. And the

whole time I talked, my heart ached, not knowing if he'd live to let me keep a single promise.

By the time Amy got to the last bullet, the wound was completely sealed, the skin smooth and soft as a newborn's.

Beside us, Alexi was cleaning up Max and himself. Cat was still and silent in the shadows, a tumult of emotion washing over her face.

"Are you sure there was a bullet there?" Amy asked, running a finger over the perfect flesh.

"I only circled bullet holes."

"And this one didn't have an exit?" She tapped his chest with the knife's handle.

Pietr had fallen into an uneasy sleep, my hand again in his, his unnaturally strong body exhausted.

"No. I'm sure something's there."

Max began to snore. Alexi gathered up the chunks of flesh. "Better burn these," he suggested to Cat. "Too good a sample for them to add to their collection."

She nodded, mute, and followed him out of the sitting room.

When Pietr convulsed, I jumped, crying in pain as his hand crushed mine. His eyes were wide and wild—unseeing—red flaring like wildfire. "Oouut!" he screamed. "Get it ouuut—"

"Shit!" Amy shrieked, losing her grip on the knife.

Pietr clawed at his chest, at the negligible circle of Sharpie marking his sealed wound. Blind with pain, he thrashed and howled, hands raking across his skin.

"Max!" I bellowed.

He was on Pietr in a heartbeat, taking him to the floor and pinning his arms over his head.

Pietr kicked out, his foot connecting with Amy's head. She crumpled where she stood, the knife she'd just retrieved clattering out of her grip. Alexi and Cat jumped on Pietr's legs, weighting them down.

Frozen in shock as he writhed, I watched all my promises to Pietr evaporating into nothing but worthless words.

"One's still in!" Cat growled. "Cut it out, Jessie!"

Gasping, I fell onto Pietr's chest, straddling him, digging the knife into his skin. "I can't—" I sobbed. "The rib—it's grown back—it's blocking my knife!"

"Hell!" Max snapped, adjusting his position and keeping Pietr's arms down with his knees. He raised a fist and slammed it down on Pietr's rib cage. Bone cracked beneath his assault, and foam speckled Pietr's gaping mouth.

"Now cut!"

I stabbed the knife in and pulled free a plug of flesh and gore, sweeping the wound with my fingers until I found the bullet. With a grunt I tore it loose, holding it above Pietr's prone body like the grimmest of prizes. It sizzled, burning the bits of flesh and blood that still clung to it.

Alexi snatched it from me. "Spiked. As if the genetic time bomb in them isn't enough."

Pietr stilled beneath me, his face taut with pain, his eyes closed, breathing finally steady. I brushed the hair, soaked with sweat, out of his eyes. I kissed him, gently, not caring that my lips came back tainted with sweat and blood.

"Amy!" I rushed to her, but Max was there already, cradling her in his arms.

"She'll be okay," he whispered. "Another bruise . . ."

"At least this one was unintentional." I pried open her eyelids, looking at her pupils. "Yeah, I guess she'll be okay."

"So fragile," Max whispered, his gaze shifting from Amy's peaceful face to my troubled one. "Maybe if we weren't . . ."

"Weren't what, Max?" My heart rattled.

"Weren't here." He picked Amy up and laid her on the love seat. "What if we weren't here, Jessie? What if the danger just left with us?"

"I'd find you."

He sighed. "Not if we didn't want you to."

"Don't you dare threaten me with leaving."

"We're threatening you by staying."

Alexi agreed from the doorway. "You'd be safer without us. You could have a nice, normal life, Jessie. Graduate high school. Go to a nice state school and get a degree. A good job. Meet a nice guy—settle down and have some kids and a dog. Live a nice, safe, long, and normal life, with a husband who will also live a good, long, normal life."

Tears prickled at the edge of my eyelashes. "Pietr can live a long life if he takes the cure," I protested, fingers folding into fists at my sides.

"He won't take it," Max said, examining the ceiling. "Not after what happened tonight. Neither of us will. We need the additional strength and abilities to free Mother."

I crossed the floor and sat on the edge of the love seat, taking Amy's limp hand. "Then stay away from her. You'll hurt her much worse than Marvin ever could if she loves you and you choose . . ." I struggled with the word. How could anyone choose *death* over a shot at life and love? "If you choose . . . to go."

Max knew what I meant. They all did.

"It's too late for me. Do you understand? I *love* Pietr."

Alexi started to open his mouth, but I stuck my hand up. "No, Alexi. I know what you'll say. It's the same thing my dad would say: I'm too young to talk about love. But I feel what I feel. I've had a lot of loss recently, you know?" I couldn't look at them, at their sad eyes, so I fixed my gaze on the bloodstained carpet. "I'd just like to hang on to love for a while now instead. It's too late for me," I repeated, stroking Amy's hand. "But it's not too late for her." I glared at the boy with the tousled curls. "Stay away from her, Max."

CHAPTER THIRTY-FIVE

As much as I didn't want to, Dad insisted I go to the match Wanda had arranged. During the day she came to pick me up, she asked, "Have you practiced enough to make this worth our time?"

"I've popped off a few rounds here and there."

"Maybe we shouldn't bother." She closed my door and sat in the driver's seat, her face drawn.

"Seriously?" A yawn stretched all the way along my spine, struggling out of my mouth.

"If you're tired . . ."

"I'm relaxed. Focused. Don't you want to go? I figured you'd put me on display—if I do well."

"You'll do well," she said, pulling into what passed as traffic on Junction's outskirts. She didn't sound like she believed it.

"Geez, Wanda, you're such a downer. Tell me good news for a change."

"Good news? How about I tell you how stupid that stunt was your boyfriend tried to pull the other night? Nearly got himself made into Swiss cheese, from what I hear."

"Yeah, he nearly died trying to free his mother. Did you even have a mother, Wanda? Do you know what it's like to lose one or know you'll lose her way too soon?" I turned to face her, straining against my seat belt. "God! Were you there? Did you have a gun on him?"

She pulled over. "No, I didn't. I wasn't even told when the shooting started. Do you know what that means, Jessie? Do you?"

I glared at her.

"I could lose everything because I keep stepping in on their behalf. The CIA wants to storm their house—drag their asses in, and I say, *Oh no, can't we be reasonable? They're kids*, I remind my superiors. *They're just confused—you know how teenagers are. Let's get them to cooperate*." She grabbed the steering wheel and shook it like she'd tear it off if she could. "I've called off so many plans to just take them in— *by force*, Jessie. And then they do this!"

"What do you expect them to do? She's dying!"

Wanda took a deep breath, shaking out her rage. "I expect them not to put me in that situation ever again. We have guys who are hospitalized."

"No one's dead?"

"No. It seems your boyfriend has pushed a no-kill policy with his little pack. I don't know if that'll help them or hurt them. By the way—where was Cat? She didn't get into the firefight at all, according to the report."

"Are we going to the match or not?"

We tore back onto the road as I sank into the seat, plugging in my MP3 player and focusing on rhythms like the beats between bringing a pistol up, firing and getting it down again. I didn't waste worry on anything—the Rusakovas were resting up at home with Cat and Alexi watching the perimeter. The CIA was still probably piecing stuff back together. I just worked to visualize my setup, the target, my moves.

In twenty minutes we came to an older rod and gun club. Wanda pulled the car to a stop on the gravel lot. She was tapping the dash.

I noticed the absence of other cars. "Huh. First ones here."

"We're early."

"Good." I liked to look at a range before anyone else got to it and

started acting nervy. It let me adjust the picture in my head and perfect my visualization before I even took out my gun.

"Jessie."

I dreaded her words.

"Do you really think I'd put you on display if you did well? Like,
make a big deal out of it? Embarrass you?" Wanda was even weirder
than normal today.

"You've coached me a little. The best thing some coaches do is
take credit."

"Oh." She turned off the car.

I caught her staring at me. "What?"

"I'm sorry I tried to push you toward that football guy and away
from Pietr." She sighed. "You're freakishly loyal, and that's a rare
thing." She picked at the steering wheel cover with one of her blunted
fingernails. "I'm . . . I'm proud of you, Jessie. You put yourself out there
for the people who matter most in your life. You can be really mature
sometimes."

"I'm the product of my environment. You grow up fast around
werewolves and CIA agents."

Wanda nodded and reached into the backseat to get my pistol
case. I thought she said something like, "Sometimes you don't grow
up at all."

"What?"

"Check out the range. In and down the hall."

I nodded.

"It's downstairs," she added.

"They leave it open?"

"Joe usually comes in, unlocks stuff, and goes in to town to get
real coffee," she nodded. "He makes the other stuff but won't drink it.
Used to be a competitor himself."

"Cool." I opened the clubhouse door. The scent of coffee greeted
me, a few empty Styrofoam cups stacked near a bottle of non-dairy
creamer, some packs of sugar, and a single spoon damp with coffee.

"Just say no." I turned down the hall, my feet echoing across the
peeling linoleum tiles and stirring up spirals of dust motes. The place
needed a good cleaning.

I took off my jacket and tucked it under my arm. Opening the door, I peered down the stairs.

"Ugh." The smell of damp places left dark too long tickled my nose. I shut the door again and turned back to the coffee. I wouldn't drink the stuff (today), but I'd try and use it to ward off the nastiness below.

Water steamed into the cup and habit nearly took over as I reached for the spoon. The damp plastic spoon. Didn't Wanda say Joe got coffee in town? Huh.

I mixed in the coffee crystals and headed back along the hall, opened the door, and started down the steps. The hair on my arms rose. Something wasn't quite right. I froze, listening for a clue, my eyes roaming.

Not good for keeping my pulse in check.

I heard something rustle downstairs to my right and I jerked, coffee sloshing.

A mouse appeared from behind a filing cabinet and raced across the basement floor.

I breathed again and continued down the stairs.

The first shot knocked me onto my butt, coffee slinging out in a long arc. Dazed, I watched Kent emerge from behind the haphazard arrangement of filing cabinets, tripods, and bullet traps—the odd assortment of metal all clubs seemed to accumulate. Light from a sliding-glass door spotlighted the gun as it wobbled in his hands, coffee dripping off him.

The damp spoon suddenly made sense. "Shouldn't drink coffee before shooting," I whispered.

"Sorry, kid. I wanted a quick kill." He sounded apologetic.

Now was the time for the heroine to blurt out something brilliant, something touching—something capable of changing a killer's mind. My mouth popped open. I gaped at him. "Not used to murdering teenagers?" Not brilliant. Not touching. Hell. My shoulder stung, and I noticed the long red line of a graze.

"Jessie!" Wanda yelled. No sense of decorum. Ranges were quiet places between shots. Didn't she realize that?

She thundered down the wooden stairs. "What the—?"

The nose of Kent's gun swung away from me, finding Wanda. Who was the greater threat: the agent—his coworker—with the gun case, or the kid with coffee streaming down her arm? "Wanda. Sorry. Headquarters decided to promote me."

"So you shoot Jessie?" She continued slowly down the steps, hands high, gun case at her shoulder. "What sort of organization are we in, Kent? I know we're far from any major hub and most of our superiors never talk to us face-to-face, but—"

"You're too close to this situation. You're not seeing clearly. You had a chance to get the cure—"

"*Jessica*," I snapped. "The cure has a name." I touched my shoulder. Nuts. Hole in my shirt. I liked this shirt. At least my jacket was okay.

Kent rambled on, "If the boy'd been able to do his part and get her under control, or if you could've kept her from the werewolves—stopped the risk of the rest of them being fixed—"

"They're sensitive about that phrase," I interjected. No, he wouldn't like me after this. But he'd shot me once already. My part in the popularity contest of life was probably nearly over.

His face pinked. "You screwed up, Wanda."

"So you shoot Jessie?" she repeated. She was beside me now. Making it easier for Kent to swing the gun's muzzle between us.

"I don't want to waste my life playing keep-away with werewolves. I'd rather eradicate the threat—the cure—*Jessica*." He moved the gun, steadying it so I was clearly in his sights.

His finger rested on the trigger. I wondered if it was a two-stage or a one-stage. It only made half a heartbeat's difference. . . .

Wanda made a bigger one.

A tooth flew out of Kent's mouth as the pistol case connected with his head and his shot went wide. Way wide.

Wanda had her sidearm in hand. "Up the steps, Jessie!"

I grabbed the pistol case and scrambled up the stairs. Behind me, I heard Wanda warn, "Don't make me—"

Then: pop-pop-pop.

I stood at the top of the stairs clutching my pistol case and still wondering what to do when Joe came in.

"You look nervous, young lady."

I nodded at the bizarre understatement.

"Have you tried sitting down and doing some visualization before the shooting starts?"

"I'm thinking it's not a good day for me to be down there."

"Mmm," Joe said thoughtfully.

"Can I borrow your phone?"

"Sure. Cells don't get a signal up here, but we've been around since the telegraph." I wondered if he included himself in the "we." He pointed to the landline.

I dialed Max with shaking fingers. He didn't ask why I needed a ride. I passed the phone to Joe for directions. And I watched the door. Waiting for Wanda. Or Kent. Either one would probably sneak out any other available exit.

Joe finished, giving Max a quick history lesson about the area (I imagined Max twitching), and handed the phone back.

"Drive carefully," I said.

Max knew what I meant.

A few competitors came through the door, nodding hellos. Coaches headed for the coffee.

"Bathroom?" I asked.

Joe pointed to the building's other end.

"Thanks." I stood before the two doors a moment, perplexed. Pointers. Setters. My eyes flicked from one sign to the other in question. Pointers. Setters. A guy slipped around me and opened the pointers' door.

Oh. Blushing, I opened the setters' door, locked it behind me, and set down the pistol case, working the cramp out of my arm. "Hurry up, Max," I begged, looking at myself in the mirror. The blood on my shoulder had dried, the sleeve sticking to it. I would've thought it strange that no one commented on my wound if I didn't understand the intensity of a target shooter's focus. Max could've shifted in front of them and they wouldn't notice.

"God, I hope he doesn't have to . . ." I opened the case, pulled out my gun, loaded the clip, and set it back down. I didn't want to use it on anything but paper. I eased my jacket on, jumping when someone pounded on the door.

"Jess!"

Fumbling with the knob, I fell into Pietr's arms. I knew he smelled blood on me. His eyes glowed, and as one arm tangled around me, he closed the pistol case, easing me toward the door. "Max is checking the area. Let's get you to the car."

I nodded.

"Any idea where Wanda is?"

"No," I whispered. "Dead? Busy burying Kent and putting in for his promotion?"

"Bring us up to speed in the car."

"This is bad, Pietr. I don't know what to do. Where to go. Is any- where safe? The Mafia's at my horse shows, and assassins are on the range. . . . I had a frikkin' gun and I wasn't safe."

His hand on the top of my head, he eased me into the backseat of the car and slid in next to me.

I touched his head, remembering his wounds. "They want to just drag you all in—cage you up. . . ." I slumped against his chest, snuf- fling and snorting, my tears sopped up by his T-shirt. "Why can't we have something normal?"

He stiffened. Clicked my seat belt together. "I'm not normal, Jess. You get out of something what you put into it."

"Oh, don't start with that crap again, Pietr. If you think you're the only not-normal one in this relationship, you really should look around." I took his arm, winding it around me. "Do you need to check on Max?"

"I'm not leaving you," he whispered, his lips in my hair.

"Good boy. Because if I'm going to be in trouble, I want you around for it."

Max came to the car grouchy. "Maybe we'll get lucky and they're killing each other in the woods."

Wanda alive wasn't what I'd qualify as helpful most times, but Wanda dead? If she'd really been trying to stand up for them—for us—"Shouldn't we try . . . ?"

"Nyet." Max backed the car up. "Just relax and let Pietr patch you up," he ordered.

I leaned against Pietr, letting him slide off my jacket. He looked at me. "I can take off your shirt. . . ."

I blushed.

"Or I can . . ." His eyebrows shoved together, deciding for me. He grabbed my sleeve and tore it, tugging the fabric away from my wound.

"Ow."

"*Eezvehneetyeh*," he murmured, cleaning and bandaging.

"I have a question," I said, my breath stirring the hair shadowing his eyes.

"*Da?*"

"I asked Cat about something, and then Mrs. Feldman asked you about the same thing. . . ."

"*Da?*" he glanced up at me. "What thing?"

"Imprinting."

Even through the rearview mirror I felt Max's eyes hot on the two of us as we leaned together like coconspirators.

Pietr sighed. "What do you want to know?"

"What is it? What does it mean to you to imprint?"

He rubbed his forehead. "It is strange in our—*kind*—the need to—procreate." He wasn't looking at me anymore. "It is probably because we live such abbreviated lives. There is a drive . . ."

"A powerful instinct," Max added.

"To mate."

"Oh. Leave it to me to ask *this* sort of question," I muttered, too embarrassed to blush.

"Imprinting . . . *Alexi speculates* . . . is a way we identify a mate capable of strengthening our bloodline, of allowing the wolf traits to dominate. It can happen anytime, but—"

"*Alexi speculates*," Max rumbled.

"It's most likely and clearest when we first change. And then it is an undeniable urge. A loyalty like no other. It is . . ."

"Nature determining the next generation's destiny," Max concluded.

"Is that why Alexi was so pissed you insisted on having me present for your first change?"

Pietr shrugged a single shoulder. Noncommittally.

"He was afraid we'd imprint." I touched my bandaged arm. "Did you want to . . ."

"*Imprint?*" Max chuckled.

Again, Pietr raised a single shoulder.

"But we're not . . . we didn't . . ."

"*Nyet,*" he whispered, leaning back in his seat belt to watch me with heavy-lidded eyes. "We're not imprinted."

"Do you wish we were?"

"*Nyet.*" A long sigh. "I don't think we get many choices in life," he admitted. "I like knowing—and I like you knowing—I *chose* you."

CHAPTER THIRTY-SIX

Pietr cupped my cheek in his hand and bowed to meet my lips, his eyes closing, lips soft as we stood in the shadows under a staircase in one of Junction High's dimmer, more distant hallways. I laced my fingers together across the back of his neck, drawing him down to meet my mouth as I pressed closer to him, pushing him into the darker shadows.

"We're going to be late," I whispered by the corner of his jaw. The footsteps on the stairs overhead rang out with less and less frequency.

"I'll take detention again for you," he volunteered, eyes gleaming. He slid his cheek along mine and nipped at my ear.

"I'm going to get a bad-girl reputation," I teased.

"As long as you only earn it with me . . ." And then his mouth was on mine again and I shivered, backpack sliding off my shoulder and hitting the floor with a slap.

He groaned, holding me tighter, crushing me to him, a sound deep in his throat boiling into a possessive growl.

A whimper and we jerked in surprise to see Sarah watching us, knuckles wedged between her teeth, tears streaming down her face as reality hit her.

"Oh, God—*Sarah!*"

With a sob she raced away, feet smacking a rapid retreat up the stairs.

"I have to—"

"Should I?" he asked, ready to accompany me.

"No. I don't think it'll help."

He nodded grimly. "See you in class." He slung my backpack over his shoulder as I flew up the stairs.

I zipped through the hallways, popping my head into each bathroom stall. Empty. Where would someone go to sob their heart out realizing their ex-boyfriend wasn't coming back and it was their best friend's fault?

I'd been so careful, trying to ease her into seeing Pietr and I together—in the open. I'd pushed him away so many times when I'd wanted to pull him close. We'd gone slowly as he built his resistance up and began taming his more canine impulses. There'd been many times I'd scowled at him when he gave me his puppy dog eyes and only recently had I let him drag me into the school's shadows to kiss me until my lips turned tender.

I froze outside Belden's classroom. He'd just turned on the overhead, displaying the day's bell work. Sitting there, prim, proper, composed, and cool was Sarah. Not curled in a bathroom clutching a toilet and bemoaning the sorry state of her love life. No. Writing down the assignment's answers. Smiling.

I stood staring just long enough for her to notice me. She turned her head and gave me a friendly grin. A wave. Stunned, I waved back. Then I noticed who sat on her far side. Macie and Jenny both leaned forward to peek at me. Jenny waved. Her smile was far too pleased for my comfort.

Back in my own class, I struggled to focus. This was bad.

When Macie surprised me by the water fountain, things got worse. "Macie, I don't want to start anything with you," I mumbled.

"Don't wet yourself, Jessica," she said with a sneer.

Across the hall Pietr pulled himself to his full height and raised an eyebrow at me. I shook my head.

"Look." Macie stepped forward, her body language threatening, her voice dropping. "Sarah's lost it. I don't know if it was seeing you two in lip-lock that sent her over the edge or what. She was teetering before, but now—*nuts*. And I'm warning you"—her eyes got big, *scared*—"things are gonna get real bad around here real fast. Jenny and I thought it would be great if she remembered . . . thought it would be great if she was her old self. . . . And she's definitely remembering, and my time—Jenny's time—ruling the school is going to end if you don't help us."

"*Help* you?"

"Think about it, Jessica. You want us running the big dogs around here, or do you want her back in charge?" She leaned in, her nose pressed to mine and I waved *no* at Pietr once more. "Because the bitch is back," she confided before she stomped off.

When I spotted Sarah in the hallway I knew things wouldn't be pretty. Except for her. She looked beautiful as an avenging angel with her perfect hair and perfect makeup.

"Sarah," I tried. "I'm sorry we hurt you." I reached out to her, but she smacked my hand away.

"You should have told me sooner. You should have been honest." She closed her eyes hard, a tiny crease appearing between her sculpted brows. "I thought we were best friends."

"We are," I insisted.

"No. Best friends don't steal each other's boyfriends."

Pietr stepped up. "Jess didn't steal me away. I chose her."

Her eyes lit up when he spoke to her; her expression softened. "Oh, Pietr." She sighed. "Guys never get it. Relationships aren't like that. There's no choosing, unless we choose to let you believe you've chosen."

"You're wasting your time here, trying to get her to see reason," Amy muttered to me.

"Sarah," I tried again. "I hope we can still be friends."

Amy puffed out an exasperated sigh.

Sarah's eyes shot wide open, a crooked smile rolling across her face. "Friends? You hope we can still be . . ." She rubbed her forehead, the scar at her hairline that her makeup helped hide. She refocused on me, her eyes glittering dangerously.

"People think I'm insane, do you realize? I've seen them stare, heard what they whisper to each other behind their hands in the hallways. The prettiest girl in Junction, all broke down and hanging with the losers. Then Pietr came along and our whole group's status jumped. Crazy what one guy can do to change so many lives. . . . But you know what, Jessica? Even if I'd lost my ever-loving mind, I'd never be as crazy as you if you believe—even for a second—I could be friends with you after what you've done."

"You raging psychopath! Jessie's the only one who stayed by you when you were *this* close to death!" Amy snapped, shoving Sarah's shoulder.

Sarah's purse whipped around her back, pencils, pens, and a single book flying. "Bitch!" she shrieked. "Don't you ever put your grubby hands on me again, trailer trash!"

Amy charged, but I grabbed her, locked my arms around her and planted my feet, grimacing as Amy fought to break free.

"Sarah, think about things again," I urged. "Remember in Ms. Wyatt's class—the quote you chose last project about life being a chance to grow a soul? I believe that. Remember that. I'm sorry we hurt you—we never meant to. Remember who your friends were after the accident. Who cared for you then?"

Macie and Jenny flanked Sarah suddenly, sneering so stylishly they could have won a snob-off competition. They looked nervous when I alluded to their abandonment.

Until Sarah laughed.

"Did you think I would ever expect *them* to spoon-feed me Jell-O in the hospital? They're a different kind of friend—the powerful, beautiful type. Are we bitches? Hell, yes! But I never expected anything more from them. *They* never disappointed me. But, you . . ." Tears wobbled at the edges of her eyes. "You made me expect more from people. You made me think there was trust to be had. You lied, Jessica Gillmansen! You lied about everything!"

Amy no longer pulled against me. Instead, she straightened, a wall to guard me from the seething devil with an angel's face.

Tears ruined Sarah's mascara. "Damn it!" She spun away and scrambled to pick up the contents of her purse while Jenny watched, amused. Macie spared me one pleading glance.

I flinched, wanting to go to Sarah, to help, but Amy changed her stance once more. She held me back, arms straight out like bars, shaking her head in mute warning.

In a moment Sarah was on her feet again, forcing her book into her purse.

Derek came up behind her, Marvin at his side. Derek watched the scene with eyes so dark they threatened to eclipse the blue that normally sparkled like cut sapphires. Beside me, Pietr bristled. The air between us hummed and I felt the growl build in him. I clutched his hand and the air stilled, the electricity between us settling.

"You're no friend of mine, Jessica Gillmansen. Don't think you ever were," Sarah declared with a hiccup of grief. She whipped away—right into Derek's open arms. He held her, whispered, and stroked the wispy blond strands of her hair, his eyes rising to meet mine.

My cheeks flamed, but my eyes fell to the book spine just peeking from Sarah's purse: *The Prince*, by Machiavelli.

I realized, watching them walk away, Sarah and Derek in front, Macie and Marvin trailing behind, with Jenny lost between, that the same brutal alpha and beta struggles that raged in wolf packs were also waged in high school.

Leaving the lunch line with only milk to complement the contents of my brown bag, I noticed Jenny grab Cat's attention and I wondered if she was also making a plea for our help to bring Sarah down. Cat seemed to have things well in hand and I glanced around the cafeteria, heading for our table.

Max was deep in conversation (as deep as Max could get) with Amy in a distant corner, out of earshot of the crowd. Try as I had to keep them apart, Amy adored Max. And who was I to stand between them? Time was short, as Pietr so frequently reminded me. Maybe we all needed to live life fiercely.

And love courageously.

Pietr stood in line and watched the clock. Catching my scent, he grinned and edged obediently forward with the line.

I sat and dumped the contents of my bag. Apple. Sandwich. So amazingly nondescript—*normal*. The standard buzz of the cafeteria shifted when I felt a hand rest on my knee and I realized someone crouched in the aisle beside me.

Derek.

Everything muted and dulled to background static as Derek filled my vision with his knowing smile. "Hey, Jessica."

"Hey."

"I enjoyed taking you out Halloween day," he murmured.

My body warmed beneath his touch, like sunlight crept through shadow. "I don't remember any of it," I admitted, feeling my eyebrows tug together. And then there was a picture in my head, a memory that bubbled up to a spot in my brain where I could grab it. The cafeteria grew hazy.

"You don't remember?" he soothed. "That's too bad—you were enjoying yourself. . . ."

I choked, my vision filling with memories of me kissing him, remembering the taste of his mouth, his tongue. Sprawled on his bed, him pushing me down . . . fingers creeping along my bare stomach . . .

I nearly tumbled backward out of my seat, scrambling to get away from his touch—my shame. "I . . ." My face burned. I sensed more than saw movement in the cafeteria as Cat rushed toward me.

Derek grabbed my wrist, stopped me from falling, and pulled me close to whisper, "It won't last with him." Another image tore into my head: Pietr and Max before the sliding-metal doors in the CIA's bunker the night they tried to free Mother, bullets ripping into them. I gasped—I convulsed—as each impact rocked their bodies.

Suddenly before me, her form wavering like a mirage in my fluctuating vision, Cat reached over, laying her palm over Derek's hand just where he held my arm. Her eyes flashed, and she jerked up so fast she nearly toppled over.

Derek grinned and pulled back, stepping away to disappear into a group of students as Cat searched the cafeteria.

My head cradled in my hands, Max's appearance surprised me. And then there was Pietr. Catherine said something to them—something in Russian.

Something I wasn't meant to understand.

Max grabbed me by the shoulders, bending down to stare into my eyes. "It's not your fault, Jessie," he assured me before turning back to Cat. "He's our wild card?"

"He saw you that night—probably saw us planning beforehand—" Cat shook her head.

"The bug was nothing," Pietr muttered as he sat down heavily beside me and curled me against him, combing at my hair with tentative fingers. "Might as well have been a decoy."

"He's been using Jessie as his eyes . . . ," Cat murmured, awestruck. "We haven't given him enough credit."

"Shhh," Pietr warned, his hand pausing over my ear.

"What?" I looked up, horrified. "What do you mean?"

"Shhh," Pietr soothed.

I pulled out of his grip, turning on him. "Don't you shush me, Pietr Rusakova—the time for keeping things from me is over," I hissed. "Are you saying Derek . . . used—*used*—me to spy on you?"

Pietr looked away, his face twisting. "You're not the only one out of the loop," he whispered, watching Cat and Max.

"Why didn't we realize this before?" Max asked, his eyes on the doors, watchful. His fingers twitched by his hip.

"We were thinking about the problems they wanted us thinking about. And he's planted right here—among the rest of a normal student body."

"There is less and less normal here," Max muttered. "We should have cleared this threat sooner, brother." He looked at Pietr.

Softly Pietr returned, "Perhaps if you had better defined the threat for me . . ." He shook his head, holding me tighter. "What would you have me do? Kill him?" he asked, spitting out the last words.

"He is why we failed. Why we nearly died that night. We need to eliminate the threat."

"You tell me how, brother," Pietr challenged.

Amy and Sophia stood back, hanging in the aisle, waiting for the fallout to stop. And probably hearing just a little too much. I watched them carefully. Soph and Amy had been my best friends for years. I trusted them. At what point did they need to know more? At what point was giving them too much information for their comfort necessary for their protection? If Derek was a threat to the Rusakovas—*to werewolves*—and a threat to me, wasn't he a threat to them, too?

"Cat," I demanded. "I want answers. Now."

CHAPTER THIRTY-SEVEN

Cat paced before me in the girls' bathroom. Sophia blocked the door, allowed to participate because I informed Cat quite clearly she was as screwed up as the rest of us. Cat trusted me and knew I wouldn't define what screwed up the Rusakovas, although Sophia probably guessed it was cultural.

Amy made it clear she wasn't ready to know anything stranger about the Rusakovas and my new, not-so-normal life. She'd chalked up the gunshot wounds from before to getting into a fight over some girl. She was far more willing to accept gangbangers in the tiny town of Junction than wonder about the truth. Maybe Dr. Jones was right: The mind did come up with all sorts of crazy things to protect itself from the weird parts of reality. So I'd let Amy hold on to her blissful ignorance a little longer if I could.

But Sophia? She and I had some stuff to learn.

"Derek is a strange mix of things, Jessie. That is why we didn't suspect." Cat's shoes clattered on the tile as she walked. She was struggling as I often did to find the right words. "A remote viewer—he can see locations from a distance, rifle through files, identify faces at covert meetings. But his job is made easier if he has a link to a direct witness."

"Like me."

"*Da.*" She shrugged. "He is also a social manipulator. He can encourage certain behaviors and attitudes in people by touching them and implanting his views. It is a trait most commonly found in successful politicians," she added. "A reason the handshaking tours used to be so very popular with people. But there are moral codes. . . ."

"Politicians have moral codes?"

Cat shot me a glance. "Do you have other questions?"

Sophia raised her hand. "Are you going to tell her the rest, or save it for a rainy day?"

"The rest?" Cat asked.

"He's capable of shifting energy, pulling and pushing it from place to place. He devours it," she explained, "gets a jolt—a high."

I blurted, "That's what Harnek meant by the stunt he pulled at Homecoming when he got the crowd all riled up because they thought he was hurt. . . ."

"Counselor Harnek?" Cat whispered.

"Wait. Derek faked that?" Sophia snapped. "Bastard. We lost the game because he was getting high."

"He's like a vampire—but not the bloodsucking type," I realized.

Cat spun from one of us to the other. "How do you—how do you know this?" she demanded.

"Derek and I went out once," Sophia reluctantly volunteered. "He tried to cut his teeth—so to speak—on me. He pulled so much energy from me, he had to throw some back. It was sloppy—maybe his first try? I think that's why . . . I think that's why I'm like I am—he flipped a switch or something."

"This is a lot," I whispered. "A lot to take in."

"Precisely why we avoided telling you," Cat said hastily. "You are already dealing with so much, Jessie, and it's such a big world. There is so much you don't know. So much that is truly frightening if you are"—Cat thought for a while—"only human. Some people do not handle the knowledge well of how wide and deep their world truly is."

"You were protecting me, too. By keeping secrets. Why is everyone trying so hard to protect me? If you'd all just frikkin' tell me what to expect, maybe I could deal with it." Chewing my lower lip, I faded out a moment, speculating.

Cat snapped her fingers in front of my face, bringing me back. "*Da*. You are handling it very well," she griped.

"So rattle off the list, Cat," I pushed. "What's really out there? I need to know."

Cat paused, eyeing Sophia.

"Soph, you okay if we broaden the borders of crazy town? A lot?" I asked. "I mean, you thought you were the tour guide, and I drive the bus, but I think Cat may just be mayor."

Sophia shrugged. "Go for it."

Cat took a breath. "Remote viewers, projectors, telekenetics, social manipulators, breakers, witches, werewolves, vampires"—she air-quoted—"zombies . . ."

"Dragons?" I asked.

"*Nyet*, though some people should moisturize more frequently to keep from being mistaken as such."

"Unicorns?"

"*Nyet*."

"Selkies, pooka, sirens, dryads, and mermaids?" I dug back into memories of research I'd done as a kid on myths and legends.

"I guess anything is possible," Cat admitted.

"In this context, that phrase is *not* reassuring."

"Ghosts," Sophie added.

Cat faced her. "Except that," she insisted, eyes wide.

"Ghosts exist," I assured.

Cat blinked. "*Pravda?*"

"Yeah. You didn't know about ghosts?" I asked.

Cat's face was pinched. "Ghosts are—creepy. They can be anywhere. Like spiders."

"Tell me about it." I sighed, remembering how my mom's ghost could be watching me almost anytime. "You guys better get to class," I said, slowly getting to my feet. "I need a minute."

"I'll stay," Cat suggested.

I looked into the mirror. There was simply no normal. I glanced at Cat. Having a werewolf babysitting only helped reinforce the fact. "A minute alone," I specified.

"I will drop my things off at class and circle around to make sure you are where you need to be," Cat said.

A moment later they left me in peace.

It only took me a couple minutes, standing clutching the sink and focusing on breathing, to adjust to my new, new—how many *news* was it now?—*new* normal. Occasional appearances of my mother's ghost, a werewolf boyfriend, a jock energy vampire ex-boyfriend, psycho ex-best friend, and a world that included zombies (ewww) but no unicorns. Things were starting to royally suck.

Barely in the hallway, I saw him barrel toward me.

"Your fault!" Marvin snapped, shoving me back. My head bounced off the wall with the impact.

"What the hell," I growled, rubbing the back of my head. "What the hell are you talking about?" *Ow.*

"My girlfriend and that—that—Rusakova!" he fumed. "Her at his house—probably in his bed—"

"Whoa," I said, my hands patting the air to try and calm him as he raged before me, pacing and cursing in the otherwise quiet hallway. My vision swam. "You're overreacting." I glanced up and down the hall for some wayward staff member or roaming substitute teacher.

Why did I have to be in the hall farthest from any of Junction's half-dozen offices when Marvin decided to go ballistic?

"Don't tell me I'm overreacting," he snarled. "She was my girlfriend. My lover . . . my *everything!*" His mouth moved, but no words came out. He just gnawed the air in a rage that bordered on psychotic.

I was finding too many reasons to use that word.

He shoved me again.

Ow.

Okay, maybe he was just south of the border of psychotic. *Damn.* I'd dealt with CIA agents trying to stop me from saving werewolves, Russian Mafia members trying to kill me to take the werewolves, and now I was faced with Amy's distraught ex-boyfriend.

A guy who thought it was okay to beat somebody he loved. What was acceptable damage to do to someone he *loathed?*

My head throbbed. I touched it again and noticed my fingers came away bloody. Not good. Where was Cat? Wasn't she coming back on some sort of patrol?

"Come to think of it," Marvin mumbled, "you're to blame for Sarah not being with her boyfriend, too. And for Jenny and Derek's split—and Jenny's ruined nose job, and . . ."

"Oh, hell, Marvin," I said through a fog. "Why not blame me for the piss-poor economy, too?" I swayed, and he pressed his nose to mine, snarling like a rabid beast.

"How stupid are you, Jessica? Taunting me? Where the hell's your protector now, huh? Probably off like your pal Max, humping somebody else's girlfriend!" he roared.

My head rocked, cheek stinging from a fresh hit.

For a second I managed to focus on Marvin. I raised my arm, rolled my fingers into a fist—and watched him disappear. "Huh?"

"Jess," someone said, and I sighed, feeling a hand warm and tender on my arm. But the voice . . . "Jess," he whispered. The voice didn't fit the name he called me. . . .

Derek's face wavered before me.

"Jessica," I insisted.

"Whatever," he said. "You're hurt. Let me help you. . . ."

I slid down the wall, Derek's fingers twisted in my hair, hand cradling my cheek, smiling. He glowed in my sight, like the first star of morning. He reached over and my eyes followed, seeing Marvin lying limp on the floor.

"You knocked him out."

"Yeah, baby."

"I'm not anybody's—"

Derek's hand grasped Marvin's wrist and I felt his other hand crawl around to the back of my head where my hair was hot and sticky. Marvin convulsed.

My vision cleared.

"Tell me what you are," I whispered, my eyelids peeling back in fear. A werewolf, I could handle. But, this . . .

His mouth clamped onto mine and my fear surged out of me, flowing into him like poison.

He laughed. "Not like poison," he insisted, bending for another kiss. And then he disappeared, too. Ripped away.

The roar I heard put Marvin's poor imitation of rage to shame.

Pietr.

"Hey, man," Derek chuckled. "It's not like she's putting up a fight. . . ."

My sight snapped into focus. Derek had his hands up.

Pietr's balled fists attached to the steel rods that were his arms. "She didn't know what you are," he seethed, lips peeling back from his teeth.

"Holy shit." Derek laughed. "*You* never told her!"

Something dangerous flashed in Pietr's eyes. Something bright and red. Bloodthirsty.

"You let me get my hands on her—I mean, *all* over her—" He leered. "You can't possibly protect her all the time, and you don't even tell her. Your own girlfriend!" He shook his head. "Stupid bastard. What do you think secrets do? Protect people?"

Pietr howled, and the classrooms emptied into the hall.

"Huh. *Witnesses.*" Derek grinned.

Pietr flinched. His options had just become severely limited.

"I've always preferred show to tell," Derek hissed, eyes narrowing, hair glinting in the thin hallway light like an awful halo. "Let's see what Little Miss Investigative Reporter thinks after a show, huh?" He turned to the crowd, shouting, "Fight, fight, fight, fight!" as he punched at the ceiling with a raised fist, punctuating the words.

They echoed him, a wild mob itching for excitement on a nasty autumn day, carrying his urgent cry, raising its volume to deafening proportions. The teachers tried everything to get them back into classes—to get past them and break it up. But it seemed all of Junction High wanted to see the football star and the new guy face off.

I knew what Pietr was capable of. Derek should have been an easy takedown. But as he turned back to Pietr and away from the chanting crowd, I doubted my werewolf boyfriend could handle him. Something was different about Derek. Something darker and more powerful. It was like he'd grown. Taller. Broader. More vicious.

They were matched.

Something sank in the pit of my stomach as he flew at Pietr, colliding with him like a linebacker, not the lighter weight receiver he really was.

The air billowed out of Pietr with the impact, and I saw the surprise in his eyes as his feet were swept out from under him and he rocketed backward.

The crowd roared.

With a bone-jarring crash they landed, floor tiles cracking like thin ice beneath Pietr's back. The crowd surged forward with a cry of "Yes!" as I screamed the opposition's part.

Pietr pulled his legs up beneath him as Derek started swinging wild punches. I heard a snap as Derek connected with Pietr's cheek.

I sucked in a breath, sickened by the sound.

Pietr's eyes flared with pain, sparking with violent red light. Growling, he shook back the change, forced back the wolf, and choked down the truth of his existence as Derek wailed on him. And then his weight shifted—so subtly, I nearly missed it—and Derek went flying through the air, flung by Pietr's muscular legs.

There was a crunch as Derek hit the wall—the crowd gasped—and he slid down its length, settling at its base, head lolling.

Out.

We were all going to have such headaches tomorrow . . . if we survived one another that long.

I dashed to Pietr, still lying on his back on the cool tile floor, eyes blinking back the red, fingers twitching as he covered his face with an arm and fought for control.

I straddled his chest and pulled his hands away. I pushed the hair back from his eyes and stared at his savaged face. "Why?"

"I can't really fight back, can I?" he muttered, turning his face from me. "If I did . . ."

I stroked his forehead and whispered little things, soothing words.

Max and Cat rushed past, herding the protesting crowd back into classrooms. The teachers lingered a moment, and I heard a bellow from behind them.

VP Perlson. "Everyone back in your classes! I'll handle this." The teachers were swept away, and I heard Perlson's walkie-talkie activate. "Yes, EMTs."

A static-filled reply.

"No. Nothing like that," Perlson responded. "A bad fight."

I was desperate to get Pietr's mind off things—like the fact he was a powerful werewolf who didn't dare fight back publicly in his strongest form.

I could have asked him to recite the scientific classification or taxonomy of biological species, or asked for his help solving a word problem including a train and a coconut-carrying swallow. But it was much easier, much more satisfying, to kiss his worries away. I fixed my lips on his, struggling to soothe him with more than simple words. My tongue slipped between his lips and I felt his teeth prick it, sharpening. I drew back, the coppery flavor of blood tainting my mouth as I searched his face.

His eyes were squeezed shut in concentration. They relaxed, opening to peer up at me. "Jess, don't," he pleaded, his eyes blaring red in warning. "You'll break my control," he groaned.

"Dammit, Pietr," I cried, tears rolling down my face to break on his. I leaned over him and as he reached up to move me aside, I caught his hands, slipping my fingers between his, and pushed his hands back over his head.

And I kissed him.

"Yee-aahh." Max plucked me off Pietr like I was nothing. "As much as he's enjoying that, his changing won't help anything," he confided.

Pietr lay there a moment more, nostrils flared, panting faintly as he held the change at bay. His fingertips twitched as if mine and his were still intertwined.

"Issues," Max said, setting me back on my feet. "You two have issues."

Perlson grabbed Pietr by the arm, tugging him to his feet. "Well, well, pup," I thought he muttered. "I see we're still thick in trouble, but getting smarter. Maybe there's a use for you yet."

The nurse showed up with the EMTs, splitting their attention between Marvin and Derek.

"You," Perlson muttered to Cat, Max, and me. "Follow me."

Cat wrapped an arm around my shoulders, turning me away, but I stopped, seeing Derek's eyes flicker open for a moment. He slumped to the side, his arm stretching out. I doubted anyone else noticed his fingers touch Marvin's ankle.

Marvin shuddered. And Derek *fed*.

Vampire. I froze a moment in the hallway, letting the word do laps in my head. I had read every book out there. I'd dreamed of vampires; I'd written short stories about them.

And now, I realized, I didn't like the reality at all.

"Let's go," Cat urged. "Perlson's office has to be safer than here."

"Where were you, Cat?" I asked.

She looked down. "Getting detention for arguing with Belden because I needed to leave the class. To come for you."

"You're still my hero."

She snorted. "Being a hero and attending high school is not so easy."

"Oh, my God!" Amy had arrived. "What the hell happened?" She grabbed me in a fierce hug.

"Girl fight," Max drawled. "Jessie and your ex."

"Shit!"

"Language," Cat reminded tersely.

"Derek and Pietr didn't want to be left out of the action, either," Max added.

"How the hell—*heck*—do I miss this sh—" Amy glanced at Cat. "Stuff?"

"I think you're the only one actually attending classes around here," I said, my eyes on Pietr and Perlson, just ahead.

She hugged me again. "You can borrow my notes."

"Miss Karlsen," Perlson warned Amy. "You'll have no decent notes to give if you don't get back to class. Now."

"Yes, sir," Amy griped, trotting off.

CHAPTER THIRTY-EIGHT

Max insisted on driving me home with Amy, Cat, and Pietr along for the ride. As Max made an excuse to Amy so he could do a quick perimeter run, Pietr and Cat hung close to me, watched by Annabelle Lee.

"I heard about the fight," Annabelle Lee mentioned, her eyes searching Pietr's battered but already healing face. *"Pietr Rusakova's suspended for fighting.* It's all over Junction. You attacked Derek?"

"That's not the whole story," he muttered.

"Rumors never are," Annabelle Lee agreed. "And Jessie"—she paused and whispered—"you look like crap, by the way."

"Thanks."

"Jessie was the victim?"

Nods all around. "I didn't even get to throw a punch."

"But at least *you* aren't suspended," Annabelle Lee muttered. "So everybody's wondering why the"—she jerked her fingers in the air— *"hot young Russian guy* was fighting the"—again she motioned— *"football star.* Over my sister. A *farm* girl."

"And what did you say?" Cat wondered aloud.

"I said they're doing it because my sister's pretty damn—"

I looked at her.

"*Darn*—awesome."

"Hey. Where are Hunter and Maggie?"

"Wanda stopped by to take them for grooming."

"Grooming?" I asked. "Wanda?" I glanced around. Something felt wrong.

"I'll stay," Pietr volunteered.

Annabelle Lee shook her head. "Dad won't have it after he hears about the fight. Amy and Max could stay, maybe Cat, but you"—she frowned at Pietr—"would get in massive trouble if Dad finds you here now."

He leaned over her and patted her head. "Perhaps you will put in a good word for me."

She tilted her head. "Maybe. If you're doing what's right by my sister," she offered.

One more protector.

"He is," I assured. "Taking care of me's not an easy job."

"Amen," Pietr and Annabelle Lee said in unison.

"Unfortunately, if I must go, we all must go. Max drives," Pietr pointed out with a shrug. But his eyes held worry.

Max jogged around the corner of the house, stopping short when he saw Amy's expression. "I had to . . ."

She frowned. "Jessie lies. Are you going to start? If you wanted to go for a run, I would have gone," she added, noting his damp shirt and hair.

"Maybe someday," he agreed.

I shot him a look of warning, but I was beyond preaching about leaving Amy alone. The way she looked at him, I had no right to tell him to stay back. Max would do his best to be good to her. Good intentions. What a road they paved. "So, you guys gonna go?"

Max nodded. The coast was clear.

Pietr grabbed me for a quick kiss. "I'm only a phone call away," he assured me.

"I know."

As they drove off, I told Annabelle Lee, "I'm going to do the horses."

She nodded.

"Going for a book?" I asked.

"Eh." She shrugged. "I was thinking about borrowing one of your monster movies."

"Go ahead," I offered. "I've pretty much had my fill of Hollywood werewolves." I strolled across the broad field separating our house from the barns, missing Hunter's and Maggie's eager, ever-sniffing presences.

When his hands grabbed me, there was no time to react. Images volleyed at me so fast my head spun and my stomach shook. Each one, Derek . . . always Derek . . . His breath was sweet and hot on my face, fingers digging into my arms brutally. "One more chance, Jessica," he whispered. "Let's get things right this time, shall we? Let's give that boyfriend of yours a good show. We'll start by getting Rio," he whispered, "and go for a nice ride by the window so Annabelle Lee calls him . . ."

Fingers dug through my mind, pulling at it and letting things I'd seen and done run through them like sand. My knees buckled and I whimpered, eyes itching and blurred.

"Okay, okay," he whispered. "A little *too* much . . ." He adjusted the way he raked through my mind, gentler now that I'd nearly collapsed in a heap. "Yes. He guaranteed he was only a phone call away. Let's see if that's true."

I heard Rio snort, a distant sound, and felt myself being lifted into the saddle. "Harnek thinks I failed the company, do you know that? But the way I see it, if I control you—I control the cure. And if I control the cure . . . well, I haven't failed, have I? So maybe I can still drive a wedge between you two," he cooed. "I mean, love and passion—it doesn't last. A heart can be splintered if hit hard enough."

Derek slid up behind me, bumping me into his lap and taking the reins. "And I do have some experience with this sort of thing. . . ." The reins snapped, his legs flexed, and I knew from the swaying of my hips that Rio was on the move.

"Excellent," he said, words blowing into my ear to scatter my brain. "She's seen us. Yep. Phone in hand . . . Now we have what? Ten minutes. Very good." The swaying stopped. "Hmm. Maybe I *should* rethink this," he muttered, staring into the shell of my skull. "The barn does have some useful things. . . . Let's return, shall we? Such a good horse," he muttered. "Too bad."

We came to a stop and he dropped me down from the saddle, my legs only holding me briefly before I flopped like a rag doll into the straw. He was tying Rio's reins to a post as my eyes began to clear, my brain began to resolidify. My body uncooperative, I tried to heave myself away from him.

"Uh-oh—not yet," he mumbled, grabbing my arm and pulling me to my feet. He wrapped himself around me, squeezing me so tight even breathing was a battle.

I flailed a moment, hands thudding against his chest. "Jess," he whispered.

"Don't call me that." The words slurred across my tongue. "Only two people have ever—*ever*"—I struggled, blinking, brain stuttering to find the words—"called me that."

"Yes," he agreed. "Your mother. And Pietr." He ran the back of his hand along my cheek, and my vision fuzzed. "The two you trust the most." His hand traced my jaw, ran down my neck, and played along my collar. "You can trust me, too, Jess," he whispered with such urgency, such blinding vehemence, something twisted in my head and for a moment I believed him.

And then it didn't matter anymore, because his lips were all over mine.

In the back of my head a little voice was muttering. Telling me it was okay, that I had always wanted Derek, that now I had my chance, he was safe—secure. Stable. That I'd never be pulling bullets out of *his* flesh after a horrific fight . . .

The scene from that awful night played out all over again in my head as our kissing deepened and my hands pushed his jacket off his shoulders and found the bottom of his sweater. My fingers ran along his stomach and chest—just like I'd imagined doing with Pietr. . . . And I was safe, the voice insisted, no rage-filled wolf eyes, no teeth, no claws . . . no danger . . . just kissing . . . heady kissing. . . . I moaned, sinking against him, just as he was torn out of my arms.

"Wha—?" My eyes came back into focus, and I fell to my knees, breath jolting out of me, head throbbing like I'd been baked in the noonday sun. Not five feet from me, Derek and Pietr battled.

"Don't you ever—" Pietr snarled, grabbing Derek by the front of his sweater and lifting him off the ground.

"She doesn't want you, Pietr." He laughed, pushing the words out as his collar choked him. "She wants safety. Normalcy."

Pietr tossed him to the ground, straw and woodchips flying up from the impact.

Derek grinned up at him, fixing his hair with a steady hand. "I know she's said it—she *dreams* of it—a *normal* life. It's in her blood, like the farm and the horses. Like the stink of manure on a summer day. A normal, *absolutely average*, life. And you can't give her that, can you, *dog?*"

Pietr roared, body quaking as he held back the change.

"Pietr," I whispered.

He turned his head to me, face red, cords standing out on his neck—so much anger bubbling, surfacing . . . My head still scattered from Derek's touch and Derek's taste, I shrank back.

"Go ahead, Pietr," Derek taunted. "Remind her of the monster you really are."

Pietr ran his hands through his hair. A breath racked his body. "Jess," he hissed, stricken.

I wanted to vomit, still feeling Derek's tongue in my mouth. I clutched a nearby haybale, dragging myself to my unsteady feet. "You *know*," I accused Derek. My eyes flew to Pietr, begging him to trust me. To know I trusted him beyond definitions of man and monster. Beyond judgments of how far he was willing to go to save me, his mother, or himself.

"What?" Derek snapped.

"You know what Pietr is."

"I've known since I first saw him," he confirmed. "Near my parents' vacation place in Farthington. A little powder blue Cape Cod."

Pietr jumped, his lips sliding back, teeth pointing.

"I didn't get to visit often," Derek said almost apologetically. "My parents liked to keep me on the Hill, watched by the help when they worked. I learned a lot in one visit, though. What pushes people apart and what slams them together."

Pietr snarled, and I reached for him.

"Yeah," Derek blustered. "My old man and your old woman," he grinned, mouth full of malice. "Who would have guessed it? Oh. Yeah. *Me.* I gave Pops the big idea." He looked at Pietr, his hand twitching toward a shovel resting by the wall.

My hand slipped along the wall and silently I pulled down a loose set of reins, weighing them inconspicuously in my hand.

"So what do you think?" Derek chuckled. "Did they do it—*doggy style?*"

I snapped the reins out, the length of leather slicing across Derek's face and cutting his cheek as Pietr launched at him with a roar, pulling the shovel from his hand as he swung it toward Pietr's head.

"You're the reason we failed that night," Pietr growled, "your vision . . . I'll pluck your eyes out. . . ."

My heart pounded and I twitched the reins in my grasp, eyes wide as Derek wiped blood off his face with the back of his hand.

"Yeah, I'm the one who got you shot," Derek grinned. "You won't get near Mother while I'm with the company. You need to just heel, boy," he said. "Cooperate. Obey. *Submit.*"

"We're not out of options," Pietr promised. "We will free Mother. Maybe Max is right," he muttered, eyes cooling by mere degrees. "Maybe we must *eliminate* you. . . ."

Derek flinched.

My eyes widened.

"Where's your audience now?" Pietr challenged him, pacing off a slow circle. "Where's your power?"

"Pietr," I warned. *Eliminate* Derek?

With a flourish, Derek bowed and pointed at me, flicking blood from his fingertips. "Jessica's all the battery I need, hound. Her emotions are *rich*. She's so easy to get going. . . . Has she told you how easy it was to *get her going* in my room? On my *bed?*" He screamed with laughter, holding his gut at Pietr's stunned expression.

"Pietr," I whispered. "Pietr, focus. Nothing happened between him and me."

"God, the way she *lies!*" Derek roared. "And the way she *lays* . . ."

I fought for words. "Nothing, Pietr. He's trying to get you to make a mistake. Focus, Pietr," I begged.

"I wonder if this is how it went down with your folks on their last night together," Derek mused, watching Pietr's face turn from him to me and back again. "Did she beg forgiveness? Did he go so nuts they *had* to put him down? What totally broke them? I wonder if it was something Pops said. What could *I* say . . . ?"

The words poofed out of him as Pietr bowled him over, their bodies rolling together in the dirt just outside the barn's open door.

No battle of titans, just two teen boys, wailing on each other like mad men with wild punches and kicks.

Until Rio stomped her hooves, snorting, as she caught a good look at the insanity. And Derek yelled, flinging Pietr off of him and all the way into the barn.

Haybales tumbled as Pietr crashed into them.

Derek was juicing up. I tried to tamp down my emotions, tried to limit his pull on my stress and fear.

Pietr stood, covered in hay, eyes blazing. He shook himself like a wolf coming out of the rain and he peeled off his shirt and unbuttoned his pants, eyes never straying from Derek—steaming with vengeance. He'd barely unzipped when the wolf tore free.

Derek scrambled to his feet in the swirling chaos of fall leaves, keeping a measured distance as he watched the wolf. "His kind are dangerous, Jess. They need to be controlled. Tamed and trained."

"What about your kind, Derek?" I whispered, struggling for calm.

"My kind's who *does* the controlling. You think a werewolf can be top dog? They can't even show their real face in public. My kind is built to hold their leashes. Teach 'em to roll over and *beg*." Just inside the barn, he reached for a pitchfork.

This time I lunged, wrenching it away from him with all the force my weight carried. It flew out of my hands, landing in a haybale, quivering. He grabbed my shoulders, shaking me, and I kneed him in the groin, falling out of his grasp, my vision clearing just as it had started to fog again.

I had to stay out of his reach.

Pietr's wild red eyes rolled from Derek to me. He leaped, knocking Derek back, their bodies rattling the stall door of one of my geldings. Derek seemed to grow a little more, and he threw Pietr back again, so hard the wolf yelped when he hit the wall.

"I guess I will need a little extra juice after all," Derek muttered, rubbing his hands together and stumbling to the haybale to pluck out the pitchfork. He smiled at me as he drew back and flung it.

Into the wall just beyond Rio's neck.

"Damn," he said. "Missed."

Rio reared up in terror, snapping the reins, hooves flailing and slicing as she screamed in fear. Pietr knocked me out of the way and falling to the ground, I heard Rio squeal as she turned and bolted from the barn.

Derek crowed with laughter. "That's a rush!" he said, his voice deepening, eyes darkening with the power brought by Rio's fear and my worry.

The wolf fell on top of me, straddling me, anger boiling in his body alongside his growl.

The horses went wild, panic-stricken by Rio's frightened departure and Pietr's fury.

"This is the problem with your breed, Rusakova—when the wolf takes over, you're quick to react but slow to learn."

In their stalls the horses whinnied, pawed, and snorted, eyes rolling as Pietr shook out his dark coat, rumbling like thunder. All shadow and stealth, he stank of a wild and untamable tundra that horses only dared dream of running. He stepped toward Derek. Away from me.

Hooves hammered against the walls and I pulled myself up, weak-kneed, to whisper soothing words to the horses. I moved down the line, stroking anxious faces, blowing my breath—so familiar— into their flaring nostrils. Filling their noses with *my* scent, their eyes with *my* face.

"You know," Derek said, hands running along the barn wall, searching for a new weapon, "when your maker first realized you actually existed, he was horrified by what he'd created. He knew he'd failed. There were so many—abominations—beasts—*monsters*. He hunted and eradicated all he could find—put them down like dogs," he sneered. "Probably some of your relatives, I guess. You all started as a government plan initiated in a single village, you know."

The wolf snorted.

"Oh. You didn't know that, either, did you? Shit. Everyone's keeping secrets around here. Everyone's telling lies." He looked at me and laughed, the noise sending shivers racing up and down my spine. "Go ahead—Bolkgorod—look it up sometime. And ignore what they say about it being wiped out by an avalanche. That happened after they had the kids they needed and the parents' bodies were at risk of being found. One big bang covered their tracks neatly. Russian ingenuity." He chuckled. "Hey. You keep track of time, right, mutt?" Derek asked.

The wolf blinked, muscles sliding beneath his thick coat, coiling to spring.

"Time's almost up!" Derek shouted, barreling toward me. His feet flew up, connecting with my knee with a crunch. I fell, twisting awkwardly, screaming, my eyes streaming. My knee burned like someone had a torch on it. Derek raced toward the barn's back door, disappearing.

Pietr, still wolf, started after him, but skidded to a stop, hay flying into the air as he spun back for me.

I gasped, struggling for breath and clutching my knee as the wolf licked my tears away and nuzzled my neck. "Shit, shit, shit!" I snapped.

And then the wolf was Pietr, his nose in my hair, warning softly, "Language," as he reached down to my aching knee, his wary eyes watching the doors.

With careful fingers he explored the joint, testing my leg tentatively. "Badly sprained."

I snarled. Mad as hell. I'd kept him from getting Derek under control. Maybe if they could catch him—not kill him—please, no more killing . . . And not be near his hands too long . . . "Crap. We need to find Rio. . . ."

Pietr leaned over and kissed me, slipping an arm under my back to raise me to him. I whimpered as my knee straightened and he re-adjusted our position, pressing his mouth along the line of my lips. "Shhh. Let her calm down. We'll get her in a moment." I opened my mouth to him—to my hero, wanting to have his taste, scent, and feel blot out the poison Derek had left in my mouth and my mind.

"Pants," I whispered into his lips, and he nodded, easing me onto a haybale.

In a flash he was back. The events of the day washed over me and I sobbed, shaking. Pietr threw his arms around me, pulling me onto his lap and rocking me ever so slightly, his mouth by my ear, making soothing sounds.

"You're safe now," he promised. "I'll have Max and Alexi deal with Derek. I'm not leaving your side. Your father will have to cope—or I'll have to tell him the truth." He sighed. "God. This isn't easy."

"Stating the obvious," I said, kissing him into silence. I didn't want to hear anything, think anything—just the pounding of his heart, the gentle panting of his breath. . . . Just another minute or two of peace in his arms and we'd go for Rio. And then we'd face my father. Together.

We could make our own normal.

We both heard the car pull up. Doors opened, feet crunched on gravel and ground across dirt.

"This is awful," Wanda whispered. "Look at her, Leon," she said to my dad. "What the hell has she done to herself this time?"

"Done to myself?" I asked, numb, pulling my face away from Pietr's fiery chest to see Dad, Wanda, and Dr. Jones watching us. "I've never done *anything* to myself. . . ."

"The gun under your pillow. The slash on your arm. The number of times you showed up to counseling late or disheveled—hurt and with no good explanation," Dr. Jones said, listing my offenses. She held out a clipboard to my father. "And here you are with a boy—"

"Who just got suspended for fighting," Dad whispered.

"He was *protecting* me!"

Dr. Jones intoned, "It's like we discussed. We need to take more drastic measures."

"More drastic . . . ?"

"We have to protect Jessie," Wanda urged.

My stomach soured as my father accepted a pen and scrawled something across the papers on the clipboard.

"Protect me . . . What are you talking about?" So far nobody's attempts at protecting me had helped me at all. "Dad," I whispered, "Rio's run off. We need to find her. . . ."

Dad glared at Pietr.

Dr. Jones walked toward me, and Pietr held me tighter, his chin on my shoulder as he curled me back into him, tucking me against him.

"We've decided you aren't making sufficient progress during weekly sessions. That you need a more exclusive environment in which to heal."

"A more exclusive . . . environment?"

"We've arranged for you to have a room at Pecan Place for a while," Dr. Jones said, smiling.

"Pecan Place—*where the nuts gather*," I muttered, remembering what the kids had said growing up. "The mental institution? No," I insisted, my voice rising. "No, no, *no!*"

Pietr clutched me closer. "I won't let them take you, Jess. I promise."

I grabbed his arm and buried my head in his chest. "Please," I whispered, "*Puhzhalsta* . . ."

A growl built softly in his stomach, rumbling and climbing toward his chest. "Don't touch her," he warned.

Dr. Jones looked at Dad.

"Now, Jessie, this is the best thing we can do for you. Your doctor has convinced me of that fact. You need additional time and treatment. You know she's trying to do what she thinks is best for you. . . ." He rubbed a hand across his forehead. "I want you to cooperate. Pietr, let her go."

"*Nyet*," he replied, biting the word off. "I will not let you take her. She does not want to go."

"Now, son . . . ," Dad drawled.

"Let go of her."

"*Nyet,* Wanda," he snapped. His breath was fire on my shoulder.

Dr. Jones made shushing noises. "It's okay," she consoled. "This occasionally happens. That's why we always bring extra help."

I heard car doors open, and two new sets of feet clomped toward us.

"Let her go," Dr. Jones suggested. *So* mildly.

I looked up to see a mountain of a man towering above us. It would easily take three of Pietr to make one of him.

Huge and thick with muscle, he was built like God forgot to grant him a neck—his head on a broad, short column that was just a narrowing of shoulders. He swung his arms at his side, and I saw the flash of a tattoo on the inside of his tree trunk of a wrist. Russian Mafia? But it wasn't any tattoo I'd seen before—it was more like a single foreign letter.

"Do it, Pietr," Wanda encouraged.

The mountain's companion—still bigger—grumbled above us.

Pietr looked up. And up. Pietr's head finally stopped when he could lock eyes with one of them. "*Nyet,*" he said.

The giants looked at each other and then lunged. The bigger one fell like a house of bricks on Pietr, pinning him to the floor while the smaller peeled me out of his arms with a grunt.

We stretched toward each other, fingers brushing a moment, as I said, "Witnesses," warning against the change. Pietr's expression was a dark echo of mine. Shock. Outrage.

Ten minutes earlier we had been readying to face the truth with my father, *together.* And now?

Pietr went wild, writhing beneath the big man's bulk. Then he stopped. Suddenly placid and still, seemingly out of breath, his eyes never left mine. And they shone like hellfire burned him from inside out.

"No," I sobbed, fists flailing against the giant. The bigger man moved off of Pietr, got to his feet, and brushed himself off. Pietr rushed us, grabbing me, nearly pulling me free, my arms and wrists popping before the big man's body slammed him down again, elbowing him to the ground, smearing his face across the dirt.

"Now—" Dad started to say, objecting, but Wanda put a restraining hand on his arm.

"We've talked about this," Dr. Jones reminded.

Pietr struggled to look at me, his nose streaming blood, a fresh gash across his forehead spilling red into his eyes. His cheek was ragged, abraded raw.

"Pietr," I whispered, his name tearing out of my throat as I choked back a cry. I was dumped on my feet and I screamed as the pain in my knee flashed through me, but the man's arms wrapped me tight, holding me up with unbreakable bonds.

The one who had toppled Pietr sat up again, rubbing his elbow.

Pietr staggered to his feet, swaying, and shoved the big man aside with one more burst of strength, coming for me.

"Stop fighting, boy!" Dr. Jones shouted.

The bigger one grabbed Pietr by the shoulders and hurled him to the earth. I heard the crunch of breaking bones.

Pietr clutched his head, his face contorted in pain. He looked at me and, with a groan, tried to rise. He reached out for me, arms shaking with effort.

The big one snarled at Pietr, readying once more, and Dad shouted, "Hey now, let's just stop—" Dad grabbed the clipboard, reaching to take the paper back.

Dr. Jones held her ground. "Mr. Gillmansen. This family is beyond broken. If you don't want me to call in Social Services and have them reconsider your youngest's living arrangements, too—"

Dad froze.

"God. No, Pietr! No," I cried, blinded by tears as he was thrown down again, his head cracking against the hardpacked dirt.

Dr. Jones continued. "You'll follow through with the treatment plan we've agreed upon for Jessica. I know this all seems very shocking right now, but it is for the best."

Pietr's body shuddered, but still he tried to pull himself back up . . . for me. "Stay down! Oh, God, Pietr . . . please, please stay down . . . ," I begged, my throat burning. "I'll go with you," I whispered to Dr. Jones, grabbing at her sleeve. "Please. Just hurry. Before he tries again."

I let them put me in the car—let them take me from Pietr, my battered hero—before they could break him anymore.

I screwed my eyes shut against the violence of the day, instead holding the memory of what I last saw tight in my mind. . . .

I remembered how, as our car pulled down the drive, Dad and Wanda gingerly helped Pietr to his feet, their faces a mix of shock and fear. And I knew that no matter where I was being taken, if they could finally come together, there was still hope for all of us.

Locked away at Pecan Place, Jessie finds her situation to be even more dangerous than she feared....

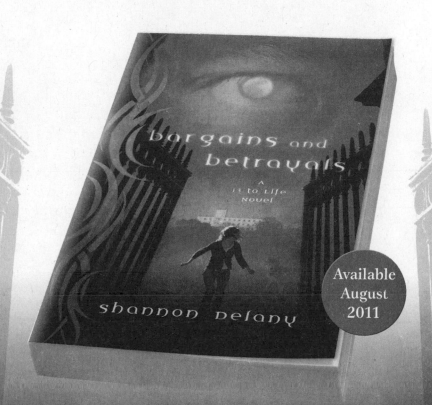

Available August 2011

In the midst of battling a secret government agency, Jessie and Pietr fight to keep their relationship alive. But what Pietr doesn't dare tell Jessie is that he made a deal that could mean the death of far more than his tenuous relationship with the girl he loves....

For everything YA—from summer loves and high school drama to vampires, werewolves, and fairies—visit WordsnStuff.net!